KAREN R̶O̶ S0-BOJ-061

FORBIDDEN LOVE

"I won't hurt you," Justin promised as he bent over her. Megan believed him. Her fingers curled against the soft brocade of his jacket and a delicate warm glow started in the pit of her stomach and pulsed outward along her veins. His hands stroked the loosened tendrils of her hair.

"Close your eyes, darling," he instructed softly, and Megan obeyed without question.

His mouth was hard and warm as he pressed her lips with a whisperlike caress. When he slid his tongue between her teeth, the bold invasion made her gasp. His body heat seemed to be drugging her; she could feel it wrapping about her like a protective cocoon.

For the first time in her life, Megan was made intensely aware of the differences between a man and a woman. He was so hard, she so soft; he needed, and it was her lot to give. His kisses intoxicated her, enchanted her, made her quake with delight.

When he began to unbutton her white shirtwaist, Megan arched herself against him, sighing with pleasure. But when her skirts were pushed up around her hips and his hands roamed higher on the bare skin beneath her pantalets....

"Justin, stop!" she gasped.

Her fault—it was all her fault. She had yearned to be close to him, but now she had ruined it all. It was a lady's responsibility to keep a gentleman's respect...and Megan knew that Justin could respect her no longer.

"Megan!" he said roughly, his hand tightening beneath her chin so that his fingers dug into her jaw. "It was *my* fault, not yours! Megan, do you hear me?"

Other *Leisure Books* by Karen Robards:
ISLAND FLAME
SEA FIRE

KAREN ROBARDS

FORBIDDEN LOVE

LEISURE BOOKS   NEW YORK CITY

To my husband, Doug, with love, and to my sister, Lee Ann, without whose cooperation finishing this book would not have been possible.

A LEISURE BOOK®

April 1994

Published by

Dorchester Publishing Co., Inc.
276 Fifth Avenue
New York, NY 10001

Printed in the United States of America.

Chapter 1

"Hell and damnation!"

Justin Brant, sixth Earl of Weston, swore furiously as a stream of icy rainwater rolled off the already saturated brim of his slouch hat to find its way with devilish accuracy to the bare skin at the back of his neck. He clenched his teeth as the freezing water trickled down his spine. Damn the ungrateful little minx to hell, he thought angrily. When he caught up with her—as he would, and before too many more hours had passed—he was willing to wager anything one liked that he would soon cure her of her disobedient tricks once and for all!

The many-caped driving coat he wore was not intended for riding down an Irish excuse for a road in inclement weather. It left altogether too much of him exposed to the rain and wind that had been nowhere in evidence when he had left Galway that morning. With the predictable unpredictability of all things Irish, the downpour had descended upon him without warning; within five minutes, he had been drenched to the skin. His usually gleaming Hessians, the pride of Manning, his valet, were all but unrecognizable, and he was reasonably certain that both his dove gray pantaloons and once snowy neckcloth were ruined past saving. Another black mark to chalk up against the impudent chit, Justin told himself, although he knew this last one was a trifle unfair, for he didn't give a damn about his clothes in the normal way of things, and regularly incurred Manning's disapproval for the disregard with which he treated his apparel. More galling by far than his bedraggled finery was the knowledge that his curricle, specially designed by himself and well-known to every sporting gentleman who fancied himself a whip, yesterday had the misfortune to encounter a damned great hole where a hole had no business to be. The upshot of this unfortunate occurrence was that his curricle had broken a wheel, and he had been forced to leave it behind in Galway for repairs, along with his horses. The only nag available for hire was one of the sorriest bits of blood and bone that he had ever clapped eyes on, and that was just his first impression! As the beast had clopped its way toward their destination, his opinion of it had grown steadily worse. He might as well have been riding a cow! The only saving grace in the whole deplorable situation, every infuriating circumstance of which could be laid squarely at the door of his step-niece and ward, Miss Megan Kinkead, was that none of his many friends and acquaintances would be caught dead riding down a dirt road in the wilds of Ireland, and so at least he was spared their sniggers at his expense.

Justin had been riding under trying conditions for hours. As his horse squelched through the seething quagmire to which rain had reduced the road, he acknowledged that he had seldom been wetter, colder, or hungrier. He had thought to be at his destination—Maam's Cross Court, his Irish estate, and, he was pretty certain, Megan's refuge—before luncheon. As it was, it was coming close to the dinner hour, and he still had some five miles to go, which in his own curricle with his own horses, would have taken perhaps fifteen minutes to negotiate. On this knock-kneed plug, he very much feared that it would take him five hours.

This bit of calculation sent Justin's temper, not placid under the best of conditions, simmering toward the boiling point. Its object could count herself fortunate if a tongue-lashing was the worst she received when he caught up with her. Although she had turned seventeen two or three months ago, and was properly considered a young lady now, she acted like a hoyden and it was as a hoyden that he would treat her. The idea of taking the flat of his hand to her backside did something to lessen his annoyance. By God, she had challenged his authority once too often, and this time he was going to make certain personally that she took the consequences! She would find dealing with him a very different kettle of fish from wrapping Charles Stanton, his woolly-headed, soft-hearted secretary, around her little finger.

This was the third time in eight months that she had run away from school—a very select and exclusive school into which it had cost him considerable effort to get her, thanks to her past record of being politely requested to leave one establishment after another for her pranks. But, considering her tender sex and age, and orphaned state (and his own lack of inclination to trouble himself about the matter), he had been, up to now, amazingly tolerant of her misdeeds. But this—this was the last straw. Returning from an evening at White's, he had been greeted by Ames, his butler, with the intelligence that an urgent message had arrived while he was out: his ward, it seemed, had been kidnapped by gypsies! Properly alarmed (although already doubting), he had driven at once to Miss Chevington's Academy for Select Young Ladies in Bath, only to discover by dint of exhaustive questioning, that the whole thing was a hoax. The minx, having taken it into her head to run off again, had somehow managed to induce a passing band of gypsies to take her with them. For which the poor fools were more to be pitied than condemned, Justin reflected, having had past experience of his ward's seemingly uncanny ability to persuade supposedly reasonable men to do her bidding. After calming the hysterical Miss Chevington, who stated quite categorically that she wanted no more to do with Miss Kinkead, earl's ward or no, Justin had set out in pursuit of the gypsies. He had come upon them after a day's hard riding, only to discover that Megan had run away from them, too, after determining that life with the gypsies was not quite as she had imagined it. Justin was as alarmed as he was angry (well, almost!) to think of her jaunting about the countryside alone and unprotected, but as he followed her trail, anger gradually gained the upper hand. It was not long before he deduced that she was headed toward Ireland, and seemed blithely prepared to take up with any chance-met stranger who offered her a ride. He supposed he should be thankful that she had made no apparent effort to cover her tracks. Wherever he went, everyone from hostlers to proper farm-wives remembered the "pretty little miss, so sweet and well-spoken, and traveling on her own like," and were able to tell him in which direction she had set off. Justin could not quite believe that she did not expect to be pursued, so he could only conclude that the thought of being followed, and eventually overtaken, with all the accompanying consequences, bothered her not at all. The thought made Justin's jaw clench. In the past it had been Charles Stanton who was sent to repair the damage wrought by the little witch, and no doubt Megan expected Stanton to be the one who came after her, to take her back to school, as he had twice before. But this time would be different. It was time to teach her a lesson she would never forget.

The girl had been an irritant ever since that day,

twelve years before, when Richard, his feckless younger brother, had drowned along with Moira, his appalling mistake of a wife, when a packet taking them from Liverpool to Dublin had sunk. Moira, a few years older than Richard, was an Irish peasant who earned her bread singing (she said) in the public houses of Dublin until she had managed to induce the soft-hearted Richard to marry her. In less than a year, they had run through Richard's considerable patrimony; at the time of their death, they had been living on his, Justin's, generosity at Maam's Cross Court, which was suitably remote from the gaming tables that, along with Moira, had been Richard's downfall. At the time of Richard's death he had been staggered to learn that there was a child, a five-year-old girl, apparently Moira's daughter by some previous, undisclosed marriage. At least, he assumed that there had been a previous marriage. He hated to think that the brat was a by-blow with an unknown father; it was certainly no spawn of Richard's, who had known Moira for less than two years at the time of their death. At any rate, the child was a fact, living at Maam's Cross Court and he was her guardian. He could, of course, have refused the charge; no one would have blamed him; in fact, many would have approved his action, for the girl was of extremely questionable birth besides being no blood kin to the Brants. However, all his life he had taken his responsibilities seriously, and this child, however unfortunately, seemed to fall into the realm of his responsibilities. So, cursing the necessity but feeling

10

duty-bound, he had reluctantly journeyed down to Ireland to see to the little changeling for himself. He had been pleasantly surprised. She was a pretty creature, all tangled black curls and huge violet eyes, with delicate bones and fine porcelain skin that seemed to belie her ignominious birth. Her pinafore was ill-fitting and stained and torn in several places, and her face decidedly dirty, but these were minor defects, easily remedied. After looking the child over, and being faintly taken aback by the cool appraisal he received in return, he had instructed Mrs. Donovan, the housekeeper, to get her cleaned up; whereupon the impudent little minx had put out her tongue at the good lady. Justin had been much inclined to laugh as his flustered housekeeper attempted to take the child by the hand and lead her from the room. He had even found it touching when the girl had run to him for succor, clinging to his leg for dear life as Mrs. Donovan, tried without success to coax her into obedience. Finally judging that this fledgling revolt had gone on long enough, he had pried her little arms from around his leg. She rewarded him by sinking a very sharp set of pearly white teeth into his thigh; to this day he bore a faint crescent-shaped scar to mark the spot.

A wiser man would have washed his hands of the hell-born brat. Justin, at twenty-four, had been too young to know that there are some contests a man simply cannot win. He was determined to make a lady of her, even if it killed him. And in the many years since, his guardianship seemed to be doing just that. If apoplexy didn't kill him, he would very likely catch pneumonia from this latest misadventure. And he had to admit it: she had defeated him at every turn. Despite his best efforts, despite the lavishing of untold sums of money on her care, comfort, and education, his recalcitrant ward seemed determined to pursue her own erratic course.

He had to admit that some of the blame was his. He had been too caught up in his own pursuits to take much interest in the upbringing of a girl-child. In fact, he had seen her perhaps for ten minutes twice a year since that first memorable encounter, leaving it to the long-suffering Stanton and a succession of girls' schools to do the necessary. During the past two years he had not seen Megan at all. This admission caused him a slight twinge of guilt, which he immediately banished by reminding himself of how busy he had been. As a peer of the realm, he had involved himself with issues of state, and they were certainly of more import than a child who was not even his own. And it was useless to expect Alicia, his wife, whose charge Megan should properly be, to bestir herself on the girl's behalf. Alicia, to his certain knowledge, had not bestirred herself since the day fifteen years before, when she had achieved the crowning ambition of her life by becoming the Countess of Weston. Indeed, he doubted if he had spent any more time with Alicia over the past twelve years than he had with Megan. Both females, for different reasons, were very much on the periphery of his life. And his Aunt Sophronsia, of whom he was marginally fond, had made it clear to him from the outset that she refused to do more than be decently civil to Megan if they should happen to meet in public. In that lady's view, he was doing both Megan and Society an injustice by elevating the child above the lowly station to which her blood condemned her. As she was fond of saying, a lady is born, not made; providing Megan with the education and other accouterments of ladyhood was of no more use than giving a mongrel a poodle's clip.

It had been forcibly impressed on Justin—by Stanton, of course, who had conceived a fondness for the girl—that Megan must soon be liberated from the schoolroom. As a young lady rejoicing in the dignity of her seventeenth year, and the Earl of Weston's ward to boot, she would have to have a come-out in the near future. The mere thought made Justin wince. He had a lively dread of being forced to guide a rag-mannered, high-spirited, disobedient minx through the pitfalls of a London season practically single-handed. His female relations would be no help. So be it. The little wretch's latest escapade had sparked in him a determination to bring the girl to heel while it was still possible to do so.

Justin's stomach rumbled loudly, bringing his attention back to his present miserable situation. He was so hungry that he could have eaten the nag beneath him, if there had been any more to it than skin and bone. It took a considerable amount of sustenance to keep his six-foot, two-inch, well-muscled and very active body at its best. He had had nothing but a mug of ale and a cold scone all day. No wonder his stomach was making its displeasure felt! And he was getting colder by the minute. It was impossible for him to get any wetter; the rain showed not the slightest sign of slacking off.

By the time he had crested the rise that brought him within sight of Maam's Cross Court, it had been dark for a full two hours. There was no moon, so it was impossible to see any of the surrounding countryside, which would in any case have been obscured by the relentless rain, but he knew the way well enough and was in no danger of slipping into one of the treacherous bogs with which the area abounded. As he drew close to the house, at last, Justin was surprised to see that the place was ablaze with light. Perhaps Stanton had managed to advise the Donovans of his impending arrival, and they were waiting to welcome him?

There was no one in the stables to receive his horse. Annoyed, he unsaddled the beast himself, rubbing it down, clapping a feedbag to its nose. Lord he was hungry. Striding toward the house, he promised himself that Megan's weren't the only ears due for a blistering. O'Bannon, who had charge of the stables, would certainly hear about this tomorrow!

As he mounted the shallow flight of stairs that led up to the front door of the three-storied stone house, he was astounded to hear music. Irish music. Wailing. Primitive. Lonely.

The music was loud as Justin let himself into the house. The hall was deserted. Donovan, the butler, wasn't there. He made his way down the long hall to the door of the blue salon, the source of the music. His booted feet and the irritable slapping of his gloves against his thigh brought no one to question his

14

presence.

He opened the door. What he saw stopped him in his tracks. Astonishment kept him silent; it was hard to believe his eyes. Donovan was flush-faced, his white hair in a mad tumble, the tails of his black coat flying. His portly, giggling wife was—well, drunk. Every one of the thirty-odd people in the room appeared to be drunk. They were dancing wild Irish dances, with much foot-stomping and hand-clapping. A rag-tag band of minstrels played long and hard. The hand-loomed carpet was rolled up; the blue salon's elegant furnishings were pushed haphazardly into corners, leaving room for the dancers to twirl madly about the center of the oak-planked floor.

Unnoticed by everyone, Justin leaned a shoulder against the doorjamb and crossed his arms over his chest, the better to observe this foolishness. A sardonic smile played about his lips as he waited for his servants to become aware of his presence.

The musicians played a fanfare; a space was cleared in the middle of the floor. A round table was pushed into that space, a beautiful Oriental table of teak with marble inlay, and a young woman was lifted to stand in its center.

"To our guest of honor!" Donovan cried, leading a round of huzzahs. The woman, slender yet shapely, laughed and bowed in response. Then, at a signal from Donovan, the musicians struck up again; the tune they played was a rollicking Irish reel.

"Give us a dance, missy!" Donovan's jovial entreaty was joined by a chorus of other voices. The

15

woman on the table tucked the hem of her blue dress into her sash, displaying a froth of ruffled petticoats and slender, white-stockinged legs. Kicking up her blue-slippered heels, she complied with a gaiety that brought a glint of appreciation to Justin's eyes. Still unnoticed by all, he admired the girl's truly lovely legs, which were on view up to the lace-edged hems of her pantalets.

Her hair, beginning to slip from its pins to cascade down her back in a tangle of waist-length curls, was crow black. He stared. Something tugged at his memory. She swung around to face him. He saw a willful little chin, laughing, rosy lips, a small elegantly-carved nose, skin as pale and silky as a virgin's wedding dress—then his gaze rose to meet head-on eyes as purple as pansies, set at a slant under straight black brows and fringed by incredibly thick lashes. Those same eyes widened to the size of saucers as they met his; recognition hit Justin with the force of a pole-ax. He straightened abruptly away from the doorjamb, an oath rising to his lips, while his ward— *his ward!*—stopped dancing with all the grace of a marionette with its strings cut.

"Get down!" he roared, striding forward to make sure she stopped her disgraceful exhibition before it could go any further. She didn't wait for his assistance, but hopped nimbly down from the table before he could reach her, prudently skipping around behind it so that its bulk stood between them before stopping to stare at him with a mixture of unease and defiance. At Justin's bellow, the music had come to a crashing

16

halt. As he stood glowering at the shameless minx, he became aware of twenty-nine pairs of eyes regarding him with varying degrees of horror. A thick silence descended over the gathering. Opening his mouth to favor Megan with a scathing appraisal of her performance, he recollected their audience and temporarily swallowed his words, although from her expression she was in no doubt of his sentiments.

"I will see you in the library in one hour!" he told her, the words forcing themselves out from between clenched teeth. She said nothing, but her chin lifted defiantly. He swung away from her before his temper could get the better of his self-control, his eyes sweeping the assembled company in a way that made them cower before him.

"My—my lord!" Donovan, trying vainly to restore some semblance of order to his person, was hurrying toward him. Mrs. Donovan, chewing nervously on her lower lip, was right behind him. The other servants gratefully yielded to the pair's seniority, looking very much as if they wished to become invisible. "We—we didn't expect you, my lord!"

"Obviously."

"My lord, we—I . . ." Donovan was stuttering as he tried to find a way to explain the unexplainable. Justin ruthlessly interrupted his faltering efforts.

"I require a bath in my chamber within ten minutes," he told his perspiring butler in a tone that boded ill for everyone. "And something in the way of dinner precisely twenty minutes after that." His eyes moved beyond Donovan to fix on his unhappy-looking

17

wife.

"As for the other," Justin's gaze flashed to the rest of the group. "I will have something to say to you—all of you!—tomorrow. For now, you will go about your business!"

"Yes, my lord," Donovan murmured unhappily. Justin did not wait to hear more. Instead, he turned on his heel and strode from the room.

The bath materialized with amazing speed, considering that he was in Ireland. Donovan, looking suitably abashed, carried the buckets of steaming water himself. (Doubtless the other servants were quaking in their boots, afraid to face him.) While the porcelain hip-bath was being filled, Justin divested himself of his wet clothes, then sat down on the edge of the enormous four-poster bed that had cradled the Earls of Weston for generations.

"Give me a hand with these, if you please," he said to Donovan, indicating his boots. Donovan nearly tripped over a footstool in his eagerness to obey.

"Manning isn't with you, my lord?" the butler ventured.

Justin eyed him. "No," he answered shortly, and thrust out a booted foot. Donovan didn't blink an eye at the shortness of his master's tone. Straddling the proffered leg and grasping the boot with both hands, he willingly presented his ample backside for Justin to push against with his other foot. Justin did, but the boot was wet and it was quite a while longer before it came free. When finally the process was complete, Donovan ventured to reopen the conversation.

"My lord!" he began impressively, looking back over his shoulder at Justin, whose eyes were glinting in a manner not calculated to encourage any confidences. "My lord, I should like to explain."

"Is there an explanation, Donovan? I should be pleased to think so."

"Oh, aye, my lord, that there is! You see, it being Missy's birthday and all . . ."

"Missy's birthday?" Justin echoed, not impressed with this argument. "Who's Missy? One off the kitchen maids?"

Donovan looked around at him again, surprise written all over his face. "Oh, no, my lord! Miss Megan! Your ward," he added in scandalized accents, as if Justin could possibly have forgotten the girl's existence. "We were wishful to celebrate her birthday! It isn't every day that a body has one, you know, my lord. Poor little soul, without no mother or papa to care! Not that you don't, my lord," Donovan added hastily, darting a look at Justin. "But with you being a gentleman and all, and busy, it is understandable that you don't make much fuss over birthdays and such!"

Justin eyed his agitated butler coldly. "For your information, Donovan, my ward, Miss Megan received a very handsome present from me on the occasion of her birthday—which was some three months ago. If she told you *today* was her birthday, then you have been hoodwinked."

Donovan was looking wide-eyed. "You don't say, my lord! Why . . ."

"Yes, Donovan, I *do* say, and I promise you I shall

have plenty to say to Miss Megan on that subject—
and several others—later. Now, I would appreciate it
if you would light the fire, see to my things, and leave
me in peace. Oh, and bring up whatever food Mrs.
Donovan has prepared. I'm famished! You and I will
discuss this entire matter at greater length in the
morning." Justin added this last as Donovan began
to look relieved at his master's comparatively mild
tone. In truth, Justin was prepared to overlook the
whole incident, now that it had been explained. But
it would not do to let the servants know that too soon.
The secret of managing a household in which one
dwelt for perhaps two weeks out of every year was
to inspire a kind of fear—no, call it awe—in the staff.

"Yes, my lord!" Donovan said glumly, kneeling to
light the fire. Justin sighed, wishing himself at home
in London. In Ireland, nothing worked as it was supposed to! Donovan was coughing, trying frantically
to get the fire going. It smoked. Justin sighed again
and told the man to open one of the long windows
despite the wetness of the night. Better to catch a chill
than to suffocate. Donovan took himself off at last.
Justin got into the tub.

The hot water felt immeasurably good as he sank
down into it. Justin relaxed against the rolled lip of
the tub, conscious of the first feeling of comfort he had
experienced all day. The tub was far too small for his
large frame, and his knees were drawn up almost to
his chest, but the warm water lapping around his legs
and belly more than made up for this minor failing. He
picked up the soap, carelessly lathering his arms and

chest. A sudden, irresistible picture of the faces of the discovered revelers flashed before him. To his own surprise, he grinned. The whole episode was really rather funny—or at least it would have been if not for the wanton display of limbs with which his ward had entertained the company. That a lady of his family could disport herself so! Shocking! And if it were to become known, there would be no end of scandal. It was time his ward was broken to bridle. She had been allowed to run wild for too long. She must learn that his hands held the reins.

Of course, the servants had no business carrying on in such a fashion in his house, but it wasn't their fault, not really. Ordinarily, it never would have occurred to them to behave in such a way. Oh, no, his little witch of a ward had cozened them into it, and it was she who must bear the full weight of his wrath.

When he joined her in the library, as he would do presently, he was much inclined to dispense with talking altogether and lay his riding crop about her backside. Perhaps that was what she needed to make her behave as a lady should.

There was a discreet tap at the door. "Come in!" Justin called, rightly supposing it to be Donovan with his supper tray. It was. Donovan placed the tray on a small table near the bed. The man's movements were so discreet that they served as a silent reproach to Justin's bad temper. He was tempted to assure Donovan that he did not, after all, hold him or his wife responsible for the events of the evening. But then he decided to hold his peace until morning; it would do

21

the staff no harm to reflect on their transgressions for what was left of the night.

After casting several unhappy looks at his master, Donovan finally tiptoed from the room. Justin resumed the business of getting clean. Then he lay back and closed his eyes.

He heard the door click open again. Donovan, he thought, not bothering to open his eyes. The man had forgotten something or come back with further apologies. The door closed and Justin heard the soft pad of feet across the carpet. Really, the man's attempts at being quiet were more annoying than anything else.

"Donovan . . ." Justin opened his eyes wearily. What he saw caused him to sit bolt upright in the tub with a suddenness that set the water to sloshing. Then, remembering his nakedness, he sank down again, cursing inwardly at the absurdly small tub which provided very little in the way of cover. He could feel his face and neck growing hot with a combination of outrage, anger, and yes, hang it, embarrassment. Because instead of finding Donovan, he found himself looking into a pair of willful violet eyes. Beautiful eyes, but far from friendly.

Chapter 2

"I want to talk to you!"

She was standing perhaps some five feet away, near the end of his bed. Her arms were crossed over her breasts and her voice was truculent. In truth, she sounded very more self-assured than she felt. Megan had never seen a man in such a state of undress, and she found the sight oddly unnerving. But having gone this far, she was resolved not to be routed until she had had her say, and it was no part of her plan to let him get the upper hand, as he inevitably must if she revealed her ridiculous attack of shyness by blushing, or leaving the room, or doing any of the hundred and one other things that young ladies were popularly supposed to do when confronted with a naked man.

Her guardian was staring at her, a dumbfounded expression on his face, which she noticed with some surprise was much more attractive—and younger—than she remembered it. As she returned his stare with a haughty look of her own, she became aware of the hot flush in his naturally swarthy face. His lordship was every bit as embarrassed as she was! The realization eased her own tension a little. Perhaps bearding the lion in his den had not been such an ill-considered idea after all! Sheer temper had driven her to it; she felt guilty that her friends should be made to suffer because of her selfish desire to have a party. But she had never had one before—and where was the harm? Besides, who could have foretold that her guardian, the inaccessible Earl, would come after her, in person, and burst in upon what had promised to be no more than an evening of innocent fun.

"May I ask what you think you're doing in here?" His voice, now that he had recovered the use of it, was positively arctic. Megan eyed him in a calculating manner, no longer put out by his nakedness. She was beginning to perceive that she had gained an un-looked-for advantage by bursting in on him in such an unconventional way. He was clearly off-balance, and Megan suspected that it wasn't a condition that afflicted him often.

"I told you, I wanted to talk to you," she replied with an insouciance that was far from feeling, and sat herself down on the corner of his bed as if she hadn't a care in the world. Deliberately she let her eyes run over him, surprised at such muscular breadth of shoulders and smooth, bronzed skin in someone she had long considered an old man. He looked ridiculous sitting all scrunched up in that tiny tub, his face beet-red under the two days growth of stubbly black beard. His eyes, a curious tawny gold color, regarded her with sheer amazement; then the look became a frown.

"You will please me by taking yourself out of this chamber, and waiting for me in the library, as I originally instructed!" The iciness of his tone was at variance with the glint in his eyes. Megan looked at him meditatively, deciding that strong men must tremble and scurry to do his bidding when he spoke to them like that. Well, her guardian had yet to learn that she was made of sterner stuff. She had embarked on this mission, and she would see it through.

"But I don't particularly *want* to please you, my lord," she remarked, her eyes unwavering as they met his fierce gaze. For a moment, he looked as if he couldn't believe his ears, and then, as his hands tightened on the rim of the tub, she was half afraid that he meant to rise and enforce his order physically. But concern for her modesty won out, as she decided it would; his sense of propriety made him her prisoner as surely as if she had somehow managed to chain him hand and foot.

"Do you realize, you impudent girl, just what you're inviting by coming into a gentleman's bedchamber like this?" he demanded.

25

Megan considered him thoughtfully, her head cocked to one side like an inquisitive bird's. He looked furious, and dangerous, and Megan supposed she should be frightened to death of him. After all, as her guardian, he stood in place of her father, and had absolute authority over her. Yet, she was not afraid.

"Of course not, my lord. As a gently brought-up young lady, how should I?" she answered demurely, a dimple quivering roguishly in her cheek. Her answer surprised him, she could see; for just a minute, she thought she glimpsed the spark of humor in his eyes. Then his mouth tightened ominously, and she knew he was reminding himself that she was his ward and not just any young girl.

"If I were you, Miss, I would take myself out of this chamber this very instant. I promise you, you'll be very, very sorry if you don't."

There was no mistaking the threat under the cloak of politeness. Megan tilted her chin at him. "Then I will just have to be sorry, won't I? Because I am not leaving until I've said what I came in here to say."

"Say it, then, and be damned," Justin snapped, clearly at the end of his patience. He glowered at her from the scant protection of the small tub. His knees rose above the water and Megan noticed that they were taut with muscle and covered with fine dark hair. His chest was covered with hair, too, in a wide V-shape that was much thicker and softer looking than the hair on his legs. The curling mat was every bit as dark as the hair on his head, which was just a shade less black than her own. But its texture was much coarser, and it waved rather than curled. At the moment, tiny droplets of water beaded it like diamonds.

"Well?" he barked. Megan jumped guiltily, realizing that he was waiting for her to state her reason for being in his bedroom.

"I won't have you blaming Donovan and Mrs. Donovan and the others for what happened tonight. It was my fault entirely." Her former belligerence had returned in full force as she recalled the purpose behind her unconventional behavior.

"Oh, you won't have me blaming the servants, eh?" he questioned sardonically. "You will forgive me, I'm sure, if I have forgotten the occasion where you were given to understand that I regarded your words as my law?"

Megan glowered at him; then, remembering the fear she had seen in the faces of Mrs. Donovan and the others when she had left them in the kitchen, she determined to try another tack. She could not bear it if they were to lose their places because of their kindness to her. Where would they go?

"I told Donovan that it was my birthday," she confessed. "And asked if we could perhaps have a small celebration. I—I've never had a birthday party..."

Although she didn't know it, Megan's voice took on a pathetic kind of dignity that touched Justin. He felt a stab of guilt as he remembered his punctilious birthday gift to her: a pair of pearl eardrops, if he remembered correctly, chosen by the excellent Stanton and posted to Megan at her school. All very correct and quite impersonal.

Justin's long silence and the frowning expression on his face made Megan swallow hard. Surely he would not vent his anger upon the servants, most of whom had been in his employ for years?

"You musn't blame them!" she cried impetuously. His eyes came to lock with hers, and his mouth tightened.

"One of the many things you apparently still have to learn, my girl, is that you never say 'musn't' to me. I will do as I please, and *you* will do as I please. That is something I want perfectly understood." The cutting words made Megan's eyes flash. "The rest I will say to you later, in more suitable surroundings. Now, I am telling you to get the hell out of here!"

Justin was beginning to lose control of his temper. The water was getting cold, his supper was getting cold; his sense of duty was under a severe strain. She appeared to find nothing particularly disturbing in his nakedness, concealed imperfectly by the soapy water. He had always thought, without really thinking much about it at all, that gently-reared young ladies were likely to faint away at their first sight of a naked man. Which led him to draw one of two unwelcome conclusions: either she was more familiar with the unclothed male form than was proper, or she was a most unusual young lady. Either way, he could see nothing but trouble ahead.

"You won't even listen, will you?" she cried passionately. "You never listen! All you care about is giving orders!"

And with that, to Justin's horror, she flung herself

28

across the bed, and burst into a torrent of tears.

"Oh, for God's sake . . . !" Justin muttered under his breath, looking at her recumbent form with exasperation. She continued to cry without restraint, her slight shoulders heaving with the force of her grief. Justin, cursing heartily, got out of the tub and pulled on his dressing gown without even bothering to dry himself. Then, ignoring the water that pooled on the floor, he crossed to the bed.

"Megan," he said, reaching out to lay a gentle hand on her shoulder. "There's no need for you to upset yourself. I have no intention of dismissing the servants."

She paid no heed to this remark, but continued to cry as if her heart was ready to break. Justin sighed again, feeling, against all reason, like some kind of monster. Hell, he hadn't even laid a finger on the chit, and yet here he was feeling guilty as could be.

"Megan," he said, this time with more authority, "that's enough. Stop crying." And when she continued to sob he applied some slight pressure to her shoulder and rolled her over on to her back.

"Let me alone!" she said fiercely, sitting up. "I'm not crying! I never cry!" Sobs punctuated her words, and tears hung like raindrops from the sooty fringe of her lashes and traced shining rivers down her pale cheeks. Those purple eyes looked like violets after a storm, all dewy and moist and glistening. Justin, watching the soft rose lips quiver pathetically, felt an unaccustomed pang of compassion.

"I see," he said gravely, tempted to smile but fighting the impulse heroically. Megan glared up at him as he towered over her; her eyes awash with tears that showed no sign of abating.

"Don't you *dare* laugh at me!" She looked absurdly fierce, and Justin could not restrain a faint quiver of amusement. To his astonishment, her mouth contorted with rage, and she launched herself at him, hissing and clawing like an outraged kitten. Justin caught her wrists without any difficulty, holding her away from him so that her kicks and writhings did not the least damage.

"Here, now," he said with some surprise, bemused by her furious struggle to break his hold. When at last she saw that it was impossible, she stood still, her slight wrists imprisoned in his hands, her head thrown back defiantly.

"Let me go!" she raged, her eyes glittering. Justin stared at their deepening color with unconscious fascination. They were beautiful. "I hate you!" she added, and then there was a fresh outburst of sobbing.

"Christ!" Justin shook his head, feeling routed before the battle had even begun. He wasn't quite certain what had brought on this deluge, but it didn't matter. Whatever its cause, he couldn't stand it. His mouth twisting in a wry grimace, he scooped her up into his arms as if she were seven instead of seventeen and, holding her cradled against his chest, walked with her to one of the two big chairs set before the fire. He sat down with her on his lap, his hands moving comfortingly over her heaving back. Megan offered no resistance. After an intital stiffening when he had first picked her up, she seemed content to be in his arms, burying her face in the curve between his shoulder and neck and weeping unrestrainedly.

"Hush now," he murmured into her hair, his hands coming up to smooth the tumbled tresses. Her hair felt like silk. "It's all right, I promise you."

Megan responded to his gentleness; her arms crept up to encircle his neck, and she clung to him. Her mouth was hot and wet against the skin of his neck as she sobbed. Justin, becoming uncomfortably aware that this was no child he held in his lap, nevertheless reminded himself that she no doubt regarded him as a sort of father, and it was in this capacity that he set himself to soothing her, ignoring the instinctive stirrings of his body. He murmured to her, petting and stroking her as if she were a ruffled kitten, until finally, her arms loosened their hold on his neck, and she lay quietly against him.

"I'm sorry," she said presently, sitting up and looking at him hesitantly. Justin found himself smiling at her. Somewhat to his surprise, he found that he was beginning to like her very much; he supposed, with an inward grimace, that he felt like an uncle with a favorite niece.

"I truly never cry," she continued, her lashes flickering down to hide her eyes. Justin noticed with interest that a deep pink blush was staining her cheeks. Then she added, with a chuckle, "Usually I don't." She peeped up at him through those absurdly long lashes.

Justin's smile widened. "That's all right," he told her blandly. "I was wet anyway."

31

This won him another chuckle, not quite so damp as the first.

"You were, weren't you? I'm sorry about ruining your bath."

"I'll forgive you—this time. But don't let it happen again." A stern note entered his voice, but he was smiling.

Megan smiled back. "No, I won't," she promised. "I really don't make a habit of invading gentlemen's bed-chambers. I was just—upset."

"Then it's to be hoped that you don't get upset too often." This was said in an extremely dry tone that made Megan laugh.

"You're really very nice," she said, as if she had made a surprising discovery. "Not at all as I remember. You always seemed so—so distant. As if you didn't like me very much!"

Justin felt another pang of conscience.

"I'm sorry if I gave you that impression." His eyes were steady on hers. "I suppose the only excuse I can offer you is that I haven't had much experience with children."

"I'm not a child," Megan pointed out. Looking at the slender yet temptingly curved shape of her as she perched so trustingly on his knees, Justin was forced to agree.

"No," he said. "But you were."

"Well, since I'm not now, maybe we can wipe the slate clean and start all over again. I'll try my best to behave like a proper young lady—Miss Chevington always said I could if I tried—if you don't stay so—so

32

far away all the time. After all, even though I know we're not really related, you're the only family I've got."

This last was said with such simple sincerity that it had the effect of making Justin feel like a villain. It also helped him to keep a tight rein on his baser instincts, which were reacting automatically to the girl's undeniable loveliness. Her eyelids were red and swollen from crying; a few tears still sparkled in the sooty blackness of her lashes. Her little nose was faintly red at the tip, and her mouth had a soft, smudged look that he found very appealing. Her hair swirled around her face and upper body in a wild profusion of gleaming ebony curls, having escaped the last of its pins during her emotional outburst. Her blue dress, with its demure, school-girl neckline and long sleeves, was damp on one side from where she had lain against him. It clung to her breasts enticingly. They were surprisingly full for so young a girl, he noted, and beneath them her waist seemed incredibly tiny. He looked up again, to find her smiling at him. His breath caught a little, and his hands clenched convulsively over the padded arms of the chair. His first impulse had been to draw her close again. Clearly she had no idea of the dangers inherent in her present position. Quite obviously, she regarded him as an ancient but surprisingly kind protector. Which was what he was to her, of course. Still, he could not help thinking of all the women who had had cause to regard him very differently, and a wry smile twisted his lips.

"Well?" she said impatiently, and he realized that

she was waiting for him to reply to her proposal.

"No more wild dancing. I'm sure you know that it's not done for ladies to show their legs."

"Limbs," Megan corrected, smiling mischievously. Justin smiled back, but continued his lecture in the same chiding tone.

"No more joining up with gypsies, and no more running away from school—or anything else improper, which I may have overlooked for the moment. Agreed?"

She gave him a dimpled smile. "Agreed," she said, laughing a little. "I just did those things—well, most of them—because I wanted you to notice me. It's not very nice, always being palmed off on someone's secretary. Although I must say that Charles has always been very kind to me."

"He's fond of you, I think."

"Yes." She was smiling. Justin leaned back in the chair, his expression indecipherable as he watched her. She was a bewitching little creature, quite apart from her physical beauty. Why had he not noticed it before? And then he realized, with a twinge of shame, that this was the first time he had ever really talked to her. Their previous meetings had all been conducted in the parlor of whatever school she happened to be attending, with either the headmistress or Stanton in attendance. Usually he had inquired about her progress at school, and if there was anything she required. Her replies were just as formal; always she ended up by thanking him, by telling him that she had everything she needed. Looking back, Justin could see that her

34

eyes had, upon several occasions, beseeched him for something, but at the time he had simply been too preoccupied to notice.

"I sincerely apologize, my dear," he said quietly. Her eyes widened, and she looked at him with some surprise.

"Whatever for?" she asked, wondering.

"I haven't been much of a guardian to you, have I?" His mouth curled with self-derision. "But I'll make it up to you, I promise. When you turn eighteen, I'll bring you up to London and give you the finest come-out a girl could wish for. You'll go to lots of parties and learn to dance and flirt, and most likely break the hearts of all the young men."

Megan cocked her head at him. "Do you think so? It seems very unlikely—that I should break hearts, I mean."

Something flickered for a moment in Justin's eyes. "I don't think it's unlikely at all," he said a little abruptly, then shifted his legs beneath her slight weight. "And while we're on the subject of things that are improper for a young lady to do, I think I should mention that sitting on a gentleman's lap would definitely fall into that category."

Megan's face flushed a deep rose; she appeared to be aware of her position for the first time. She slid off his knees at once and stood rather awkwardly by his chair, looking at her hands which she had clasped in front of her. She looked like the innocent schoolgirl she was. Justin felt a stab of irritation at himself. In his sudden need to get her off his lap, he hadn't meant to embarrass her.

"I'm sorry," she said in a stifled voice. "I didn't think . . ."

"Don't worry about it." Justin got to his feet and looked down at her bent head. The top of her head did not quite reach his shoulder. Suddenly, he felt very impatient with himself. Despite her maturing body, she was a child, after all, and he was the closest thing to a parent she possessed. He vowed to keep that fixed firmly in his mind. In his own defense, he supposed that it would take a while to become accustomed to the fact that he—he, Justin Brant, noted connoisseur of beautiful females—had so unexpectedly acquired yet another beautiful female as his ward.

"I put you there, after all," he said easily, tilting her chin with a careless hand and smiling into her upturned face. "So if anyone was improper, it was I."

After a moment, she smiled back at him. They were smiling rather foolishly at each other when Justin's stomach interrupted with a loud rumble.

"Oh, I'm keeping you from your dinner," she said politely. "I'll go."

Justin dropped his hand from her chin. He was conscious of an impulse to ask her to stay and share his supper, but the impropriety of her being alone with him in such intimate circumstances held him back. A young lady's reputation was her most precious asset, and if it became known, even among the servants, that she had been alone with him in his bedroom—to say nothing of the fact that she had seen him in his bath—their relationship would inevitably become suspect.

"Megan," he said, sounding as uncomfortable as he felt but feeling that he had to warn her. She had already taken a few steps toward the door, but as he spoke she looked back over her shoulder.

"Yes, my lord?"

"My dear, it would be best if you didn't mention your visit to my bedroom to anyone, even the Donovans. I realize you might not understand why, but . . ."

"Is it because people might think we were lovers?" Megan asked. Justin felt his jaw drop. He stared at her for a moment without speaking. Damn it, he was blushing like a schoolboy. The pictures her words conjured up stunned him with their vividness.

"That is a most improper question!" he snapped, still shaken.

Megan did not look particularly abashed. "I know," she acknowledged, smiling a little. "Young ladies are supposed to pretend that they don't know about such things. But I thought that you and I could speak frankly. Can we not?"

Justin felt harassed. This whole day had turned into a disaster of major proportions. Quite how it had happened, he wasn't sure, but he knew that it was somehow all tied up with this maddening girl who was even now looking at him so guilelessly with her violet eyes. He thought of his plan to break her to bridle, and inwardly acknowledged that this particular filly might well give him more trouble than he had anticipated. The problem was, she was so goddamned beautiful. . .

"Oh, yes, of course you can speak frankly to me," he said, giving up the battle for the moment. What he needed most now was time alone to recover his balance. "Run to your bed, like a good girl, and we'll sort this whole thing out tomorrow."

"All right." She smiled seraphically at him. "Good night, my lord."

"Good night," Justin answered automatically. Megan was just reaching out to touch the door handle when a sharp rap sounded on the door. She and Justin both started.

"Wait!" Justin called out imperiously, consternation plain in his eyes as he met Megan's. She was chewing nervously on her lower lip as she backed quickly away from the door.

"I've only come to put a warming pan in your bed, my lord." Mrs. Donovan's voice sounded from the other side of the door. "Them sheets get dreadful musty!"

"Just a minute, Mrs. Donovan!" Justin responded. He was tempted to tell her to forget the warming pan, that he didn't need it, but he was afraid that she might think there was something strange in that. After all, the night would be cold.

"Get under the bed," he whispered to Megan, coming swiftly to her side. She looked up at him, surprised, and then started to giggle.

"Hush!" he warned her, pushing her, one arm over to the side of the bed. "It won't do for her to find you here. Now get under there, and for God's sake be quiet until I tell you to come out."

38

"Worried about your reputation, my lord?" she whispered saucily, but when Justin glared at her without answering, she did as she was told. He waited just long enough to make sure that no part of her showed before crossing to sit before the fire. When he was settled, he told Mrs. Donovan to come in.

She threw him a quick look before moving to the bed to pull back the covers and push the warming pan between the sheets. From her silence, Justin gathered that she was very much on her dignity; probably she thought he held her to blame for Megan's wild behavior at the so-called birthday party. Justin would have set her mind at rest if Megan hadn't been under the bed. He was afraid that she might pop out like a jack-in-the-box and cause all three of them no end of embarrassment.

Mrs. Donovan plumped the pillows, then turned away from the bed. "If that's all you require, my lord?" she asked, eager to please. Justin nodded, wanting to be rid of her, but she wasn't ready to go.

"Was there anything wrong with the meal, my lord?" she asked, glancing at the untouched supper tray. Justin sighed inwardly, knowing that of all things, she prided herself on her cooking. And, as he thought with some longing, it was indeed something to be proud of. He had no doubt the dinner was delicious.

"No, not at all, Mrs. Donovan," he said hastily. "I just felt a trifle unwell, that's all. All that traveling, you know."

Her face softened. A bad traveler herself, he had

picked on the one excuse she understood.

"You should have said something, my lord," she reproached him, moving closer to stare at him with motherly concern. " I would have prepared you one of my own special purges. Nothing like it for setting a queasy stomach to rights again."

"That's not necessary, Mrs. Donovan." Justin tried to keep her from seeing his shudder. Once, as a young boy, he had been visiting Maam's Cross Court and had eaten too many green apples. Mrs. Donovan had dosed him with one of her famous purges, and the cure had been far worse than the ailment. Not even for the sake of his ward's reputation would he suffer through that again.

"Very well, my lord, if you say so." From her tone, Mrs. Donovan would have dearly loved to argue with him, if she had dared. "With your permission, then, I'll take the tray back downstairs. When a body's sick, he don't want to smell food!"

She barely waited for Justin's faint assent before snatching up the tray and heading for the door. Justin watched his dinner disappear with a feeling of inevitability. Going hungry to his bed would put the cap on a miserable day, he thought bleakly as the door closed behind the housekeeper.

She had barely gone before Megan was scrambling out from under the bed. The minx was covered with dust—apparently the maids didn't consider it necessary to sweep under his bed!—and grinning from ear to ear. Justin regarded her with a jaundiced eye, not bothering to get to his feet.

"I hope you're happy," he said morosely. "You just cost me my dinner."

"I'm sorry." The grin vanished; she sounded genuinely contrite as she crossed the room to stand looking down at him worriedly. "If you're really hungry, I can raid the kitchen for you later. I used to do it all the time at school."

"I think I can live without eating for one night. Now get along to your own bed. Scoot!"

"Are you sure? I'm really very good at it, you know!"

"I'm sure!" Justin's voice was firm. "Now get going before Mrs. Donovan decides to come back with one of her purges. And if she does, I swear I'll strangle you!"

Megan, who had experienced Mrs. Donovan's purges herself, giggled at the image of her lordly guardian being forced to swallow a sickening draught while Mrs. Donovan looked on. Justin glared at her, then grinned reluctantly. Her laugh was infectious.

"Get out of here!" he ordered, standing up. Megan, still chuckling, went to the door. "And for God's sake, don't let anyone see you!"

"I won't," she promised, smiling at him over her shoulder. Then, with one hand on the knob, she turned back to face him, saying, "I didn't mean it, you know!"

"Mean what?" Justin asked.

"I *don't* hate you, my lord," she said softly, and before Justin could reply she whisked herself away.

Chapter 3

Megan was humming tunelessly to herself as she came downstairs the next morning. The rain had stopped during the night, and the soft September sunlight matched her mood. She felt as if she'd been reborn, as if the person she'd been last night had been replaced by someone altogether different. Justin had come for her at last, making her feel as though he had some personal interest in her for the first time in all the years he had served as her guardian. It seemed as if she had spent her life in an ever-changing procession of schools. She had craved Justin's attention; for the smallest sign that he cared about her. It hadn't happened. Gradually, she had learned to resent and fear him. His word, it seemed, was law, and must be obeyed absolutely whether she liked it or not. Her letters to Justin, written dutifully once a week under the watchful eyes of her teachers, were answered just as dutifully by Charles Stanton. Her sole contact with Justin was for a few minutes perhaps twice a year. As a little girl, she had been sick to her stomach for days before one of Justin's visits, hoping against hope that this time, *this* time, he would unbend a little, perhaps smile at her with more than the bare civility that was all he ever showed her. Perhaps he might even take her out for a macaroon and an ice as all the other fathers did when they visited their daughters.

But it never happened, and Megan had finally brought herself to accept the fact that it never would. She had told herself rather fiercely that she should be grateful to him for troubling himself about her at all, when she had no real claim on him. The other girls, with smug schoolgirl superiority, assured her that, if Justin hadn't made her his ward, she would be lucky to work for one of them as a maid. Megan had blackened more than one eye in defense of her background, and had, in consequence, been disciplined for her unladylike behavior. Over the years, she had built Justin up into a combination of ogre and savior, while still convincing herself that one day, when she was a grownup lady, he would be proud of her and tell her so. Comforting herself with this fantasy, she nevertheless deeply resented her guardian's neglect. It was this resentment, coupled with her natural high spirits, which was

44

constantly getting her into so much trouble at school.

Then, when Justin stopped coming at all, her first deep hurt had turned to anger. She vowed to make him take notice of her, and had exerted every ounce of her considerable ingenuity toward achieving that end. Last night, when she had seen him glaring at her from the door of the blue salon, her feelings were a mixture of triumph and apprehension. At last, she had succeeded in attracting his attention.

Anger had prompted her impulsive visit to his bedroom; when she discovered him in his bath, she had almost run away. Instead, she had squared her shoulders, raised her chin, and vowed to make him listen to her for once. His attitude of icy command was just what she had expected; she had hated him so much she could have killed him. But then, when her overwrought sensibilities had betrayed her, and she had burst into tears like some ninny, she had gotten the shock of her life. The inaccessible Justin had actually been kind! When he held her, sobbing on his lap, she had felt more warmth and security than she had ever known in her life. It seemed that he did care about her, after all, and that knowledge had turned her world around.

"Morning, Miss Megan," Mrs. Donovan called placidly from the breakfast room, where she was setting a place at the table. Megan blinked once, brought back to the present with a start, then leapt gaily down the remaining three steps, careless of the wide skirt of her girlish white muslin dress that billowed upward as she moved. Smiling, she crossed the hall to join

45

Mrs. Donovan.

"Isn't his lordship up yet?" Megan asked with some disappointment. There was only one place setting on the long, polished oak table.

Mrs. Donovan awarded her a warm smile. "You can rest easy, my lamb. He's eaten and been out this hour and more. Likely we won't see him again until dinner."

"Oh." Megan sat down at the table, feeling that the morning had fallen flat. She had looked forward to sitting down to breakfast with her guardian for the first time. But then she remembered that he had had no dinner the night before, and must have been fairly starving this morning. Of course he had hurried down to breakfast. A small smile curved her mouth as she remembered how loudly his stomach had growled.

"I don't think you have to worry overmuch, lamb," Mrs. Donovan told her. "His lordship don't seem to be in a temper. Why, he told Tom—Donovan, that is— that he was prepared to forget all about last night, so that probably means that he won't be too hard on you neither."

"I'm sure you're right, Mrs. Donovan," Megan answered with a smile. Apparently last night's unorthodox call on her guardian was going to be every bit as successful as she had hoped! And with that cheering reflection, she bestowed another smile on Mrs. Donovan and allowed herself to be helped to sausages and eggs.

Megan had just finished eating when she heard the front door open and the sound of booted feet on the wide-planked hallway. Justin was back. She dabbed at her lips with a napkin and hurried out to greet him. It was only as she reached the doorway that she recalled being held on Justin's lap while she cried into his shoulder. For a moment she was overcome by shyness.

Justin was handing his gloves and hat to Donovan. Megan had a few minutes to study him while he was still unaware of her presence. Her eyes ran over him from his booted heels to the rough black disorder of his hair. Wide-shouldered, lean-hipped, and hard-muscled, he towered over Donovan's rounded figure. His face, turned partly away from her, was all rough-hewn planes and harsh angles, the skin bronzed and toughened by exposure to sun and wind. He was clean-shaven this morning, which allowed her to get a clearer look at a determined jaw and a straight, beautifully-formed mouth. Why, he's handsome, Megan thought with some surprise, doing her best to reconcile her new impression of her guardian with the cold haughty autocrat whose affection she had schemed to win for so long. Why had she never noticed the way he looked, in all the years she had known him? Then he turned to face her. The golden gleam of his eyes met hers head on. Megan was dazzled by his sheer physical appeal. Although her experience with men was so slight as to be non-existent, she realized that he was magnificent. She found herself blushing.

Justin, noting her confusion, cocked an eyebrow at her. "Good morning, Megan," he said coolly, moving down the hall toward her. "I trust you slept well?"

There was nothing in this civil inquiry to cause her

47

embarrassment, yet Megan felt her blush deepen. She could have kicked herself. What a fool he must think her, she thought despairingly. Last night she had behaved like a ninny pot, and this morning she was blushing like a schoolgirl.

"Yes, thank you, m-my lord," she stammered, feeling more uncomfortable by the minute. "And—and you?"

"Like the dead," he answered good-humoredly, running speculative eyes over her face. Megan, thrown into hopeless confusion by his openly questioning gaze, looked helplessly at the floor. She had no idea what a charming picture she made in her childish high-waisted white frock, with its blue sash emphasizing her blossoming curves. She had left her hair loose this morning, catching the sides back with a ribbon, and the night-black cloud fell past her waist in back while a few wayward tendrils curled enticingly over her shoulders. The sooty length of her lashes veiled her eyes as she stared at the floor, and Justin felt a grin tug at the corners of his mouth as he divined the reason for her shy refusal to look at him. Of course she was remembering all that had passed between them the night before, and he was inordinately pleased that the memory had the power to make her blush. It appeared that she was not lost to all sense of maidenly modesty after all.

"However, I must confess that my rest was not entirely undisturbed." His voice dropped to a conspiratorial whisper. "Circumstances forced me to do a little pantry-raiding in the middle of the night. I live in terror that Mrs. Donovan will discover that the better part of her roast beef is missing, and instigate an inquiry into the identity of the culprit."

As he had intended, this nonsense made her laugh and look up at him. Her incredible violet eyes, now bright with amusement, were enchanting. Justin had to warn himself to be on guard against their spell. He stood in place of a father to this beautiful creature, and it was as a daughter that he must think of her.

"Have you had breakfast?" he asked abruptly. Megan's eyes flickered at his sudden change of tone, and the smile died slowly on her lips. She nodded.

"Then you will please come with me to the library. I think we have a few things to discuss."

He moved off down the hall without waiting for an answer. Megan trailed behind him, bewildered at his quick change of mood. One moment he was charming, smiling at her, teasing her, and the next, for no apparent reason that she could see, he was coolly formal.

Justin opened the door to the library and then stood aside so that Megan could go in first. He closed the door behind them, then crossed to sit behind an ancient mahogany desk that had dominated the room for generations. He motioned Megan into a leather chair facing him.

Justin leaned back in his own chair, surveying her across the width of the desk. She looked up, meeting his eyes, her own unconsciously appealing. Justin experienced a sensation that he didn't care to define; not for the first time, he wished that he had let Stanton undertake this mission.

"I see no need to rake over the matters we discussed last night," he began at last, his eyes on the ornately carved ceiling. "What I want to discuss is your future: I am fairly certain that I can get Miss Chevington to take you back—or, if you prefer, we can find another school that is more to your liking. I am sure that Stanton will be more than equal to the task." A glimmer of a smile lit his eyes as he looked at her.

Megan felt as if he had kicked her in the stomach. Her eyes sought to engage his. "But I thought you said I would go to London and have a come-out!"

"And so you shall, my dear. When you turn eighteen. But in the meantime, I think it would be best if you returned to school. As I said, I am prepared to consider your wishes in the matter: You may choose whichever school you prefer, within reason."

"No!" Megan sat abruptly upright, her eyes catching fire.

Justin stared at her. "I beg your pardon?" he asked at last, with careful civility.

"I said, no!" Megan reiterated, looking militant.

"Perhaps you would care to elaborate on that statement?" Justin was keeping a careful hold on his own temper; defiance was something he hadn't expected; it was beyond his experience. Usually, when he made a decision, his dictates were obeyed without question.

"I won't go back to school!" The light of battle gleamed in her eyes. She felt betrayed. Last night she had thought that he understood at last, that he had recognized her loneliness and need. But it was now clear that he had merely been humoring her, getting

50

through a difficult situation as easily as he could, all the while meaning to banish her from his life as soon as he was able. The knowledge hurt unbearably; glaring at him, Megan fought the urge to cry.

"Do you have some other suggestion to put forward instead?" Justin congratulated himself on his control. His first impulse had been to roar out that she would do as he said and be done with it, but the memory of the woebegone little creature who had sobbed in his arms the night before stayed him. He was prepared to admit that perhaps he had neglected her in the past; that could be remedied in the future. But he was not prepared to put up with insolent disregard of his wishes.

"You could take me back to London with you!"

Justin thought of his bachelor existence in London, and slowly shook his head. It would not do. If Alicia were a proper wife to him, living in his house instead of taking herself off to stay with friends whenever he came up to town, then it might have been possible. But as it was . . .

"I'm sorry, but that's not possible," he said, looking at her steadily. Megan's eyes sparkled with unshed tears; her mouth set mutinously.

"Admit it, you just don't want me!" she cried, jumping up from her chair. "You've never wanted me! I thought last night that you were different—kind, even—that I might have misjudged you all these years! But I hadn't! You're cold and cruel and hateful!"

"Sit down!" Justin did not raise his voice, but it bit

51

like a whip for all its civilized softness. Megan, used to causing a furor when she allowed her Irish temper free rein, was stopped in mid-tirade.

"I have put up with quite a bit from you, my child." He was speaking through his teeth; Megan found the effect strangely intimidating. "I am prepared to overlook your recent behavior—which has been that of a self-willed hoyden in need of a good paddling—but I will not tolerate insolence or disobedience. Is that perfectly understood?"

Megan had never allowed anyone to dominate her, and she was not about to start with her impossible guardian. She returned his look with a fiery one of her own, and lifted her chin in instinctive challenge."

"I won't go back to school," she said stubbornly. His eyes flashed; it was all Megan could do not to cower away from him.

"By God, you'll do as I say!"

"I *won't* go back to school," Megan said. Justin jumped up from his chair and was around the desk before she could move. His hands bit into the tender flesh of her upper arms as he jerked her from her chair. Megan gave a cry of pain and alarm, but he ignored it, his hands continuing to grip her cruelly. He glared down at her but her eyes continued to defy him.

"You're hurting," she said in a cold, clear voice, then winced as his grip tightened. He looked furious, angry enough to enjoy causing her pain. Megan felt a little stab of fear. After all, there was really nothing to prevent him from beating her, or punishing her in any way he wished.

"I'm sorry," he said stiffly after a moment. His hands eased away from her, dropping to his sides. Megan realized, with an exquisite sensation of relief, that however much he might threaten, he was not a man who would use physical violence against a woman. With that realization came a sudden sense of power. He would not beat her, or harm her in any way, she was almost sure. And in any contest of wills, she was his equal!

"Nevertheless, you will obey me," he added grimly, daring her to contradict him. She could smell the faint scent of horses and cigars and what she vaguely recognized as pure man smell that emanated from him. The mixture was oddly pleasant, and soothing to the nerves, if she had been of a mind to be soothed. But she was not. She glared at him, her head tilted back. He loomed over her, far taller and bigger than she, but she refused to allow his physical size to intimidate her.

"If you make me go back to school, I'll only run away again," she warned him truculently. He muttered an oath, and he gripped her arms again, crushing the puffed muslin sleeves but not really hurting. He gave her a slight shake. Megan met his black frown unflinchingly.

"You run away again, my girl, and I really will paddle you," he promised. From the set of his jaw, Megan knew that he meant what he said. The sheer hopelessness of her position infuriated her; her eyes glittered with all the reckless fury of her Irish ancestry.

"Why can't I come to London with you?" she demanded fiercely. "I'm too old for school! I'm not a child anymore: I'm a woman!"

His eyes, swiftly running the length of her, acknowledged the truth of that. She was a woman—physically, at least. But her mind was that of a wayward child, determined to get her own way at any cost. And Justin knew he couldn't have that.

"I told you, it isn't possible," he answered, his voice harsh. "Next year, when you turn eighteen, will be time enough. In the meantime, you're going back to school. And that's all I intend to say on the subject!"

This autocratic pronouncement was like a match to the fuse of Megan's temper. "You can't make me!" she screamed, struggling against the hands that still gripped her. He pulled her closer in an attempt to control her rebellion. For one brief moment Megan was conscious of the hard strength of his body against hers, the warmth of him, the half-painful, half-pleasurable sensation of his chest against the softness of her breasts. Then she jerked away from him, catching him by surprise; she was able to put perhaps a foot of space between them. Drawing back her slippered foot, she kicked him squarely in the shin.

The kick hurt her far more than it hurt him. He barely flinched while she felt like howling with pain. But it did serve to ignite his anger; she could see it blazing in his eyes.

"Why, you little . . ." he rasped, biting off the epithet. Before Meghan realized what he intended, he had swept her off her feet and was striding around the desk with her, sitting down and putting her across his knees. Megan fought like a wildcat, kicking and scratching with frantic strength, but he held her easily. Megan felt him lifing her skirt; she writhed furiously against the hard shelf of his knees, but there was no stopping him. He delivered three stinging slaps to her backside, which was protected from his blows only by her muslin pantalets, then stood up abruptly, setting her on her feet.

"Beast!" she cried, jerking free of his hold. He merely looked at her, his eyes glinting in a way she found impossible to decipher. She saw that a deep red color had risen to stain his hard cheekbones, and put it down to his loss of temper.

"Get your things together," he ordered, turning away and striding across to the long window that overlooked the back lawn. It was as if he couldn't trust himself to keep his hands off her. "We'll be leaving right after luncheon."

"I won't!" Megan quivered with outrage, but, clearly, he wasn't in the mood to stand any more of her tantrums. For once in Megan's life, prudence raised its cautious head, and she was silent. She could feel his eyes boring into her back as she whirled and stalked from the room.

After she was gone, Justin drew a long breath and sat down at his desk, staring unseeingly into the cold embers of last night's fire. He had not intended to lay a hand on her—indeed, he had never before touched a woman in violence—but she was behaving like a spoilt child and what else could she expect? But there was more to it than that, for as soon as his hand had encountered her soft, rounded bottom he had been conscious of an almost overwhelming desire to let his fingers linger, to stroke and caress her quivering flesh instead of bruising it. Disgust at his own thoughts rose like bile in his throat; he had released her at once. But now, more clearly than ever, he could see the need to get her safely out of harm's way before any damage was done. Something about the chit aroused him; this was the second time in as many days that he had found himself wanting her in a way no guardian should want his ward. In the last twenty of his thirty-six years of life, he had desired many women, and taken most of them. But never had he found himself battling such an overwhelming sexual attraction, or one that was so clearly impossible to pursue.

He was still staring moodily into the darkened fireplace when Donovan came into the room. Seeing Justin, he stopped, and with a muttered word of apology began to back out.

"Did you want something, Donovan?" Justin asked wearily, feeling more annoyed at himself than ever as he observed the butler's attempts to escape his notice.

"Oh, no, my lord," Donovan assured him hastily, regarding his master with every appearance of trepidation. "I thought your lordship had gone out with Miss Megan!"

Justin eyed his butler. Plainly Donovan was disconcerted to find him still in the library, and he suspected that the bottle of Irish whiskey that was always kept in a bottom desk drawer had been the man's object.

"What do you mean you thought I'd gone out with Miss Megan?" he asked sharply. "Miss Megan has gone upstairs."

Donovan looked even more unhappy.

"Oh no, my lord, if you'll excuse me saying so. Miss Megan went out through the kitchen dressed in her riding clothes just a few minutes ago. She was saying something about your lordship under her breath, and we—that is, Mrs. Donovan and I—assumed that she was going riding with you. Seeing that she was wearing her riding dress and all, my lord!"

"Damn it to hell!" Justin surged to his feet, looking so furious that Donovan backed away. "The disobedient little wretch! This time I really will peel the skin from her backside!" He rushed past Donovan and went up the stairs, two at a time. He stopped to shout down to Donovan. "Have someone saddle me a horse. A good one, mind you, and not that nag I arrived on!"

According to Justin's calculations, by the time he had changed clothes and mounted, Megan had a good twenty minutes' start on him. Jem, the young groom, had seen his mistress head off down the road toward the tiny village of Maam's Cross, a few miles away. Justin realized that this time the baggage really meant to give him the slip. There was nowhere she could hide in so small a place. So he went the other way. After an hour's hard riding—his mount, a mettlesome black stallion was the fastest thing in the stables—he saw her. She was mounted on a small gray gelding, and she was setting a brisk pace.

As he quickly closed the distance between them, he noticed that she sat her mount with innate grace. She didn't hear him until he was less than forty feet away;

then the sound of his horses' hoofbeats caused her to cast a quick glance back over her shoulder. When she saw him, her face reflected fear, then anger, then sheer determination. Clapping her heels into the gelding's side and uttering what sounded for all the world like a wild Indian's war cry, she was off. Justin grinned savagely as he sent his mount streaking after her. This time, when he caught up with her, he'd definitely cure her of running away. And no amount of tears and pleading were going to sidetrack him!

It was an unequal contest, as he had known from the first. His horse was faster and larger than hers, and he was by far the better rider. In seconds he was pulling up alongside her. She was bent low in the saddle, doing her best to give him a run for his money, but both he and she knew he had won. He flashed her a savage grin as he leaned forward, reaching for the gelding's reins.

"No!" she cried, trying to jerk the animal's head around, but it was too late. He grabbed the reins, and as both animals began to slow, once again she cried "No!" and brought her riding crop down hard on his stallion's rump.

After that, everything happened in a blur. His horse reared furiously at such unaccustomed mistreatment. Justin, already off-balance from reaching for the reins, went somersaulting through the air. Megan screamed as he landed with a thud, hitting the rain-softened ground so hard he bounced. The stallion, eyes rolling, went streaking past his fallen rider, his hooves coming within inches of Justin's head. Megan dragged her own horse to a stop, flinging herself from the saddle and running to kneel beside her guardian's body. He was lying on his back, sprawled at what Megan knew instinctively was an unnatural angle; all the blood had drained from his face, leaving it a pasty white. Megan, shuddering convulsively, was very much afraid that he was dead.

Chapter 4

Megan sat huddled in a tall armchair near Justin's bed, her chin resting on her drawn-up knees, her arms wrapping her slender calves. Her nightgown, all she had on, was of fine white lawn and offered scant protection from the chill of the room which was not noticeably lessened by the fire which blazed and crackled in the hearth. To keep warm, she had taken a quilt from her own bed. She snuggled into it and waited.

From the depths of the cavernous four-poster she could hear the steady rasp of Justin's breathing. He had not awakened since she had caused him to be thrown from his horse. Megan was suffering from a remorse so intense that it was like a physical pain inside her. The doctor, who had left hours ago, long before night had fallen, had assured her with bluff sympathy that Justin would not die, but this was small comfort. If he was not on the verge of death, he had been gravely injured in the fall; the doctor said so. Besides the blow to the head which had knocked him unconscious, he had broken his left leg high up in the thigh where it would take a long time to heal. The doctor had assured her that this was the worst of his injuries: the rest, except for the blow to his head were little more than scrapes and bruises. But despite the doctor's well-meaning assurances, Megan knew that her part in what had happened was inexcusable.

Mrs. Donovan, at Megan's insistence, had gone to bed about an hour before. Despite the lady's offer to sit with the Earl—and everyone had agreed that he shouldn't be left alone at least until after he had regained consciousness—Megan was determined to stay with him herself. After all, she had been the cause of his injury, and it was up to her to make what amends she could. She meant to nurse him devotedly. She was the cause of it all, and she would accept his chastisement without complaint.

The only light in the huge chamber was the soft glow cast by the fire and a single flickering candle on the bedside table. The rest of the room was bathed in deep shadows. Megan cast an occasional apprehensive glance at the dark corners, and wished that the rich walnut paneling the walls had not been so artfully decorated with the heads of grinning gargoyles and demons. Megan knew that she would never be able to sleep a wink if her own bedroom had been embellished in such a manner.

While she was lost in thought, Megan's eyes had drifted away from the figure in the bed. Some change in his breathing made her look at him. He was moving. His long body, made cumbersome by the splint on his leg, jerked spasmodically. Anxiously Megan arose from the chair and bent over him. She was astonished to find herself looking into the golden depths of his eyes.

"What the hell . . .?" he muttered, frowning as his eyes moved over her slender shape so imperfectly concealed by the thin nightgown. Megan smiled mistily at him, so relieved that he was awake that she could have cried.

"Be still, my lord," she said, her voice low. "You've been injured."

His eyes traveled over her body, which was clearly silhouetted by the glow of the fire behind her.

"I remember."

Megan was surprised at the wryness of his voice. He sounded blessedly normal.

"I'm so sorry," she murmured, hovering helplessly over him. He tried to hitch himself up against the soft pillows, his face twisting in a grimace at the pain the movement caused him. Megan instinctively put a hand on his shoulder, which was as bare as the rest of him. After the doctor left, it had been decided that it would subject him to too much discomfort if Donovan tried to dress him in his nightshirt.

He looked at her hand, so small and cool and pale against the bronzed width of his shoulder. "Next time you're feeling murderous, it would be more sporting if you gave me advance notice. Then I'd take care to stay clear."

Her mouth quivered at his words, which were meant mostly in jest. She looked stricken. Justin swallowed an oath, and reached for her hand which she had pulled away as if he had burned her.

"I was only teasing," he said impatiently, capturing her hand and holding it firmly despite the pain that shot through his abused body. "Don't worry about it: it was as much my fault as yours, for being such a damned cow-handed rider."

Megan laughed with a little catch in her voice. Justin saw the liquid sheen of tears in her eyes. Before he realized what he was doing, he lifted her hand to his mouth, brushing it with his lips. The faint scent of jasmine—a sachet tucked in with her night-clothes and undergarments—teased his nostrils. He half-closed his eyes, instinctively savoring the sweetness of her. Then an awareness of what he was doing snapped his eyes open again, and he quickly released his grip on her hand.

"Is there any water?" he asked gruffly. She was looking down at him with a soft glow in those violet eyes, and he was desperate for something to distract her attention. On no account must he let her know of this ridiculous attraction that he was finding harder and harder to ignore. If she had any inkling of the effect she had on him, their guardian-ward relationship

64

would become impossible to maintain.

"I'll get some." She turned away from the bed to the small table, where Mrs. Donovan had left a jug of water and a glass along with a sleeping potion recommended by the doctor if his patient should suffer too much pain. Megan filled the glass with hands that were not quite steady, feeling the imprint of Justin's mouth on her skin as if he had branded her. Never had she felt anything like it before; she had to fight to keep from pressing her lips to the spot on her hand where his lips had been.

Megan turned back to the bed with the glass in her hand. Justin was watching her with an odd, hooded look that she supposed could be put down to the pain he must be feeling.

"Let me help you," she said, when it became obvious that he couldn't drink while lying flat on his back.

He waved her away. "Tuck another pillow under my head, and I'll be fine." He sounded irritable. Megan bit her lips, and did as he ordered, now he was able to drink and he drained the glass thirstily.

"How do you feel? Are you in much pain?" Megan asked hesitantly when he handed the empty glass back to her. He grimaced, his face looking very dark as he leaned wearily back against the pillow.

"Aside from my leg, which I assume from this damned uncomfortable thing around it must be broken, my head, which aches like the devil, not to mention various cuts and bruises, I feel wonderful."

His dry humor, accompanied by a twisted smile,

65

made Megan laugh again, but she sobered immediately. "I really am so very sorry," she told him remorsefully. "My teachers are always telling me that I act first and think later, and it's perfectly true. I do. But I never meant to hurt you. I just—didn't consider the consequences."

"If murder really wasn't on your mind, then I suppose I must forgive you," he said with a thoughtful air that was belied by the smile in his eyes. "Besides, you don't have to explain to me about temper. I have a most inconvenient one myself."

Megan smiled. "I've noticed."

"I thought you might have."

"Dr. Ryan left you a sleeping draught, if you should be in pain. Would you like it?" She was anxious to make up for what she had done by nursing him as best she could. A worried frown puckered her brow; her teeth nibbled thoughtfully on the rosy fullness of her lower lip. Justin was fascinated. She was truly lovely, he thought for what must have been the tenth time since he had seen her making such an exhibition of herself—was it only one night ago?—in the blue salon. Her face, with its small round chin and elegantly carved cheekbones, had a delicate perfection of feature that would not have been out of place on the most exquisite of Chevres' porclain ladies. Her skin was the color of smooth, heavy cream; against it, the darkness of her brows and lashes seemed almost startling. Her hair was drawn softly away from her face to hang in a braid over one shoulder. The curling tendrils that had worked themselves free formed an entracing frame for the huge purple eyes which were regarding him so solemnly.

"Don't you have a dressing gown?" he asked sharply as his eyes touched on the demure white nightgown with its high, ruffled neckline and rows of tucks that did such an inadequate job of shielding her slender body from his gaze.

"I do, but I left it at school," Megan answered, bewildered at the abrupt change of topic.

Justin stared at her. "For God's sake, didn't they teach you anything in those schools? I paid them enough money!" He sounded thoroughly annoyed, and Megan felt her bewilderment grow. What on earth did her education have to do with it?

"My lord?" The words were a soft question. Her eyes were puzzled as they searched his lean face.

Justin looked at her sharply, saw the uncomprehending innocence in her eyes, and sighed. "Never mind," he said roughly. Then, taking a deep breath, he asked, "Where's Mrs. Donovan?"

"I sent her to bed. She's old, and she was tired."

"So you thought you'd play the ministering angel for a while, did you?" Justin asked sardonically. Harsh lines of what Megan assumed to be pain appeared around the edges of his mouth. "Well, you can take yourself off to bed, too. I assure you that I won't expire in the night if I'm left alone."

"But what if you should want something? You can't possibly get out bed to get it yourself," Megan pointed out. Justin, looking at her impatiently, saw that she was shivering, and that she had wrapped her

67

arms over her breasts for warmth.

"You're freezing. Go on to bed," he ordered abruptly. Megan's mouth took on the stubborn curve that he was beginning to know all too well.

"I have a quilt over there in the chair," she said. "I'll curl up and be very quiet, but I'm not leaving you alone."

The spark in her eyes told him that she would not be persuaded, and he was in no condition to argue about it. Sighing, Justin gave it up.

"Oh, for God's sake," he muttered furiously, trying not to look at her. He closed his eyes. "Give me the damned sleeping draught!"

When Justin awoke at last it was to find the bright autumn sunshine streaming in through the many-paned windows that gave him an excellent view of the Irish countryside even from his bed. He was relieved but a little sorry to see Mrs. Donovan sitting in the chair Megan had occupied the night before. When she saw that he was awake, she put down the mending she had been working on and bustled around making him comfortable in a way that was a great improvement over Megan's inept ministrations of the night before. There wasn't much she could do for him besides straightening his bed and settling his breakfast tray, but at least she presented no threat to his peace of mind. When he had eaten, he sent Mrs. Donovan away, preferring her husband's assistance in performing his morning ablutions, and helping him into his dressing gown.

By the time Megan put in an appearance, Justin was sitting up against his pillows, a book of plays forgotten on the bedspread beside him and a decidedly peevish look on his face. Dr. Ryan had been in to see him, and had ordered him to stay in bed for at least the next few days; with his leg out of commission—and it pained him damnably!—he had little choice but to obey. Without the aid of a crutch, which would take perhaps three days to make, he had no way of getting around. To add insult to injury, Mrs. Donovan seemed convinced that his injury relegated him to nursery status, and she addressed him in motherly tones that annoyed him unbearably. She called him Master Justin, which she hadn't done since he had inherited the title at the age of sixteen, when she brought him his lunch she warned him to eat it all like a good boy! She had told him that he was feeling cross because he was tired, and that he should try to take a nap. And then, thankfully, she had left him alone. That had been perhaps three hours before; by the time Megan tapped on his door, he was facing the fact that he was utterly bored.

When she entered in response to his curt summons, she looked so young and unconsciously appealing in her jonquil-colored day dress that Justin glared at her. She came to stand at the foot of the bed, her hands curving around the ornately carved footboard.

"Shall I go away again?" she asked with a small smile. Justin's scowl deepened. His dark hair was wildly mussed; his tawny-gold eyes snapped irritably. He looked very big and powerful propped up against the mound of fluffy white pillows.

"You got me in this shape, so you can damn well entertain me," he growled. Megan had to laugh; she couldn't help it.

"Mrs. Donovan said you were as sore-headed as a hedgehog with its quills pulled. I see what she meant."

"I wouldn't get too saucy, miss. I won't be tied to this bed forever, you know." Despite his threatening words, Justin could not control the responsive quiver of his lips. Minx, he thought appreciatively. Then, unwilling to abandon his ill-humor, he added accusingly, "You're loving every minute of this, aren't you? As long as I'm laid up here, you don't have to go back to school."

The smile faded from Megan's lips. "I admit it. I am glad not to be going back to school," she told him, her eyes grave. "But I am truly sorry that you were injured. I would gladly undo it, if I could."

She sounded so conscience-stricken that Justin immediately relented. He had not meant to remind her of the fact that she had caused his accident, and he was heartily ashamed of himself for having done so.

"Well, you can make it up to me by singing to me, or some such thing: I am as bored as be-damned."

This made her smile again. "My lord, I am afraid that you took very little notice of my reports from school: as far as singing is concerned, I fear that I wouldn't give the hoarsest frog any competition!"

Justin looked at her doubtfully, and saw, to his surprise, that she was serious. He had always assumed

70

that well brought-up young ladies could sing at least passably.

"As bad as that, eh?" he asked, grinning. "Well, then, pray don't deafen me as well as lame me! Look in that drawer over there, and bring me a pack of cards: If you don't object, I'll teach you to play baccarat."

"I don't object at all, my lord," Megan answered calmly, and did as he told her.

At the end of two hours' play, both were chuckling companionably, and Megan had lost the equivalent of two years' pocket money to her ruthless guardian.

"Just think of it," he said wickedly, his eyes laughing as they surveyed the untidy mound of Megan's scribbled I.O.U.'s that were piled high before him. "No more ices or trinkets, or packets of ribbons or lace, or whatever else you females do with your money. In fact, you will probably have to hire out as a chambermaid or something to pay these off. After all," he added virtuously, "you can't expect me to permit you to use your allowance to redeem them: People might say that I was encouraging your unfortunate predilection for gaming!"

"Then I will just have to sell the ear-bobs you gave me for my birthday to pay them off!"

Justin grinned at her. "Oh, will you? In that case, I suppose I shall have to forgive the debt. The gossip would be never-ending if it should get out that you had to sell your jewelry to pay your gaming debts! And all the dragon-mothers would warn their sons against you. It would never do to ally themselves with a hardened gamester!"

Megan wrinkled her nose impishly.

"Then you would be stuck with me forever, so I wouldn't laugh so hard, if I were you!"

"That aspect of the situation didn't occur to me. I can see that I really have no choice but to forgive the debt. To be forever fated to bear-lead a naughty, impertinent chit would be a penance too heavy to be borne!"

He was grinnning crookedly at her, so Megan had no trouble accepting this sally in the spirit in which it had clearly been meant.

"You're funny!" she said, smiling warmly at him. His eyes twinkled at her.

"What makes you think I'm not serious?"

For a moment she looked uncertain. "You're not, are you?" she asked, sounding worried.

He looked at her, his expression softening. "I'm not," he assured her, and might have said more if a brief knock on the door had not distracted them.

It was Mrs. Donovan.

"I brought you your supper, Master Justin," she told him as she entered. "It's a bit early, but I thought you might be feeling hungry since you ate so little of your luncheon." Her faded blue eyes sharpened at the sight of Megan perched comfortably on the side of Justin's bed. The girl's cheeks were flushed and her eyes sparkled with laughter, and the Earl himself looked much more cheerful than he had earlier. The cards that littered the coverlet between them told their own story.

"You don't want to be playing them devil's games

with the likes of him, now, lamb," Mrs. Donovan said to Megan with the merest suggestion of a smile. "The Brants have always had the devil's own luck with cards. It's in their blood." She put the tray on the small table beside the bed.

"I always heard it said that the devil takes care of his own, Mrs. Donovan," Megan said with such an angelic air that Justin burst out laughing.

"That's right, my lamb, and you remember it, too," Mrs. Donovan said, glancing at Justin. He was still chuckling.

"Thank you for bringing up my dinner, Mrs. Donovan," Justin said.

Mrs. Donovan eyed the steaming tray complacently. "You can best thank me by eating it all up, Master Justin," she told him with a stern look. "It's good food, and it will do you good. You need to keep up your strength."

With a nod and a wink at Megan, she left the room. As Justin lifted the cover off the tray, Megan stood up, smoothing her skirts rather self-consciously. She remembered how he had warned her that first night about letting the Donovans find out that she had visited him in his bedroom, and wondered what that good lady might be thinking.

"Well, I'll leave you to your meal," Megan said, feeling a surge of color creep up her face. Justin paused to look up at her. Faint rays of light were still wandering in through the windows, but her face was in shadow, and he could not read her expression. Something in her stance, however, told him that she was uncomfortable.

"Why don't you draw the curtains, light a couple of candles, and join me?" he suggested casually, wondering what he might have said to disturb her. She hesitated before answering. Justin peered at her closely. "Is something the matter, Megan? You're not still worried about these damned I.O.U's, are you? I was only joking. I wouldn't take your money."

"I know that, my lord," she answered quietly.

"Then what's wrong?" he demanded, impatience plain in his voice. " And don't tell me, nothing! You've gone as quiet as a bird when a hawk flies over!"

Megan smiled a little at that.

"It's only—the first night I was in here—you remember," she hesitated, then finished in a rush, "You were afraid that if the Donovans found me in your bedroom, they might think it wasn't perfectly respectable. But last night, and just now, Mrs. Donovan didn't appear to mind at all. I was wondering what the difference is."

Justin looked at her, his mouth slanting wryly.

"The difference, my child, is quite simple. On the occasion of your first visit I was in perfect health. Now I am incapacitated, to all intents and purposes, which puts quite a different light on the matter. It's perfectly respectable for you to visit your guardian in his chamber when he is ill; in fact, it *wouldn't* be proper if you didn't. The servants would think you unfeeling. And if you want it in plainer terms, now that I am a broken man, the consensus will be that I won't be thinking in terms of making improper advances to you."

Megan looked both amused and faintly incredulous. "You wouldn't anyway," she stated positively.

Justin regarded her a little ruefully. "No, I wouldn't," he agreed, and if there was anything odd in his tone Megan didn't notice it.

With that small point cleared up, after having been once again assured that he truly wanted her company, Megan had no hesitation about sharing his supper. She munched companionably, if inelegantly, on a chicken leg, using it to gesture as she talked while Justin ate with a little more decorum and watched her with amusement. With grease rimming her mouth and her eyes sparkling merrily, she looked absurdly young; Justin had no difficulty at all in recognizing the mop-haired, dirty-faced urchin of twelve years before beneath the surface loveliness of the young woman. He encouraged her to state her views on everything from educating females to the world situation, and found to his pleasure that she was as intelligent as she was beautiful. Her views were rather naive, colored noticeably by both her youth and sex, but they were perceptive for all that. Justin marveled at the thought that he had had such a creature under his care for a dozen years and done almost nothing about it. He should have made her acquaintance long before now, instead of waiting until she was nearly grown up. Besides all the other advantages, it would have made his present situation so much easier.

Over the next several days, Megan blossomed under Justin's attention. He was obivously growing fond of her, and the knowledge brought a pretty flush to her cheeks, a sparkle to her eyes. For herself, she thought he was the most magnificent man she had ever known—not that she had known many. The rector who conducted services at the school every Sunday, and the fathers and brothers of her schoolmates, were about all she knew about the opposite sex. But Justin was everything she had ever dreamed a man should be: kind and funny, tender and strong all at the same time. The fact that he was so handsome made it even better. Megan knew that he was quite old, thirty-six he said, which sounded like a great age to her. But when he was laughing and teasing her he didn't seem much older than she was herself. Megan knew she was fortunate to have such a man for her guardian. If she had been ordering one made to measure, she wouldn't have changed a thing about him.

She spent a great portion of the day with him, playing cards, reading to him, although he was perfectly capable of reading to himself. He liked the sound of her voice, he said. They talked. She would have spent even more time with him if he had not insisted that she get out in the fresh air for several hours each day. He told her sternly that her chatter tired him; that he needed to rest, so would she please go away and leave him in peace for a bit. Megan knew that he had no intention of resting while she was gone, and suspected that he actually missed her, because he always seemed pleased to see her when she got back.

Justin found Megan both a delight and a torment. Her unselfconscious beauty attracted him more every day, and it took a great deal of control to keep in mind that she was his ward. Quite apart from the appeal she made to his senses, he found himself liking her very much. She seemed a precocious child one moment, a wise old granny the next. Her way of thinking amused and intrigued him, and he found the smallest things about her, from the dimple that appeared in her cheek when she smiled at him to the husky, three-noted sound of her laugh, ever fascinating. All too clearly he realized that he was being drawn into treacherous waters with each day that passed. But he was confident that his self-control would prove more than a match for the unwelcome stirrings of his body. Besides, the only way to be totally safe from temptation was to remove it firmly from his vicinity; and, chained by his leg to the bed, he saw no easy way of getting Megan out of his life. To tell the truth, he didn't even want to, although he knew that when he was well again, it was the only responsible course of action to take. If she was dead set against school, then he would not force her to return, although he had not told her yet. Instead, he would bully or bribe his Aunt Sophronisa, who was chronically embarrassed for funds, into providing a home for Megan. He would hire a governess to oversee the remainder of her education, and would himself call upon her as frequently as he could manage. But for now, until his leg healed, he was content to let things ride. After all, what possible harm could come from simply enjoying a few weeks of his ward's company?

A week after the accident, Dr. Ryan called, bringing

with him Justin's crutch. He would have brought it sooner, he said, but knowing the Earl of old he had guessed that, once he had a means of getting out of bed, he would not hesitate to use it, and the leg had needed a certain period of rest. Justin was too thankful to get the crutch to make a fuss about the slowness of its delivery. With Dr. Ryan carefully monitoring his efforts, he managed to lever himself out of bed and balance precariously with the crutch's support. By the time the doctor left, half an hour later, Justin could stand with tolerable assurance and even walk across the room with a fair degree of ease. Dr. Ryan warned him strictly against attempting to negotiate the stairs, telling him frankly that another bad fall before the leg had healed might lame him for life. Justin faithfully promised to limit his perambulations to his bedroom and the hallway outside.

Megan had been out for her daily ride during the doctor's visit, and it was Mrs. Donovan who insisted that Justin rest after trekking back and forth across the room perhaps two dozen times. Justin, who was more tired by the small exertion than he cared to admit, was agreeable, although he absolutely refused to return to bed. Mrs. Donovan, with many disapproving noises, was persuaded to pull a chair up to the window so that Justin could sit and enjoy the view.

When she had done all she could to see to his comfort, including tucking a quilt about his legs, she left him at last to his own devices. Justin rested his head against the high back of the leather chair, idly watching the antics of a gaggle of geese as they chased each other across the lawn.

When Megan strolled into view, the skirt of her black riding habit tucked carelessly over one arm to expose a ruffle of petticoats and neat leather boots, Justin smiled a little and leaned forward so that he could get a better view. He realized that he had been watching for her without knowing it, aware that she must cross this particular stretch of lawn on her return from the stables. With her hair confined in a loose knot on the top of her head and the severe lines of her habit emphasizing the lissome grace of her form, she was dazzling. Justin saw her laugh as the geese clustered around her skirts, squawking and scrabbling for any crumbs of food she might have brought them. She had nothing, as she tried to convey to them by holding out empty hands and shaking her head. When they refused to believe her, growing more vociferous in their demands, she laughed again, and picked up her skirts before sprinting for the house.

When she had disappeared from sight, Justin leaned back in his chair. She would be up shortly, he thought, and he was right.

She swept into the room with only the briefest of knocks.

"What did Dr. Ryan say?" she demanded breathlessly, addressing her question to the bed before she saw that it was empty. Justin grinned at her from his chair; he liked the way her eyes lit up with surprise and pleasure when she saw that he was out of bed at last.

"He said that you may not have crippled me for life,

after all."

She stuck out her tongue at him. "Very funny, my lord."

Justin's grin widened as she danced across the room toward him. With her rosy cheeks and wide smile, she reminded him of sunshine and fresh flowers and the carefree days of his own youth. As she neared his chair, he could not resist the impulse to tease her a little. He pretended to cower, throwing up both hands to ward her off. She stopped to stare at him.

"Before you make any more nefarious attempts at murder, I think I should tell you that you no longer have a motive: I've decided not to send you back to school, so you see, you really have no reason to get rid of me."

Justin grinned broadly as he watched her eyes widen with incredulous delight.

"Oh, Justin!" she cried. Before Justin could ponder the wisdom of permitting this familiar form of address, she effectively distracted his attention by flinging herself at him in an excess of joy. Her skirts brushed the splinted leg, which was thrust out stiffly before him, and then her arms closed about his neck in an impassioned embrace.

"Careful," he warned, still laughing as his hands came up to her waist. And the laughter died in his throat and he felt her soft lips brush his cheek. With a stunning rush of desire, he realized that he would only have to move his head a fraction to touch her lips with his.

Chapter 5

Justin's jaw felt bristly against her lips; although he had shaved that morning, his beard grew fast, and it was now late afternoon. Megan tasted the rough saltiness of his skin with lips that were slightly parted. The now familiar smell of him—a combination of good cigars, soap, and sweat—enveloped her as she kissed his cheek with impulsive fervor. Her arms were wrapped around the strong column of his throat, squeezing tightly in an effort to communicate her joy; her fingers touched the thick hair at the nape of his neck, vaguely registering the alien texture. Her kiss was as innocent as a young child's, and when her lips brushed his, she did not even consider drawing away.

Megan felt his hands go hard on her waist, digging into her flesh with a force that should have hurt but didn't. Then he kissed her mouth, very gently; a soft, butterfly kiss. At first Megan was a little surprised at his action; she was not used to being touched, much less kissed, having never been around anyone who cared enough about her to physically demonstrate their affection. Her eyes opened instinctively, and she found him looking at her with a strange hot gleam in his golden eyes that she had never seen there before. Hesitantly, she smiled at him, deciding that she liked his kiss very much. The gleam intensified so that it seemed as if it would burn her, and he made a sound that was midway between a laugh and a groan. Then he was pulling her down so that she was sitting on his good leg, nestled against his shoulder; his arms slid all the way around her waist. Her head was tilted back across the hard muscles of his upper arm; against her ear she could hear the heavy thud of his heart. Her smile quivered and died as she stared up at him, mesmerized by that unreadable something in his dark face.

"Am I frightening you?" he asked with a husky note in his voice that made it sound as if he was having trouble speaking at all. Megan's eyes widened as she looked at him, then she slowly shook her head. Whatever this feeling that he was arousing in her was, it certainly wasn't fear.

"I won't hurt you," he promised as he bent over her. Megan believed him. Her fingers curled trustingly against the soft brocade covering his chest as he kissed her lightly. He dropped soft little kisses on her cheeks, temples, forehead, nose, and chin. She lay quietly in his arms, perfectly still except for her hands, which curled and uncurled against his chest, feeling a delicate warm glow start in the pit of her stomach and then pulse outward along her veins. His hands moved to stroke the loosened tendrils of her hair. She looked at him gravely, her eyes deep purple pools in the pale oval of her face. Justin smiled the ghost of a smile as he looked down at her; his golden eyes still held that hot, excited glow, but the curve of his long mouth was tender.

"Close your eyes, darling," he instructed softly, touching her eyelids with a gentle forefinger. Megan obeyed without question, feeling a tremulous excitement begin to spiral inside her as he laid his mouth against hers again.

His mouth was hard and warm as he brushed it back and forth across hers; he stroked her lips with his in a whisper-like caress, careful not to hurt or alarm her. When he felt her mouth quiver beneath his, he touched her lower lip with the tip of his tongue, tracing the outline of her lips before sliding between them to probe the smooth surface of her teeth. At the intimate touch, Megan felt an odd melting sensation.

"Justin," she whispered shakily, her hands moving with blind sureness to clutch the back of his neck. As she murmured his name, Justin took advantage of her parted lips to slide his tongue between her teeth. The bold invasion made Megan gasp, and she stiffened instinctively as his tongue began to explore the hot, sweet recesses of her mouth. Justin felt her uncertainty and slowly withdrew his tongue. He kissed her lips again, briefly, gently. With a sense of wonderment, Megan felt the tremors that racked the long muscles of his arms as they enclosed her. His body heat seemed to be drugging her; she could feel it wrapping about her like a warm, protective cocoon.

She was very conscious of the hardness of his chest against her breasts. Beneath her she could feel the steely muscles of his thigh as she half-lay across it.

For the first time in her life, Megan was made intensely aware of the differences between a man and a woman. He was so hard, she so soft; he was strong, she was weak; he needed, and it was her lot to give. His kisses intoxicated her, enchanted her, made her quake with delight. From the answering shudders that rippled his arms as he held her, from the dark rush of blood to his high cheekbones, from the piercing heat of his eyes as they moved over her, she knew that he was as enthralled by the touch of her mouth as she was by his. All question of right and wrong fled from her consciousness as she looked dazedly into his lean, handsome face. Her body had come awake at last, and it yearned for him fiercely, with an instinctive knowledge that transcended the innocence of her mind. He was as entrapped by passion as she was herself, and yet she knew that she had only to utter the slightest sound of protest to secure her instant release. The knowledge only increased her longing to be sheltered in his arms forever.

"Justin," she said. He gave a long, moaning sigh, and then his mouth was on hers, hot and shaking, kissing her with a hard passion that would have terrified her had anyone else been doing it; but from him, it excited her almost past bearing.

"Open your mouth, darling," he whispered in a queer, raspy undertone. Eyes closed, nearly mindless in the grip of sensations she had never even dreamed existed, she obeyed. This time his tongue was a welcome guest, caressing her tongue and the softness of her mouth until she was gasping for breath. She thought, it feels so strange, to be kissed like this, and then she couldn't think at all. The slow seduction of his mouth was driving her wild. Shyly at first, and then with increasing confidence, her tongue began to reply to his. Her untutored response seemed to set him afire. He kissed her over and over again, his mouth bruising her softness without meaning to, hardly aware of what he was doing. Megan gloried in his frenzied kisses, crying out against his mouth, clinging to him like a limpet to a rock. She could feel him shaking as if with a fit of ague. Her own body was at the mercy of similar tremors. When at last his mouth left hers to trail across the side of her cheek to her neck, Megan felt that she might expire at the sheer wonder of his lips against her skin.

His fingers were unsteady as they unwrapped the white silk stock from about her neck so that he might have better access to her skin. Megan felt his lips in the hollow of her throat, burning her, and her nails dug convulsively into the thick wavy hair at the back of his head, holding him to her. When he began to unbutton her white shirtwaist, greeting each centimeter of newly liberated flesh with a kiss, Megan arched herself against him, sighing with pleasure. He unbuttoned the garment down to the edge of her plain white chemise, laying aside the edges of her shirtwaist so that a deep V of creamy flesh was exposed to his mouth. His lips and tongue stroked with rough insistence from the hollow of her throat to the first pale swellings of her breasts where they were just visible above the top of her chemise. At the touch of his mouth on her breasts, Megan felt the world begin to whirl around her. She moaned, tightening her grip on him, writhing against him in an attempt to ease the mingled agony and ecstasy that had her in thrall. Justin shuddered in answer, gasping out her name, and Megan felt the hot touch of his hand as it found its way up under her voluminous skirts. He slid the flat of his hand over her slim calves in their white stockings, exploring the curves of her legs, touching her knees; his fingers moved up beneath the hem of her pantalets to a soft thigh, running gently over the stockinged flesh until he reached her lacy garter. Then he moved on, lightly caressing the silkiness of her bare skin before his hand slid all the way around to the inside of her thigh. The touch of his hand where no one had ever touched her before shocked her. Her nails slid down his head to curve into the brown flesh of his neck, impaling him. As his hand slid ever higher, she squirmed uncomfortably. The increasing intimacy of his touch was bringing her back to an awareness of herself that

86

brought waves of embarrassment in its wake. With a hot flood of color to her cheeks, she suddenly realized how she must appear, lying in his arms with her shirtwaist half unbuttoned and her skirts pushed up around her hips while he pressed hot kisses to her breasts and his hands roamed ever higher on the bare skin of her thighs beneath her pantalets.

"Justin, stop!" she gasped, self-disgust thick in her voice as she pushed against his shoulders with her hands. For a moment she feared that he wouldn't heed her, so caught up in his own rising passion that he was now deaf and blind to her pleas. But she was wrong. As she continued to push against his shoulders, he drew in a deep, shuddering breath; she felt his hands clench on her flesh, and then he was smoothing down her skirts. She couldn't look at him; instead she looked down at the whiteness of her flesh above her chemise, marred now with rosy marks where his lips had been, and blushed furiously. Her hands were shaking so badly as they tried to do up her shirtwaist that she couldn't fit even the first button into its hole. Justin, with a harsh sound, brushed her hands out of the way and fastened the garment for her. Megan blushed anew at the brush of his knuckles against her flesh.

"I'm sorry," he said awkwardly when this task was completed. Megan risked a quick look at him; saw the rigid set of his mouth and hooded glitter of his eyes. She looked away quickly. She wanted to scramble off his lap, but she feared that her quivering knees would refuse to support her weight and she would end up crumpled in a heap at his feet. What had taken place between them was her fault; she had not the slightest doubt of that. She had kissed him first. Her smiles and gestures had encouraged him to kiss and touch her in return. He no doubt thought she was a wanton. Among the girls at school, it was common knowledge that it was a lady's place to conduct herself at all times so as to keep a gentleman's respect, because if he ever ceased to respect her he would try to take awful liberties with her person and then she would be ruined, which was the worst fate that could overtake any gently-reared girl. Clearly she was well on the road to ruin; remembering how she had sighed and quivered in Justin's arms, she thought she deserved to be.

"Megan, did you hear what I said?" Justin's voice sounded more normal now, and was tinged with just a hint of exasperation. "Look at me!" His hand slid beneath her chin to enforce his command.

She met his eyes with a flicker of her lashes, then fastened her gaze obstinately on his tightly compressed mouth. She couldn't bear to see the contempt he must be feeling for her reflected in those golden eyes. For years she had yearned for his affection, and now, just when she thought she had begun to earn it, when they had been such friends over the past week, she had ruined everything. She despised herself, and was very much afraid that he must despise her, too.

"For God's sake, don't look like that!" he said roughly, his hand tightening beneath her chin so that his fingers dug into her jaw. "It was my fault, not yours. Megan, do you hear me?"

It was kind of him to take the blame. Megan darted another quick, unhappy glance at him and saw that he was frowning blackly. Her mouth quivered. Suddenly all she wanted was to get away from him, to go off somewhere by herself and cry and cry.

"Please let me go," she said in a stifled little voice. Justin's grip tightened for an instant, then he slowly released her. Moving like a sleepwalker, Megan got up and began to turn away toward the door. Justin tried to catch her hand, to hold her there, but she eluded him. Her eyes were almost blind with tears.

"Megan, come back here!" he ordered furiously as she continued to walk with careful, measured steps toward the door. "Megan!"

As she let herself out, Megan winced at the string of furious oaths that fell from his lips.

Over the next few days, Megan made it her business to stay well out of her guardian's way. The visits to his room, the friendly card games, the intimate suppers were a thing of the past. She knew he roamed the upstairs corridors and guessed that he was on the lookout for her. Not wanting to confront him, she spent nearly every hour of the day on horseback or in the stables. At night, she took the precaution of locking her door, although she knew instinctively that he would not seek her out in her bedroom after what had passed between them. Whenever she remembered those moments in his arms, the way he had kissed and caressed her, the way she had responded, she blushed to the roots of her hair. Logically, she knew she could not avoid him forever; his very position as her guardian made that impossible. But with every ounce of her being, she longed to put off the inevitable meeting with him for as long as she could. She thought that he was probably as embarrassed by her behavior—and his, although, being a man, he could not really be held at fault—as she was herself, and wished that she could feel confident that he would just ignore the whole deplorable incident. But, secretly, she knew he would not. Like the gentleman he was, he would apologize as he had tried to do before she so ignobly fled, and she didn't think she could bear to hear him pretending that she was the blameless party. Besides, if just the thought of him could make her blush, what would his physical presence do to her composure? She had kissed his mouth, felt those long, strong hands on her body, dug her nails into the strong column of his neck. If she had to look at him, to speak to him, she thought she might die of shame.

The servants, particularly the Donovans, were clearly aware of the rift between their master and his ward, but they had no knowledge of its cause. Megan shuddered to think of how they would treat her if they ever learned the truth. She would be a scarlet woman; even the servants would feel nothing for her but contempt. Realizing this, Megan had never felt more miserable in her life.

To Mrs. Donovan's discreet inquiries as to what had happened to make her refuse to spend even so much as a quarter hour in the Earl's company, Megan said only that they had quarreled. Knowing how high-handed all the Brants could be when the mood was upon them,

Mrs. Donovan had no trouble believing this. But as she told her husband, it must have been a peculiar quarrel to have Miss Megan avoiding her guardian like he had the plague, while he paced and prowled his rooms and the upstairs hallways like a caged tiger. It was plain that he missed Miss Megan's company; it was equally plain that Miss Megan was not going to relent in her refusal to see him until she was forced to.

Justin, for his part, could have cheerfully kicked himself down a flight of stairs. His behavior to his innocent young ward had been inexcusable. Telling himself that he had been unable to resist her did no good at all. No matter how charming or beautiful he found her, no matter how strong her onslaught on his senses, nothing should have been allowed to outweigh the fact that she was a seventeen-year-old schoolgirl in his care. That she had aroused feelings in him that he hadn't felt in years was neither here nor there; it was his job, as her guardian, to protect her morals, not to allow her to be compromised or especially to compromise her himself. He had always heard that men approaching their fortieth year acquired a taste for very young girls. Remembering the intensity of his physical reaction to Megan, he began for the first time to believe that this might be true. Nothing else could account for the way he had quivered and moaned, ached and burned for her like some damned snot-nosed schoolboy; and for nothing more than a few kisses and gropes with a pretty—all right, very pretty—girl! Mentally he reviewed all the elegant ladies of the *ton*, all the gorgeous actresses and dancers, all the coquettish demimondaines he had known, and shook his head at himself. He must really be getting senile, to let an innocent schoolgirl affect him in such a way!

Whenever he thought back over that scene with Megan—which he did, frequently—guilt rose to swamp even the incredible force of his passion. The fact that she had been willing enough, at least in the beginning, made no difference. Of course the girl had been willing! She was as innocent as a baby, with little idea of where a few sweet kisses could lead. But he had known full well, and he had kissed her anyway, to his everlasting discredit. He had told himself that he would kiss her just once, and he might have been able to keep to that resolve if she had not smiled at him so sweetly after he had first brushed her lips with his. That beguiling smile had tempted him past bearing, and he had thought to kiss her just once more. After that, it had been all over with him. At his age, with all his experience with women, he should have known what would happen. And yet he had no way of knowing how warm and tender her flesh would be, how like the inside of a juicy ripe peach her mouth was. Kissing her, he had lost control. What happened next was totally unforgivable. If any other man had used his ward as he himself had, he would have called him out, and been more than justified in doing so. Then, if he had managed to curb his anger sufficiently to wound rather than kill the blackguard, there would have been a quick, quiet wedding whether the bride and groom were willing or no. A young lady's virtue was her most precious possession; he, Justin, had hopelessly compromised Megan's. An *amende honorable* would be in order, but, as he was already married, there was no possibility that he could make such traditional reparation even if he wished to.

The fervor of her response was something that he firmly refused to think about. She had been as overwhelmed with desire as he had himself; the knowledge still had the power to excite him unbearably if he did not keep a tight rein on his imagination. It would be fatal to allow himself to speculate on what she would be like in bed once she learned a little more of what it was all about, and had been coaxed past her first virginal shyness. Most of the women he had known carnally could be grouped into three categories: frankly cold, which described Alicia perfectly; cold but faking, something women often did to lure a man back to their bed; or frankly lecherous, which strangely enough could apply to as many fashionable ladies as to their less reputable sisters. Megan, he knew instinctively, would be none of these things, if handled correctly. Unless a cruel or clumsy lover frightened her, she would be a warm passionate bed partner, accepting and returning caresses with joyful abandon. Justin was aware of a crushing longing to be the one to initiate Megan into the rituals of lovemaking. Given the chance, he would be as careful and tender as he knew how. The images thus conjured up made his loins ache. But it could never be, as he knew, so it was best not to allow himself such dangerous fantasies.

The one memory that had the power to cut him to the quick was of her face after she had very properly

called a halt to their lovemaking. She had looked so—
so ashamed. Her face had been frantic with embarrassment, and her long, silky lashes had veiled her
eyes as she had steadfastly refused to look at him. Her
mouth, red and swollen from the force of his kisses,
had trembled pathetically, and he had been conscious
of an almost overwhelming urge to soothe it with yet
more kisses. With more restraint than he had ever
credited himself with, he had managed to refrain from
doing so, and had even permitted her to get up off his
knee. But he had meant to talk to her, to tell her that
she had no reason to blame herself for what had happened; that any fault, if fault there was, rested solely
with him. But she had not given him the chance to say
more than a few words. Instead, he had not so much as
set eyes on her in the five days since. He was very
much afraid that he had irreparably damaged their
guardian-ward relationship, but he was determined to
salvage what he could. They must agree to put the incident behind them, and he must school himself to
think of her strictly as a daughter. But first, he had to
find some way of getting her to listen to him. He did
not want her to be eaten up with guilt for something
that was none of her doing.

On the sixth day of Megan's careful avoidance, Justin could stand it no longer. He had to talk to her, and
he would, damn it! If she would not come to him, then
he would go to her. For a moment he considered waiting until evening and confronting her in her bedchamber, then dismissed the notion as being too fraught
with temptation. No, he needed to talk with her on

neutral ground, and he was determined to do so. When, from his bedroom window, he saw her ride out from the stables, he made up his mind. He would be waiting for her when she returned.

Megan, mounted on Rufus, the same gray gelding she had been riding when she tried to run away, felt as despondent as she had every day since she had so disgraced herself. The soft-falling rain, really little more than a mist, exactly suited her mood. It cast a cool veil over everything, graying the lush hills and dales, lowering the usually limitless sky. Megan chose to ride cross-country, not wanting to bother with the muddy mess into which rain inevitably turned the road. Her thoughts, as she went, were not happy ones.

When at last she turned back, it was early afternoon. A slight rumbling in her stomach reminded her that she had just picked at her breakfast, to Mrs. Donovan's displeasure, and had missed lunch. She had an apple in her pocket, which she would share with Rufus when they reached the stables. That should tide her over until dinner.

Riding into the barn, Megan looked around for Jem. He usually came running to take Rufus when she returned from her ride, but today he wasn't there. Not that it mattered. She had fallen into the habit of unsaddling and rubbing down the horse herself. It filled up the time she spent away from the house.

Kicking her foot free of the stirrup, she slid from the saddle, then turned to unfasten the girth. Rufus stood patiently while she lifted the sidesaddle from his back, glad that it was small and light as she lugged it toward its peg. It was dark inside the barn, the only light coming in from the large double doors that led to the stable yard. The corners of the huge barn were lost in shadows. As Megan returned to slip off Rufus's bridle, he nickered suddenly, lifting his head to look in the direction of the stable door. Megan turned to look too, expecting to see Jem, or perhaps O'Bannon. But instead, to her profound dismay, she found herself staring at the tall figure of her guardian, leaning heavily on his crutch. A wry smile flickered across his mouth.

Chapter 6

"If Mohammed won't come to the mountain . . ."
Justin said ironically, moving toward her, awkward on
the unwieldy crutch.

Megan felt fiery color creep up her neck and face to
her hairline. Jerking her eyes away from him, she bus-
ied herself with removing Rufus's bridle. She was actually conscious of Justin not five feet away, his eyes
quizzical as they rested on her averted face.

"I thought Dr. Ryan said that you weren't to try to
come downstairs," she managed to say, knowing that
she had to say something. The bridle slid off Rufus's
nose to dangle unnoticed from her hand. The horse im-

mediately began to move away toward his open stall. Megan, looking after him with a feeling akin to despair, felt as if her last source of protection had been spirited away.

"If any harm comes of it, I shall have no hesitation in placing the blame squarely where it belongs. On you."

She couldn't look at him. She knew he was waiting for her reaction. "But as it happens, I was very careful."

She nodded once in reply, then turned away with relief; the bridle she held gave her an excuse to do so. She took her time about hanging it on its peg, then went to close the stall door after Rufus. Finally, when she could not avoid doing so, she turned back toward Justin. He still stood squarely between her and the door, leaning heavily on his crutch as he watched her. Without volition, her eyes met his. Immediately she panicked, her lashes fluttering down to hide her eyes, red spots burning her cheeks. He inhaled sharply, then tok a step forward. She backed away in embarrassed confusion. He stopped where he was, and from the corners of her downcast eyes Megan could see his knuckles whiten as he clenched his fist over the handpiece of the crutch.

"Megan, look at me," he said after a moment. She hesitated, then unwillingly lifted her eyes in obedience to his command. Her hands came up to try to cool her burning cheeks. Justin's jaw tightened, and his long mouth thinned as he observed her reaction.

"This is ridiculous." He sounded annoyed. Megan

was looking at the straw-covered ground. With the best will in the world, she could not keep her eyes on him for longer than a few seconds. He looked very handsome, with his rough black hair waving wildly from the dampness; and the chiseled hardness of his features seemed swarthier than ever against the stark white of his plain linen shirt. His shirt emphasized his broad shoulders and wide chest, the muscled strength of his arms and torso. He had not bothered with a neckcloth, and the shirt was open at the throat, revealing the thick mat of hair she remembered all too clearly. His long legs were clad in well-worn buff-colored pantaloons that had been slit up one side and then pinned to allow for the bulk of his splint. One foot wore a Hessian boot, restored by dint of much hard work on Donovan's part to something resembling its former glory, while the other one, the one that extended from the wrappings of his splint, was rather incongruously covered by a soft slipper. Megan would have smiled at the idea of his arrogant lordship wearing such a homely item out of doors if she had been in the mood for smiling. As it was, she could only remember how hard and strong his body had felt against hers. She blushed with renewed heat.

"If you get any redder, I wouldn't be surprised if someone didn't mistake you for a fire and throw a bucket of water over you."

The sardonic voice won him another quick look. Justin released his breath on a long, drawn-out sigh when her eyes fluttered away from him again.

"For God's sake, Megan, you're making me feel like

a first-class swine. Can't you even look at me?" The roughness of his voice brought her eyes up to his at last. He read both defiance and shame in their violet depths. With her black hair tumbling down her back in wayward curls, her slender figure clad in the black riding habit, she was a study in black and white silhouetted against the weathered gray wood of the stalls. "I've said I'm sorry," he continued in the same harsh tone. "What more do you want?"

The only sign of her agitation was the clenching of her hands. "Please don't play the gentleman and apologize," she said, so low that he had to strain to hear. "You know as well as I do that the blame is mine."

Justin's mouth tightened. "Don't be absurd! The whole regrettable incident is entirely my fault. You are not to blame in any way. Do you understand?"

Her huge eyes were made even larger with shame. "Please—I don't want to talk about it any more," she said, hanging her head and turning slightly away from him. Justin choked back an impatient curse and moved cumbrously until he stood directly behind her.

"Megan." His voice had gentled. "Megan, you're a very beautiful girl, and when you kissed me—a very proper kiss from a very proper young lady to her not so proper guardian—I lost my head. It was my behavior that was at fault, not yours. You did absolutely nothing of which you need be ashamed."

She looked very small and defenseless with her bowed head and her slim back turned to him. There was something about the erect way she held her spine, about the shamed yet gallant stance of her, that touched him profoundly. He clenched his teeth as he fought down the urge to stroke the thick profusion of curls that cascaded down her back.

"I kissed you back."

Again he had to strain to hear her. "What?"

"I said, I kissed you back." At last she turned around to face him, squaring her shoulders proudly as she refused to allow him to claim responsibility for the fault which she knew was hers.

He shut his eyes briefly. When he opened them again, he reached for her, not able to help himself. Still, there was very little of the sexual in the way he pulled her resisting body against his, enfolding her with his free arm, tenderly stroking her silky hair. His intention was to comfort and protect; Megan, sensing this, gradually let her body relax against his until her face was hidden in his chest.

"Of course you kissed me back. All the ladies do. I'll have you know that I'm held to be a very good kisser."

The intentional lightness of his reply was calculated to still the convulsive shudders that ran lightly over her skin. Her arms found their way around his waist, and she clung to him. Justin, without in the least meaning to, bent his head so that his face was buried in the shining sweetness of her hair.

"You are," he thought he heard her murmur.

"I am what?" he asked absently, absorbed in the tantalizing scent and feel of her. Against his will, he found himself caught up again in the mystical web of wanting, the physical attraction she held for him increased a hundredfold by the heart-shaking memory

101

of her previous response. With one dim part of his mind he realized that touching her again had been a monumental mistake, but it was one that it was too late to do anything about. He couldn't have released her now if he had tried.

"You *are* a very good kisser," she said distinctly, her head tilting back so that she could look up at him. Justin saw the uncertain smile that trembled on the rosy fullness of her lips, and knew that he was lost. He bent his head, moving with conscious slowness so that she could elude him if she tried. She merely closed her eyes. As her mouth parted sweetly beneath his, Justin knew one last moment of clairty, then he was conscious of nothing but the hot blood drumming through his veins and he kissed her with a fervor that set them shaking. She had learned the lessons of her first kiss well, and she responded to him without shyness or fear, her lips and tongue returning touch for touch, caress for caress. Her arms were tight around his waist; he could feel the whole perfect shape of her pressing against his body.

Megan, for her part, felt as if she was moving in a dream. This had been the biggest part of her shame— the secret wish that he would do it again. And now he was kissing her, and it was the most wonderful thing that she had ever known. She surrendered to him utterly, reveling in the sheer size and strength of him as his big body bent ardently over her; rejoicing in the feel of his mouth on hers and the harsh rasp of his beard against the softness of her cheek. His arms were locked around her now, with one large hand cradling her head through the thick fall of her hair. Vaguely Megan wondered how he was managing to stand, then the increasing urgency of his kisses drove every thought from her mind.

It was Justin who broke it off at last, pulling his mouth away from hers with obvious reluctance, steadying her when she sagged weakly against him.

"I should be shot for that," he said ruefully to the top of her head. Tremors still coursed through Megan's body, and her arms still hugged his waist for support, and she tilted her head back to look up at him with a tiny smile.

"I don't think so," she told him, feeling suddenly more at ease with him than she ever would have dreamed possible. The last vestiges of shame over their previous encounter had vanished with the re- newed hunger of his kiss.

"You're just a baby, my darling. You don't know anything about it." The curve of his mouth was tender as he looked down into her upturned face. Megan was very conscious of the intimate way that he continued to hold her. Against the softness of her breasts she could feel the rocklike fortress of his chest; and the muscles of his good thigh pressed with demanding strength against her own thigh and hip. There was also a pulsating hardness pressing against the yield- ing flesh of her belly. Its presence could not be ac- counted for by what little she knew of human anatomy. Puzzled, her hand slid around from his back to touch the odd protuberance. At the tentative brush of her hand against him, Justin sucked in his breath sharply. Megan snatched her hand away, and looked up at him.

"Did I hurt you?" she asked, puzzled.

Justin's ragged laugh sounded more like a groan.

"No, you didn't hurt me," he replied, his mouth twisting wryly.

"Then what is it?" she demanded, totally bewildered by his odd reaction.

"You really are a baby, aren't you?"

"Are you going to explain or not?" Megan practically stamped her foot. His superior smile was galling.

"Not."

"But why?" Megan's curiosity was thoroughly aroused. She moved her hand against him again, this time tracing a finger over the bulge through the soft cloth of his pantaloons. It was iron-hard and seemed to be pulsating with heat, and extended at a slant from just above his thighs to almost as high as his waist. Justin groaned at her action, and his hand flew to capture hers in an unbreakable grip, holding her hand away from him.

"Don't do that," he told her, his voice thick.

"But what is it?" Megan persisted, thoroughly mystified. She stepped back a pace and looked down at the object in question. She could clearly see the cylindrical object straining against the buff-colored material of his pantaloons.

"If you're not careful, I may show you," Justin threatened, sounding suddenly hoarse. But there was a wry tenderness in his face as well as he looked down into her questioning eyes; the hand holding hers was gentle for all its strength.

"All right." She was willing. She had never wondered so much about anything in her life. To cause such a reaction from Justin, this object must be quite out of the ordinary.

He laughed. "Don't tempt me," he muttered, bending forward to press a quick kiss to her lips. He straightened almost at once, his hand still gripping hers. "I am both relieved and sorry to have to tell you, my darling, that this very interesting discussion will have to be postponed. If I don't sit down pretty soon, I may fall down."

"Oh, Justin, of course!" Instantly, she was all concern. How could she have forgotten his leg, and allowed him to stand there for so long? He was not even supposed to come downstairs, and yet he had walked all the way to the stables, and then supported her weight as well as his own. "Can I help you?"

"I think I can manage," he told her with a slow smile. Megan hovered close beside him as he released her hand and started to move with halting care toward the door. Although his leg really hurt him, he wanted to get them safely to the chaperoned confines. He mustn't lose his head again. But his infirmity defeated him. He was able to ignore the throbbing discomfort of his injured leg, but when his good leg, began to cramp, he knew he would have to rest before he could get back to the house. Grimacing at his own weakness, he cast his eyes around for a likely place to sit. Bales of hay were stacked neatly in an empty stall almost directly opposite where he was standing, and he headed for them, his movements growing more and more labored. When at last he reached the piled-up hay, which extended like a shelf from the stable wall, he sank down onto it with a groan of relief, his hand moving automatically to massage his aching thigh.

"Are you all right?" Megan hovered over him. Justin looked at her, smiling despite his pain. She was the most beautiful creature he had ever laid eyes on. He watched the graceful flow of her body as she gently removed the crutch from beneath his arm and set it aside. He wanted her more than he had ever wanted a woman in his life. But her innocence, even more than her position as his ward, prevented him from taking what he most desired. Only a complete bounder would undertake to seduce such a child, and he had already gone further than he should. But at this point, no real harm had been done to anything except his own frustrated senses. And really, he thought, although such kisses and caresses as they had exchanged might go far beyond the boundaries of what was considered proper, he might even have done her and her future husband (the mere idea of whom cost him a wince that had nothing to do with his leg) a service. He had always thought it was barbaric to expect a young lady to enter into marriage with no more idea than an infant of what was expected of her in the marriage bed. His own disastrous wedding night was a case in point. Alicia, when confronted with his eager, adoring lustiness, had gone into screaming hysterics which had robbed their union of its first bright promise within six hours of their having entered into it. It had taken him weeks of painstaking effort to coax her into allowing him to consummate their marriage vows; it took the threat of an annulment before she consented. The whole experience had been a disaster. She had lain unmoving beneath him, stiff with distaste, tears trickling down her face, sobs racking her throat while he made her his wife. Afterwards, she had cried even more bitterly. Then she saw the virginal blood staining her legs, and started to scream. Nothing he could say or do would convince her that he had not rent her in two.

For a while after that, he had tried to get her to take pleasure in the sex act, but she continued to despise it—and to despise him. Within six weeks of their wedding, he went to her bed only reluctantly, aware of his duty to sire an heir; but as months passed and her dread of what she called "the marriage act" continued unabated, he had finally given up. Not even a son and heir was worth having to force himself upon the frigid body of his wife.

Initiating Megan into the joys her body could give her would be a far different experience, Justin thought, eyeing her as she came to sit beside him. He envied her inevitable husband-to-be very much.

"Let me do that." He had been rubbing his thigh in an effort to ease the cramping, and now her soft little hands brushed his aside and kneaded the aching muscles with surprising strength.

"That's good." He was surprised at the way she found the painful knots with unerring accuracy. He knew he should call a halt to even these most practical of ministrations, but her touch was easing his discomfort too well. She smiled whimsically at him as her hands continued to massage his leg, and he gave up the struggle with his conscience and lay back against the hay, his hands linked behind his head. His expression was absorbed as he watched those small, slender hands with their elegantly tapered fingers and oval nails. She rubbed his leg quite unselfconsciously, her fingers alternately pressing and releasing every inch of flesh from his knee to his crotch.

"You should never have come downstairs!"

Justin, to his own amusement, liked being scolded by her. She sounded very bossy, and very proprietary, and easily old enough to be his mother. He grinned at her.

"You should never have tried to avoid me," he retorted amiably.

Megan sent a quick look flickering his way. "I was embarrassed," she answered.

"I realized that," he said. She continued to work, without looking at him. Justin stretched out a hand to turn her face to his. "You're not embarrassed now, though." It was both a statement and a question. Megan looked at him and smiled.

"No," she agreed softly. Satisfied, he released her, and settled back again to enjoy being fussed over.

After a few minutes more, her hands stilled against his leg, and she looked at him enquiringly.

"Is that better?" she asked. He smiled at her, thinking what a lovely picture she made with her hair tumbling in wild curls all around her face, her cheeks

108

glowing with color. She frowned as she waited for his reply.

"I think you just shifted the ache." The suggestive words were out before he could stop them. Justin swore inwardly at her puzzlement. He hadn't meant to bring up that subject again.

"What?"

She looked so bewildered, and so damned unknowing, that he grinned wickedly. He couldn't help himself. Well, thank God she hadn't understood what he had been referring to.

"Never mind, little girl." His voice was teasing, and his golden eyes had a droll twinkle as they swept over her. She frowned at him again, her expression severe, and his grin broadened.

"I wish you wouldn't call me that!" Her hands rested unmoving against his leg, as though she had forgotten all about them. Justin wished that he could.

"All right," he said obligingly. He took her hands and pressed them to his lips. It was a relief to get them away from the too-vulnerable area of his thigh. "What would you rather I called you instead? "

Her face softened as he touched his lips to the back of each hand in turn. "I think 'my darling' has a very nice ring to it." The glimmer of a smile lit her eyes as she looked at him. His eyes lifted from her hands to meet hers, an arrested expression in their depths.

"I think so, too," he said, his voice thickening, and he made no move to repel her as she leaned forward to press her lips with gentle ardor against his mouth.

He let her kiss him for as long as he could stand it,

making no move either to help or to hinder as her mouth coaxed and caressed and pleaded. But finally, when her little tongue found its way between his lips, he could bear it no longer. He groaned, and his arms came up to close about her, turning her so that she lay flat on her back on the hay and he loomed above her.

"My darling," he muttered hoarsely, his eyes feverish on her face, and then he was kissing her as she had longed for him to do with every fiber of her being.

Justin's heart thudded furiously. Megan pressed her hand against his chest. Her fingers encountered the slightly coarse material of his shirt. She could *easily* feel the pounding of his heart. Two of her fingers found their way between the buttons of his shirt. At her touch his breathing quickened, and the arms that were holding her tightened so much that she feared for her ribs. Emboldened, Megan withdrew her hand to work loose first one button and then another, making enough room so that her whole hand could slip beneath his shirt to caress his chest. As she touched him, his lips left her mouth to press hotly against her neck. He groaned as if in torment.

Her hand explored the hard muscles of his chest, delighting in the soft pelt that curled around her fingers. She was entranced by the male nipples so like a woman's and yet so different.

"God!" The word was breathed against her neck as she traced teasing circles around his nipples with her nails. It told her how profoundly she was affecting him. With a feeling of triumph that she could arouse him so, Megan withdrew her hand again and unbuttoned the rest of his shirt.

"Justin," she whispered after a moment, her hands pushing lightly against his chest. Desire blazed in his eyes.

"Let me look at you," Megan murmured.

His eyes narrowed passionately at her barely audible words, and he allowed her to push him back without protest. Now it was she who leaned over him, her eyes wide with admiration. Truly, he was magnificent.

Her hands followed the trail of hair down to where it disappeared beneath the waistband of his pantaloons. He could stand her sweet torture no longer. His hands came up to capture hers, holding them tightly when she would have pulled them free and continued with her exploration. When he refused to release her, she pouted a little.

A lopsided smile twisted his mouth as he met her reproachful look. "I was taught that turnabout is fair play," he said softly.

"So was I," she agreed in a husky whisper, and thought she would die with the sheer wonder of it as he reversed their positions and began to gently remove her shirtwaist.

This time she helped him with the tiny buttons, helped him ease the severe black jacket from her shoulders, and then the shirtwaist itself. Her thin white lawn chemise with its rows of prim tucks was all that remained to cover her breasts. He pulled it down from her shoulders with teasing slowness, his breath catching painfully when at last her small, high breasts with their milky-white skin and rosebud nipples were exposed to his view. For long moments, he didn't touch her, seemingly content to devour her breasts with his eyes. Then, finally, when Megan thought she could wait no longer, he lifted one hand to run a finger lightly from her left side over both swelling peaks. As his finger brushed across her nipples, they tautened with a suddenness that sent shudders coursing through her body. Her hands flew to his shoulders, her arms straining against the flimsy cloth of her chemise which bound them just above the elbows. Instinctively, she tried to pull him down to her, longing to feel his hair-roughened chest against the quivering bareness of her breasts. He resisted, smiling crookedly at her, his golden eyes hot as they touched her face. Both hands came up to cup her breasts, weighing them in his palms as he teased her nipples with his thumbs. Megan's hands tightened on his shoulders. Her nails dug into his flesh at the unexpected shaft of pure pleasure that shot through her at his touch. She watched him, eyes heavy-lidded with newly awakened passion. He leaned over to take her right nipple gently between his teeth.

Her hands slid up to cradle his head. Her eyes closed as he bit lightly on her nipple. Behind her closed eyelids was painted the image of his dark head against the whiteness of her breasts. What he was doing to her was against every moral principle she had ever been taught, but she was beyond caring. The touch of his mouth on her breasts drove everything else right out of her head.

He circled first one nipple and then the other with

his tongue. She moaned. He reached up to kiss her mouth, drinking in her soft cries. His hand again sought her breasts. Megan returned his kiss with passionate abandon, her arms coming up to encircle his neck, writhing beneath him as she gloried in the feel of his naked chest crushing her breasts. He lay half on top of her, kissing her with a slow, heady expertise that made her head reel while his hand continued its teasing play with her breasts. His good leg moved restlessly against her thigh, and Megan became aware of the heat and pressure of that unknown part of his anatomy pressing against her hip. Curious, one hand left his head to move down his chest, her fingers raking through the thick pelt covering it as she stealthily approached her objective. When at last her fingers found the rock-hard bulge, he groaned, as she ran her fingers exploringly up and down the puzzling thing between his legs. From the sound of his breathing and the strength of his grip, she was clearly giving him much pleasure by her touch. She tried to grip it, her attempt not entirely successful because of the tight-fitting pantaloons. She squeezed it experimentally and felt it seem to grow even larger in her hand.

"Sweet Christ!" he moaned as if in pain, and then his hand left her breast to press her hand even harder against him as his mouth moved back up to take hers in what was almost a frenzy of desire The heat of his passion made the sweet clamoring of her blood increase a thousandfold. She pressed herself tightly against him, writhing mindlessly, as his hand began to

113

pull up her skirt.

Justin heard the sound of approaching voices before she did. He stiffened, lifting his head to listen. Megan moaned a protest, writhing against him, doing her best to pull his head back down.

"Someone's coming," he said, his voice still hoarse with passion. It took his words a few seconds to penetrate the haze of longing which enveloped her. By the time she became fully aware of what was happening, he had already pulled away from her and was buttoning his shirt with hands that were not quite steady.

"It's O'Bannon and Jem," he told her in a quick undertone. "I sent them into Maam's Cross on an errand so that we could talk without interruption. Then I forgot all about them." His mouth quirked with wry humor. Megan, horrified as his words sank in, sat up abruptly, struggling to pull her crumpled chemise back up over her breasts. Justin finished tucking in his shirt, then reached over and fixed her chemise for her. Megan's expression of panic was not lost on him.

"Don't worry about it, I'll get rid of them," he told her softly. "Then you can get dressed and come up to the house. Hand me my crutch, please." This was said hurriedly as the sound of voices came ever closer.

Blushing violently, Megan did as he asked. Justin tucked the crutch beneath his arm and got to his feet with one heaving motion, then leaned over to press a quick, hard kiss on her soft mouth. When he drew back, she smiled rather tremulously at him.

"That's my girl," he murmured encouragingly,

114

then, after dropping another quick kiss on her still smiling mouth, he swung around and prepared to divert the intruders.

Chapter 7

Justin felt like a drowning man. He had done his best to steer both himself and Megan back into calmer waters, but instead, without quite knowing how it had come about, he found himself in deeper than ever before. His shameful desire for her was growing by leaps and bounds with each passing hour. Even now, in the privacy of his bedroom long after the rest of the household had retired to bed, he was kept awake by the aching of his loins. He wanted her fiercely, and he was afraid that if they continued in their present close proximity, his need for her might escape the bonds of decency with which he tried to bind it. It had so nearly happened this afternoon, and he thanked God for the interruption which had threatened to drive him right out of his mind at the time. He was absolutely determined to conquer the almost desperate longing which held him in thrall whenever he so much as thought of her. It would be easy, so very, very easy, to take her, to ease this gnawing ache he sensed within the softness of her body. She wanted him, he knew, and would put no obstacle in his way. Which was all the more reason for him to keep a tight hold on his self-control. She was the merest child for all her impassioned response to his kisses; to take her innocence would be an act of infamy. If he could, he would have offered her marriage, and then bided his time with what patience he could muster until she should grace his bed as his wife. But that path was not open to him. And if he could not marry her, then he could not have her. It was as simple as that.

Sometime in the hazy hours of the morning, Justin sat himself down at his writing table and proceeded to pen two letters: one to Stanton, instructing him to send the traveling coach and a maid to accompany Megan to London. The other letter was to his Aunt Sophronsia, informing her that Megan was presently at Maam's Cross Court with him, and that while he himself would be laid up a while longer because of a regrettable accident, he would like to send Megan to her in London. He assured her that the girl was a raving beauty, and would doubtless snare a husband within mere weeks of coming up to town, so that her hospitality would be required for only a relatively brief period.

He also mentioned the handsome allowance he would make to her as Megan's chaperone, and trusted that he could consider that matter as settled. If he heard nothing to the contrary, Megan would arrive in London within three weeks. Sealing these messages, Justin heaved a sigh of mingled regret and relief. He felt as though he had just reached out his hand and found a lifeline.

He was up very early the next morning, dispatching Jem with his letters to Galway before he could change his mind. Then he breakfasted sparingly on tea and rolls, to the accompaniment of Mrs. Donovan's disapproving clucks. When he had finished eating, he took himself off to the library, instructing Mrs. Donovan, who looked skeptical, since she had no idea that he and Megan had reconciled their differences, to send Megan to him when she had risen and breakfasted. Then he settled down to wait, thumbing desultorily through some estate books that could have been in Greek for all the sense they made to him in his current state of mind.

It was nearly ten o'clock when a brief knock on the library door heralded Megan's arrival. She barely waited for his answering "Come in!" before dancing into the library and closing the door behind her. She leaned back against it for a moment, a warm smile curving her mouth as she looked at him seated behind his desk. Apparently *she,* at least, had had no trouble sleeping, Justin thought wryly, his eyes not missing a single detail of the healthy color that bloomed in her cheeks or the brightness of her eyes. She was dressed in another

119

of those girlish white frocks with a modest round neckline
and elbow-length puffed sleeves. To differentiate this one
from its fellow, it was adorned with a violet sash that exactly matched the color of her eyes; posies of embroidered
violets were scattered across the fullness of her skirt. A
ribbon in the same shade of violet confined her hair at the
back of her neck. The simple style threw the beauty of her
bone structure and slanted eyes into sharp relief.

"Planning to administer another beating, my lord?" she
asked with a twinkle. Remembering their other unfortunate encounter in this room, Justin could not control the
answering grin that twitched at the corners of his mouth.

"If I were, it would be to myself," he responded a shade
grimly. "Come in, Megan, and sit down. I want to talk to
you."

"That sounds very ominous and guardian-like," she observed with no visible abatement of her good humor. Justin eyed her with as much sternness as he could muster in
the face of such overwhelming loveliness. His every in-
stinct screamed at him to take her in his arms and kiss her
until she was breathless, but he doggedly ignored such
base promptings as she obediently settled herself in the
chair opposite his desk.

Justin had had hours to prepare what he wanted to say
to her, to make her understand that while nothing had
happened of which she need be ashamed, their relationship must return to what it was before it had got so out of
hand. Looking at her, his carefully prepared speech flew
out the window. Searching the book-lined walls for inspi-
ration, he found none. He looked from the many-paned
windows with their heavy velvet drapes to the bright-

colored carpet without any more success. Finally his eyes returned to Megan's face, where they lingered with guilty intensity.

"What is it, Justin?" she prompted softly, her smile fading as she divined the subject that he was finding so hard to introduce. His eyes rueful, he leaned forward, his fingers drumming on the surface of the desk.

"I've made arrangements to send you to stay with my Aunt Sophronsia in London," he said abruptly. "I wrote to her last night, and sent for my traveling coach at the same time. It will take you to your destination. The coach should arrive in a week to ten days. In the meantime, I think it would be best if we saw as little of each other as possible."

Megan's face had whitened during this terse speech; now she looked totally stricken. Justin was aware that he had been far harsher than he had meant to be, but he couldn't help himself. He longed to touch her but steeled himself against the impulse.

"Will you be coming to London, my lord?" she asked. Justin noticed with a sharp pang of regret that she had reverted to the formal mode of address.

"Later," he said in clipped tones. "At the moment, as you know, I am in no state to travel. But I will do my best to be there for your come-out. As your guardian, it will doubtless be my lot to discourage the legions of your importunate suitors."

This last heavy attempt at humor fell sadly flat. Megan didn't even smile, but continued to regard him steadily. "And won't that bother you, Justin?" she questioned, her voice soft as she looked at him with what he refused to rec-

121

ognize as pleading.

"Undoubtedly it will," he answered coolly, bracing himself to disregard the hurt his words must cause her. It was better, by far, that this feeling growing between them be nipped in the bud before it shattered her life forever. He realized that he had made her care for him a little, and he realized too that her healthy young body had responded to his with the first burst of passion that it had ever known. But she was only seventeen, for God's sake; he had no doubt at all that he was the first man who had ever laid a finger on her in that way. But he would not be, could not be, the last. In the natural way of things, she would of course meet a boy of her own age, and fall in love with him without any of the shame that had marred this, her first sweet flowering. They would marry, and it would be her husband who would initiate her into womanhood. And long before this happened, Megan would cease to think of him, Justin, as anything but her guardian, that is, if she thought of him at all. The kisses and caresses they had exchanged, that had such a galvanizing effect on him, would fade away with all her other barely-remembered childhood memories.

"It will undoubtedly be something of a bore, having to fend off dozens of stammering boys who aren't dry yet behind the ears," he added with just enough humor to be convincing. He saw her face whiten at the cheerful callousness of his words. But there was no help for it. Painful as this was to both of them, it had to be done. For her sake. "But I'm sure I shall survive it. Just so long as you don't take too long picking out a husband."

Her lips quivered. Justin, watching her, wanted to pick

her up in his arms and carry her off and make love to her forever. She looked so lovely, so soft and appealing, that she wrung his heart. But he restrained himself with a powerful effort of will, and her reaction told him that he had done the right thing. Her mouth firmed, her shoulders straightened. Her little chin came up, and those gorgeous eyes, bright with unshed tears but with the beginnings of a healthy anger smoldering in their depths, looked at him squarely. Admiration for her courage rose in him. When she had matured a little, she would be a woman in a million. And he could never have her. For a brief, raging moment, Justin felt like cursing the fate that would deny her to him forever, but allowed nothing to show on his face.

"I will do as you wish, my lord," she said with great dignity, rising from her chair. Only the pallor of her face betrayed her pain. Justin had to clench his jaws to keep from throwing all his good intentions to the wind. "If I may be excused?" she added with careful politeness. Justin could only nod in reply. His eyes never left her slender back as she left the room.

Over the next few days, Megan avoided her guardian as studiously as she had before, with one major difference: this time, he was just as careful to avoid her. He kept pretty much to his room, even taking his meals there. Megan returned to her previous habit of whiling away time in the stables, not wanting to make him a prisoner in his own house. Justin seemed to divide his time between his bedchamber and the library, and whichever one he happened to be occupying, the door was always closed firmly behind him.

Just thinking of him hurt Megan more than anything

123

had ever hurt in her life. She had heard the other girls at school talk ad nauseum about falling in love, but she had never realized that it would hurt so much. For she knew that she had fallen hopelessly, helplessly in love with her guardian, the inaccessible Earl who had figured in so many of her childish dreams. He was the handsomest man she had ever seen, so tall and muscular that she felt tiny beside him. She loved everything about him, from his thick black hair to the roughness of his swarthy skin to the golden gleam of his eyes. He could be kind, too, when he wished, and very, very tender. Remembering the gentle care with which he had kissed her, Megan wanted to cry. How could he have kissed her like that, whispered such sweet words to her, if he didn't care for her at least a little? Megan knew that the answer was obvious, although she hated to admit it. Kisses and caresses were nothing new to him. He kissed ladies all the time, as he had admitted himself. And, undoubtedly, did far more than kiss them. He was a grown man, not a boy, and she must have seemed like a child to him. No doubt she bored him with her inexperience, and that was the real reason why he was sending her away.

Ten days passed, and then eleven, and there was still no sign of Justin's traveling coach, or an answer to his letter. He was much improved, and had taken to swinging himself about the grounds on his crutch whenever he thought she was safely out of the way. Megan, watching him sometimes from the vantage point of the stable loft, thought her heart would break. Her love grew stronger every day, feeding on her stolen glimpses of him, and the dreams in which he appeared by night and day, dominated all else that touched her. The idea of going to London, which had once held so much appeal, had lost its savor. She knew that once she left Ireland, what she and Justin had shared would be gone forever. He would revert to being the inaccessible Earl, and she would once again be nothing more, or less, than his ward.

She was having trouble eating and sleeping, and she knew that her looks were suffering as a result. Always before, she had taken the silky smoothness of her complexion for granted, but now there were faint smudges of weariness beneath her eyes, and her skin was ghostly pale despite the time she spent out of doors. Her clothes were getting looser, and she realized that she was losing weight. Even Mrs. Donovan had noticed these changes in her appearance, and asked with concern if she was feeling well. Megan knew quite well what was wrong with her, but she was unable to tell Mrs. Donovan the truth, so she said she was perfectly well. She did not know that Mrs. Donovan had felt obliged to mention these alarming symptoms to the Earl, and had her head bitten off for her pains.

Justin, too, was suffering. Like Megan, he had quite lost his appetite and his capacity for sleep. He was as gaunt as she, and if he wasn't as pale, it was due entirely to the natural darkness of his skin. He craved her fiercely, and not only for her body: he missed the sweetness of her smile, the sound of her laughter which had come easily and often, the sparkle in those violet eyes when she was amused. He missed the adoring way she had of looking at him, as if he was the most marvelous being in the world. He missed her conversation, her company, the very scent of her. The hardest thing he had ever done in his life was to make no move to heal the breach between them.

Justin had never been in love, in fact did not believe that such a state existed. When his friends confessed sheepishly to having fallen in love with some bewitching creature, Justin had taken their words with a large grain of salt. It had not escaped his notice that his friends tended overwhelmingly to fall in love with ladies who held out for a wedding ring before allowing them into their beds, and there he thought was the answer: they were suffering from a severe case of sexual frustration. Being gentlemen, once the desired objects became their wives, they were forbidden to discuss them in such terms, but Justin had often wondered how long after the ceremony the so-called "love" lasted. From what he had seen of most marriages, not very long at all.

Sexual frustration was how Justin diagnosed his own problem. If he could just get Megan into his bed once or twice, he thought that this craving he felt for her would be assuaged and die a natural death. But that was the crux of his problem: in all honor, he could not follow this most sensible course of action. If he had been in town, he would have found someone else. But there were no other women available at Maam's Cross Court except serving girls and local peasant wenches, and Justin drew the line at cold-bloodedly seducing one who was not up to the rules of the game. Therefore, he had no course but to restrain his baser impulses as best he could, and wait for the coming of the traveling coach to solve his difficulty for him. Knowing that Megan was so near was hell, but he was determined to grit his teeth and keep his distance. He knew he would be glad of his self-control when this madness had finally run its course.

The twelfth day since Justin had dispatched his letters came and went, and thre was still no sign of the coach. Megan didn't know whether to be glad or sorry. She hated to leave Maam's Cross Court, to leave Justin, but in a way it would be a relief. The strain of loving him and knowing that he did not love her in return was beginning to wear her spirits down completely. She had barely eaten all day, and now, hours after she had gone to bed, she had not slept. Getting out of the bed, which was a smaller, more delicate version of the four-poster in Justin's room, she disconsolately lit a candle. Maybe if she forced herself to eat something she would then be able to sleep.

Her room was near the end of the second floor hallway which bisected the right wing of the house. Justin's room was some distance away, but on the same corridor. She knew he was asleep, knew he would not even be aware of her presence and would be furious if he was, but still she walked past the hall leading to the stairs and along to Justin's door. Her candle cast a flickering pool of light as she stood in the corridor outside his room. She made no sound, had no plans to enter his room. In fact, the very thought made her shudder. To do so would be to lose all sense of shame.

The house was dark and silent. The servants had been in bed for hours.

No sound came from Justin's room; no tell-tale light showed beneath the door. Well, what did she expect? she asked herself. That he would be unable to sleep for love of her?

Biting her lip, Megan turned away from the door. How

foolish, to stand mooning about out here in the cold darkness! He didn't want her, and there was an end to it. The sooner she accepted that as fact, the better off she would be.

She had taken several steps away when a crashing sound reverberated from within Justin's room. It was followed by a loud thud, a groan, then a string of muffled curses. Megan had no touble at all in recognizing that voice. It was Justin, and he sounded as if he were in pain. Forgetting all her scruples in her concern for him, Megan fairly flew back along the hall to his door. She hesitated for one brief moment; then as the curses continued unabated, she took a deep breath, turned the knob, and went in.

Chapter 8

"Justin?"

She stopped just inside the door, lifting her candle high in an effort to penetrate the gloom.

"Damn it to bloody hell!"

The muttered exclamation made Megan turn in the direction from which it had come. Still holding the candle high, she advanced a couple of steps into the room. Frowning, she scanned the two big chairs near the fire, which had been allowed to die down to a few flickers amid glowing embers. The chairs were empty.

"Remind me to buy you a dressing-gown. Those frilly things you wear to sleep in are damned indecent."

This growled remark came from the floor.

"Justin?" she said again, and then she saw him. He was sprawled flat on his back on the floor midway between the fireplace and his bed. A stool lay overturned nearby, and Megan surmised that he must have tripped over it. That would account for the crash, the thud when he fell.

"Are you all right?" She hurried toward him. Her movement made the candle flicker. Her thin night-dress billowed out behind her.

"I was a few moments ago."

Megan ignored this as she sank to her knees beside him. She set the candle down on the carpet.

"What are you doing in here?" Justin, still flat on his back, scowled at her. Megan bent over him with some concern, thinking that he looked pale. As she did so, the unmistakeable odor of whiskey assailed her nostrils.

"You've been drinking!" she said accusingly, straightening and giving him a look in which surprise and disapproval were mingled.

"What if I have?" Then, as she continued to eye him coldly, he was goaded into adding, "And what business of yours is it, anyway, miss? I'm a grown man, and I'm answerable to no one for my actions. Particularly not to a seventeen-year-old chit who is so lost to all sense of propriety that she repeatedly comes to my bedroom in the middle of the night!"

"I do not! I heard you fall! It would serve you right if I left you to get up all by yourself!"

"I wish you would!"

"You can't! Without your crutch, and drunk to boot!"

"I am not drunk!" He sounded indignant. "I have had one or two small glasses of whiskey! If you knew anything about anything, you would know it is not enough to make me even the slightest bit drunk!"

"Then why did you fall?" she asked, with the air of one holding a trump card.

"Because I tripped over the bloody stool!"

They glared at each other, golden eyes clashing with violet. Megan, looking at him properly for the first time since she entered the room, saw that his hair was wildly mussed, and he badly needed a shave. With that fierce scowl on his face she thought that he looked far more like some sort of brigand than a belted earl. And his manners were far closer to a brigand's, too.

"If you were as much of a gentleman as you like to think, you'd know better than to swear in the presence of a lady!"

"If a *lady* was present, I might watch my language!"

"Why you . . . !" Angry color rose in her face; her eyes flashed violet fire. She was the most beautiful thing Justin had seen in his life. He ached with wanting her.

"What's the matter, don't you know the words? Remind me to teach you sometime!" Justin taunted, his mouth curling sardonically.

"I don't need you to teach me anything, thank you

very much!"

"Don't you?" They were both silent a moment. "Anyway, how did you come to hear me fall? I couldn't possibly have made enough noise to carry all the way to your bedroom." Justin had started his inquiry at random, merely wanting to get his mind off how much he would enjoy teaching her to make love. But by the time he had finished speaking, his words were sharp with suspicion, and Megan had turned even pinker.

"I was on my way downstairs for something to eat," she said defensively.

"Oh, were you now? Maybe I am drunk after all, because I don't seem to remember that you have to go past my bedroom to get downstairs!"

"Maybe you are!" Defiance was all she could offer. She knew as well as he did that there was no reason why she should have had to pass his room.

"I don't think so," Justin said.

His eyes, as he stared at her, were opaque. Megan had to force herself to return that probing look without flinching. She felt vulnerable, with her deepest emotions exposed to view. She prayed that he wouldn't see how she felt about him. That would be the ultimate humiliation.

"Go back to bed." His words were abrupt, but the anger seemed to have died in him.

"But you . . ."

"I don't need your help. Go back to bed."

"All right, I will. And I hope you have to lie on the floor all night and catch your death of cold!"

132

Megan jumped to her feet as she spoke. Struck by her shoulder, the door slammed shut. The sound reverbrated through the house, making her start guiltily.

"Now you'll have the whole household up here!" Justin muttered angrily, sitting up for the first time since Megan had entered the room. She turned back to look at him. He glared at her.

"Go on, go to bed!"

Annoyed by his tone, Megan gave him a haughty glance, and flounced around, meaning to leave him to his own devices. He richly deserved it. If he caught pneumonia, that was his look-out, not hers. She stalked toward the door; behind her, she heard the harsh intake of his breath.

"Christ, Megan! Stand still!" She turned back to look at him with some surprise, stunned to see him lurch to his feet with the aid of a nearby table and practically hurl himself towards her.

"Justin?" she said, terrified that he would injure himself. And then she felt the hot lick of flames as they shot up the back of her nightdress.

She didn't even have time to scream. Justin was upon her almost instantly, moving with a speed that seemed impossible in view of his splinted leg, tearing her gown from her shoulders, smothering the flaming remnants in a corner of the rug. It was all over in a matter of seconds; Megan, shivering, wrapping her arms around herself as tremors began to rack her body. She wasn't aware of her danger until it was safely past.

133

"My God, are you all right?" There was panic in Justin's voice. His face was very white beneath its tan.

She was surprised to hear her teeth chattering. "I'm all right."

"Come here and let me look at you." The harsh tone brooked no disobedience. Moving like a sleepwalker, Megan took the few steps needed to bring her within arm's reach of him.

"Turn around."

Megan turned.

"You don't hurt anywhere?" His voice was sharp. Megan shook her head, turning back to look at him. She was trembling from head to foot. She felt so cold.

"That damned nightdress was almost the death of you! You little fool, what possessed you to set the candle on the floor? My God, you could have been killed!"

"You saved my life." She had trouble speaking. The image of her nightdress going up like a torch with her still in it made her shake. She turned to look at the candle, lying on its side, its flame snuffed against the carpet.

"Yes."

Megan continued to stare at the blackened wick of the candle while shudders rippled over her skin. Justin reached for her. Megan felt his hands on her shoulders, and turned into his arms with a little choking cry. Her hands clutched at the front of his dressing gown, and her face burrowed in between its lapels to rest in the soft nest of hair on his chest. He cradled her against him, leaning back against a bureau for support, murmuring soft words of comfort into her ear. It was only as his arms came around her, sliding over her skin, that Megan realized that she was totally naked.

At first it didn't seem to matter. It felt so right to be held against him, to feel his hands stroking the satiny skin of her back and shoulders, to hear him speaking to her so soothingly. He held her protectively, possessively; Megan, still shaken by convulsive shudders, was warmed by the heat and strength of him. Like a small animal blindly seeking warmth, her hands released their death grip on his dressing-gown to creep beneath it, sliding about his waist and clinging to him. She felt the hardness of his muscles and the raspy softness of his body hair against her as she pressed herself to him.

"Megan . . ." His voice was hoarse. His arms tightened around her.

"Hold me, Justin. Please. I feel so—so cold." Megan's voice, no more than a whisper to begin with, trailed off at the end.

"You should go back to your own room." But his words lacked conviction, and his arms did not release their grip on her. Megan snuggled closer without answering, and shut her eyes. The musky scent of him, combined with the faintly sour odor of whiskey, rose in waves to envelop her. Against her cheek, she felt the tensing of his chest muscles.

"You scared me to death." His breathing had slowed and deepened. His voice was even hoarser than it had been before. "I thought you were going to burn to death right before my eyes. I thought I wouldn't be able to reach you in time to save you. This damned leg . . ."

"But you did, Justin. You saved me." The words were murmured into his chest. Her arms tightened their grip on his waist.

"Yes." It sounded like a prayer of thanksgiving. Megan felt her heart speed up as he bent his head to kiss her.

"Justin?"

"Yes?"

His head was still bent, his lips resting against the side of her neck. He was merely holding her, not kissing her, but Megan felt the warmth of his breath against her skin.

"I'm cold," Megan said.

He lifted his head to look at her. Megan felt the weight of that steady gaze, but refused to return it.

"You should be in bed. If you'll help me find that blasted crutch, I'll walk you back to your room."

His voice was not quite steady. Megan heard that slight unevenness, and took heart.

"I don't want to go back to my room. I want to stay here with you." The words were muffled against his chest, but she knew he understood what she was saying.

"Megan . . ."

"Please let me stay with you, Justin. I'll probably have nightmares, if you leave me alone."

"Megan . . ."

"Please, Justin." She lifted her head to look up at him; her eyes beseeched him to let her stay. On one level she knew that she was inviting his lovemaking, pleading for it in fact, but on another level, the level she allowed to show in her eyes and her voice, she truly needed the comfort of his presence. What she had said was perfectly true: If he took her back to her bedroom and left her alone, she would almost surely have nightmares. She had come so close to death.

"All right." His voice was harsh as he capitulated. "You can stay here—for a little while. But when you're warmer, and over your fright a little, you must go back to your own room. Understood?"

"Yes, Justin," she said submissively, and allowed him to put her away from him for a moment.

"Good God." His eyes were on her body; he was seeing her nakedness for the first time. His gaze raked over her, missing nothing from the quivering pink-crested breasts, to the tiny waist and flat abdomen with its shadowed navel, to the delicious curve of her hips and long, lissome lines of her thighs and calves. She made no attempt to shield herself from his eyes, but stood unmoving before him, a Mona Lisa smile curving her lips and a shy tenderness shining from her eyes. Her hair in its thick, childish plait hung over her shoulder. Tied at the end with an absurd bit of red ribbon, its ebony blackness contrasted sharply with the paleness of her skin.

"Get a blanket from the bed." The words were abrupt as he forced himself to take his eyes away from her. His hands clenched into fists at his sides as he fought to control his body's base urgings. He knew that he should send her away, at once, before things got out of hand, but before he could put the thought into words, she moved toward the bed, apparently intent on obeying his instructions. Justin allowed himself to relax a little, thinking that once she was decently covered it would be all right. They would sit in separate chairs before the fire, as decorous as a nun and a bishop, until she felt recovered enough to return to her own room.

Megan sent these good intentions away by crawling into his bed and pulling the covers up to her chin. Justin gaped at her as she returned his look with angelic innocence. Her face was very small and delicate against the snowy white pillow.

"What in the name of all that's holy do you think you're doing?" Justin demanded when he had recovered his power of speech. She smiled at him rather hesitantly.

"You said I could stay with you." She sounded confused and a little hurt.

"You know damned well that I didn't mean in my bed."

"But I'm so cold."

Justin ground his teeth. Seeing her like that, in his bed, knowing that she was naked beneath the piled covers, was almost more than he could stand. And she knew it, the little witch, and was deliberately tormenting him!

"That's just too damned bad. Come on, get up. I think you'd better go back to your own room after all."

Megan took a long look at him, standing tensed against the bureau not ten feet from where she lay.

138

With only the dying fire to shed light, she couldn't see his face. His big body looked very powerful, almost menacing, despite the splint on his leg. The maroon brocade dressing gown did little to conceal the muscular contours of his body, and his shoulders were every bit as wide as the bureau. He could easily remove her from his bed by force, despite his handicap, if he were so inclined. And she didn't want that. She wanted him to hold her, wanted him to whisper sweet words to her as he had done earlier. She wanted his tenderness— and his love.

"If you want me to go, I will," she said, not meaning it. "But I'm so cold, and scared, and . . ." She let her words trail off with a little intake of breath that sounded suspiciously like a sob. From her previous experience with him, she knew that the one thing that he was not proof against was her tears.

"Oh, hell!" But he sounded resigned. "All right, don't cry! You can stay there if you want to!"

This blatantly ungracious concession made Megan smile inwardly. With another of those little intakes of breath, she rolled over onto her stomach and buried her face in the pillow.

"Megan!" She could hear him swearing as he hesitated, plainly in two minds about whether to approach her or not. The he finally limped and lurched his way across the room. "Megan!" he said again, when he was at last standing over her. Megan did not look up, but continued to keep her face buried in his pillow while her shoulders shook suspiciously.

"Hold me, Justin," she whispered from the depths

of the pillow.

"Damn it, you know I can't!" He sounded angry, frustrated, and concerned. Megan turned over so that she could see him. His face was set as he battled with temptation.

"Please, Justin," she begged, wanting to reach out and touch the hard brown thigh that was just inches away from her. But she didn't dare. "Just hold me. What's the harm in that?"

Justin could have told her, but he didn't. An awful temptation possessed him: he was ready to give everything he owned to be able to do as she asked, to hold her in his arms until she was warm and sleepy and completely over her fears. As she said, what was the harm in that?

With a sinking feeling in the pit of his stomach, Justin surrendered, knowing all the while that he was making a mistake.

"All right." He sounded strangled. "But just for a few minutes; just until you're warm. Then you go back to your own bed. Understood?"

Megan agreed, as she had once before. Then she moved over in the bed, making room for Justin to lie beside her. He got under the covers almost gingerly, lying stiff as a ramrod with perhaps a foot of space between them. It was left for Megan to snuggle close.

"Justin," she murmured reproachfully, "I'm cold." He put his arm around her, his movements almost reluctant, and drew her closer, so that when they were settled at last her head was lying on his broad shoulder.

He still wore his dressing gown, but Megan could feel the heat and strength of his powerful body. His arm was heavy about her shoulders; she could hear the steady thudding of his heart. He wanted her, she knew, and rejoiced in the knowledge. She also knew that he would do everything in his power to keep their relationship within the bounds he had set. But this might be the last chance she would ever get to find out if he loved her as she loved him. The realization made her bold.

"Justin?"

"Hmmm?" The murmur had a distinctly irritable edge. Megan let her own voice go even softer.

"Do you remember the first time I ever saw you? When you came here to Maam's Cross Court to get me, when I was just a baby?"

A faint smile twisted the corners of his mouth. Megan, peeping up at him, saw that smile, faint though it was, and took heart.

"You're still just a baby, but yes, I remember. Why?"

"I always wanted to tell you how sorry I was that I bit you."

His smile was broader now. "Not as sorry as I was, believe me," he said humorously, impulsively hugging her closer.

"You frightened *me.*" Her head was tilted back on his shoulder so that she could see his face. It felt very good to be lying with him like this, with his head on the pillow beside hers, and the deep shadows shrouding the room making it seem as if they were alone on some deserted island. "You seemed so big."

"You frightened *me*," he said, looking at her. His long mouth with its curling smile enticed her madly. She wanted him to kiss her. "I thought you were a little cannibal."

"I've loved you ever since that day, I think." Her voice caught on the words. His arm stiffened beneath her head; for a moment, she thought he had stopped breathing.

"You certainly had a funny way of showing it!"

He was trying to pass the moment off lightly, she could tell. But she wasn't going to let him.

"I had to do something to get your attention."

"You certainly got it." He meant the words to be teasing, she knew, but they had a flatness to them that spoke of their underlying truth.

"Yes." Megan rubbed her head against his shoulder, her eyes searching his face. Seen from this angle, the line of his jaw was hard and unyielding, unsoftened by the black stubble of beard that shadowed it. His cheekbones were harsh, jutting out from the brown leanness of his cheeks. He looked down at her with those hooded golden eyes that made her think of some great cat. She smiled back at him, her eyes as soft as her lips.

"I love you, Justin," she said clearly. He stared at her without speaking. Then his jaw clenched, and he shut his eyes. When he opened them again, he didn't look at her but at the frescoed ceiling high above them.

"You don't know what you're talking about." His

142

words were abrupt, his voice harsh. Megan felt his muscles tense.

"Yes, I do. I love you."

"You want me to make love to you. That's all it is, except you're such a baby you think you're in love."

"Don't you?" The question was steady.

"What?"

"Love me."

"No!" he practically shouted, turning suddenly so that she lay flat on her back while he loomed over her, his face as black as the devil's.

"Don't you, Justin?" She refused to be intimidated. She didn't think she was wrong.

"That's what you want, isn't it?" he muttered furiously. "You want me to tell you I love you, and then everything your body craves will be all right: Blessed in the name of love! Well, it isn't true, and you may as well learn it now: What you want, and what I want, is sex, pure and simple! It has nothing to do with love!"

Megan winced, but she kept her eyes locked to his.

"That may be true for you, but it isn't for me: I said I love you, and I meant it!"

Her stubbornness made him grit his teeth.

"So you love me, do you, little girl? Well, let's see if you love me after this!"

With that savage challenge, he lowered his mouth to hers and kissed her with brutal strength. He had never kissed her like that before. He seemed to be deliberately trying to hurt her, to humiliate her, and Megan was unprepared for the fierce onslaught. She whimpered, trying to turn her head away as he purposely bruised her mouth. His hands came up to clamp on either side of her face, holding her head in place. Megan felt the harsh rape of his tongue, felt her lower lip split as he ground it back against her teeth, tasted the saltiness of her own blood. He was lying half across her now, his big body crushing hers. Her hands came up, to push him away. But instead of pushing at him, instead of bruising him as he was bruising her, her hands crept around his neck, and she clung to him.

At last he lifted his mouth from hers.

"And do you love me now?" he demanded, his voice almost a snarl. Megan's stared back at him with huge defenseless eyes. Her mouth, swollen and red, had a little trickle of blood at the corner. Justin looked at it, and felt his heart contract.

"Yes," Megan said simply. Justin groaned, and propped himself up on one elbow while his other hand came up to touch her abused mouth.

"I hurt you," he said. "I didn't mean to."

"Justin? Do you love me?"

At that moment he knew he was lost. "All right," he said heavily, his eyes burning deep into hers. "All right, my darling, you win: I think I love you, too."

144

Chapter 9

When he kissed her this time, his mouth was absurdly gentle. It moved over her bruised lips with all the tenderness of which he was capable. She returned his kiss without restraint, her body beginning to burn and quiver although his hands stayed firmly on the sides of her head and he never touched her anywhere else. When she felt him lick away the little trickle of blood at the corner of her mouth, a long shudder rippled through her. She wanted him fiercely. And she loved him.

When at last he lifted his mouth from hers, he buried his face in the hollow between her neck and shoulder. Her hands came up to lovingly stroke his hair. She felt so happy, so warm, so peaceful. Justin loved her. Beside that, everything else paled into insignificance.

"I ought to paddle your luscious little bottom and send you back to your own bed." The words were muffled against her skin. One of his hands slid down from the side of her head to stroke her neck, his fingers brushing against her as lightly as a moth's wings.

"Please don't send me away, Justin." She turned her face as she spoke, so that her cheek rested beseechingly against his ear. He laughed, a curiously husky sound, and lifted his head to look at her.

"I don't think I could if I wanted to. But if you have any sense, you'll jump out of this bed and run away from me just as fast as you can. Because if you don't, I'm going to make love to you."

Megan smiled lovingly at him, her trust and belief in him shining from her eyes. Justin looked down at her, his heart twisting at her innocent beauty. He knew that what he was about to do was criminal, but even that knowledge, even the love he seemed to feel for her, was not enough to stop him. Only she could do that.

"I never did have much sense." That ravishing smile widened, showing the pearly perfection of her small teeth. Unable to help himself, Justin bent down and traced the outline of her parted lips with his tongue, then drew back a little.

"Megan . . ." he began, determined to give her one last chance to escape him.

She shook her head at him, lifting a finger to press it

146

against his mouth. "Don't talk, Justin," she chided softly. "Kiss me. Please."

Even the knowledge that he would be damned for all time couldn't have kept Justin from obeying. His mouth took hers hungrily, but even under the sudden onslaught of possession he was careful not to hurt her. Megan reveled in the hot passion of his mouth, in the steely strength of his arms as they lay tensed on either side of her, supporting his weight. She was shaking by the time he lifted his mouth from hers.

She looked into his dark face, her eyes tracing the hard line of his jaw, the chiseled firmness of his mouth with its sensuous lower lip, the long, straight nose, the rugged cheekbones, the broad forehead beneath the thick, waving blackness of his hair. Then her gaze shifted to his eyes beneath the level black brows: They were gleaming at her, gold as money and hot with wanting. She felt as if she were melting under their steady regard.

"I love you," she whispered, reaching up to stroke the bristly line of his jaw. He sucked in his breath sharply, his eyes darkening with passion.

"My darling," he said, and bent his head to kiss her again.

Megan could feel the unsteadiness in his fingers. The knowledge that she, so young and ignorant in the ways of men, could have such an effect on this man whom she loved was intoxicating. Fiercely she longed for him to finish what he had started, to touch her breasts and the rest of her. She wanted him to love her until she died of it.

Her eyes were wide purple pools of longing as she stared at him. His hand untied the ribbon that held her hair back, and she shook it loose until it was spread out around her, black as midnight against the white pillows. Megan, watching him, was weak with love and wanting.

Justin's expression was serious, and at the same time very tender. "Megan, if I scare you, or hurt you, you have only to tell me. I'll stop." The thickness of his voice told her that it was an effort for him to speak at all. She smiled at him, her mouth soft and tremulous.

"All right, Justin," she agreed. Her hand reached up to draw his head down to her. He kissed her with an almost desperate need.

This time, when his hand slid over her throat and shoulders, it did not stop, but continued on down to close possessively over her breast.

She arched her back against the warmth of his hand, loving the feel of his calloused palm against her softness. When he followed his hand with his mouth, pressing soft, teasing kisses to both breasts before finally taking a nipple between his teeth, she gasped, her hands twining mindlessly in his hair, pulling on the thick strands. He groaned against her breasts, and his hands slid down over her rib-cage to trace the inward curve of her small waist before following the line of her body outward to the slender roundness of her hips. His hands molded the shape of her all the way down to her thighs, pushing aside the pile of covers in the process, stroking her flat belly, exploring

148

the indentation of her navel.

Megan felt a tight spiral of need begin deep in the pit of her belly and spin out to consume her entire body. She was restless, impatient for something more even though she did not have the faintest idea exactly what it might be; she only knew that her body craved something desperately, something that only he could give her.

He was nibbling very gently at her nipples, his hands stroking the smooth front of her thighs from her knees to her dark, secret place. Megan writhed beneath his expert touch, wanting him to hurry.

"Justin. . . ." she murmured achingly as he continued to tantalize her, arousing her emotions to a fever pitch without satisfying the burning need that had begun to throb inside her.

He looked up from where he was licking careful circles around her quivering nipples, a slight smile curving his lips.

"Don't be impatient, my darling," he said softly. The hoarseness of his voice, his smoldering eyes, revealed a ravening hunger. "We have all night. I want to make love to you properly, so that you tremble in my arms, so that your beautiful body opens like a flower for me . . ."

"I am trembling. Can't you feel it?" She meant the words to be tart, wanting to egg him on to finish what he had started; to show her where this mysterious feeling that he had aroused in her could lead. But her voice sounded drugged; her words were so blurred and husky that she feared he might not be able to understand them.

Justin smiled and shook his head. "Not enough," he said, sounding judicious. She struggled to feel indignation, knowing that it was humiliating to be so much at his mercy while he remained in control. But as he pressed a lingering kiss to her mouth before returning to his leisurely exploration of her body, she could not summon the will to be angry. All her energy was focused on the delicious things he was doing to her with his mouth and his hands.

Finally, when she thought she could bear his teasing no longer, his hand slid softly between her thighs, touching her as she had longed to be touched without even knowing what it was that she longed for. Her legs parted instinctively; she gasped as he ran his hand back and forth between her thighs.

He lay on his side beside her, still clad in his dressing gown, his head propped on one hand as he studied her reactions to his touch. Her eyes were half-closed and she bit down on her lower lip as she squirmed beseechingly against the large, dark-skinned hand that seemed bent on tormenting her past endurance. He stroked the delicate silkiness of her inner thighs, the warm, moist flesh between them, the little triangle of hair that rose to press pleadingly against his hand as he caressed it. When his hard fingers began to probe her softness more intimately, Megan lifted her hands to clutch at his shoulders, trying to close her legs against the sudden discomfort as he found her virginal softness.

"Justin, you're hurting me!" she gasped. She

opened her eyes and pushed at him. But he did not remove his fingers; instead, he leaned over to kiss her passionately on her protesting mouth, silencing her and distracting her while his fingers did their work. When he lifted his mouth from hers, her arms were twined around his neck and she lay pliantly beneath his hands. The discomfort had eased, its going marked only by a slight tenderness that left when he removed his hand.

"Do you want me to stop?" he asked, mindful of his earlier promise. But Megan, soothed by his kisses and by the easing of the hurt he had caused her, silently shook her head. She loved him and wanted him. She would follow blindly wherever he led her.

He kissed her again, his lips both hard and tender at the same time. Then he trailed kisses down over her breasts to her flat belly, where he explored her navel with his tongue. Megan's eyes opened wide with shock as she felt him lick his way from her navel over the smoothskin of her belly to the place where her thighs joined. She looked down, horrified to see his dark head nestling between the whiteness of her thighs, and her hands flew to clutch at his dark hair, meaning to pull him away. She had never even dreamt that he would want to kiss her *there!* But his lips were warm and very gentle against hers, and his hands were gentle too. They slid beneath her to cup her buttocks and draw her even closer to his mouth. Her hands, which had meant to stop him, instead caressed his dark head; as his tongue moved inside her. She moaned, and moaned again. Strange chills began to

151

course through her body. Her whole being seemed focused on what he was doing to her. Her eyes closed, and she writhed feverishly against him, feeling as if tongues of flame were licking at her very soul. The odd pulsing feeling that he had ignited in her earlier grew more intense, sending hot little shivers shooting along her nerves, and she whirled away on a tidal wave of pure bliss.

When she came floating back to earth, he was lying beside her, propped up on his elbow, a half-smile curving his lips.

"And did you like that?" he asked, as if he were making some casual inquiry. Megan looked at him, saw the knowing glint in his eyes, the crooked smile on the mouth that had just made love to her with such fevor. She blushed hotly. Justin's teasing smile widened to a grin.

"You know I did," she said, half-crossly, feeling horribly embarrassed that he should laugh at her. She sat up in bed, pulling the sheet up almost to her neck holding it tight as she wriggled toward the edge of the bed. His arm snaked lazily around her waist, stopping her.

"Where do you think you're going?" He was still grinning, but the tenderness in his eyes went a long way toward soothing her embarrassment.

"I—want to wash."

"Right now? I thought that you wanted me to make love to you."

"But—you did."

His grin widened; and those golden eyes danced with humor. Megan glared at him. His arm tightened around her waist, drawing her resisting body back against him.

"No, I didn't. Not by a long shot. I was just getting warmed up."

"You mean that's not all?" She sounded so aghast that Justin burst out laughing. Megan glared furiously.

"No, my darling, that's not all," he agreed when he could speak. Then, meeting her indignant stare, he did his best to eliminate the lingering traces of amusement from his expression.

"You're beautiful," he said contritely, possessing himself of one small hand and pressing his lips to her palm. The half-angry, half-embarassed light died out of her eyes, to be replaced by a warm glow.

"I love you," she told him. "What do you want me to do?"

Her practical tone nearly set him off again, but he managed to control his mirth.

"Touch me," he instructed solemnly. Her eyes slid speculatively down the length of his body and he suddenly lost all desire to laugh.

Megan realized that she had pulled the covers completely off him. He looked very big and dark as he lay there against the white sheet, so handsome that he took her breath away. He was still smiling a little, but those smoldering eyes told her how very serious he was. Megan's eyes touched on the deep vee of hair-covered chest that the loosened lapels of his dressing gown exposed almost to the waist, and slid down over the maroon brocade that discreetly veiled his hips and

153

thighs to the single, powerful-looking calf and bare foot that she could see. Megan's eyes slid back up his body to his face to find that he was watching her intently.

"Well?" Justin prompted her.

"I—don't know what to do." The look she gave him was pleading.

"I know." With that, he relented, reaching out to catch her hand in his and place it against his chest. Megan realized that she was as curious about his body as he had been about hers. She wanted to see it, to feel it, to understand its workings. Justin's hands moved to rest lightly on her waist, then tugged gently at the sheet until her body was once more exposed to his gaze. Megan was hardly aware of what he was doing until it was done, so engrossed was she in discovering the hard contours of his body. But as the cool night air touched on her bare skin, she realized that she was naked. Blushing anew, she reached for the sheet. Justin's hand around her wrist stayed her.

"Please," he said huskily. "I want to look at you."

Megan saw the aroused tenderness in his face. She nodded. Then she looked back down at the hard length of his body, still clad in his dressing-gown.

"I—want to look at you, too."

Justin said nothing, but his hands moved to the belt of his dressing gown. He shrugged free of the encumbering garment and tossed it aside. Megan's eyes slid down his body to the hard, flat muscles of his abdomen. As they reached the juncture of his thighs, they widened with amazement. This huge *thing*, was the

154

bulge she had felt in his pantaloons when he kissed her that day in the stable. It was enormous, jutting up from his flesh, looking like nothing she had ever seen before.

"What is it?" she whispered, awed, still staring. Justin, who had been watching her expression with growing amusement, roared with laughter. She turned on him, indignant that he should laugh at her and this time determined to let him know in no uncertain terms how she felt. He saw the militant sparkle in her eyes and reached up to pull her down to him. Still laughing, he held her stiff body against him until he had recovered a measure of control.

"You are a constant source of joy and delight to me, my darling," he told her.

"But what is it?" she insisted. A small smile still played around his mouth as he told her, whispering the words into her ear. When he had finished, Megan was both embarrassed and intrigued. Her hand slid down over the taut muscles of his stomach to hesitantly touch the huge thing. It jerked spasmodically at the feel of her cool little fingers. She snatched her hand away, her cheeks burning.

"Go on, it won't hurt you," Justin encouraged, and when she still hesitated he took her hand in his and guided it to him. He gasped as her hand closed over him, and Megan looked at him, surprised. He was watching her, his eyes very dark and passionate. Experimentally, she moved her hand; his lips parted as he drew in a harsh, shuddering breath.

"God, Megan," he groaned, his hand reaching out

155

to stop her. His fingers closed over her wrist and he pulled her down so that she sprawled across his chest.

"Justin . . . ?" she murmured, not knowing what to expect.

"I can't wait any longer, sweetheart," Justin murmured. He began to kiss her with wild abandon.

"I don't want you to, Justin," she whispered.

His arms were hard and powerful as he turned her over on to her back, positioning himself above her. Megan's own arms were wrapped tightly around his neck, her head thrashing from side to side on the pillow. She never even noticed when he pulled the pillow from beneath her head and threw it on the floor with a single impatient movement. Then he pressed down into the mattress and held her steady. The quickening that he had earlier assuaged with his lips began again inside her as he kissed her pastionately, running his hands which were slightly unsteady along the silken length of her. He touched her breasts and belly and thighs, caressing her, loving her. By the time he parted her thighs with his knee she was trembling as much as he was. She felt the hard strength of his thigh against hers, felt the unyielding bulk of his splinted leg join its fellow, felt the crushing weight of his big body as he covered her. He murmured, hoarse love words to her. The room around them was thick with shadows, almost completely dark as the fire continued to die. The only sounds were the occasional popping of the embers, the harsh rasp of their breathing.

She felt him pressing against her softness, and instinctively stiffened. Despite his burning need of her, he was gentle as he eased himself that first little bit inside. He had prepared her for this as well as he could, but there was no way he could completely ease the pain of their first joining. When he thrust deeply into her, she cried out against his mouth, her nails digging hurtfully into his shoulder. She had not expected the pain. . . . He held her against him, keeping himself buried deep inside her, soothing her with kisses and soft words until he could contain himself no longer. He began to move, thrusting into her, his whole body shaking, his breathing like harsh sobs in her ears. At first Megan lay unmoving beneath him, stunned by the sudden explosion of his passion, but gradually, as she felt him thrusting inside her, she began to get caught up in the urgency of his rhythm. This is Justin, the refrain played over and over again in her mind. Justin, my love. Her arms slid around his neck to hold him tight, and she began to move, instinctively responding to the demands of his body.

"Oh, God, Megan!" she heard him gasp against her ear, and then he was deliberately slowing down, waiting for her before getting caught up again in the immediacy of his own need. This time he took her with him. She whispered his name over and over against his mouth as he kissed her with fierce desire, feeling heat building inside her until it flashed along her limbs in a raging conflagration. She cried her joy out loud as the whirlwind took her again, this time carrying her higher, faster, and further than before. Justin, hearing her cry and feeling the convulsive shudders that shook her, drove into her fiercely one last time, his big body shaking, and matched her ecstasy with his own.

They lay together, panting, floating slowly back down to earth. Gradually Justin eased himself off Megan's limp body, taking her with him as he rolled on to his side. He cradled her against him, his arms holding her tightly, moving so that her head was pillowed on his shoulder. He had hurt her, he knew, despite all his care and the pleasure he had given her at the end. He was suddenly sorely afraid.

"Megan?" he murmured huskily after a moment, unable to stand her silence any longer. If she hated him, he had to know it.

"Ummm?" That sleepy murmur told him nothing.

"Are you all right?"

"Ummm."

Justin's jaw clenched. Anything, even tears or abuse, was better than not knowing.

"Do you still love me?" There was a curious catch in his voice, and the last two words—words he never thought he would find himself asking—were whispered. Megan heard the strangled sound of his words, and opened her eyes to look at him. She was puzzled. How could he possibly doubt it, after...?

"Insanely," she whispered, pressing a soft little kiss into the hard skin of his shoulder. She felt his tense muscles slowly relax against her, and heard his breath expel in what sounded like a sigh.

"Justin," she said after a moment, still curled contentedly against his side. He murmured something she didn't catch.

"I was taught that turnabout is fair play."

It took him a few seconds to recognize the phrase he had used once before, and to understand her meaning. When he did, he hesitated, then with a feeling of inevitability felt himself plunging deep into the dangerous waters he had always sworn to avoid.

"I love you," he murmured, glad of the darkness so that she could not see his face.

"That didn't hurt, now, did it?"

He smiled at the smugness in her voice.

"No," he admitted.

"I told you." She sounded like a very-satisfied little cat who has discovered a whole pool of goldfish for its very own.

"Yes, you did."

"Justin."

"Hmmm?"

"Was I totally shameless?"

Justin lifted his head to look down at her. "My darling, you were marvelous—what every man dreams of finding in a woman. I adore you."

"Do you mean that, Justin?" She sounded a little shy, still unsure of herself—and of him.

"More than I've ever meant anything in my life," he assured her. Reassured, she settled back down against his shoulder, surprised to find herself yawning. Justin felt the movement against his skin, and smiled.

"Go to sleep, darling," he teased fondly. She yawned again, snuggling deeper into his shoulder even as she protested.

"I should go back to my room," she murmured, picturing Mrs. Donovan's horror if she should find her tucked up in Justin's bed in the morning.

"There's plenty of time for that. Go to sleep. I'll wake you in a little while."

Megan didn't want to let thoughts of the morrow intrude on their idyll, so she quickly banished the image of Mrs. Donovan's scandalized face.

"All right," she agreed sleepily, and drifted off to the sound of Justin's heart beating steadily beneath her head.

Chapter 10

It was late when Megan awoke, far later than she was accustomed to. She could tell by the way the sun slanted through the green damask curtains that she had closed only part way before going to bed the night before. Sunbeams trailed across the wide-planked floor and bounced across the matching green damask of her coverlet. Watching the sun play around her feet, she smiled, stretching like a lazy kitten, her arms extending above her head. She yawned. She felt wonderful—on top of the world. Happiness radiated from her like sunrays. For a while she lay back against her pillows, smiling foolishly as her eyes took in the green and cream bedroom which suddenly seemed incredibly beautiful to her. Then, with a surge of energy, she bounded out of bed and pattered across to the windows to pull the curtains wide and admit the full glory of the September morning.

Moving, she was conscious of a faint soreness between her thighs. She blushed, remembering its cause. She laughed, then danced around the room with her arms flung wide. Justin loved her. He had told her so, and had proved it beyond any need for words. He loved her, and she loved him. It was the most incredibly perfect thing that had ever happened to her.

Justin! She said his name out loud as she went over to the wardrobe, flinging the doors wide and looking through it for something to wear. She wanted to look beautiful this morning—for Justin.

Mrs. Donovan hadn't awakened her, as she usually did, and Megan puzzled over this as she critically inspected the small store of dresses she had brought with her from England. There wasn't much to choose from. She couldn't understand why Mrs. Donovan hadn't called her. Perhaps Justin had told the housekeeper to let her sleep, although how he would explain away his knowledge of her tiredness she couldn't imagine. The one thing she was sure of was that Justin would do anything to keep their love a secret. He was far more concerned about her reputation than she was herself.

Megan hated to wear another of the childish white dresses, but they were all she had left. What she had would have to do. She knew that they were woefully lacking in style, and made her look like a schoolgirl, but Justin had seen her in them before and appeared to find them pleasing. A secret smile curved her mouth as she whirled away from the wardrobe, dress in her hand. Yes, Justin found her—very pleasing. He had made her a woman, his woman, and she would have liked to look like a woman this morning. But from the passionate way he had made love to her, not once but twice more before he let her leave him, she thought that she could come downstairs in a blanket and he would find her beautiful.

She hummed as she washed herself with water from the basin by the window, stipping off the nightdress which she had donned after returning to her room the night before, and proceeding to sponge herself off from head to toe. Bold reminders of Justin marked her body: a curling black chest hair adhered the creamy skin of her breast, faint purplish marks from his lips dotted her pale flesh indiscriminately, traces of her virginal blood smeared the inside of her thighs. He had wanted to bathe her before she left him, but the suggestion had seemed too outrageous, and she had blushingly denied him. She had washed herself before tumbling into her own bed, but she had been so tired, and washing in the dark left something to be desired . . . But this morning she scrubbed herself vigorously, and by the time she stepped into her undergarments, she felt as fresh as the morning.

It did not take her long to pull on the stockings and garters, the lace-trimmed muslin pantalets, the che-

mise and single petticoat that was all she customarily
wore beneath her clothes. Custom decreed the addition of at least one more petticoat, for modesty's sake,
and a pair of stays to nip her in at the waist, but
Megan had never been one to worry much about custom. Wearing multiple petticoats made her hot, and
her waist was small and firm enough without any arti-
ficial enhancement. If her teachers had known of her
laxness in dress, she would have been punished, but
the very fact that they had never noticed told Megan
how useless such garments were.

The white dress she had chosen to wear differed
from her others. Pale roses bloomed across the full
muslin skirt, and the deep rose-pink of the wide silk
sash. Megan tied the sash in a big bow in the back,
leaving the ends to trail behind her. Then she slipped
her stockinged feet into little rose pink slippers. She
would have liked to do her hair up in a more adult
style, but she was not very handy with her hairpins
and it would have taken too much time to arrange it
properly. So she brushed it quickly, impatiently, and
caught the sides up at the top of her head with a ribbon that matched her dress. The curling mass hung
down to her waist.

After she dressed, Megan spent a few seconds ob-
serving herself critically in the cheval glass, curious as
to how she would look when she appeared before him.
The mirror reflected a slender girl, not tall but regally
erect, with masses of jet black hair, skin as white as
her dress, huge slanting violet eyes under the straight
black brows, and a slightly swollen lower lip that

smiled as she remembered how it came to be bruised. Her nicely rounded breasts (beautiful, according to the very best authority) were covered demurely by the snug-fitting bodice which had a modest round neckline edged by a frill of lace. Her waist (also beautiful, said the same source) looked incredibly tiny clothed in a wide band of pink silk which emphasized its smallness. Her simple round skirt flared out in a nice bellshape. Beneath the edge of the skirt her little pink slippers were just visible.

Running her eyes over the girl in the mirror one last time, Megan made a face at her then turned away to leave the room. She was anxious to get downstairs—to see Justin. Would he kiss her at once, or would he wait until they were completely on their own?

She skipped along the upstairs hallway, then ran down the stairs, her hand sliding easily over the polished wood banister. When she was almost two-thirds of the way down, the breakfast room door opened and Justin came out. Apparently he had overslept, too, because it was long past his usual breakfast time. She smiled impishly. He looked up and saw her descending, but didn't return her smile. Megan's eyes twinkled as they met his, which were unusually grave. No doubt he was going to apologize again. The fact that he was her guardian seemed to cause him considerable qualms of conscience. He was dressed in a plain white shirt with black pantaloons slit up the side and pinned over the splint. The inevitable Hessian adorned his one good foot. He was leaning on the crutch, watching her as she came down the stairs, his golden eyes brooding. His mouth was set in a straight uncompromising line, and lines of strain had etched themselves from his nose to his mouth. His hair was neatly brushed for once, but deep waves were already springing back into it to mar its smoothness. He looked very handsome, very big, and very much as if he was going to be difficult. Megan shook her head. She felt no regrets for what had happened between them, and didn't intend to let him fret. After all, they had merely anticipated that which would be perfectly proper on their wedding night.

"Good morning," she called, wanting to call him darling but not quite daring in the face of his stern look. He limped forward, meeting her at the foot of the stairs. She still stood two steps above him, which brought her almost to his eye level. His hand shot out to close about her waist, and she stopped on that second from the bottom step, waiting resignedly.

"I've got to talk to you," he said in a low voice, tightening his hold on her. Megan did not claw him, or struggle in any way. She merely placed her hand over his, and after a moment he let her go.

"I expect a very large apology this time," she told him softly, smiling at him, hoping to coax him out of this guilty mood. He didn't return her smile; if anything, he looked bleaker than before, and Megan began to feel the first small pangs of uneasiness.

"Justin, what . . ." she began, then stopped.

"We can't talk here," he said impatiently, his voice still curiously quiet. "Come into the library."

"All right."

Megan moved down to the bottom of the steps, feeling as if she had somehow been caught up in a bad dream. Something was very wrong, she knew. Not all the guilt pangs in the world could account for his manner. Her heart began to pound as she followed him docilely toward the library. What on earth could have occurred to put that look in his eyes?

Justin took her wrist again and towed her after him like a barge pulling a small boat. The door to the drawing room opened. Megan looked up, surprised. Justin dropped his hold on her and moved to get between her and the door. Megan cast him a quick, questioning look, but he was looking over her head. Bewildered, growing more uneasy by the moment, Megan turned to see what he was looking at.

Framed in the drawing room door was a perfect lady of fashion. She was beautiful, from the top of her perfectly coiffed silver-blond head to the toes of her little kid half-boots, which were plainly visible beneath daringly shortened skirts. She was dressed in the very height of the current mode in an ice-blue walking dress with a little matching jacket. Several inches of lace-trimmed petticoat were artfully visible at the hem of her gown, which did not quite reach her ankles. Megan saw the cool perfection of her features, the pale, rather thin lips that were the only flaw in the lady's beauty, the eyes that were the same color as her dress. As she gaped, wondering who on earth this vision could be and what she could possibly be doing at Maam's Cross Court, the lady stepped out into the hall, moving languidly toward them, an amused smile curving her lips.

"La, Justin, is this your little ward? You were right—she's really very, very pretty. But a little ah—uncultivated, as you said. But we can soon fix that." She directed her remarks to Justin as though Megan were not present. The lady's manner irritated Megan. She had called Justin by his name, and seemed to be on very familiar terms with him. Megan's eyes were cool and a little watchful as the lady halted some three feet away.

"Really, Justin, where are your manners? Aren't you going to introduce me to your ward? She looks rather bewildered."

Megan said nothing, but looked quickly back over her shoulder at Justin. Spots of dark red color simmered high on his harsh cheekbones, and a muscle twitched in his jaw. His golden eyes met hers for a second, and there was something very much like pain in their depths. They shifted to the strange lady.

"Alicia, as you guessed, this is my ward, Miss Megan Kinkead," Justin said heavily, as if the words were being forced out of him. "Megan, this is Lady Alicia Brant, Countess of Weston—and my wife."

The words took a few seconds to penetrate Megan's protesting brain. At first, she simply refused to believe them. But, looking at the smug expression in the woman's eyes, hearing Justin's tortured voice, she knew they were true. She thought for one terrible instant that she was going to faint.

"Why, Justin, the poor child's gone white. I do believe that she's been nursing a schoolgirl crush on you, and I've quite broken her heart."

Megan hated that cooly malicious voice and its pos-
sessor more than she had ever hated anything before
in her life. Justin married! Why had he not told her?
But she couldn't think about it now, not with that
woman watching her so closely. She knew that the
lady had picked up something, some hint of tension in
the air, between herself and Justin. A courage she had
never realized she possessed stiffened her spine and
stilled the trembling of her knees. She would not make
a fool of herself before this smirking creature—and
Justin.

"On the contrary, my lady, I have been ill lately, and
have not yet breakfasted. I assure you, when I have
something to eat, my color will return."

Lady Alicia's eyes grew sharp, as if she had not expected Megan to speak. Behind her, Megan heard Justin take a deep breath, a harsh, ragged sound. Why
hadn't he told her, she asked herself? But she mustn't
give way to tears, to anger, to panic.

"Well, I'm very pleased to hear that you don't have
some dreadful Irish accent." Lady Alicia addressed
Megan for the first time. She eyed Megan speculatively, silently disparaging the childish, outmoded
frock and untamed hairstyle. "I can see that I have
my work cut out for me, but as Justin said, you're
very pretty. I'm sure that with a little effort on both
our parts, we will succeed admirably."

"But I haven't the faintest idea of what you are
talking about. Perhaps you had better enlighten me:
Succeed at what, my lady?" Megan's tones were cool,

and she lifted her chin and returned Lady Alicia's haughty stare. She had no intention of allowing herself to be intimidated by this terrifyingly modish lady. For the first time in her life, she was thankful for the years she had spent at the various academies for young ladies: They had taught her well in spite of herself, and now, in this moment of crisis, she could face this condescending woman on equal terms, knowing that her own speech and manners were every bit as proper.

"Why, at finding you a husband, of course. My dear, I assume that is what Justin had in mind when he wrote suggesting that you be introduced to the *ton* immediately rather than wait for your eighteenth birthday."

Megan turned to look at Justin. Anger was building inside her, and she knew that he could see it burning in her eyes. His expression was stony, but some indefinable emotion flickered in those golden depths as he returned her look steadily.

"Is that what you had in mind, my lord?" she asked him. Only her eyes told him of her rising fury and contempt.

"Yes." The single word grated in her ears. Her heart felt as if it had turned to stone. She would never forgive him for this, she told herself, then firmly locked all thoughts of him away.

"It is very kind of you to go to so much trouble on my behalf," Megan said civilly to Lady Alicia. She didn't want to look at Justin.

Lady Alicia smiled at her. "Not at all," she said

pleasantly. "Justin and I have wanted children for years." Megan barely managed to conceal a grimace. Alicia, whether she knew it or not, had struck a blow clear through to her heart. "But so far we have not been blessed. Although I am not nearly old enough to be your mother—" here she smiled a little—"I quite expect to be as much a mother to you as Justin has been a father."

"Thank you, my lady, but as you said you are not nearly old enough to be my mother," Megan replied smoothly, deflecting the little dart that she suspected had been meant to emphasize Justin's age and his position as guardian. "And as for me, I am too old to need mothering or fathering, though I thank you for the kind thought."

Both women stood smiling at each other with patent falseness. Megan could read the hostility in Lady Alicia's eyes. The woman clearly recognized Megan as a threat and was ready to fight to hold her man. Megan wondered why she bothered. She was Justin's wife, after all, and no matter how many other women he took to his bed nothing could change her legal position.

"Alicia, I know you are dying to go upstairs and rid yourself of your travel dirt, so if you will excuse us I will take Megan off to the library. I have a few things to say to her." Justin's voice was still harsh, but other than that it was impossible to guess what he was feeling, if indeed he was feeling anything.

"Don't be absurd, Justin," Alicia said, smiling archly. "You just heard the poor child say she hasn't

171

breakfasted. And she's been ill lately! And I will confess that I could do with a tiny nibble of something myself. Do go on and do whatever it is that you do in the mornings, and let your ward come with me."

"Alicia . . ." Justin began impatiently. Megan could feel the restless movement of his big body behind her. She turned to smile sweetly at him; only he could see the daggers that shot from her eyes.

"Your wife is right, my lord. I would dearly like my breakfast. And surely there is no longer any need to discuss your plans for my future, when Lady Alicia is here with plans of her own."

Justin stared down at her, his own eyes hooded.

"As you wish," he said abruptly, then swung around on his crutch to disappear into the library, shutting the door behind him with what was almost, but not quite, a crash.

"Really, my dear, you must excuse my husband. Men can be such boors at times! But of course you wouldn't know about that yet. Do come along and we'll see what the housekeeper—what is her name?— can give us for breakfast."

The day passed in a blur of pain for Megan. She found it hard to believe that this was the same world she had greeted with such rapture only that morning. Her new found happiness had been shattered before she had had a chance to enjoy it. And her love? Shattered too, shown up as the pipedream it was. If Justin had loved her, he would never have done such a thing to her. To take her love (to say nothing of her virgin body) when he was a married man was dastardly. She

172

hadn't known about his wife; how could she have? When he had paid her those duty visits at school, she had been a child, and all they had ever discussed was her progress in various subjects. Nothing personal had ever been mentioned. Charles Stanton too, had never mentioned the existence of a Countess of Weston. Had it all been some huge conspiracy of silence? But as tempted as she was to believe it, Megan reluctantly dismissed that idea almost as soon as it had occurred to her. Despicable Justin might be, but she was sure that he had not planned her seduction since he had first taken her under his wing as a five-year-old child. No, she had to absolve him of that. But he had known, at any time over the past three weeks, that she was falling in love with him. Or if he hadn't known, he should have. And he had certainly outstepped the bounds of propriety with her! Megan thought of the kisses they had exchanged, the caresses, and wanted to weep. She remembered the ecstasy she had found in his arms the night before, thinking herself loved, knowing that she loved him. She thought the sheer agony of remembering would tear her apart. He told her that what he wanted was sex, pure and simple; she had to admit that. He told her he loved her only when she had practically forced him into it. She saw now that he must have done it because he thought it was the easiest, shortest route to get him what he wanted. She couldn't accuse him of forcing himself on her against her will: She had wanted him as badly as he had wanted her, and even now the memory of his lovemaking could make her shiver through the haze of pain. But the difference was that she had loved him, adored him, worshipped him, in fact. She would have given him anything he wanted, never counting the cost. And in return for her love, he had used and abused her, robbed her of her virginity and her self-respect. Now what was she but soiled goods? If anyone ever found out what Justin had done to her she would be ruined, disgraced, cast out of decent society. No man would want to marry her.

As Megan considered these aspects of the situation, she hated Justin so much she could have killed him. He had done this to her, knowing the consequences far better than she did. She had loved him, and he had exploited her love for his own ends.

During the course of that day—Megan thought it the longest day in her life—Lady Alicia gave her to understand that she had only journeyed to Ireland (which she hated) to escort her back to London. She meant to stay no longer than she absolutely had to, and suggested that they start the journey back after only a day's rest. This meant, of course, that Justin with his broken leg would have to stay behind, but that was all right: Justin would not expect them to wait for him, and must be getting rather tired of being forced to endure female companionship day in and day out. Justin didn't much like women, Lady Alicia said, and would probably be glad to see the last of his troublesome ward. Megan agreed coolly that it would probably be best to start for England at once. Inwardly, she told herself the sooner she got away from Justin, the sooner she could start getting over him.

Stamping out her love for him was a matter of survival—and she meant to survive.

She escaped from Lady Alicia at last; by then it was after dinner. Justin had kept out of her way all day, and, although he had appeared for dinner, he had been silent and grim-faced, replying only when spoken to, and always briefly. He toyed with his food while downing glass after glass of wine. Lady Alicia seemed to find nothing odd in his behavior. Megan, thinking fleetingly of the laughing, teasing companion who had charmed her into loving him, could only suppose that such moroseness was normal for him. After all, Lady Alicia, his wife, would know far more about him than an ignorant little girl he had managed to lure into bed.

Hurt and rage combined to stifle down any compassion she might have felt for him. If he was suffering from guilt pangs, well, surely no one ever more richly deserved them.

By the time she managed to get up to her room, she was exhausted from the effort of pretending everything was as it should be. If she had to smile one more time, she thought her jaw would drop off; if Lady Alicia made one more sweetly poisonous remark, Megan was sure nothing would be able to stop her from scratching out the lady's eyes. She knew that it was ridiculous to hate Lady Alicia for being Justin's wife, but she couldn't seem to help herself. The real object of her hatred and scorn should be Justin. Toward that end, she would have to stamp out this ridiculous affection she still felt for him. He had betrayed her, and she would be damned before she went mooning after him like a lovesick schoolgirl. He had taught her a brutal lesson, and she knew that she would never be so blindly trusting again.

Long after she had pulled on another of the filmy lawn nightdresses—the very sight of which made her want to cry—and climbed into bed, she lay awake, staring blindly up into the darkness. Her eyelids ached and burned, and her throat felt scratchy, but she would not, could not, allow herself the luxury of tears. If only Lady Alicia had arrived twenty-four hours earlier, before Justin had taken every scrap of love she had to offer. Futile, too, to torture herself by remembering the very different bed in which she had slept the night before. If she was to salvage anything from this debacle, she had to put the past behind her. From now on, her only concern had to be herself, and her own well-being. If she could not completely eradicate all thoughts of the black-hearted swine who had reduced her to this, it would not be for want of trying.

Megan listened to her heartbeat, hoping that the rhythmic sound would lull her off to sleep without allowing any troublesome thoughts to intrude. She was dozing when she heard the faint sound of her bedroom door being opened. Jolted from sleep, she opened her eyes and sat bolt upright in bed. Someone—or something—was in her room. Maam's Cross Court was said to be haunted, although Megan had never seen any trace of the ghost. Her nocturnal visitor had to be either spectral in origin—or it had to be Justin. She wasn't sure she would not have preferred the ghost.

176

"Who is it?" she called out sharply, gathering the bedclothes around her.

There was a scraping sound, a brief flare of light, and then a candle flickered into life. By its sallow light, Megan had no trouble recognizing Justin's muscular shape, large and menacing as the candlelight threw him into sharp relief.

"Get out of my room!" Megan's voice quivered with outrage.

"Keep your voice down," he growled, moving closer, the candle safely deposited on a nearby table. "Do you want the entire household to know I'm in here?"

"I don't give a damn if the entire world knows you're in here! I want you out of my room."

"Don't swear," he said, frowning at her. He continued to approach the bed, not stopping until he stood beside it. "I want to talk to you. I want to explain."

"What is there to explain, Justin? The situation seems perfectly obvious to me!" Megan's voice was cool, but her eyes shot daggers at him. "And I'll swear at you if I damned well please."

Justin looked at her for a long time without speaking. His skin looked curiously gray, and the lines of strain around his mouth had deepened, making him look far older.

"Megan, I want you to know that—I mean what I said—last night." His voice was low; his eyes were full of pain. But Megan refused to pity him.

"I don't want to talk about last night!"

"Megan, my darling, we have to talk about it."

"Don't call me *that!*" Her voice rose shrilly on the

177

last word. She rose to her knees in the bed, the covers still clutched to her breast, her eyes feral as she glared at him. Justin winced at the naked agony he heard in her cry.

"I'm so desperately sorry," he said quietly, his eyes dropping to stare at the carpet as if it fascinated him. "I never meant to hurt you."

"You never meant to hurt me!" She had to fight back an urge to laugh hysterically. "God, you never meant to hurt me! What did you think would happen? You seduced me and you were already married."

"At that point, I was beyond thinking. I've never been in love before."

Megan stared incredulously. "Love!" she gasped viciously. "Don't you dare talk to me about love. If you loved me, you would never have laid a hand on me. I thought you wanted to marry me."

He looked at her quickly.

"I did. I do! I would divorce Alicia if I could, but I have no grounds. And she'll never divorce me. She likes being Countess of Weston too much." Bitterness twisted his mouth.

"Well, isn't that convenient! You would marry me, but you can't divorce your wife, and she won't divorce you. How very sad. But at least your intentions were honorable! Which is why you never bothered to mention to me the little fact that you're married."

Justin winced under the harsh lash of her words, the lines around his mouth whitening. "You knew I was married."

"The hell I did! How could I? I'd never met your

178

wife." She fairly spat the word at him. "And neither you nor Charles nor anyone else ever mentioned her. Do you think I would have behaved as I did if I had known you were *married?"*

Justin looked stricken. "I've been married to Alicia for fifteen years. I thought you knew. We don't live together. Alicia doesn't love me, doesn't even like me very much, and I don't love her. I didn't write to her. She happened to be visiting my Aunt Sophrinsia when my letter arrived, the letter I wrote describing you and asking if she would let you stay with her, and bring you out. Something in the letter frightened Alicia and brought her running. She must have realized that her position was in real jeopardy for the first time. She knows I don't love her. It's never bothered her before, and it doesn't bother her now. Just as long as I continue to keep up appearances and pay her bills, she's happy. But I think she guessed how I feel about you. She's made enough snide remarks. Oh, she doesn't have any idea that I—that we —about how far it's gone, but she is astute enough, and has known me long enough, to sense that you are a threat to her. That's why she's here, why she's so eager to take you to London and find you a husband. She wants to get you safely out of my way."

"You must want that, too, or you would never have written that letter." His explanation had in no way softened Megan's bitter anger, and her words were as nasty as she could make them. Even if what he said about his wife was true—and she tended to believe him—it didn't change what he had done to her. He had

179

made her love him, taken her virginity and broken her heart, all the time knowing that he could offer her nothing but disgrace. Talk of divorce was just a way of smoothing her down. No one got divorced. Once a couple got married, they remained husband and wife until death did they part.

"I wrote that letter before I came to love you. I wanted to protect you. I knew that if I didn't send you away soon, I would make love to you. I wanted you so much. I still do."

"Don't say that."

"It's true!" His eyes darkened with passion. "I want you so much I'm going out of my mind. I would marry you if I could, but I can't! And I can't ask you to stay with me without marriage, though I would cherish and protect you all the days of my life. It wouldn't be fair to you."

"How noble!" Megan sneered. "Then tell me something, my lord. If you can't ask me to marry you, or to be your mistress, just what is your purpose in coming to my room? Surely you're not conceited enough to imagine that I'm going to let you get into bed with me again."

"No!" His head flew back as if she'd struck him. "I wanted to apologize, to explain, and—something else. Megan, my darling . . ."

"Don't call me that!" Her voice rose angrily.

Justin held up his hand. "I'm sorry," he said quickly. "Hear me out. After what we did last night, there may be—results. If you should find that your monthly course doesn't come as it should, I want you to tell me at once. Do you understand?"

Megan felt her face burn with humiliation. "How dare you speak of such things to me!" she gasped. She put her hands to her flaming cheeks, hoping to cool them. Even among women, such subjects were not discussed. For a man to bring it up was hideously embarrassing.

"Megan, do you understand what I'm telling you?" he asked fiercely. "The way I made love to you last night is the way people make babies: if your monthly course doesn't come as it should, then it means that you are with child."

"Oh, my God!" Megan felt herself go white. She had had no idea that such a thing could result from that single night of rapture. She stared at him, not really seeing him, sickened at the picture of herself in an unmentionable state, the object of scorn and, from the more charitable, pity—later bearing a bastard child. She would be better off dead.

"Megan, I want you to promise that you'll tell me!" Seeing her turn pale with shock, he reached for her, but at the touch of his hand she became a tigress, launching herself at him with her fingers curled into claws, scratching him and hitting him, knocking him backward with the force of her assault. He regained his balance with some difficulty, dropping his crutch and falling to the bed with his arms around her to stop her struggles, holding her in an iron grip as she bit and kicked and writhed with all her strength, desperate to do him any injury.

"Darling, don't! You'll hurt yourself! Megan, be

still!'' He murmured to her anxiously, pinning her body with his to keep her quiet. Finally, Megan realized that she was not going to get away. She stopped struggling, and lay unmoving beneath him, her eyes glaring like a wild thing's.

"Get away from me!" she hissed into the dark, strained face that was only inches away.

"When you promise me." His words were final sounding. Megan, shuddering from his touch, which she could feel along the whole, barely covered length of her body, would have agreed to anything to get him off her. She loathed him so much that her skin actually crawled.

"I promise," she spat at him. "Now get off me, you disgusting swine! I despise you! I feel sick at the very thought of having your baby! It makes me want to throw up!"

Justin got up with the help of his crutch. Megan rose to her knees on the bed, still cursing him. Justin made no attempt to fend off the blow he knew was coming. Megan drew back her hand and slapped him full across the face. His head snapped back from the force of her blow. He said nothing. He just stared at her. There were red marks on his face.

"I hate you!" Megan told him, her voice trembling. "Get out of my room!"

Still Justin said nothing. He just looked at her steadily. Then he turned and went out.

Chapter 11

It was in mid-November, almost a month after Megan left Maam's Cross Court, that Justin returned to London. The weather was cold and blustery as he drove himself along the cobbled streets of the town at a fast clip, anxious to get home to his own fireside, complete with a hot dinner and a bottle of his best port. He had been on the road for some days, traveling far slower than was his custom because of the necessity of pampering his healing leg, which had been liberated from its splint less than a week before. Dr. Ryan had strongly disapproved of Justin's determination to drive himself back to town, recommending a closed coach with a driver, but Justin had turned a deaf ear to the good doctor's protests. He was sick and tired of being mollycoddled, and besides, he hated being driven.

Weston House, an imposing four-storied brick house that had been the town residence of the Earls of Weston for the last hundred years, was located in the fashionable Grosvenor Square. As Justin drew close, he saw that the square was nearly deserted. It was after nine o'clock in the evening, and the gas lamps sputtering at the street corners gave the park an almost menacing aspect. Justin scarcely noticed this as he reined his horses to a halt in front of number 14. All his thoughts were concentrated on the coming meeting with Megan.

The ornately carved door swung open as if by magic, and a liveried footman came hurrying down the steps as Justin descended from the curricle. Ames, the butler, stood framed in the open doorway, his imposing figure clad in sober black. The lamplight spilled out behind him.

"Take them around to the stables," Justin instructed the footman, and didn't even wait for the murmured "Yes, my lord" before ascending the steps to his house.

"Good evening, my lord," Ames greeted him as he passed through the door, showing no more surprise than if he'd been absent for a quarter-hour instead of nearly three months.

"I'll have dinner served in my study immediately," Justin said, handing his driving coat and hat to Ames.

Ames received the garments impassively, and passed them on to a footman who had materialized behind him.

"Yes, my lord."

"And send up a bottle of port."

"Yes, my lord."

Justin turned away, preparing to walk down the thickly-carpeted hallway to his study, which was near the back of the house. Then, as if by afterthought, he asked, "Are the ladies at home? I don't expect the Countess, but perhaps my ward?"

"No, my lord," Ames said. "Both ladies are out for the evening. I believe that they were planning to attend Lady Castlereagh's ball."

Justin's lips compressed. "I see. Thank you, Ames. Oh, and what about Mr. Stanton?"

"I believe that he is still here, my lord. I will have one of the maids inquire. If Mr. Stanton is in the house should I send him along to your study?"

"Yes, thank you, Ames." Justin bestowed a fleeting smile on his butler, then adjourned to his study.

When Charles Stanton arrived, knocking discreetly on the door before being bidden to enter, Justin was ensconced in a deep chair before the fire. His dinner sat half-eaten on a small table before him, but he was nearly three-quarters through his first bottle of port. He smiled at his secretary, who had been in his service for nearly twenty years. Stanton, a thick-set fellow with sandy hair who was some few years Justin's senior, returned the smile. They shook hands.

"Have your supper, Charles?" Justin asked, gesturing to the meal before him.

Charles shook his head. "No, thanks, I ate two hours ago. But I will have a glass of that excellent port, if I may."

Justin filled a glass and passed it to him, then took another large swallow from his own glass. Charles, used to Justin's taciturnity from long years of association, waited to see what was wanted. When it became apparent that Justin was more interested in the contents of his glass than in conversation, Charles Stanton spoke. "Leg paining you, Justin?"

Justin looked up, a frown furrowing his brow as he stared at his old friend. The other man returned his look blandly.

"Not particularly. Why do you ask?"

Stanton's mouth twisted into a wry smile.

"I don't think I've ever seen you go through a bottle so fast. And that's your best port, too."

Justin glanced from the nearby empty bottle to his glass, then tossed off what was left of the port. Charles looked faintly scandalized at this desecration of a fine wine, but wisely said nothing.

"What's been going on in London since I've been away?"

Justin was forced to listen impatiently as Charles recited the latest gossip.

"And how has my ward been getting on? And my wife?" he tacked on hastily.

Charles grinned. "We were all very surprised when Lady Alicia took up residence here with Megan. Caught us all napping. Thought the lady was fixed in

186

Bath for a while."

"Until I left for Brant Hall, you mean," Justin interjected dryly, referring to his country estate in Worcestershire. Charles was well aware of the unhappy state of his marriage, and Justin saw no reason to pretend for his benefit. "Believe me, she was quite a surprise to me, too."

"You could have knocked me over with a feather when she arrived here demanding a carriage so that she could race to your bedside in Ireland. First time I've seen her in the role of the devoted wife."

Justin grimaced. "It surprised me too."

Charles thought better of continuing this line of talk knowing that Lady Alicia was a sore subject with Justin. Instead, he sought to turn his employer's attention in a less painful direction.

"And what did you think of your ward, Justin?"

Justin looked at him sharply. But Charles' face was completely unconcerned. He relaxed.

"A beauty," he said dispassionately, leaning back in his chair so that the curved wings cast a deep shadow over his face.

Charles chuckled. "She is that," he agreed. "Since Lady Alicia has been taking her around, the house has been knee deep in her admirers. Made quite a hit, has our little Megan."

"Has she?"

"Oh, yes. She's got them all after her, I believe. Not just the puppies, but Resenick and Ivor, too, I hear."

"Resenick and Ivor are paying court to Megan? They are not serious, surely." Resenick and Ivor were two of London's most notorious rakes. The Earl of Resenick was a childless widower of forty whose fortune was reputed to be nearly as great as Golden Ball's; Lord Ivor was younger, in his early thirties, and had never been married. He, too, was very rich. Both were famed connoisseurs of beautiful women. Justin had frequently done battle with one or the other of them for the favors of some beautiful woman. Justin's good looks gave him an edge that the others lacked.

Charles shook his head. "As to that, who can say? But they have certainly been assiduous in their attentions. As a matter of fact, it is Lord Ivor who escorted Megan and Lady Alicia to the Castlereagh's ball tonight."

"The devil you say!" Justin shot to his feet, nearly oversetting the small table. "What were you thinking about, to permit such a thing, Charles?"

Charles looked up at him in lively surprise.

"I had nothing to say in the matter. The decision was Lady Alicia's—and Megan's."

Justin swore viciously.

"Good God, Justin, don't tell me you're going to be a strict guardian?" Charles was about to laugh; the look on Justin's face stopped him.

"Where are you going?" he asked in consternation. Justin looked angry enough to do a murder.

"To the Castlereigh's," Justin snapped. "Megan has no more sense than a baby, and Alicia would just love throwing her to the wolves. And Ivor's the biggest damned wolf I know."

"Really, Justin!" Charles expostulated, but he

found himself talking to thin air. Justin had gone.

By the time Justin had summoned Manning from the nether regions of the house, got into evening dress and made his way to the Castlereagh's, it was nearing midnight. The ball was in full swing and would continue until dawn, perhaps later than that. Justin handed his evening cloak to a liveried footman. He could hear the gay music floating down from the ballroom. It was mixed with the sound of laughter and voices exchanging the latest gossip. Justin glowered as he moved up the stairs to the ballroom, acknowledging the greetings of friends and acquaintances alike with a terse nod. The Castlereagh's elegant townhouse seemed to be bursting at the seams; Justin reflected sardonically that the ball would probably be termed a "sad crush", which was the ultimate in praise.

"Weston! Didn't expect to see you here, old man. Lady Alicia has been telling everyone some tale about your being laid up for months. Ain't true, obviously."

"Obviously." Courtesy dictated that he reply to the Honorable Mr. George Seavors, whom he had known over the past fifteen years. Ordinarily, Justin had no objection to Seavors, who was not a bad sort for all his giving himself the airs of a Macaroni, but tonight he was not in good humor. The idea of Ivor—Ivor!—making Megan the object of his gallantries annoyed him to the point where he could think of little else.

"Yes, um, well . . ." Seavors was at a loss to understand how he could possibly have offended Justin. The man was looking like a thundercloud, and in

189

Seavors' experience that meant trouble. Weston was famous for being a deadly shot, and had more than once killed his man in a duel. And his temper was such that prudent fellows steered clear of him when he was looking the way he looked tonight. Seavors cast a hasty glance into the ballroom, hoping to be rescued, and had the happy notion of something he could say that could not possibly be open to misinterpretation.

"Allow me to compliment you on your ward, Weston! A real stunner!"

"Ahh." Seavors had Justin's full attention. "Thank you, Seavors. Have you seen her tonight?"

Seavors beamed. "Who hasn't? She's the belle of the ball. Say, Weston, do you suppose you could introduce me? I've been trying to ask her to dance all night, but there's no getting near her."

"I will be delighted, Seavors—later. But in the meantime, I would be in your debt if you could point me in her direction."

"Nothing easier, old man," Seavors replied, turning to peer into the ballroom, grinning at the same time. "See that knot of fellows over there? Last time I saw her—just a few minutes ago—she was in the center of it, trying to decide which of her admirers to honor with a posy of violets. Both Ivor and Peter Marsh requested it, you see."

"I do indeed." Justin bowed ironically and left Seavors to his own devices. Seavors, staring after him, wondered briefly what ailed Weston, then with a shrug dismissed the matter from his mind, and took himself off to the card room.

By the time Justin had made his way through the crowded ballroom to the place Seavors had indicated, he was just in time to see Megan sweep off to the dance floor on the arm of Lord Ivor as the musicians struck up a country dance. Justin halted, gritting his teeth and watching as Megan laughed and chatted with Ivor in the friendliest manner imaginable. He scowled as Ivor took her hand in his and led her through the steps of the dance. If anyone spoke to him—and several did—he didn't hear them.

Megan, looking lovelier than he had ever seen her, was dressed in a satin ballgown the color of wisteria, with a full flounced skirt that must have been yards in circumference. The bodice tightly molded her slender shape, emphasizing the proud young tilt of her breasts and the slimness of her waist. Above the dropped-shoulder styling of the neckline her bosom peeked shyly forth. Her hair, piled in masses of ebony curls on top of her head, was ornamented at the side by an amethyst clasp securing a cluster of violets. Justin had no trouble in recognizing the clasp, and the matching necklet which adorned Megan's white throat, as being part of the Brant family jewels. He could only suspect that Charles had fetched them from the locked cabinet where they were kept for Megan to wear tonight.

As Justin watched, a movement of the dance brought Megan around to face him. She was totally unconscious of his presence as she exchanged gay repartee with her partner, whose scarlet balldress nearly rivalled Megan's own for magnificence. Justin curled a lip at Ivor's foppishness, wondering why he had never noticed it before. Then Ivor laughed aloud at something Megan said, and raised her slim white fingers to his lips. Justin, seeing this, felt such a surge of rage that it was all he could do not to stalk out onto the middle of the dance floor and drag Megan away by force. Only the thought of the scandal that must ensue, and the damage it would inevitably do to Megan's name, stayed him. Smoldering, his eyes never leaving Megan and Ivor, Justin leaned against a pillar and waited for the dance to end.

Megan was enjoying herself as much as could be expected under the circumstances. Her heart was bruised and battered from Justin's callous use of her, but she was determined that no one should guess it. She laughed and danced and flirted as if she were having the time of her life. She thought she had succeeded in convincing Lady Alicia that she had totally banished Justin from her mind, if indeed she had ever thought of him at all. She was not about to wear her heart on her sleeve, or to allow one man's base betrayal to ruin her life.

Timothy Crichton—Lord Ivor—was one of the many gentlemen who had flocked to her side as soon as she had appeared on the London scene. Megan liked him, and Lady Alicia seemed to approve of him as an escort for both of them. The Castlereagh's ball was the fourth social event to which he had squired them, and Megan was growing quite comfortable in his presence. He treated her with a great deal of respect, as if she was, in truth, a grown-up lady (which

Thrill to the most sensual, adventure-filled Historical Romances on the market today...

FROM ![LEISURE BOOKS logo] *LEISURE BOOKS*

As a home subscriber to the Leisure Romance Book Club, you'll enjoy the best in today's BRAND-NEW Historical Romance fiction. For over twenty years, Leisure Books has brought you the award-winning, high-quality authors you know and love to read. Each Leisure Historical Romance will sweep you away to a world of high adventure...and intimate romance. Discover for yourself all the passion and excitement millions of readers thrill to each and every month.

Save $5.⁰⁰ Each Time You Buy!

Six times a year, the Leisure Romance Book Club brings you four brand-new titles from Leisure Books, America's foremost publisher of Historical Romances. EACH PACKAGE WILL SAVE YOU $5.00 FROM THE BOOKSTORE PRICE! And you'll never miss a new title with our convenient home delivery service.

Here's how we do it. Each package will carry a FREE 10-DAY EXAMINATION privilege. At the end of that time, if you decide to keep your books, simply pay the low invoice price of $14.96, no shipping or handling charges added. HOME DELIVERY IS ALWAYS FREE. With today's top Historical Romance novels selling for $4.99 and higher, our price SAVES YOU $5.00 with each shipment.

AND YOUR FIRST FOUR-BOOK SHIPMENT IS TOTALLY FREE!

IT'S A BARGAIN YOU CAN'T BEAT! A Super $19.96 Value!

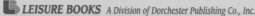

![LEISURE BOOKS logo] **LEISURE BOOKS** *A Division of Dorchester Publishing Co., Inc.*

Get Four Books Totally
FREE— A $19.96 Value!

▼ Tear Here and Mail Your FREE Book Card Today! ▼

PLEASE RUSH
MY FOUR FREE
BOOKS TO ME
RIGHT AWAY!

Leisure Romance Book Club
65 Commerce Road
Stamford CT 06902-4563

AFFIX
STAMP
HERE

she seldom felt herself to be). His courtesy after Justin's continual scathing references to her youth and inexperience was very pleasant.

She was laughing at something he said when he happened to glance over her shoulder. His eyes narrowed. After a moment, he looked back down at her, his expression quizzical.

"What have I done to earn such black looks from Weston, Miss Kinkead? Do you suppose someone has been carrying tales of me to him—tales which must of necessity be quite untrue, I might add?"

Megan turned to look in the direction Lord Ivor had indicated. Sure enough, Justin was there, leaning against a pillar with his arms crossed over his chest, a scowl darkening his face. Before the dance claimed her attention again, she saw that he appeared to be as strong and healthy as he had been. The splint was gone.

Justin's evening coat was black, his waistcoat severe charcoal gray brocade. His shirt and cravat were snowy white. Megan felt her heart trip a little as she registered his sheer physical splendor. Then she encountered those tawny gold eyes and took herself firmly in hand, tilting her chin defiantly, daring him to interfere. He had no right to look at her in that way, to glare at Lord Ivor—whose conduct had been a thousand times more circumspect than his own—so fiercely. He had no rights at all where she was concerned. She refused to allow him even those of a guardian. He had forfeited all right to dictate her behavior, as she meant to demonstrate. She turned away from him without so much as nodding, refusing to acknowledge the sardonic little smile with which he favored her.

"Perhaps Justin has a stomach-ache," Megan said. Lord Ivor laughed, and began to talk of other things. During the remainder of the dance, Megan laughed and chatted for all she was worth, while striving to appear unconscious of Justin's steadfast regard.

Megan and Lord Ivor were close to Justin when the music stopped. Megan had planned it that way. She knew Justin was listening.

"I am positively dying of thirst," she said plaintively, fluttering her lashes. "Do you suppose we could find the punch bowl?"

Lord Ivor grinned knowingly. He was tall, about Justin's height, but very thin, with a shock of light brown hair and a narrow, intelligent face. Megan, despite her three weeks in London, had not yet got quite used to seeing a man rigged out in red velvet. But she had discovered that he was really quite sensible. From the twinkle in his hazel eyes, Megan guessed that he knew her object was to avoid Justin at all costs.

"Running scared, Miss Kinkead?" he suggested, offering his arm so that she could lay her fingers on it in the approved manner. "Are you sure it's you he's frowning at? I would rather have supposed it was me. Weston, being of the same stamp himself, could conceivably hold the opinion that I am not exactly a proper companion for his very charming ward."

Megan remembered to smile prettily at the compliment, but her thoughts were elsewhere. Several young

194

ladies of her acquaintance had taken great pains to warn her of Lord Ivor's reputation as a rake; had let fall several tidbits about Justin's similar notoriety that she had hoped were exaggerated. Now here was Ivor confirming all that she had been told about both of them. As far as Lord Ivor was concerned, it made not a farthing's worth of difference, but it sickened her to think that Justin made a habit of seducing women. Well, he had seduced her, hadn't he—and for that she was going to make him pay.

"I've changed my mind," she murmured sweetly. "Please take me out on the balcony. I'm feeling a trifle faint."

Ivor looked at her, wondering what her game was. She returned his look with a limpid look of her own, an innocent flutter of her lashes. After a moment he shrugged and obediently led her toward the long french windows which opened out onto the balcony.

"Far be it from me to turn down what the gods offer, Miss Kinkead," he said as they approached the heavy drapes that shielded the french doors. "But are you absolutely certain you want to do this? Weston's not a pleasant fellow when he's angry."

"I'm sure he's not," Megan said, then added with a breathless laugh, "We don't get along. Haven't for years. He's terribly tyrannical, and I'm getting tired of having everything I do vetted by him. He doesn't seem to realize that I've grown up."

"He must be blind," Lord Ivor said. They went out to the balcony.

Megan paid no heed to Lord Ivor's remark, but

walked over to where a wrought-iron railing protected the unwary from ending up in the garden below. The iron felt cold against her palms as she gripped it. The night was pitch black, very cold. Megan breathed deeply, finding the cold air invigorating. Behind her, she could hear the muted sound of the musicians striking up again, and she wondered briefly how long the young man she had promised this dance to would look for her before giving up.

Lord Ivor came up behind her and put his hands lightly on her bare shoulders. Megan stiffened at his touch.

"Shall I do the expected thing and kiss you?" he murmured. "Anyone who saw us come out like this will be certain that's what's happening, and I really hate to take credit for something I haven't done."

The halting quality of this last statement and the tightening of his hands on her shoulders told Megan he was serious.

She looked over her shoulder, frowning slightly. "I would really prefer that you did not," she said. His hands tightened for a moment, then fell to his sides.

"So I'm to be used but not rewarded, is that it?" he murmured wryly. "Very well, Miss Kinkead, I bow to your wishes."

"Thank you." Megan turned toward him, smiling warmly, touched at the gallantry. In comparison to some she knew, he was a true gentleman.

They were like that when Justin found them. He had come through the french doors silently, pulling them shut after him. He was furious. Ivor had no right to bring Megan out here, and Megan; damn her, had no business falling victim to his practiced blandishments.

"If you touch her, Ivor, I'll throw you over the railing." Justin spoke through his teeth. Lord Ivor and Megan turned to face him.

"That sounds remarkably like a threat, Weston," Ivor drawled.

Justin smiled unpleasantly. "It is," he said, and as the two men bristled at each other Megan moved between them. Justin ignored her, his eyes issuing an angry challenge for Lord Ivor. Megan felt her face blanch. She had not meant to cause trouble between the men, only to use Lord Ivor as the handiest weapon available in her private war with Justin.

"Thank you for your kindness, my lord," she said to Ivor. "But I believe it would be best if you returned to the ballroom."

She accompanied this statement with a small, placating smile as she silently begged him to do as she wished.

Ivor hesitated. "I will be more than glad to stay if you should feel yourself in need of company, Miss Kinkead." There was no mistaking the meaning of that.

Justin stiffened, with rigid menace. "I assure you, Ivor, that my ward is perfectly safe in my company," Justin grated.

Ivor looked questioningly at Megan. "Please go," she said, recognizing the danger signals. "And thank you," she added, as Ivor gave a stiff little bow and left the balcony. With a haughty look at Justin, Megan gathered up her skirts in her hands and prepared to do the same. He stopped her by gripping her wrist.

"Where do you think you're going?" he asked.

"Back to the ballroom," Megan answered, trying vainly to pull her arm free. "In case you haven't noticed, it's cold out here."

"Oh, I noticed," Justin's voice was unpleasant. "Too cold to stand out here and talk to me, but not too cold for you to welcome that cretin's kisses."

Megan winced. She was beginning to feel cold—and not just because of the weather.

"Lord Ivor," she said with emphasis, "was a perfect gentleman."

"Oh, yes?" Justin sneered. "It didn't look like it from where I was standing. I absolutely forbid you to have anything further to do with that man. Good God, if you were stupid enough to let him lure you out onto a balcony at a ball, I shudder to think what he might be able to talk you into if he were to get you alone."

"Do you speak from your own experience of me, my lord?" Megan asked. Justin's face grew pale. "As it happens, Lord Ivor did not lure me onto the balcony; I asked him to bring me. It was hot, and I was feeling faint."

"That's a damned lie!"

Megan smiled mockingly. "What is a lie? That I was feeling faint, or that I asked Lord Ivor to bring me out on the balcony?"

"You did it to punish me, didn't you?" he demanded hoarsely.

Megan smiled again, a slow, taunting smile that wasn't reflected in her eyes. He was beginning to get the idea. If there was any possible way she could make him suffer as he had made her suffer, she would do it.

"Did I?"

"You little bitch." He said it deliberately. Megan winced at the word before she could regain control of herself. "You brought Ivor out here to punish me. My God, do you have any idea of what you invited? He eats little girls like you for breakfast!"

"So I've heard," Megan said softly. "But then, I've heard the same about you, my lord, and have good reason to know it for the truth. Besides, it's a little late to be worried about my virtue, isn't it? I have none left to lose."

Justin's face was suddenly etched in sharp lines of pain. Megan would have felt sorry for him if she had not hated him so much.

"Megan . . ." he began, his voice faltering. Then his jaw clenched and all trace of expression was wiped from his face by a strong effort of will.

"I meant what I said about Ivor," he said, his face and voice suddenly remote. "You're not to see him again. If you do, I'll find a means to stop it. If I have to call him out to do it."

Megan wrenched her arm away, and at last he let her go.

"Do you know what's the matter with you, my lord?" She went to the french doors, opened them,

199

then turned back to spit her words at him. "You're not worried about Lord Ivor, or my reputation. You're jealous!"

And with that she swept through to the ballroom, leaving Justin behind. When finally he did leave the balcony, he paused only long enough to collect his cloak. Then he went to his club, where he proceeded to get very, very drunk.

Chapter 12

Over the next few days, Megan tightened the screws as best she could. She flirted outrageously, encouraging her many admirers to ridiculous excesses. The house was positively aswarm with young men; they brought flowers and books and boxes of chocolates as a tribute to her beauty. She was out every night until long past midnight, and then rose very early to drive through the park with one or the other of her swains. Lady Alicia, in her element when partaking of the *ton's* glittering pleasures, was as eager as Megan to gad about to soirees and parties and balls. An acknowledged beauty herself when she had come out some sixteen years before, Lady Alicia did not let her poorly disguised jealousy of her protege's success stop her from enjoying herself enormously. She was an established leader of London society, and her social position with its accompanying priveleges meant all the world to her. After all, it was why she had married the distressingly earthy Earl of Weston. He had been the catch of the season, rich and handsome and blessed with impeccable lineage. It had been quite a feather in her cap to get him to propose, and she had made haste to accept with her family's full blessing. And, from her point of view, the marriage was a success. Oh, it had taken her some few months to teach Justin that a high-born lady such as herself could not be expected to pander to his male appetites, but once he had learned that she had no intention of acting the whore for him he had left her alone. The last fourteen of their fifteen years of marriage had been ideal. She had all the advantages of being the Countess of Weston without having to suffer the disagreeable burden of her husband's presence.

Unlike Lady Alicia, Justin had no stomach for the never-ending social round of London in November. Even at the best of times, he preferred the peace and quite of Brant Hall, or even the independent bachelor life that he led in London without Lady Alicia. But now that it was Megan tormenting him, he could barely stand to enter his own house. The sight of so many young puppies slobbering over his ward set his teeth on edge. He wanted to kick them down the steps, and since he could not his anger built each day.

202

In self-defense, he spent most of his time at his club, playing cards for high stakes and not coming home until dawn. He was drinking heavily, and it made his temper hair-trigger quick. More than one of his cronies refused to play with him in such a mood, for his skill with the pistols was well known.

If Megan had known how well her punishment was working, she would have been delighted. But she saw very little of him, just an occasional glimpse as he entered or left the house, and she had no idea that the torment she had devised for him was so effective. She began to encourage Lord Ivor, although she realized that she was playing with fire. Justin would be furious if he found out that she was openly defying bans on Ivor. But she wanted him furious, she told herself. She wanted him so furious he couldn't see straight. She would not be sorry if he died of rage.

She had agreed to ride out with Lord Ivor at the fashionable hour of two o'clock. Justin was occasionally home at that time, and she hoped that he would see her leave. But if he did not, she could be fairly sure that some gossip would tell him. It was not proper for a young lady to be in the company of any man who was not related to her without a chaperone, and as Lady Alicia invariably spent the daylight hours in her room resting for the evening's exertions, Megan would be riding out with Ivor alone. She was not even taking her maid, and that was intentional, too. She badly wanted to get a rise out of Justin, even if she had to create a tiny scandal to do it.

Her maid, procurred for her by Charles Stanton

after her arrival in London, was a positive genius when it came to styling hair, so Megan was feeling pleased as she looked at her reflection in the dressing table mirror before going downstairs to wait for Ivor. The maid had arranged a simple chignon at the back of her head, and the severe style emphasized the porcelain purity of her features. It was topped of with a shako hat of soft white fur. Her riding habit was a deep burgandy wool, and a little matching muffet of white fur curled around her neck to frame her face. Black boots and warm black gloves completed the outfit; surveying these last additions to her toilette, Megan knew that she looked as well as she ever had.

Lord Ivor was punctual, as usual. Megan greeted him with a pretty smile, and allowed him to help her into the saddle of the black mare that had been provided for her use by Justin's stables. Ivor himself was mounted on a big gray gelding; watching him as he jogged along beside her, Megan privately thought that riding was not one of the areas in which he excelled.

The park was deserted because of the weather, which was quite cold. Megan loved the crisp bite of the air, and if Ivor didn't quite agree with her he didn't say so. They chatted casually as they put their mounts through their paces, pausing now and then to exchange greetings with various friends who happened to pass by.

"Do you go to the Chetwood's soiree tonight, Miss Kinkead?" Lord Ivor inquired politely as they slowed their horses to a walk.

"Don't tell me that you are planning to attend, Lord Ivor?" she murmured teasingly. "Somehow, an evening of operatic music doesn't sound like your cup of tea."

Ivor smiled disarmingly. "Only the prospect of your presence makes it bearable, Miss Kinkead."

Megan laughed. "In that case, my lord, I shall certainly be there!"

"I would be honored if you would accept me as your escort," Lord Ivor murmured, giving her a sidelong look.

Megan hesitated. Instinctively she knew that going to the soiree with Ivor would bring Justin's rage to the boiling point. And yet . . . and yet . . .

Megan's eyes widened as she watched the approach of an elegant black curricle. She knew those horses; she knew that carriage; and she undoubtedly knew the man holding the reins with such cool confidence. She didn't know the woman sitting beside him. Megan stared at the lovely face with its crown of improbable red hair, watched the way she smiled at Justin from her nest of black sables.

Megan felt sick. "Who is that?" she whispered to Ivor.

"I presume you are referring to the lady with Weston?" Ivor drawled. "That, my dear Miss Kinkead, is a someone you should pretend to be unaware of. She is not of your class, and you should not trouble yourself with thoughts of her."

Megan could not take her eyes off the rapidly approaching curricle. "Never mind all that," she said impatiently. "Who is she?"

"Her name is Clorinda Barclay. At least, that's what she calls herself. She is—was—a singer at the opera house before Weston took her under his protection some eight months ago."

"She is his—his mistress?" Megan could barely get the words out. She hurt so much, she wanted to die.

"If you would have plain speaking, yes."

The curricle was almost even with them before Justin cast a casual glance at the two riders approaching on the edge of the road. His eyes blazed as he recognized Megan and then her escort; his mouth tightened ominously. Megan exchanged one look with him, then immediately averted her face, her nose in the air as she kicked the black mare into a canter and rode past. Justin and the woman drove on.

Megan was silent throughout the rest of the ride, and felt secretly relieved when Lord Ivor suggested cutting it short. As he escorted her back to the house, she responded politely to his attempts at conversation, but heard scarcely a third of what he said. Her thoughts were too occupied with pictures of Justin holding that woman in his arms, making love to her with the same tenderness he had shown to her.

"You never did tell me whether I might escort you to the Chetwood's tonight," Lord Ivor reminded her as they drew rein outside her door. A footman immediately ran out to take hold of the mare's head. Megan slid down without assistance. She looked up at Lord Ivor, really seeing him for the first time since she had caught sight of Justin with that creature.

"I would be very pleased to accept your escort, my lord." Megan's eyes flashed as she spoke. Her hurt was rapidly turning into rage, and she no longer felt the slightest compunction about making use of Lord Ivor to fan Justin's anger.

"I will call for you at eight, Miss Kinkead," Lord Ivor bowed, and took himself off.

Throughout the rest of the day, Megan's temper remained at boiling point. She refused to recognize the emotion she felt as jealousy, telling herself that her anger sprang from being made a fool of. And Justin had made a fool of her very capably, with his charming smiles and teasing remarks, his tender kisses, the final humiliation of his lovemaking. Just remembering the way they had been that night still had the power to make her shiver. So she refused to think about it. She also refused to calculate the days that had passed since her last monthly time. It would come, she knew it would come. Fate would not be so cruel as to force her to bear his child.

Anger was very becoming, she thought as she watched her maid put the finishing touches to her toilette that night. It brought a rosy flush to her high cheekbones and added sparkle to her eyes. Dressed in a deep rose pink taffeta gown with a heart-shaped neckline that exposed most of her shoulders and quite a bit of her breasts, Megan thought she looked ready for battle. With her hair caught up high at the crown of her head, to fall in a cascade of dusky ringlets down her back, her only ornament a single rose, Megan was well satisfied with her arsenal of weapons. She had declared all-out war on Justin, and she meant to win.

"You look a real picture, miss," the maid said shyly as Megan gathered up her spangled shawl before going downstairs. Megan smiled at the girl.

"Thank you, Mary," she said, and with her shawl draped negligently over her elbows she went down to join Lady Alicia and Lord Ivor, who were waiting for her.

The soiree was held in the Chetwoods' first floor salon, and it was crowded. It seemed as if everyone had turned out to hear Madame Minerva Diaz, the famous Spanish diva. Lady Alicia, elegantly turned out in her favorite ice-blue, abandoned Megan immediately to chat with some of her particular friends. Megan was left to entertain Lord Ivor, which she did with enthusiasm. Ivor, watching her determined efforts to flirt with him, began to get a gleam in his eyes that should have given her pause, but she was too caught up in what she was doing to see it. She meant to set all of London talking about her relationship with Lord Ivor by the end of this night!

Madame Diaz sang. Megan listened with genuine appreciation. The lady had a fine, unusual soprano, and it was a pleasure to hear her perform. But when their hosts' eldest daughter took the lady's place after Madame Diaz retired to her seat, Megan was not the only one to become restless. Madame Diaz' voice was a true gift of the gods; Miss Chetwood's was a penance.

"Let us get some refreshments," Lord Ivor whispered into her ear when Miss Chetwood paused for breath. Megan nodded. She felt Lady Alicia's eyes on her as she left the room on Ivor's arm, and knew that nearly every other lady in the room was watching, too. She smiled inwardly. If Justin didn't find out about this night's work, he would have to be deaf and dumb and blind.

"And how are you enjoying the soiree?" Lord Ivor asked blandly, steering her toward the room where the refreshment table had been set up.

"Very well. And you?" Megan smiled up at him, thinking that he was not nearly so black as he had been painted. He had never once stepped beyond the line of what was proper in all the weeks she had known him, and that despite some pretty blatant provocation on her part. Despite his rakish reputation, and the absurdity of his clothes, which she had come to suspect he affected for amusement, Megan found herself quite liking him.

"I think the best is yet to come," he replied cryptically, and before Megan realized what he was about he had whisked her through a pair of heavy velvet curtains that concealed a small alcove where they were quite alone.

"My lord . . .?" Megan turned to look at him, confused, when she saw where they were. He smiled at her, his hands behind him holding the curtain shut. The expression in his eyes made her uneasy.

"Time to pay the piper, my dear," he said pleasantly, but his eyes were very far from being pleasant. "You've been making use of me quite shamelessly, and I intend to collect my reward."

"What do you mean?" Megan was afraid she knew very well, but surely she could talk him out of the intention she read so clearly in his eyes.

"Come, my dear Miss Kinkead, you're not so naive as all that," he said dryly, moving away from the curtains toward her. "You know very well what I mean."

Megan backed away from him. "Lord Ivor, if you touch me, I'll scream," she warned, beginning to feel frightened. Her common sense told her that there wasn't much he could do to her in a house full of people, but perhaps she was wrong. Her experience with Justin had taught her how to recognize the signs of a man's arousal. Lord Ivor was unmistakeably aroused.

"And cause a scandal?" he asked cynically. "Somehow I don't think you'll scream, Miss Kinkead. But if you wish to, please feel free. Because I am going to claim my reward no matter what."

And with that he reached out and pulled her close.

After taking Clorinda home, Justin returned to Grosvenor Square. It had taken several hours to assure her that he meant what he said when he told her that he wanted to end their liaison. It was past eight o'clock by the time he walked wearily through his own front door. Today had been the first time he had seen Clorinda since he had left London in pursuit of Megan three months before, and he had sought the woman out with the express intention of relieving his sexual frustration with the body of one whom he paid to be available. Instead, he had wound up giving her the congé as his mistress. As she had thrown herself at him in ecstatic greeting, he could not help comparing her lush appeal to Megan's slender beauty; the full charms that had been more than acceptable to him once now seemed grossly overblown, and to his own disgust Justin could not dredge up the smallest flicker of desire. Disengaging his mouth from hers after her first breathless kiss, he had told her gently to dress warmly because he was taking her for a drive. He had been breaking the news to her as painlessly as he knew how when he had caught sight of Megan in the park. For a moment he had felt absurdly guilty that she should see him with Clorinda, and then as he had recognized her companion his guilt had been swamped by rage. He had nearly stopped his curricle and confronted the pair of them there and then, but the simple practicalities of the situation had prevented him. He could not present Clorinda to Megan, nor would he want to. And he owed Clorinda the decency of an explanation. She had been good to him, in her way, and he felt no animosity towards her. If Megan had emasculated him to the point where he could want no other woman, that was not Clorinda's fault. But the fury he had felt upon seeing Megan with Ivor had not been dimmed because of having to wait to vent itself. He meant to be waiting for her tonight when she got home from whatever function she was attending, and he meant to be stone cold sober, something that he hadn't been very often lately. So instead of going to his club after leaving Clorinda, he had come home.

As he expected, Ames informed him that both ladies were out. Justin accepted that information with a nod, and started to go on to his study. He would spend the time catching up with some paperword that he had grossly neglected of late. Then, thinking about it, he changed his mind. Instead of waiting around until all hours for Megan to get home, he would join her at whatever party she happened to be. He smiled grimly to himself as he pictured her consternation when he appeared. She must think herself safe until morning.

Ames was able to tell him about the Chetwoods' soiree, and Justin, grimacing at the dull sound of it, almost changed his mind again. But his smoldering anger demanded action, and he knew that he would have no peace until he had torn a strip off Megan's hide for her willful disobedience. If she wanted to punish him—and he admitted that she had every right to—she was going to have to find another means. He had no intention of standing idly by while she flirted with a bounder like Ivor.

It was nearly half past ten by the time he walked into the Chetwoods' salon. A yellow-haired chit was caterwauling to the accompaniment of a piano; Justin winced at the sound, and nearly decided to leave again. But Lady Chetwood had caught site of him, and hurried to make him welcome.

"This is a pleasure, my lord," she gushed, her plump, matronly faced wreathed in smiles. The Earl of Weston was notoriously elusive, and his presence would lend quite a bit of cachet to a party that even she, with her incurable optimism, had to admit was nothing above the ordinary.

"The pleasure is mine, my lady," he said in a civil tone that he hoped would adequately mask the boredom that was already starting to claim him.

"You've come to join your wife," the good lady said happily. Justin raised an eyebrow at her. Surely she must be the only person left in London who was not aware of his long-standing estrangement from Alicia.

"I was told she would be here," Justin replied smoothly without giving a direct answer. "And my ward, as well."

"Yes, they are. Let me see, Lady Alicia is over there," Lady Chetwood indicated Alicia, who was seated next to her very dear friend Sally Jersey and gossiping madly. They ignored the singer. "And your ward—why, I believe that Miss Kinkead must have left us. You'll probably find her in the refreshment room, my lord."

"I thank you," Justin bowed. She smiled at him, simpering a little, then withdrew her hand with a reluctant sigh and went to speak to a guest who had the good sense to plead a headache as an excuse for leaving early.

Left to himself, Justin walked briskly across the room, intent on finding Megan as quickly as possible. Alicia saw him, and raised her eyebrows in exaggerated surprise at his presence. She knew from bitter experience that he hated functions of this sort, and usually avoided them. He ignored her and left the room. His whole purpose in coming here was to find Megan, and he meant to accomplish it as quickly as possible so that he could leave.

She was not in the refreshment room, nor in the hall, nor in any of the other chambers that he checked. His frown deepened with each passing minute. Where the hell could she be? His anger increased as he searched again, more carefully. Still no luck. He was standing in the hall, undecided about whether or not to question Alicia, who after all was the girl's chaperone and ought to have some notion of her whereabouts, when he heard a slight sound from beyond the curtains at the far end of the hall. Justin crossed to them, and stood for a moment listening. He had no wish to intrude on some couple's private moment, as long as it wasn't Megan. Though he heard nothing further, some sixth sense persuaded him to push aside the curtains and enter the room. What he saw froze him in his tracks for the space of two heartbeats.

Megan was pushing and shoving at Ivor's scrawny shoulders as he bent her back over his arm, his mouth searching for hers. Justin clenched his teeth as he realized what Ivor's intentions were. Then he was across the room, his hand hard on Ivor's shoulder as he tore him away from Megan. Ivor barely had time to register the identity of his assailant before Justin was hitting him, his fist slamming with satisfying force into Ivor's face. Justin felt bones and flesh disintegrate under his hand, and smiled savagely as he repeated the blow. Then Ivor seemed to come to himself, and parried Justin's blows with punches of his own. One caught Justin on the side of the nose, making him bleed a little, but he barely noticed the pain as he sank his fist deep into the other's midsection.

214

"Justin, stop it! You'll kill him!" Megan had recovered from her shock enough to fly at him, catching his arm and trying to pull him off Ivor's groaning body. Justin paid no attention to her entreaties, concentrating on beating the man to a bloody pulp. Finally, when Ivor sagged to his knees with a groan of surrender, Justin backed off but stood over his downed opponent, fists still clenched, breathing hard.

"Justin?" Megan's voice was shaking, and her hand was unsteady as she put it on his arm.

Justin turned his head to look at her. Blood from his nose covered the lower half of his face and dripped onto his elegant evening clothes, but he was unaware of it. His eyes were fierce as they moved over her.

"Did he hurt you?" he rasped.

Megan shook her head. Justin saw the swollen state of her mouth, the little rip in the shoulder of her gown, and swore furiously.

"By God, you'll meet me for this, you damned blackguard," Justin snarled at Ivor, who now lay flat on his back on the floor. One whole side of his face was unrecognizable from Justin's blows, and his breath rattled painfully from beneath his bruised ribs. "Tomorrow morning, six o'clock, on the Heath. Do you hear me?"

Ivor looked up at him then, his eyes vicious as they slid from Justin to Megan and back again.

"I'll be there," he said.

Justin stared at him a moment longer, his fingers curling and uncurling at his sides as if he would like to wrap them around Ivor's neck there and then. Megan

215

noticed this and moved closer to him, her eyes raised beseechingly to his.

"Justin, take me home," she said low. Justin's mouth compressed as he looked down at her, and then he reached out an arm and drew her close against his side.

"Six o'clock," he said tersely to the man on the floor, and then, keeping Megan pressed closely to his side, he led her away. Fortunately Madame Diva had begun to sing again, so no one witnessed their dishevelment as Justin whisked them through a side door and into the night.

Chapter 13

Long after the house had quieted for the night, Megan paced the floor in her bedchamber. Justin had refused to say a syllable to her during the hansom ride home, and upon entering the house he had immediately ordered her to her room. Megan, frightened and trembling, took one look into those golden eyes and obeyed without question. Justin was in a mood to do murder if he was defied in any way, and she was uncomfortably aware that her conduct that evening had been far from blameless. But surely she had been punished enough? Her skin still crawled as she remembered the way Lord Ivor had kissed her; the greedy thrust of his tongue in her mouth and the feel of his hands sliding over her body had made her quiver with revulsion. He had paid no heed to her frantic struggles to escape him, and Megan shuddered to think what might have happened if Justin had not appeared so opportunely.

Justin's violence had terrified her. She had never witnessed anything like it. For a few moments she had thought that he meant to beat Ivor to death with his bare fists, and that was when she had flown to his side. Ivor's conduct had been atrocious, he had frightened and repelled her, but it did not deserve death. And Megan was very much afraid that Justin intended to kill Ivor tomorrow.

Or he might be killed himself. Megan closed her eyes and groaned. All her professed hatred seemed to melt away at the thought of Justin's life blown from him because of her folly. Justin had warned her about Lord Ivor; she had wanted to revenge herself upon him so much that she had taken positive delight in flouting his express command. Tonight she had paid for her hardheadedness; tomorrow either Justin or Ivor would pay.

They could not be allowed to meet. But how to prevent it? Megan had not the slightest notion. She could only go to Justin and beg him, for her sake, for the sake of the child she might or might not be carrying, not to go through with this madness. In her mind she pictured two lonely figures facing each other across a width of green field, pistols rising, firing, smoking— and then one of the figures falling, bleeding, dying.

She shuddered convulsively. It could not be allowed to happen.

She would go to him and plead with him not to persist in this folly. She would crawl on her knees if necessary.

Clutching the high neck of her blue-sprigged wrapper about her throat, Megan blew out the candles in her bedroom and then let herself out into the hall. It was lit by a single cluster of candles in a silver candelabra afixed to the wall. The feeble light showed her that the hall was deserted. Lady Alicia would most likely not be home until dawn; the servants, except for Alicia's maid, who would be waiting wearily in her mistress' chamber, had long since retired. Still, Megan was very swift and silent as she sped toward Justin's suite. With all the other difficulties besetting her, it would be the last straw to have one of the servants see her creep into Justin's room in the middle of the night.

She hesitated for a moment with her hand on the knob, her heart pounding in her throat, listening for any sounds from within that might mean that Manning had not yet left his master. She heard nothing. Taking a deep breath, she turned the knob and went in.

The room she entered was the small sitting room which connected the master's and mistress' bedrooms. Lady Alicia had long preferred to sleep on the other side of the house, so the bedroom that should have been hers was unoccupied. Megan was glad of that. If Bettina, Alicia's maid, should hear her talking with Justin, there would be hell to pay.

The sitting room was furnished in an intensely masculine fashion in shades of brown and gold with touches of orange. The delicate Louis XIV furniture which was Alicia's taste and which was so much in evidence throughout the rest of the house was absent here. The chairs flanking the fireplace were large, dark leather wing chairs, and a leather settee sat against one wall. A hand-loomed Indian carpet covered the wide oak planks of the floor; a pair of crossed duelling pistols adorned the space above the fireplace. They gleamed in the firelight which was blazing strongly. Looking at them, Megan felt her mouth go dry.

"Up to your old tricks again, I see." Justin's sardonic voice came from across the room. Megan whirled, startled, to see him standing in the doorway which connected the sitting room to his bedroom. He was dressed in the same elegant black evening breeches that he had worn earlier; his coat and waistcoat had been discarded, and he had changed his blood stained shirt for another, a frilled white one that was open halfway down his chest to show a tantalizing amount of hair-roughened flesh. As she stared at him, wide-eyed, he leaned his shoulder negligently against the doorjam, his eyes moving over her in an insulting fashion. It was only then that Megan saw the half-empty bottle which dangled from one hand. As she looked at it, she realized that it was all the explanation she needed for the wildness of his hair, and the faint redness which rimmed those golden eyes.

"You're drunk," she said accusingly, her eyes moving up to fasten on his. He laughed, swinging the bottle idly to and fro, his eyes mocking as they returned her angry glare.

"Oh, yes, my darling. This time, you are exactly right. I am very drunk."

Megan was too afflicted with contradicting emotions to object to his calling her his darling; in fact, she scarcely heeded it. Relief and terror warred for supremacy inside her. If Justin was drunk, surely he couldn't be intending to engage in a duel with Lord Ivor in approximately five hours. On the other hand, if he was intending to meet Lord Ivor at six o'clock that same morning, he wouldn't stand a chance. He couldn't even stand without swaying, much less shoot a man.

"You've thought better of it," she said slowly, her eyes, although she did not know it, faintly pleading.

"Have I?" He smiled. "Tell me, my darling, just which of us are you so worried about? Ivor, the slimy bastard, or me? It occurs to me to wonder why you didn't scream for help. Surely you were not worried about disturbing Lady Chetwood's guests in their enjoyment of her daughter's atrocious singing?"

Megan glared at him furiously. "I didn't want to make a scandal." She told the exact truth. The consequences attendant upon screaming for rescue from a man's embrace at a soiree had been too horrible to contemplate.

"Oh, yes?" he said politely, as his eyes slid over her from head to toe and then came back to rest on her face. They were lit at the back by tiny demons; Megan, looking at them, nearly shuddered. He looked as

221

if he were on the brink of hell itself, and was having thoughts about dragging her there with him.

He continued softly: "Or was there another reason for your damnable silence, my darling? Were you so hungry for what I taught you that any man would do? Did you want Lord Ivor, Megan, the way you wanted me that night in my room?"

Megan stiffened, feeling furious color flood her face. "How dare you? How dare you suggest such a thing—or remind me of an event that fills me with shame every time I think of it? You're contemptible! I despise you!"

"Do you?" he said, still terribly polite. "You relieve my mind. I can see that I have nothing further to lose."

He straightened away from the doorjam; Megan, frightened by something that had sprung to life in his face, began to back away.

"And where do you think you're going, my own?" he said, moving toward her very slowly. Megan looked at him, saw the wild flicker of his eyes, and swallowed. He did not look sane. She continued to edge toward the door, her movements stealthy.

"Frightened of me, darling?" He laughed; the sound sent a chill down her spine. He was stalking her. With his black hair rioting around the harsh lines of his dark face, with the powerful length of his body clad in stark black and white, with the little golden demons glaring at her from the depths of his eyes, he looked like the devil himself. "Why, I believe you have reason."

That mocking voice sent a chill down her spine. Megan took another step backwards, relieved to feel the polished wood of the door against her back. In just a minute, she would be safe.

"Justin," she began, her voice placating. She never got a chance to finish. With an oath, he drew back his hand and hurled the bottle into the fireplace. It landed with a splintering crash. The whiskey caused the fire to flare hungrily; its fumes permeated the room. Megan jumped, her eyes flying fearfully to his face.

"You little bitch," he rasped, stopping in his tracks and glaring ferociously at her. "Did you call him by name as he kissed you? Timothy, did you say, oh, Timothy?" His falsetto imitation of a female voice husky with passion made Megan cover her ears with her hands.

"I don't have to listen to this!" she cried, her eyes full of sudden rage as they met his savage ones. "How dare you insult me in such a way? You know perfectly well it wasn't like that. Your mind may live in the gutter, my lord Earl, but mine does not. I came in here tonight to try to make you see sense about that damned stupid duel, but now I see that it's just the thing: I hope he kills you. I hope he blows a hole through you so big that a camel could pass through it. I hope. . . ."

She paused for breath, panting as she searched for words to describe the awful fate she hoped befell him. He smiled sardonically.

"Never mind," he said softly. "I get your general drift."

Megan glared at him furiously. "Goodnight, my

lord," she said with what dignity she could muster as she fumbled at the door knob. "I'm going back to bed."

Justin smiled again, his expression frightening. Panicing suddenly, Megan whirled, attempting to turn the knob and jerk open the door at the same time. With a sound like a snarl he lunged. Megan, panting, her heart drumming loudly in her ears, pulled frantically at the door, but to no avail. He was too fast. In an instant he was beside her, his hard arms catching her around her shoulders and knees as he lifted her high in his arms. Instinctively Megan screamed. He muffled the sound with his mouth.

"Doesn't the scandal worry you anymore?" he mocked harshly, striding with her toward his bedroom. Megan was still reeling from the brutal possession of his mouth, with its pungent whiskey fumes enveloping her.

"Put me down!" she cried when she could speak. "Damn you, you swine, put me down!"

The curl of Justin's lips was ferocious. His gleaming tiger's eyes raked her face with humorless intensity. Her frantic struggles seemed to have no affect on him except to make him tighten his grip.

"With a great deal of pleasure, my darling," he said tightly, and before Megan realized what he was about she felt his arms loose their grip on her. She was falling, arms and legs flailing, her eyes and mouth opened wide with surprise, to land with a bounce in the center of his huge bed. For just an instant she lay where he had dropped her, too stunned to move, and then, reading his intention in his eyes as he towered above her, she began to scramble frantically for the side of the bed.

"No!" she cried as his hard hands caught her, dragging her back. "No, no, no!"

Justin laughed, his face cruel with harsh mockery. He was beside her in the bed, stilling her cries with his mouth, his hard thigh imprisoning hers so that she could not move, his hands capturing her flailing hands as she tried to claw his face and imprisoning them in one of his above her head. She was trapped, pinned by his weight, practically immobile.

"Oh yes," he whispered savagely against her mouth. "Yes, my darling, yes."

He was kissing her, his mouth hard and hot against her own. His tongue was like a fiery rapier as he forced her lips apart; when she would not open her teeth for him he bit down warningly on her lower lip until her faint cry of pain allowed him the opening he sought. His tongue invaded her mouth, thrusting savagely into her softness, piercing her, violating her. Megan tried desperately to turn her head aside, but his hand was under her chin, holding her in place as he ravaged her mouth. His kisses continued until her struggles ceased, until she lay shivering and still beneath him.

"Justin, don't do this," she whispered as he reared his head back to look at her. He looked like a dark frightening stranger with his flesh taut over the hard bones of his face and his eyes blind with wanting. The violence he was showing terrified her. Never in her darkest dreams had she imagined that he could behave like this.

He paid no heed to her barely audible plea. Instead, his hands shaking, he began to tear ruthlessly at her wrapper and the demure white nightgown beneath it, ripping it from the throat clear down to the hem, tearing it from her shoulders with long ripping sounds, his eyes brutal as he watched her squirming attempts to escape him.

"Justin, please." she gasped when he had her naked and lay propped above her, his eyes scalding her as they raked her body.

"I aim to, my darling," he muttered thickly, and then his mouth was closing over the small pink rosebud of her nipple, making her gasp with sensation.

He had been gentle with her, before; this time he was barbaric in his passion, taking what he wanted, forcing her to submit to him. Megan's mind rebelled furiously from the burning mastery of his hands and mouth, but her healthy young body revelled in it. She wanted him, and he was forcing her to acknowledge it; quivers raced over her from head to toe, centering from whatever vulnerable part of her flesh he was branding with his hands and mouth.

"You beast," she moaned in a last desperate attempt to deny him. But the hands which he had freed minutes before were clinging to him, and she knew he could read desire in her eyes. Faced with the tantalizing demands of his hard body, she was helpless; she knew it, and so did he.

When he drew away from her to remove his own clothes, she whimpered a protest, a strange mewling sound that came from deep within her throat. The sound of her own voice shocked her. Her eyes fluttered open to see him looking down at her. He was jerking off his shirt and breeches with shaking hands, and his eyes were alive with passion as they moved over her slim body. She could feel his gaze burning like molten lava on the quivering fullness of her breasts; the creamy peaks were crowned with small, rigidly erect nipples that screamed without words how weak were the dictates of her mind when compared with the needs of her body. Then his eyes moved lower, to the ivory flesh of her small waist and flat belly, to the silkyblack triangle of hair between her thighs, to the slender beauty of her long legs. She trembled beneath that gaze, her thick black lashes coming down to veil her eyes from his as they rose to probe her face.

He took her almost without preliminaries, his body a hard, driving instrument of exquisite torture. Megan felt the tremors that racked his long limbs as he plunged ever deeper into her soft flesh, heard the harsh rasp of his breathing which sounded almost like sobs in her ears, felt the staccato thudding of his heart against her breasts. She gasped out his name as he entered her, her nails digging deep into his broad, bronzed shoulders, her legs lifting of their own accord to encircle his hard waist. Only once did she open her eyes, trying desperately to escape the ultimate surrender that she knew was waiting for her. He was looking at her, his eyes hot on her face, avid as they watched the response that was reflected there. He was exciting her madly, driving her wild, beyond anything she had

227

ever dreamt existed, and he knew it. The hard triumph was there in his eyes for her to read.

She closed her eyes again, not wanting to see him glorying in her degradation. He had reduced her to the status of animal, conscious only of the demanding pleasures of the flesh with no thought for right or wrong, religious principles or morals. He was making a whore of her, an adulterer of himself, and the horrible part of it was, she didn't care. With his hot, powerful body joined so intimately to hers, she felt as if he was forcing her to a form of devil worship. And he, of course, was the devil.

"Megan," he groaned at the end, thrusting deep inside her and holding himself there while wild tremors quaked through his body. Megan felt the pulsating warmth of his seed inside her and gasped with pleasure. Her arms clutched his back and her legs held him to her as she was drawn down into the dark abyss of a hellish ecstasy.

It was some time before he heaved himself off her exhausted body and shrugged into his dressing gown. Megan refused to look at him. She kept her eyes tightly closed as he wrapped her in the coverlet that had been beneath them, then lifted her into his arms.

"Look at me, Megan," he whispered, his arms tightening around her as her head fell back limply against his shoulder. Unwillingly, Megan did as he bade; her lashes lifted with slow reluctance to let the smoky-violet pools of her eyes touch on his face.

"I'm not going to apologize this time," he said, still holding her cradled against him and staring down at her with a grim expression. "You asked for everything you got, and you enjoyed it. You're just damned lucky it was me, and not Ivor. This is what he had in mind for you, you know."

Megan gasped with shock. "No."

Justin's mouth curled unpleasantly. "Yes. I almost feel sorry for the poor bastard. You were probably driving him crazy, an innocent little baby with the face of an angel and the instincts of a temptress. He had to be going out of his mind to do what he did; he knew I'd kill him if I found out, and he knew damned well that I would find out."

"Justin, please, you can't mean to go through with that silly duel. He didn't hurt me." Megan was shaking. Her eyes were wide with anguish as she remembered what had prompted her disastrous visit to his room.

"I can and do." He said it brutally, beginning to walk with her, carrying her through the bedroom into the sitting room and then out the door into the hall. "How does it feel, my darling, to know that in just a couple of hours a man will be dead for love of your beauxyeux?"

"No." The word was a moan, and she looked up at him beseechingly as he shouldered his way into her bedroom and carried her over to her bed. The room was pitch dark, and she could not see his face.

"Justin, please don't go through with it. You could be killed."

He laughed harshly. "I thought that was what you wanted," he taunted. "I seem to recall you saying something about hoping he blows a hole through me big enough for a—what was it? A camel?—to go through."

"Justin, you know I didn't mean it. Please." The words trailed off as he dropped her without ceremony on the bed.

"Justin." she cried as he turned and started for the door. "For my sake. . . ."

He laughed again. Then he was through the door, and Megan listened incredulously as he turned the key from the other side.

"To keep you from meddling in things that don't concern you," he said through the panel. "But don't worry, my darling, I'll be back in plenty of time to let you out before anyone even knows I've locked you in."

"Justin!" she wailed, leaping from the bed and flying to the door to press herself against the cool wood. She heard footsteps receding, and beat her fists impotently against the door. "Please don't do this. Justin, I think I'm going to have your baby."

But the continued silence on the other side of the door told her that he hadn't heard.

Chapter 14

A heavy fog obscured Hampstead Heath, but Justin paid scant attention to it, as he leapt nimbly down from his curricle and threw the reins to his diminutive tiger, Todd. Charles, whom Justin had chosen to serve as his second out of a desire to keep the business as quiet as possible, climbed laboriously down. A note delivered at his lodgings at the ungodly hour of four in the morning had half-convinced him that Justin must be going mad.

"Buck up, Charles. Looking at you, anybody would be forgiven for thinking that it was you whom I was meaning to put a bullet through instead of Ivor,"

Justin told him grimly.

"It might as well be," Charles said gloomily. "If you kill him, you'll most likely have to fly the country, and make your home on the continent these next twenty years. And I'll be out of a job."

Justin grinned a little in spite of himself at this lugubrious prediction. "And if he kills me?" he asked lightly.

Charles snorted. "Not bloody likely. Drunk or sober, you're the best damned shot I've ever seen. Take my advice, Justin, and don't kill him. Think of the scandal."

Justin's mouth tightened. "I don't give a damn about the scandal."

"You should," Charles said gently. "If not on your own account, think of Megan and Lady Alicia. Word of this is bound to get out, you know, and people will assume that Ivor either compromised Megan or seduced your wife. No other reason for you to meet him."

"I'm meeting him because I am sick of his damnable taste in clothes," Justin said, his eyes narrowing. Charles sighed.

"And if you think that anyone will believe that, you're drunker than I thought you were."

"I'm not drunk. I was, I admit, but I've been sober these two hours past."

Charles turned to look at his friend, who stood perhaps half a head taller than himself. Justin's hair waved wildly around his head despite the careless brush he had run over it before they had left Weston

House. As usual his clothes were impeccable: A claret colored wool coat fit his broad shoulders to perfection, his buff pantaloons encased the long, hard-muscled legs without a crease, his neckcloth was elegantly tied, and his Hessians gleamed despite the dulling effects of the fog. It was his face which showed how he had passed the night. His eyes were bloodshot from lack of sleep and overindulgence in alcohol. Lines of dissipation creased the corners of his mouth and eyes. Looking at him, Charles reflected that, if he hadn't known Justin so well, he would have been much afraid of the outcome of this day's work. But as it was, his only qualm was whether or not Justin would come to his senses at the last minute and merely wound Ivor. Justin was deadly with pistols. Charles could only wonder what had possessed Ivor to agree to this meeting. Justin's reputation as a duellist was well known.

"You never did say exactly what this is all about," Charles hesitatingly remarked. Although, he could guess. Ivor had stepped beyond the bounds with either Megan or Alicia, and Justin had caught him at it or the lady had run to him bearing tales. And, knowing that Justin wouldn't give a damn if Alicia cuckolded him with every man in England (not that it was likely), Charles assumed that the cause of the duel had to be Megan. Not for the first time had Charles wondered about the exact nature of Justin's feelings toward his beautiful ward. Justin had been as grumpy as a bear with a sore paw for the last few weeks, and he had been drinking heavily ever since his return from Ireland. Charles was very much afraid that Justin found himself attracted to Megan, who was a lovely thing in all truth, and despised himself for it. For Justin, despite his other failings, which Charles would be the first to admit were many, was a man of honor. His treatment of Alicia was a case in point. Charles knew full well that that haughty lady had denied Justin her bed for years, and yet Justin still treated her with the respect and courtesy due his wife. Many men would, at the very least, have beaten the cold bitch, and quite a few would have divorced her for failure to fulfill her conjugal duties. But Justin had done neither of these things, and, while Charles had lost track of the number of paramours that Justin had taken over the years, the man had even been discreet about them. So if Justin found himself wanting Megan, as Charles very much suspected he did, he would make a hell on earth for himself before he so much as considered giving into temptation.

"I told you," Justin said grimly just as Ivor's carriage swept into view. "I don't like his damned dandyish clothes."

In addition to Ivor, and his particular friend, Mr. Nettleston, there was a doctor in the carriage. Justin observed this good fellow descending with raised eyebrows, and turned to grin sardonically at Charles.

"It seems as though my lord shares your faith in my abilities," he said cynically.

Charles merely shook his head, and hurried over to meet with Mr. Nettleston and inspect the weapons. As the challenged party, it was Lord Ivor's right to choose what weapons would be used, but as Ivor had no skill with swords, the choice of pistols was a foregone conclusion. Nettleston was as upset about the business as Charles, but, as there was no possible way of persuading Lord Ivor to apologize, and Charles was doubtful that Justin would accept it, there seemed nothing to do but allow the duel to proceed.

Frowning heavily, Charles waited while Lord Ivor selected a pistol from the pair that was offered to him, and silently congratulated the lord on his courage. Except for a certain whiteness of face, Lord Ivor looked perfectly composed, although he had, Charles noticed, arrayed himself in sober black so as to make as small a target for Justin as possible. Having seen Justin snuff the flame of a candle at forty yards, Charles could have told him that such precautions were in vain, but he held his peace.

The fog had begun to lift by the time Charles made his way back to Justin's side. Faint fingers of sunlight wandered down to sparkle on the droplets of water that still clung to the grass. A grove of tall pines at the far end of the field stood like mournful sentinels. It seemed impossible that in just a few minutes two shots would ring out, and one of the men standing in the field would die.

"For God's sake, don't kill him, Justin," Charles urgently whispered as Justin moved to take his place in the center of the field. Justin gave no sign that he heard.

The doctor, as the only impartial one present, gave the instructions: "I will count to ten, gentlemen, and as I call out each number you will each take one step forward. On the count of ten, you will turn and fire, with no holding back on either side. Is that clear?''

''Perfectly clear, Mr. Rollins,'' said Lord Ivor. Justin merely nodded tersely. His eyes were hard as twin topazes as he looked at Ivor. The picture of Ivor as he had seen him last, holding Megan in his arms while she struggled to escape him, was imprinted on Justin's brain.

''You'll die for that,'' he promised Ivor silently. Ivor, catching the murderous glint in Justin's eyes, visibly paled.

The two men stood back to back, one clad arrogantly in deep red as though mocking by his very choice of clothes his opponents' skill as a marksman, the other was prudently dressed in black. The doctor began his count. Backs held stiffly erect, pistols pointed at the ground, they paced apart. Charles, watching the tableau, felt little fear for Justin's life. But he did fear most grievously for Ivor's, and as the count neared its end he muttered a little prayer.

''Nine!''

The sound of hoofbeats caused Charles' attention to be momentarily distracted from the field. The horse was coming fast, and he was just able to note that the rider was a woman when the doctor cried, ''Ten!''

''Stop!'' cried the newcomer as the men turned and fired. Charles recognized first the voice and then, as she galloped closer, the rider herself as Megan. Justin's head jerked around even as he pulled the trigger; in that instant it was all over. Megan halted her horse and leapt down, her skirts flying up to reveal ruffled

236

petticoats. Charles saw that she was clad in a pale yellow morning gown that looked, from the wildly askew buttons and sash, as if she had thrown it on at a moment's notice.

Megan had seen all she needed in a glance. Since Mary had released her from the locked room, she had been terrified that she would be too late to even try to stop the proceedings. Galloping on to the scene, hearing the short little man in the sober gray clothes call "Ten" even as she approached, she had feared that she really had been too late. Now, as she ran toward Justin, her skirts flying behind her and her unbound hair blowing in the breeze like a silken banner, she was sure of it. Lord Ivor lay sprawled on the ground at the far end of the field while two men bent anxiously over him, but it was on Justin that her attention focused. A bright scarlet stain was beginning to mar the smooth perfection of his coat.

"Oh, my God, Justin," she moaned, reaching his side and staring with fearful eyes up into his face. Charles, his mouth open at the sight of blood on his friend's coat, was right behind her.

"What the bloody hell are you doing here?" Justin rasped furiously. Her face was white as death as she stared at that spreading stain; her hands were frantic as she clutched at him.

"Darling, are you badly hurt?" Her mouth quivered as she looked up into Justin's harsh face. Charles, hearing that 'darling', stopped in his tracks, his eyes moving from Megan to Justin with visible shock. Both were completely oblivious to his presence.

"No, no thanks to you," Justin growled, reaching out to take hold of Megan's arm in a grip that looked brutal. "What the hell do you mean by coming here? You've got no business here, and you could have got me killed, distracting me at such a time! Anyway, how did you get out of your room?"

Charles listening to this conversation, which was growing more incomprehensible by the moment, felt his ears pinken. The one thing that was as clear as sunlight was the intimacy between the two of them. It was clear that they were far more than guardian and ward; Megan's face as she looked up at Justin was the face of a woman looking at the man she loves. Justin's face was less easy to read, but that hand on her arm and the harsh voice told its own story.

"Mary let me out," she said impatiently. "Justin, how badly are you shot?"

"The merest scratch," Charles heard Justin say as he raised a hand to his shoulder, and then Charles turned and went over to see how Lord Ivor fared. The exchange between Megan and Justin was too private to be witnessed by outsiders.

Lord Ivor was not mortally wounded. Justin, distracted by Megan's cry, had fired wide. The ball had pierced Ivor's chest, and though he was presently unconscious, Dr. Rollins assured both Charles and Mr. Nettleston that Ivor would recover.

"And what of your man?" the doctor inquired, after instructing Ivor's lackeys to carry their master into his carriage and convey him home at all speed.

"He is shot, but he feels it is not serious," Charles

answered curtly.

Nettleston's eyes widened. "Ivor actually shot Weston? Famous!" he crowed, then, lowering his voice, added, "Distracted by that wench, I know, but still . . . Who is she, anyway, Stanton?"

But Charles prudently refrained from answering.

When he returned to Justin's side with the doctor at his heels, both Megan and Justin seemed to have recovered themselves. Megan no longer clutched at Justin's coat, and Justin had released his vice-grip on Megan's arm. But nothing could conceal the look in the girl's eyes.

"Put her in my curricle," Justin instructed Charles, giving him a hooded look. Charles tried his best to return that look blandly, but his consciousness of the true state of affairs between Justin and Megan must have shown in his face, because Justin's face tightened suddenly so that the hard bones sprang into prominence.

"My lord . . ." Megan began to protest, sounding worried and oddly decorous at the same time. Justin flashed her a commanding look.

"Go with Charles," he ordered, and with a single anxious look up into Justin's face Megan allowed herself to be led away.

"Now then, my lord, if you will remove your coat," they heard the doctor say punctiliously. As Charles handed Megan up into the curricle and went to retrieve her horse to tie it to the rear, he saw that Justin had obeyed. It was some fifteen minutes before Justin joined them, disdaining Charles' offer to drive and taking the reins himself. Only the tiny blackened holes high up on his shoulder and its darkening scarlet stain revealed that he had been wounded. Otherwise he appeared as healthy as when he and Charles had left Weston House that morning.

It was still early when the little party returned to Weston House, and except for Ames, whose discretion was legendary, no one saw them enter the house. A single hard glance from Justin's golden eyes sent Megan scurrying upstairs. She went meekly enough, exhausted from the sleepless night she had passed and the emotional turmoil that had accompanied it. Charles adjourned with Justin to the study, where Justin rang for breakfast to be served. Charles thought about commenting on the exchange he had witnessed between Megan and his employer, but something in the flinty set of Justin's face stayed his tongue.

Over the next several days, there was some little tongue-wagging about Megan's hasty and unheralded exit from the Chetwoods' soiree in her guardian's company, but Megan explained that she had developed a sudden headache and, not wanting to disturb the enjoyment of the rest of the company, she had persuaded Justin to take her home. Justin curtly endorsed this explanation, and the talk died for lack of fuel to feed it. No one seemed to connect Lord Ivor's sudden indisposition with Megan's headache, and so all was well in that quarter.

As that week passed, and then the next, Megan's suspicions were confirmed. She was with child. She

240

trembled when the realization dawned, knowing that, as soon as her condition became obvious, she would be ostracized by the very people who were so anxious to know her now. Her condition would be the talk of the Season, and speculation about the fathers identity would be rife. Megan speculated that Lord Ivor would probably be named as the most likely candidate. She doubted that Justin's name would enter into consideration.

He had asked her, not long after that nightmarish duel, if she was "all right." Correctly interpreting his meaning from the speculative look he bent on her, she had assumed the most angelic face and boldly answered yes. Knowing Justin as she did, she guessed that, if he knew that she was expecting his child, he would never let her go. For her own sake, she might not have objected too strenuously to being set up in a discreet little house on a London sidestreet as his mistress. She loved him, after all. But for the sake of the unborn child, she could not allow such a thing to happen. She wanted her baby to be born in all honor, to grow up able to look any man or woman in the eye, to need feel no shame over his origins or parents. Already she loved the child; she shuddered at the thought of it carrying the label "bastard", and she vowed that it would not happen. If she could contrive it, this child would have the best of everything the world could offer, no matter what it might cost herself.

She would have to marry. Megan came to this inescapable conclusion only after hours of careful thought. If she married immediately, she could pass the child off as her husband's, contriving a fall or some such accident to account for the fact that it would be born early. For her purposes, it would be best if she accepted the proposal of a boy not much older than herself, who would presumably be fairly innocent in the ways of the world. As she had been, Megan thought bitterly, before Justin had educated her so thoroughly. If such a course of action might be unfair to the prospective bridegroom and father, Megan didn't care. She was prepared to be utterly ruthless, if that was what it took to protect her baby.

Accordingly, she encouraged the more callow of her swains, and within the week no less than three of them had asked Justin for her hand. To her horrified anger, he turned each one down, sending them about their business with a flea in their ear that made them reluctant to do much more than exchange common pleasantries with Megan. After the fourth and then the fifth boy was sent on his way by Justin, Megan knew that she had to have it out with him. At this rate, the baby would be born before she was even engaged, and then it would be too late.

Justin had been staying out of her way lately, and Megan had to bribe one of the footmen to tell her when he next entered the house so that she could speak to him. When the footman passed word to Mary that the Earl was in his study, Mary in turn told Megan. Megan lost no time in freshening herself and then proceeded downstairs as quickly as she could. Justin usually spent no more than an hour in the house before heading out again.

Conscious of Ames and a footman watching her with disapproval from the hall, Megan knocked on the study door and discreetly waited for Justin to call out "enter" before going in. The curtains were drawn back today, allowing the cold November light to flood the room. Justin, dressed in a pale blue coat and cream pantaloons, stood with his back to her, looking out the window into the garden at the rear of the house. His hands were clasped behind his back. Looking at those long, strong hands, so brown against the pale blue cloth, Megan felt a pang of love for him that stabbed clear through to her heart. Quickly she brought her feelings under control, reminding herself that she had to be strong for the sake of her baby. She was no longer a young girl in love but a woman fighting for her child's very life.

By the time Justin turned to look at her, Megan had herself well in hand. She met his faintly enquiring gaze with a level look of her own. His eyes narrowed.

"Yes?" he said coolly.

"Several gentlemen have lately asked you for my hand; you have refused them all without even an appearance of politeness. I want to know just what you think you're playing at," Megan said baldly. Justin's eyebrows rose; he was silent as he made a leisurely inspection of her indignant face, and then ran his eyes over her young body clothed in the soft pink dress. Except for the sparks emanating from her lovely eyes, the effect was one of angelic innocence.

"I'm playing at being your guardian," Justin replied finally with just a hint of mockery. "Why? Was there one particular gentleman that you wished to have as a husband?"

The wicked glint in his eyes told Megan that he was certain the answer to that was no. That last night in his bedroom had told him more clearly than words how she still felt about him, and she had merely reinforced his opinion of her affection for him when she had run to him the morning of the duel. But Megan raised a defiant chin, determined to do whatever she must to secure a respectable future for her baby.

"Yes, there is," she answered. "Lord Donald Winspear."

Justin's eyes widened. "That puppy? Don't be ridiculous. Why, he's barely twenty!"

"I'm only seventeen myself. Or had you forgotten?" Megan smiled at him with psuedo-sweetness. He stared at her incredulously.

"Are you actually going to stand there and tell me that you've fallen in love with that—boy?"

Megan looked at him, saw the powerful body in the elegant clothes, the hard, handsome face with the straight mouth and the golden eyes gleaming at her, and she felt her courage falter. Then the thought of the child in her womb gave her the strength she needed.

"I have a considerable regard for him," Megan answered with dignity, knowing that it would be useless to plead a deathless love for young Lord Winspear. Justin quite simply wouldn't believe her. "And I believe that he would make a good husband. I want to marry him."

Justin frowned, looking suddenly pugnacious. "Well, you can forget it. I am your guardian, remember, and as your guardian it is my prerogative to approve your husband. And I don't approve young Donny Winspear."

"Would you approve of anyone?" Megan cried, incensed. Her hands clenched at her sides, and her eyes warred with his. She knew as well as he did the reason he would not approve any of her suitors.

"No," he answered brutally, turning away from her. "At least, not for a couple of years. You are too young to marry."

"You are too dog in the manger to let me, you mean."

Justin flashed her a brief look over his shoulder. "Oh, not dog in the manger, my darling," he said softly, mockery in his tone. "You see, I do want you."

Megan glared at him, and opened her mouth to tell him, untruthfully, that that was just too bad, because she didn't want him. The words were never uttered. A brief rap on the door interrupted.

"Come in," Justin said, with a taunting smile at Megan. As Charles came in, looking from Megan to Justin with some embarrassment, Megan threw a fulminating look and flounced from the room.

The week passed slowly, as Megan helped Ames and Mrs. Lamb, the housekeeper, with the preparations for her very own coming out ball, which was to be held at Weston House on Wednesday next. As the lady of the house, Alicia should more properly have been in charge of the arrangements, but Alicia said that she

245

was far too fatigued by the rigors of the Season to even contemplate so much as drawing up a guest list. Charles proved invaluable at this chore, and Ames and Mrs. Lamb between them took care of most of the other things that needed to be done. Megan was left mainly to approve of disapprove of their suggestions, and to select a gown to wear to the ball.

Wednesday was greeted with the first snow of the season. Just a few large flakes drifted down, but it sent Mrs. Lamb into a tizzy as she worried that it might keep many of the guests from attending. Her fretting so enraged Anatole the cook that he threatened to walk out, and as the Earl was from home and Lady Alicia was abed, it was left to Megan to soothe Anatole's ruffled feathers. This required considerable time and ingenuity, and it was past four o'clock before Megan felt able to retire to her chamber and begin her preparations for the ball.

She took a leisurely bath, then ate a light supper. Finally, she sat down before her dressing table and allowed Mary to do her hair. The style Mary had suggested was a charming one. She piled Megan's hair high atop her head in a shining swirl of curls, allowing a single fat curl to spiral down to caress one bare white shoulder. Looking at her reflection in the glass, Megan agreed with Mary that the effect was extremely becoming.

The dress she had chosen for the evening was of mauve satin. The color would have been a trying one for most young women, but on Megan it was magnificent. Her shoulders and the tops of her breasts rose creamy smooth from the folds of gleaming satin, and the pointed waistband and yards of flounced skirt reduced her waist to nothingness. A simple necklet of pearls—Justin's gift to her for some long ago birthday—was her only ornament. The long cheval glass in the corner of her bedroom told her that she looked lovlier than she ever had in her life.

Justin was waiting for her when she went downstairs. Megan paused halfway down the stairs to stare at him. In his formal evening clothes with his hair brushed severely away from his face, he was the handsomest man she had ever seen. Then she heard Alicia coming down the stairs behind her, and hurriedly resumed her own descent. It would never do for Alicia to guess that Megan had been standing there frozen in admiration of her husband.

The evening passed in a kaleidoscope of colors and sounds. Megan stood in the receiving line with Justin on one side of her and Alicia on the other until nearly midnight. She was so nervous that she was barely conscious of what she said to anyone, although from the nods and smiles that greeted her words she supposed she must have made sense. Only Justin cast her a sharp look once or twice. But Megan couldn't help it. She had planned a surprise for the company at precisely midnight. Justin in particular would be stunned—and furious. It had taken all her considerable ingenuity to arrange it, to say nothing of her feminine wiles. Her only hope was that Lord Donald would remember his part in the conspiracy. She had discovered to her satisfaction that he was not particularly bright.

When finally the last guest had arrived and been dully greeted, Megan escaped from Justin's side as quickly as she could. For her plan to work, she had to be far away from Justin, but close to Lord Donald, else he might forget what he was supposed to do.

It was just before the stroke of midnight when she spied Lord Donald. He was a thin young man, fair-haired and moderately handsome, clad in neat brown evening clothes of no particular style. He was obediently stationed just beside the musicians, and she hurried to join him.

"Oh, there you are, Miss Kinkead," he said as she touched his arm. His formality under the circumstances was a trifle absurd, but Megan refused to allow herself to become irritated with him. He would be a kind husband and a good father, and she was lucky he wanted to marry her. "Are you sure you want to go through with this?" he asked, his voice dropping to a whisper, looking at her worriedly.

"Yes." Megan barely stopped herself from snapping. At all costs, she had to keep him sweet. She smiled meltingly at him. "Don't you want to marry me, Donald? You know this is the only way."

"More than anything in the world, Miss Kinkead," he replied, looking dazzled, as he usually did when he looked at her. Megan stifled another stab of impatience. Total adoration could be very wearing, she had found—and this after only three weeks of Lord Donald's acquaintance. But for the baby's sake, she could not back out now.

As she had arranged, the musicians sounded a fanfare hard on the stroke of midnight. All attention focused on herself and Donald, standing as they were directly before the musician's stand. Lord Donald seemed momentarily dumbstruck.

"Go ahead," she hissed, poking him in the ribs in a most unladylike way. Lord Donald looked unhappy, but as a sea of curious faces stared at him he could see nothing for it but to comply.

"A-hem," he cleared his throat, then turned beet red. Megan, swallowing her exasperation, nudged him again. "Ahem. L-ladies and gentlemen, I-uh-I have an a-anouncement. Miss Kinkead has done me the very great honor of consenting to become my wife."

He finished the last in a rush, and then as a babble of talk arose he turned to look proudly at Megan. He had done it, by jove, he had done it. After such a public declaration, not all the stuffy guardians in the world could refuse to allow Megan to marry him. Megan didn't even see the look he bent on her. Across the oncoming tide of faces, her eyes met and locked with Justin's burning gold ones. In an unguarded moment, she saw agony flare in their glittering depths.

Chapter 15

Megan saw Justin making his way across the crowded room to her side, the pain in his eyes changing in the space of a few instants into smoldering anger. But he was waylaid on all sides by well-wishers and the merely curious who were anxious to know all the details of this surprising engagement. He had to stop, to respond politely, and this gave Megan a chance to escape. Clutching at Lord Donald's arm, she practically dragged him toward the dance floor.

"Dance with me, Donald," she ordered, masking the command with a saccharine smile.

"Of course, Miss—Megan," he beamed down at her

fondly. It was plain from his expression that he considered her the most beautiful girl he had ever seen, and himself the luckiest man.

Megan managed to smile and blush demurely in answer to the joshing comments and questions that were addressed to her; Donald, both pleased and embarrassed at the sudden attention accorded him because of the surprising, unorthodox announcement of his engagement to the Season's reigning beauty, could manage no better than a blush and a stammer himself. Megan watched him impatiently as he turned beet-red in response to some of the jocular comments thrown his way by the more dashing of his male contemporaries, and redoubled her efforts to drag him off to the dance floor. He might not have been the husband she would have chosen if she had been free to choose with no restrictions, but she was not. The very bumbling innocence that so annoyed her was exactly what made him ideal for her purposes. An experienced man of the world would no doubt recognize her lack of virginity within hours of their marriage, and would undoubtedly, therefore, question the birth of a child seven months later. With Donald, she was almost certain that she need have no such qualms. She told herself fiercely, as her conscience pricked at her, that it was not as if she meant to cheat him. She would be a good wife to him if it killed her. Indeed, if he were a good father to her baby, she would do anything humanly possible to please him.

Lady Alicia was waiting for them on the edge of the dance floor. A tiny smile curved her lips, and she seemed both pleased and secretly amused.

"You sly boots, you," she greeted Megan, her pale blue eyes warmer than Megan had ever seen them. "I had no idea that you were contemplating getting engaged to Lord Donald." The slight emphasis she put on the young man's name told Megan, if not Donald, exactly how negligible she felt him to be. "But I must tell you I am delighted. I hope you're very happy, my dear."

She presented her powdered and perfumed cheek for Megan to kiss. Megan complied with an inward grimace, just brushing her lips against the cool, dry skin.

"And as for you, young man," she assayed playfully to Donald, tapping him coquettishly on the arm with her intricately painted silk fan. She was dressed in an elegant ballgown of cloud-pink brocade with touches of gold, and even Megan had to admit that she was looking quite beautiful. Donald smiled as foolishly at her as he did at everyone else. "I am sure you are as aware as I am that Weston is likely to be extremely wroth with you. However, you may count on me to stand as your friend. It's been so long since we were wed, I don't doubt that he has forgotten just what it is to be young and in love. I will endeavor to remind him, and thus explain to him why you must need announce your engagement so precipitately, instead of referring it to him for approval in the usual way."

"Th-thank you, ma'am," Donald said rather doubtfully, beginning to look alarmed at the inevitable prospect of an interview with Weston. The Earl was a dangerous man to cross, and Donald began to feel that announcing his engagement to the Earl's ward in such a hurly-burly fashion might not have been just the best way to get in on the man's good side. But Megan had insisted that, if he wanted to marry her, this was the only way to go about it. Weston, it seemed, was determined not to let her marry for years, and she wanted to marry Donald, oh, so much. Therefore, Donald would have to be as resolute and brave as she knew he was and circumvent Megan's stern guardian by a public announcement. After such a declaration, there could be no drawing back. The scandal would be ruinous. Donald, infatuated beyond belief and incredulous that this vision of loveliness actually wished to marry him, allowed himself to be persuaded. And it was now too late to alter anything about it. A gentleman could not cry off from an engagement, not that he wanted to, so he would just have to brave Weston's wrath as best as he could, and hope that the coming close connection between them was enough to keep Weston from calling him out. The Earl was reputed to have a trigger temper and an aim truer than William Tell's.

"If you will excuse us, Lady Alicia, this set is just forming,"Megan said desperately, spying Justin's formidable figure approaching. Lady Alicia cast a comprehensive glance over her shoulder, her eyes alight with a combination of malicious enjoyment and triumph.

"Certainly," she almost purred, and moved with stately grace to meet Justin as Megan practically dragged Donald into the dance.

Donald danced as he did nearly everything else: with mediocrity. Megan smiled and nodded in response to his comments as he led her through the dance, hearing scarcely a single word he said. She was growing more apprehensive by the second of what Justin's reaction would be to her engagement. He would be furious, she knew, and since she could not tell him the real reason behind her sudden, urgent desire to marry, she would have to make him think that she had fallen in love with Donald. Acknowledging that Justin knew her and her responses so well, that would be no easy task.

He was waiting for her when she came off the dance floor on Donald's arm. Megan, with a feeling of inevitability, saw him watching her. She could not avoid him forever, so it might be best to get this initial confrontation over now, while she was protected from the full explosion of his wrath by the presence of so many watching eyes.

Donald's eyes widened as he saw Justin, and knew that the meeting he was now dreading with all his heart was upon him.

"My—my lord," he achieved as Justin strolled to meet them, his tall figure intimidating and the slight smile which curved his lips looking more like a snarl. Justin spared him a brief, dismissive glance.

"I shall have plenty to say to you tomorrow," Justin told him in a gravelly voice, his eyes cold as winter as they flicked on the younger man's reddening face. "You may call upon me at Weston House at ten o'clock. Megan, my dear, I would like a few words with

255

you NOW, if you please. If, of course," his glance at Donald was ironic, "Lord Winspear can be persuaded to excuse you."

Donald nearly swallowed his tongue in his attempts to assure Justin that he would be only too happy to do so. Justin made no effort to conceal the contempt with which he looked at him, and even Megan threw him an annoyed look. Why couldn't he show more poise? Justin was reducing him to the status of a wayward schoolboy with little more than a single look from those heavy-lidded eyes.

"If you'll forgive me, my lord, I prefer to dance," Megan interrupted Donald's stammers to stare defiantly at Justin. She clutched Donald's arm in such a grip that it would fairly have been torn it from its socket if he had attempted to leave her. "I'm sure whatever you have to say to me will keep until tomorrow."

Justin smiled urbanely. Only Megan could read the grim warning in his eyes. "So you prefer to dance, do you, my charming ward?" he purred. "Then of course you shall. I'm sure Winspear here will excuse you to dance with me."

Justin's manuever was so deft that Megan was not sure exactly how he managed to detach her from Donald and steer her on to the dance floor where he pulled her into his arms. The musicians had struck up a waltz; it was only the second time that she had danced it, the first being shortly after her arrival in London, at Almack's with the permission of the patronesses. For the first few minutes she was so taken up with minding her steps that she could only spare an occasional dagger-glance for Justin. He danced as well as he did nearly everything else, his big body leading her in the graceful turns of the waltz with careless mastery.

"Smile, my own," he murmured satirically. "Else people might think we're quarreling."

Megan looked up at him to see that a polite smile was plastered on the straight mouth. One had to be quite, quite close to see the glittering hardness of his eyes.

"Now why should they think that?" She gave him a smile as blatantly false as his own while their eyes clashed. Being held so close to him in public was playing havoc with her senses; his hard arm around her waist, his large strong hand enfolding her small one, the occasional brush of his thighs against her skirts sent tingles chasing up and down her spine. Three months ago she never would have dreamed that it was possible to feel like this about a man; now she wondered with a sudden sense of despair how she would ever manage to live the rest of her life without him. But for the sake of the child she was carrying, she had no choice. She had to marry quickly, and she could not marry Justin. Lord Donald could secure her child's future, and her own, in a way that Justin never could even if he wanted to. Donald offered her a life of respectability, and her child a chance to be born and grow up in all honor. Justin could offer only dishonor to them both.

"Suppose you explain yourself, my darling," Justin

said after a moment. At the endearment, Megan's fingers curled involuntarily into the charcoal gray velvet of his coat. Beneath her hand she could feel the tensing of his shoulder muscles as he responded to the instinctive movement.

"I don't know what you mean," she said mendaciously, her eyes flickering away from the slight, false smile that still twisted his mouth. Her head did not quite reach his shoulder, and it was a simple matter to regard the snowy folds of his neckcloth as if she found them fascinating. Simpler by far than looking up to meet those gleaming eyes.

"Don't you, my own?" Something in the timber of his voice made Megan shiver. He was angry, furiously angry, and he meant her to know it. She dared a quick glance up into his dark face, and saw that his jaw was clenched tightly while his eyes smoldered. That hideous smile was still pinned firmly to his lips. He added, "Then you must allow me to elucidate: What the hell do you mean by allowing that puppy to make such an announcement? It will cause the devil of a dust when I refute it, as I have every intention of doing as soon as I kick his ass all the way back to Lincolnshire."

Megan smiled at him, and saw his eyes narrow into twin golden slits.

"I love him, Justin," she said with as much conviction as she could muster. "I mean to marry him."

"The hell you do!" The exclamation brought several heads swinging in their direction. Justin stared down at her, and Megan noted that, for the moment at least, his face was innocent of that frightening smile.

"You love me," he added in a hoarse voice. Megan saw hot color stain his high cheekbones. A stab of feeling so intense that it shook her pierced Megan to the heart. It took every ounce of her will-power not to melt against him there and then, to tell him the truth about the child they had made, and beg him to do with her and their child as he would. But her love for the child, growing inside her, stopped her. Justin was a grown man, and would forget her in a little while if she were out of his reach. Her baby would be helpless, dependent upon her for whatever its life would bring. She had to choose the baby, even though the choice threatened to break her heart.

"I have no stomach for being your paramour, Justin," she answered quickly. His arm tightened around her waist almost convulsively, and for a moment Megan felt the hard muscles of his chest against her breasts before he loosened his grip, allowing her to put a more decorous distance between them.

"Don't you, my own? If my memory serves me correctly, so far you have managed to stomach it very well indeed. Divinely, in fact."

Megan looked around, her face coloring a little at the thought of anyone else hearing those sneering words. They would be left in little doubt of what she had been to Justin.

"Would you keep your voice down?" she demanded in a fierce whisper. "You have no right to say such things to me here, of all places."

"Where would you prefer that I say them to you,

259

my darling? In my bed?"

Megan gasped, and tried to pull away from him, not caring about appearances nor anything else except that she put as much distance between herself and Justin as possible. His arm tautened into a steel band as he forced her to continue in the movements of the dance.

"Let me go." she raged at him, trying her best to pull away. She retained just enough presence of mind to keep her voice low. Justin's grip did not loosen an iota. Looking up at him furiously, she saw that his eyes were glittering with anger even while that travesty of a smile curled his lips.

"Oh, no, my darling," he answered softly, and the words seemed to apply to far more than his present unbreakable grip. Megan quivered in his hold, but knew that there was no possible way to break it until he was himself ready to let her go. Justin was a strong man; against him, she was as weak as a baby chick.

They danced silently for some minutes, dipping and swaying and turning in beautiful rhythm while the musicians played the lilting tune. Many eyes were upon the tall, powerfully muscled man, handsome in his formal evening dress despite the rather menacing smile on his face, and the slender, lovely young girl in the satin ball-gown. Megan was oblivious to the looks they were receiving; she was conscious only of the proximity of Justin's beloved body, the familiar man-smell of him, the achingly pleasurable touch of his arm around her waist. All her bravado threatened to leave her as she felt her full skirts swishing about his long legs, sensed rather than saw the intimacy with which he bent over her.

"So you don't wish to be my paramour." There was a quality to the musing statement that brought Megan's eyes swinging up to his. He did not sound angry, or even particularly mocking. He sounded almost—tender. The violet of her eyes deepened to purple as she stared questioningly into his golden ones.

"What would you say if I asked you to be my wife?"

The question, put in an off-hand manner in that oddly tender tone, made Megan's heart stop. She blinked at him disbelievingly, wanting what he offered her so much she could have died for it. To be Justin's wife, to have his baby in all honor, to give it his name and see it grow up under his guidance, that was the stuff of which dreams were made. But, Megan reminded herself with a sudden, painful return to reality that there was one very large obstacle in the way: Lady Alicia, Justin's wife.

"I would say that I have as little stomach for bigamy as I have for being your paramour," she responded tartly, tramping ruthlessly on those wayward dreams of hers. This surprised a genuine grin out of Justin.

"You never say the expected thing, do you, my darling?" he asked, still with that slight grin playing about his handsome mouth. "Is that any way to respond to a gentleman's proposal of marriage? The proper answer is, I believe, 'Oh, my lord, this is all so sudden!' " His falsetto imitation of a simpering girl's voice would have made her laugh if she had not been feeling so heartsore.

"When I receive a proper proposal, then perhaps I will return a proper answer." Megan's voice was cool. She did not appreaciate his mockery.

"What, to your mind, constitutes a proper proposal? Do you want me to go down on my knees?" He was still smiling, Megan saw, but the passion that blazed from his eyes stunned her. He almost looked as if he were serious.

"Don't be ridiculous," she said sharply. "You know perfectly well that you can't offer me marriage, even if you would. Or have you forgotten your wife?"

"No, I haven't forgotten Alicia," Justin said. The golden blaze of his eyes was threatening to make Megan go weak at the knees. "But I could get a divorce. It's been done before; it's not impossible."

"The scandal. . . ." Megan whispered, wide-eyed. The idea tempted her so much she could have screamed. To be Justin's wife would be everything she had ever wanted.

"I don't give a damn about the scandal." Justin's hand tightened on hers. "Do you?"

Megan said nothing, just stared up at him, dumbfounded.

"Of course, it would take a while," he continued softly. "Maybe several years. Would you wait for me, Megan?"

There it was, the fly in the ointment. Even if he was serious about getting a divorce, even if it could in fact be done, it would take several years. And she didn't have several years. This baby was going to put in an appearance in a little more than seven months time, and unless she married someone quickly it would carry the stigma of bastardy for the whole of its life. For herself, she would have waited for Justin forever, if need be. For her baby, she could not.

"I thank you for your very flattering offer, my lord," Megan's forced coquettishness sounded horrible even to her own ears. "But I find after all that I prefer to marry Donald." She smiled as she said it, hoping that he could not read the pain in her eyes. Apparently he did not, for his face tightened until the hard bones were clearly visible, and a tiny muscle began jumping in the side of his jaw.

"You little bitch," he grated harshly, and would have said more except the dance came to an end with a flourish of violins. Megan was able to pull away from him under the cover of the general exodus from the dance floor, and without causing a scene Justin had no way of reclaiming her from the circle of her friends to which she quickly fled for protection.

Megan's refusal of his offer hit Justin in a vulnerable spot. His heart was damaged, but he refused to recognize it; instead he chose to focus on the blow to his pride. For the first time in his thirty-six years of life, he knew what it was to be in love with a woman. No, not a woman, he corrected himself harshly, but a maddening chit of a girl who haunted his mind through waking and sleeping hours, never giving him a moment's peace. He loved her, wanted her, and she had said she loved him—but that was when she was expecting him to offer her a marriage untainted by years of waiting. He told himself savagely that hers had been no more than puppy love, that she had been more interested in his title and fortune than in Justin Brant the man. When their romance had run into stormy waters, she had elected to jump ship rather than ride it out with him. A wise man once said that a bird in the hand was worth two in the bush, and Justin supposed that Megan considered Lord Winspear as the proverbial bird in the hand. Winspear could offer Megan a marriage with no taint of scandal to mar it, an assured place at the very pinnacle of society, and a fortune that was respectable, if not as large as Justin's own. She would be secure with him, if not ecstatically happy. Justin knew that his love for Megan was such that he would have waited the rest of his life for her, if need be. If she could not wait a scant few years until he would be free, the love she had expressed for him must have been a paltry emotion, if indeed it had ever existed. Or perhaps it had not been love at all, as he had feared from the beginning. Perhaps it had been a case of her healthy young body responding of its own accord to the arousal she had sensed in his; or, worse, it might even have been a case of hero-worship for the guardian who had served as a distant father figure for her for years. It was a well-known fact that young girls often got crushes on their fathers at a certain stage in their development. Justin was horribly afraid that this was how Megan had felt about him. She had had a crush, and it had passed. Now she had found another man, the one with whom she wanted to spend her life.

As Megan's guardian, Justin would have been well within his rights to veto the proposed marriage, and send young Winspear on his way with a flea in his ear. But his pride wouldn't let him. If Megan wanted to marry the young slow-top, then she was welcome to him. He made no demur even when Megan used the failing health of Lord Winspear's father as an excuse for scheduling the ceremony a scant two weeks in the future. If she was that anxious to become the bride of another man, he thought with a fury that didn't quite erase his pain, then let her. He would find himself another woman, one with a little experience to recommend her this time, and forget all about the violet-eyed little temptress. She was not worth another of his thoughts.

The two weeks passed with alarming swiftness. As frantic preparations for the wedding continued, Megan felt as if she was caught up in a dreadful nightmare. Every atom of her being rebelled at the idea of being Donald's wife, of sharing with him the heart-shaking intimacies that belonged by right to Justin. Her heart bled whenever she saw that tall, powerful form, and it was all she could do not to call the whole thing off. But for the sake of her unborn child, she could not. Her child's future was the important thing.

The wedding was scheduled for a Thursday evening during the second week in December. Megan's gown, in which she felt only a perfunctory interest, would be delivered the day before. Tonight, Tuesday of the same week, was the last social function she would be

265

attending as Miss Kinkead. In less than forty-eight hours, she would be Lady Winspear, forever.

They were to attend the assembly at Almack's. Megan did not particularly want to go, but on the other hand, there was no point in sitting at home brooding. What was done was done, and she must needs make the best of it. There could be no turning back now.

The gown which she had allowed Mary to choose for her was of white silk cut in a chemise style with gold thread glinting through the material and embroidered gold fleur-de-lis edging the neckline and hem. It clung closer to the body than most of her dresses, and the effect was both unusual and arresting. Mary had chosen to dress her hair with a simple gold cord woven through the piled black curls. Looking at her reflection, Megan knew that she was looking beautiful despite the pallor which had robbed her cheeks of their usual healthy color, but she could take no pleasure in the knowledge. The white dress reminded her forcibly of her wedding gown, and if there had been time she would have changed it. But she was already late, and of all things Lady Alicia disliked being kept waiting. Donald, who had volunteered to escort them, was more patient, and Megan told herself quite fiercely that she should be pleased at this evidence of his thoughtful nature.

When she went downstairs, however, she was surprised to find only Justin waiting for her. He was correctly attired for an evening at Almack's in black satin evening breeches and a swallow-tailed coat, but

Megan barely managed to stop herself from gaping at him. He had avoided her assiduously since the disastrous evening of her coming out ball, and Megan had had no notion that he even knew of their intention to visit Almack's that evening, much less that he meant to join them.

"Where is Lady Alicia? And Donald?" Megan asked quite sharply as she stepped down into the hallway where he awaited her. She hated to admit it, but being left alone with him set her nerves on edge in a way she could ill afford if she was to keep up this pose of indifference to him.

Justin merely smiled in reply. Ames hurried into view with Justin's cloak and her own over his arm. Justin took Megan's cloak from Ames and placed it carelessly around her shoulders, then fastened his own while she eyed him with some trepidation. He looked both determined and oddly pleased with himself, and Megan decided that she didn't trust him an inch.

"I asked you where Lady Alicia and Donald are," she said again. This time Justin shrugged his broad shoulders.

"You know how Alicia is. She refuses to wait for anyone. And she prevailed upon your fiance to escort her on to Almack's. So you and I, my dear, are left to bring up the rear. As soon as you are ready."

Somehow this didn't seem terribly plausible to Megan, but with Ames interested gaze upon them she hesitated to say anything. After all, what could Justin say or do in the short ride to Almack's that he hadn't already said or done? So she allowed Justin to usher her out the door and into the waiting carriage without another word of protest.

He climbed into the carriage behind her, closing the door and sinking back into the luxuriously upholstered seat opposite where she sat. The coach began to move. Megan noticed with a slight frown that they were in the larger traveling carriage, the one which had conveyed her from Ireland, but she supposed that, if Alicia had taken the lighter vehicle, this must have been the only closed carriage available. And it was far too cold to make an open carriage practical.

To her surprise, Justin said nothing on the journey, just settled against his seat with his arms crossed over his chest and watched her with a sardonic look in his eye. By the light of the lanterns set into the curving walls on either side of the coach she saw that he looked almost amused. His straight mouth was twisted into what could have passed for a wry smile, and his golden eyes seemed to hold a wicked twinkle as they moved over her. He looked very large and dark in such close quarters, and Megan found herself growing absurdly apprehensive. Then she scolded herself. He was trying to make her nervous, she thought, and she mustn't allow him to even suspect that he was succeeding admirably.

Megan was so caught up in ignoring Justin that it was some time before she noticed that the brief ride to Almack's was stretching to considerable length. With a sudden sharp frown at Justin, she leaned over to pull the pale blue velvet curtain from the window and look out. It was difficult to discern any landscape through the pitch blackness that greeted her gaze, but that very darkness told her that they were no longer in any part of London that she knew, where the streets were all lit with flaming torches.

"Where are you taking me?" she demanded of Justin, lifting her dumbfounded eyes from the unenlightening window to glare at him. He met her furious query with a lift of his brows.

"Oh, forgive me, did I forget to mention that there had been a-uh-slight change in plan?" He smiled grimly. "You've been called into the country to visit a dear relation who is even now on her death-bed asking for you."

Megan stared at him. "You know I don't have any relations."

"You don't, do you?" There was a wealth of satisfaction in the words. "But only you and I know that. The truth is, I'm offering you the not inconsiderable compliment of abducting you, my own."

Chapter 16

Justin had come to a decision only that morning. The night before he had gone to White's as had become his custom, and had passed the hours before dawn drinking and gaming recklessly. As he drank, his anger at Megan, and himself for letting her reduce him to such a state, grew to nearly ungovernable heights. It was fueled by a tender scene he had witnessed earlier in the day in the parlor of his own house: He had come home to change clothes, and had found the parlor door, which usually was left ajar, closed. Naturally intrigued, he had pushed it open to find Megan caught close in her fiance's embrace. The sight riveted him to the spot. He had clenched his fists, conscious of an almost overwhelming urge to close his hands around the whippersnapper's neck. But then he reminded himself forcibly that Megan had chosen to spend her life with this man. He had every right to kiss her as he was doing, and it was obvious that Megan was not struggling to escape. In fact, they were both so caught up in their mutual bliss that neither of them was aware of his presence. Acknowledging this, the pain Justin felt was so great that he could have screamed. But he did not. He did nothing. Gritting his teeth, he managed with a truly heroic effort to turn on his heel and leave the two of them. And then he had taken himself off to White's and gotten soddenly, numbingly drunk.

Always before, he had scorned and mocked those of his friends who were foolish enough to fancy themselves in love. Now he was in love, something which he had once thought impossible, and he was learning that it was no laughing matter. He had offered Megan his heart, and she had callously trampled it underfoot. It galled him unbearably to think that a seventeen-year-old schoolgirl, and his own ward to boot, should have the power to make such a fool of him. He had been one of the prizes of the marriage mart the year he had married Alicia, and he knew without conceit that, if he were to rid himself of his wife, he would be an even bigger prize today. He was older, richer, handsomer. Not even the stigma of divorce would deter most of Society's females from scheming to become the next Countess of Weston. But Megan, whom he loved so much that it was threatening to drive him insane, had made it very clear that she wanted no part of him, except in her bed. By God, he had created a monster, introducing her to the pleasures of the flesh so well that she was prepared to take her fun where it was offered like a man, and then look elsewhere for a marriage partner. When she had turned down his proposal of marriage, saying blithely that she preferred to wed that wet-behind-the-ears boy rather than wait the necessary time required for him to get a divorce, Justin had scarcely been able to believe his ears. The only interpretation he could put on her refusal was that she didn't want him. At least, not for marriage and not enough to wait. She would have injured him less if she had taken a sword and stabbed him through the heart. This way she had left him to slowly bleed to death, and he was suffering agonies.

Along toward morning, it began to occur to him that he now despised Megan almost as much as he desired her. She had played him for a fool, and if she had been a man he would have blown a hole through her. But she was very much a woman, with a woman's weapons against which those of a mere man were ineffectual. She had snared him in a silken web from which there was no escaping, baiting her trap with such sweet inducements that he had walked into it without a struggle. Now, like a female spider, she was intent on devouring him. The very thought of another man calling her wife, sleeping by her side at night, kissing her and bedding her and giving her children was enough for him to break out in a cold sweat. Then she very coolly chose to kick his love aside as if it was a thing of little value. The more Justin thought about that, the more furious it made him. She had made him love her, damn it, and she could damn well pay the consequences.

Justin told himself that he had been a fool to offer her marriage. He wouldn't marry her now if she begged him, but he still wanted her. As his mistress. He dwelled on the title, which previously he had refused to even think of in the same breath as her name, with vicious satisfaction. Yes, she was eminently suited for the role of his mistress, and he deserved some recompense for the time and trouble he had invested in her. Why, he had even taught her how to make love, and he would fry in hell before he would let her practice her new-found expertise on another man until he himself had tired of it. Oh, yes, he would make her his mistress. He would bed her until he had worked her out of his system, and then, if she wished and could persuade her precious Donald to it, she would be free to marry the man of her choice. But until then, she was his, his possession, his prisoner, to do with as he willed.

Putting his plan into execution was ridiculously easy. The fact that he was her legal guardian and that she resided under his roof simplified things. After all, he had the ultimate authority over Megan until she married, and she was not married yet. He had only to tell her idiot of a fiance the story about her relation, and that was that. No possibility of scandal, while he whisked Megan off with the most dishonorable of intentions.

Looking at her now, as she stared disbelievingly at him from the other side of the carriage, he felt a welling of fierce triumph. She was his now, whether she liked it or not. And the sooner she accepted the fact the better it would be for her.

"You're either drunk or mad," Megan said with conviction, her eyes enormous in her pale face. Justin allowed his own eyes to roam insolently over her, touching on each exquisite detail with savage satisfaction. Her raven curls were piled high atop her head, showing off the delicate perfection of her features and the porcelain purity of her skin. Except for the gold cord binding her hair, her jewel-like eyes were her only ornament. Justin looked at them, slanting violet gems fringed by feathery black lashes and set beneath silken brows, and thought that a man could be forgiven for believing in her angelic innocence. The expression in those eyes said everything of heaven and nothing of hell, and yet it was to hell that they had driven him. Now he meant to bring her down with him. Her lips were as red and delicious looking as the ripest of berries, and beneath the flimsy silk of her dress the fullness of her breasts was clearly visible. The straight lines of the garment hinted at rather than revealed the narrowness of her waist, but Justin didn't need any help remembering exactly what lay beneath her dress. The image of her body was seared on his brain forever.

"Do you think so?" he asked negligently, stretching

his long legs out in front of him and smiling at her. Annoyance began to replace the sheer astonishment with which she had been regarding him.

"Where do you think you're taking me? You know perfectly well that no one is admitted at Almack's after eleven, and if you don't turn back at once, we'll be too late."

"Then I suppose you must resign yourself to being too late, because I have not the slightest intention of telling the coachman to turn back."

"I will then," Megan glared at him, then sought to open first the window and then the door while he watched her with a satiric grin on his face. Neither would budge.

"They're locked," he said laconically as she turned a flushed and angry face to him. "From the outside. And I've instructed the coachman not to stop until we reach a certain inn in Abingdon."

"You are mad!" she spat furiously. He raised a mocking eyebrow at her.

"If it pleases you to think so."

Megan looked at him, uncertainty battling with the anger in her face.

"Where are you taking me?"

"I own a house on the coast of Wales. It's a beautiful place, quite peaceful, and almost totally isolated from the world. My great grandfather, I believe, named it Windsmere, and it is every bit as lonely and as magnificent as the name sounds. I thought you might like to see it."

"I am getting married in two days' time."

Justin smiled again, but this time there was no mistaking the underlying nastiness.

"I don't think so," he said with unhidden satisfaction.

Megan stared at him with growing horror.

"Dear God, what have you done?" she whispered, her hand coming up to cover her mouth.

At the honest dismay he saw in her face, Justin's mouth took on a hard, straight line.

"So anxious to marry young Donald?" A sneer laced the words. "That's just too bad. Because I have a prior claim, and I intend to exercise it."

"I can't marry you! You're married!" She was practically wailing with despair.

One corner of his mouth twisted up mockingly.

"I don't recall mentioning marriage," he drawled. "You can consider my previous offer withdrawn. I have since decided that you will fill another position in my life most admirably. I've been out a mistress for some weeks."

"If you think I'm going to be your mistress," she spat the word at him, "you are crazy. As soon as we stop, I'm returning to London, and I'm marrying Donald the day after tomorrow."

"I think not," he said, as if that settled everything.

"You can't stop me." The words were mere bravado on her part. She was beginning to feel truly alarmed. Justin's only reply to that statement was a derisive smile. He could stop her, and they both knew it.

"You don't understand," she said desperately, biting down hard on her lower lip in an effort to make him see reason. He watched the betraying gesture as if it fascinated him. "I must marry Donald. I love him."

His brows snapped together as if he'd been stung, and he looked quite furious. Megan visibly quailed from the menace shooting from those golden eyes.

"I wouldn't marry him on that score, if I were you," he spat out. "Think how fickle your emotions have already proven to be. Less than a month ago, you were saying the same thing to me."

"I was mistaken," she said lamely. His eyes flashed golden fire at that.

"Were you now?" he drawled. "What a pity. You see, you whetted my appetite for your delicious little body, and I don't intend to let you go until it's quite appeased."

Megan stared at him. "I won't let you do that to me again. I tell you, I love Donald, and I mean to marry him."

His eyes narrowed, and his jaw clamped shut.

"The hell you will," he growled, and reached for her.

Megan fought as his hands closed hurtfully over her upper arms, hauling her across the carriage into his arms, but pitting her puny strength against his powerful muscles was like trying to turn back the sea. He dragged her across his lap so that her head was cradled on his shoulder, and when she would have rolled to the floor he twined his hand in her long hair and twisted it cruelly, holding her in place. His mouth closed on hers with a ferocity that shook her to her core. His lips and tongue were brutal as they possessed her, forcing her to submit to him whether she

278

would or not. Megan could only moan helplessly into his mouth as he bent her back against the plush velvet upholstery, bending over her and holding her in place with the weight of his body. Megan's hands were crushed between them, and she could feel the heat and strength of him in every fibre of her body. Weakly she tried to avert her head from his kiss, but the hand that was twisted in her hair jerked on it so fiercely that she cried out. After that she lay quietly beneath him, making no effort to escape but protesting his action by her very passivity. When at last her silent resistance seemed to penetrate the thick fog of angry passion which held him in thrall, Justin lifted his head to look down at her. His face was so close that Megan could see every little detail of the harsh lines that bracketed his mouth, and the smaller ones that radiated from the corners of his eyes. A thick swathe of his black hair had fallen over his forehead; Megan was conscious of an instinctive urge to push it back. In the flickering light from the lanterns, his face looked very dark; the hard straight mouth that had so unfeelingly ravaged her own was set in a cruel line. The feeling blazing from his eyes was barbaric in its intensity, and the primitive effect was not lessened by the elegant black evening suit that fit him to such perfection. Megan felt as if she were seeing through to the true, uncivilized nature of the man for the first time. He was an animal, she thought, and not all the elegantly tied neckcloths or superbly tailored coats in the world could ever blind her to the fact again. He was revealed at last in his true form, and she would never forget it.

"Kiss me back," he growled at her, his eyes aflame as they bore down into her own. "Kiss me back, you little bitch, or I'll take you here and now."

Looking into those glittering eyes, Megan had no doubt that he meant it. Something in him wanted to hurt her, to punish her. She supposed that it was his way of revenging the blow she must have dealt his monumental male pride by seeming to prefer Donald to him. When she returned his stare with a bitter one of her own, she felt his fingers digging hurtfully into her scalp. Despite herself, she whimpered.

"I mean it, so help me God," he whispered threateningly.

Defeated, Megan closed her eyes and waited. He was beyond the stage where any sort of reason could reach him, and he was far bigger and stronger than she. She had no doubts that he would do just as he had threatened if she did not obey him.

He looked down at her, saw the submission implicit in her closed eyes and laughed harshly.

"I said for you to kiss me," he grated. "Damn you, put your arms around my neck and kiss me. I want to feel your soft little mouth begging me."

Megan's eyes fluttered, and she looked up at him through the shield of her thick lashes. He looked totally capable of any cruelty. Her hands fluttered against his chest, trapped still between their bodies, and he lifted himself slightly so that she could free them. Moving slowly, so slowly, she slid her hands up to his shoulders, then around to the back of his neck. Against her breasts she could feel the lower part of his

280

chest crushing her. The beat of his heart reverberated throughout her being.

"Now kiss me," he muttered. Megan saw the excited flare of those thin nostrils as she lifted her head to obey. As her mouth touched his she felt the convulsive tremor that shook him, and then he was assuming total control of the kiss, taking her mouth with a fierce passion that demanded her total response. By the time he lifted his head again, Megan was breathless, her senses aswarm with the delicious way he could make her feel. She had betrayed herself utterly with that kiss. She hadn't been able to help herself. Her traitorous body went crazy if he so much as touched her. He had taught her passion, and her flesh recognized its master.

He looked down into her face with bitter triumph, reading there the response that she couldn't even begin to hide.

"So you love Donald, do you?" he rasped. "Does he know how much you want me? Does he know how very wanton his future wife can look when she's being kissed senseless?"

The sneering words lashed her like a whip. He saw her involuntary response and abruptly sat up, running a hand through his black hair and staring down at her with barely disguised contempt.

"Sit up," he ordered coldly. "And straighten your clothes. I think I've made my point. No matter how much you may protest for the sake of propriety, we both know that you won't find being my mistress any hardship. Who knows, if you're a good girl and do your best to please me, you might even do quite well. Many 'ladies' have emerged from similar positions, as quite wealthy women."

His words were meant to hurt, to insult, and they succeeded. Megan's eyes widened as if from a blow, and for just a moment she could only stare at him. With a grimace, he reached out and hauled her into an upright position, then nearly flung her over onto the opposite seat.

"Tidy yourself," he instructed briefly. "I fancy we are nearing Abingdon. And be patient. You'll have everything you want, and possibly quite a bit more, very shortly."

Megan couldn't bring herself to reply to the cruel words. Her response to his brutality had left her without any defense. He had made her want him, and they both knew it. It was shameful, but horribly true.

As Justin had predicted, in a very short while, the carriage rocked to a halt. Megan blushed to the roots of her hair as she heard the bolt drawn back from the door, and drew her cloak tightly around her shoulders, hoping desperately that the mark Justin had made on her showed only on her soul, not her body. Throwing a quick, unhappy glance at him, she was humiliated to notice that, for him, the degradation of the last few miles might never have occurred.

"My lord." The door had opened, and the coachman, one of Justin's servants, was standing anxiously by it, waiting to help them alight. Justin sprang lightly down, then turned around to lift Megan out. Her weight might have been nonexistent for all the trouble it caused him. He held her against him, and to her shame she felt her body melt obligingly as it touched his hardness. He smiled with grim mockery, and Megan knew that her involuntary response was not lost on him.

"I would advise you not to try anything foolish for I have known the innkeeper who will shortly be greeting us for many years, and I assure you that there is no help for you here. If you were misguided enough to try to enlist his or his staff's sympathy, all you would accomplish would be your own humiliation, or worse."

He didn't bother to wait for a reply, but set her away from him and turned to his coachman.

"Be sure and rub them down, Pryor, and bring the carriage around at first light. We have a long drive ahead of us tomorrow."

"Aye, my lord," the man said, pulling deferentially on his forelock as he stepped back. Justin paid no more heed to him, but ushered Megan before him into the inn. The warmth and light within was very welcome after the cold darkness of the night.

"Welcome, my lord," cried a voice, and Megan looked around to see a giant of a man in a stained white apron advancing on them, his face wreathed in smiles. For just an instant Megan felt a flicker of hope. This man was Justin's match physically, and if he could be persuaded to champion her cause all might not yet be lost. Then she looked back at Justin, absorbing his air of command that was as much a part of him as his skin, and knew that Justin was exactly right in his assessment of the situation. If she appealed to this man to help her to get back to London, he would undoubtedly defer to Justin. A simple inn-keeper, no matter how brawny, was no match for the Earl of Weston.

"Thank you, Rogers," Justin said civilly, halting Megan with a hand on her arm. "I trust rooms have been prepared, as I instructed?"

"Oh, yes, my lord," the man rubbed his hands together, smiling servilely. He seemed totally oblivious to Megan's presence. With a tiny spurt of shamed anger, Megan wondered whether he supposed her to be Justin's mistress and was being discreet. Then, she thought, "But I am," and felt all the color recede from her face as she wondered if Justin meant to openly display her as such.

"Yes, my lord. If you will follow me, my lord." Rogers' continual scraping and bowing was beginning to grate on Megan's nerves, but she followed him silently as he led the way up the stairs, Justin hard on her heels. She could feel his hand possessively in the small of her back, and tried to pull away from the contact. But he refused to let her.

"My best room, my lord," Rogers said proudly, throwing open a door and standing back so that Justin could precede him. Justin barely glanced inside.

"And for the lady?" he asked impatiently.

"As you instructed, my lord," he murmured, looking embarrassed. He moved to open the next door along the hall, and when that was done handed Justin the key.

"Thank you." Justin turned to look at Megan. "In

with you, my girl. I warned you that I would not tolerate your running away from school a third time, and now you will see that I meant it."

Megan gaped at him, totally taken aback, while he propelled her inexorably forward with his hand in the small of her back. When at last she stood inside the room, he bid her a curt good-night, and shut the door in her face. She was still standing there, dumbfounded, when she heard the key turn in the lock. He had locked her in.

Chapter 17

Megan was left alone for some time. When finally she realized that Justin was not intending to come back—at least, not for a while—she shook herself out of the lethargy she had fallen into and looked around the room. It was a rather small chamber, not up to Weston House standards by any means, but then Megan supposed that Justin had taken good care to avoid one of the larger, more luxurious posting houses where they would be in danger of running into friends and acquaintances. In addition to the bed, an austere single with a spool headboard, there was a dressing table and a washstand. Megan dropped her cloak, shivering a little as the night air struck the bare skin of her arms and shoulders. The fire had not yet been lit, although wood and kindling bits had been laid in the hearth in readiness. Megan rubbed her hands up and down her arms in an effort to warm them as she made her way over to the washstand. First she would wash, and make use of the chamber pot which had so thoughtfully been provided. Then she would see about lighting the fire, if no servant came in the meantime to do it.

Megan splashed her arms and face with the luke-warm water, and thought longingly of a bath. But there was none in evidence, and under the circumstances she didn't care to request one even if there had been someone available to ask. So she contented herself with a quick sponge bath, not removing her clothes but washing under them as well as she could. She had not missed the door in the middle of one wall which more than likely connected her chamber to Justin's. It was closed now, but if she were a gaming person she would wager that it would not long remain so. If she were to succeed in thwarting Justin's probable plans for the night, and she had to admit that her chances of that were slim, it would not do for him to come in and find her undressed and tucked up in bed.

She was relieved that he apparently did not intend to make the role he intended for her to be public knowledge. She would have died of shame to be openly presented as his mistress, and she was reluctantly grateful to him for maintaining the outward appearance of their guardian-ward relationship. His voice when he had locked her in this chamber had been strictly authoritarian, and Megan had no doubt that the innkeeper thought them exactly what they seemed: A stern guardian pulling in the reins on his rebellious ward. Megan smiled mirthlessly to herself. If only their relationship was still that simple.

Her ablutions completed, she crossed to the hearth and sank to her knees beside it. Reaching for the box of matches kept nearby she proceeded to light the fire. Though it took several attempts the tiny flames provided scant heat. Megan realized that it might be some time before the fire emanated any appreciable warmth. She stood up, crossed to the bed and pulled the coverlet around herself for warmth. Then she sat down on the edge of the bed to await Justin.

For the sake of their child, he must be persuaded to let her go. Only by marrying Donald, as scheduled, could she hope to prevent a horrifying scandal.

Megan had been sitting in the same position for what seemed like hours when the door connecting the two rooms opened. She looked up to see Justin framed in the doorway. He was still dressed in his elegant evening clothes, but he had discarded his coat. His rough black hair was wildly untidy, and his dark face was guarded. As he saw her sitting there, he leaned negligently against the doorjam, his arms crossing over his chest, a sardonic smile playing across his mouth.

"Waiting up for me? How touching."

Megan flushed, but she tilted her chin at him, and her eyes sparked with defiance.

"I was hoping that, now you've had time to consider a little, you would recognize the sheer idiocy of what you're doing. You can't force me to be your mistress, Justin."

"Can't I?"

Megan looked at him, correctly interpreting the glint in his eyes, and decided to try another tack.

"You are too much of a gentleman, Justin," she said quietly, her eyes never leaving his. "If you force me to submit to you, it would be rape. And you are not a rapist."

"Oh, I doubt I'll have to resort to rape," he responded, thrusting his hands deep into his pockets and smiling at her. "Correct me if I'm wrong, but I have always labored under the impression that the term "rape" implied the lady was unwilling."

His meaning was unmistakeable. Megan flushed angrily, and glared at him.

"Damn you, I am unwilling."

"I've told you before not to swear. Little girls with dirty mouths usually end up getting them washed out with soap."

The derisive glint in his eyes was infuriating.

"I am unwilling. I am, I am."

He smiled brutally. "No, you're not. We both know that. So why don't you quit wasting your time and mine with these theatrics and come to bed."

"If you mean to your bed, no, thank you. I prefer to sleep here."

"And I prefer otherwise. Which one of us will get his own way, I wonder?"

Megan eyed him. He looked very tall and broad in

his white dress shirt and black evening breeches; the silver brocade of his waistcoat hugged his muscled chest like a second skin. His neckcloth was intricately arranged, and secured in place with a diamond pin. He looked handsome and a little dangerous, and she knew that if he chose to exert himself, there was little chance she could hold out against him. She realized her vulnerability to his masculine attraction with a sinking heart, and a renewed determination not to give in.

"What do I have to do to get it through to you, Justin? I don't love you, and if you can make me want you it's no more than any other man with your expertise could do. I love Donald, and I want to marry him. Surely you will not stand in the way of my happiness?"

His face hardened.

"Fickle little bitch, aren't you?" he said quite pleasantly, then called her a name that brought the blood surging into her cheeks.

"How dare you?" she gasped, jumping to her feet and scarcely noticing as the coverlet slipped away from her shoulders to fall in a heap on the floor. She was left standing in the white silk evening dress she had donned for Almack's; her beauty as she faced him breathing fire and defiance only served to fan Justin's rising anger.

"Oh, I dare," he remarked unpleasantly. "I dare quite a lot, as you may find to your cost."

"I want you to let me go, Justin."

"Presently, my love. When I tire of you."

"Have you no shame?"

"Very little," he drawled. "And none at all where you are concerned." He straightened away from the doorjamb, looking very formidable. "Now, enough talk. Come here."

"No!"

"Don't make me fetch you, my own."

Megan backed away, keeping one eye warily on him. He made no move to come after her, but Megan did not fool herself that he would not. He would, if she continued to defy him, but this time the Earl might be in for quite a surprise. She had had enough of being humiliated at his hands, and she meant to fight.

"Go away, Justin!" Her fingers curled around the handle of the china pitcher that had earlier held the water for washing.

His only response to that was a harsh laugh. He strolled toward her as if he had all the time in the world, but the fierce glitter of his eyes belied his casual movements. She had aroused him, and she had no illusions as to what his intentions were.

"Stay back, Justin," she said warningly, the pitcher held behind her back out of his sight, ready for use as a weapon if he drove her to it. She was backed into a corner already, and there was no place to run even if she somehow managed to slip past him.

He continued to advance on her. Megan had no idea of what a lovely picture she presented, with her black hair working loose from its pins to cascade down her back and her creamy skin flushed with color. Her slender body was alluring despite the belligerence of her stance, and her eyes had deepened to purple with either fear, anger, or excitement, or some combination of the three. Watching her closely without giving that impression at all, Justin found himself wanting her so much he ached. And he meant to have her.

"I mean it, Justin." Megan warned again, and when he continued to advance she hefted the pitcher threateningly. He looked at it with a little twitch of amusement on his face.

"And do you really think that will stop me?" he asked almost conversationally, and while Megan was considering how best to reply to that he pounced.

Megan screamed instinctively, jumping back, and swung the pitcher in a wide arc that just missed his black head. Instead it slammed into his shoulder as he caught her in his arms, shattering into fragments as it hit the floor. Justin barely flinched. Megan's eyes were huge as she stared at him, held fast in the prison of his arms, one hand pressed between their bodies and the other trapped by one of his hands. She had hit him with the pitcher, and she knew it must have hurt for all his lack of outcry. As she waited the punishment he was sure to inflict upon her, her mouth was dry and her heart was beating like a frightened rabbit's.

"Hellcat," he said without heat, scooping her up and bearing her back through the opened door to his bedroom. Megan's eyes fastened on the bed, and her mouth went dry. To her shame, she realized that she wanted him fiercely. Remembering the things he did to her in bed, her cheeks flushed a wild rose color and her bones seemed to turn to water.

"No, Justin," she cried desperately. To her amazement, he stopped his slow advance toward the bed, and set her gently on her feet. He stood a little away from her, his arms folded across his chest and his head cocked a little to one side.

"It would be a shame to tear that beautiful dress," he said, his eyes glinting over it. Then, as Megan stared up at him wordlessly, he added, "Take it off."

Megan blinked at him in disbelief. "N-no."

He smiled. "You have precisely one minute to take it off. If you don't, I'll rip it off myself, and while I will enjoy it you might not. Besides, you will be left with nothing to wear tomorrow. But if it doesn't matter to you to appear in public in your shift, it doesn't bother me."

"You can't be serious." Megan wished she was as confident of that as she sounded. She had a horrible feeling that he meant precisely what he said. She had a choice: She could remove her dress, or he would do it for her.

"I am completely serious. And you have forty seconds left." He pulled a gold watch from his waistcoat pocket and stood watching her while it dangled tauntingly from his brown fingers.

"Ohh!" With a little exclamation of furious capitulation, she reached behind her back and tried to undo the fastenings of her dress. She managed to work one or two tiny hooks loose at the very top of the dress, but the ones further down defeated her.

"Having trouble?" he asked as she struggled with

the recalcitrant hooks.

"Yes," she hissed, glaring at him. She felt very tempted to hit him, and if it wasn't for the awful certainty that he would wreak some terrible vengeance on her she would have done it.

"Turn around," he said, surprising her, and pocketed the watch. "I have no objection to acting as lady's maid."

Megan stopped reaching for the hooks, letting her aching arms drop to her sides while she glared at him.

"No, thank you."

"Turn around," he said, his hand reaching out to catch her by the shoulder and turn her so that her back was presented to him. Megan stood stiffly while he worked the hooks loose with practiced ease. The touch of his warm fingers against the skin of her back sent shivers coursing up and down her spine. She bit her lip doing her best to control her treacherous body so that her reaction would not betray her. He slipped the dress from her shoulders at last, and Megan caught at it for a moment before allowing it to fall in a heap on the floor at her feet. Her eyes closed in mute response as he lifted aside the heavy fall of her hair to touch his lips to her nape.

"No stays?" he asked with a mocking inflection as he straightened, his hands on her shoulders turning her back to face him. Megan was dressed only in her chemise and the single narrow silk petticoat that went with her dress. The tops of her breasts swelled above the low, rounded top of her chemise, and Justin's eyes rested on their creamy flesh with blatant desire.

"I don't like to wear them." The look in his eyes was doing funny things to her voice. She knew he had to hear the husky note in it, and guess at the havoc he was wreaking on her system.

"You don't need them." His hands came out to measure her small waist, spanning its circumference between them. "You have the most incredibly tiny waist I've ever seen."

"And I suppose you've seen hundreds." Her voice was waspish as the face of Clorinda Barclay swam before her mind's eye. She was glad of the little spurt of anger that accompanied it. It prevented her from melting like butter under his hands.

His eyes glinted down at her with a spark of humor in their tawny-gold depths. "I would say that is an exaggeration," he drawled, his hands tightening around her waist. "More like dozens."

"Let go of me." Outraged, Megan pushed at his hands, which refused to be dislodged. After a moment, Megan ceased trying to push them away and stood panting and glaring at him.

"Jealous, Megan?" He was watching her closely.

She laughed scornfully, her head tilting back so that she could meet his eyes. "Of you? Don't make me laugh."

"Ah, yes, of course, I forgot: Of course you wouldn't give a damn about my lady friends. After all, it's nothing to do with you. You're in love with young Donald Winspear."

"Yes," Megan answered defiantly, praying he wouldn't read the lie in her eyes. "Yes, I am."

"You're going to have to prove that to me," he growled, and his hands slid from her shoulder to close around her neck as he covered her mouth with his. His kiss was both brutal and seductive, and Megan's initial resistance soon faded away to nothingness under the hot tutelage of his mouth. Her arms crept up around his neck, clinging to him; her body pressed instinctively against the hard length of his. His arms were tight around her waist, and he bent her backwards as his mouth devoured hers. When he drew back at last, she could only blink at him mistily as his eyes raked her face.

"Now tell me you love Winspear," he grated.

From somewhere deep inside Megan found the strength to lie to him.

"I do."

"Like hell you do." He caught her close in his arms again, swooping down on her like some giant dark bird of prey. His kiss was devastating, his hands busy as they stroked from breasts to thighs. Megan felt their hard sureness burning through the layers of her clothes, and her knees went weak. She moaned against his mouth, struggling against the overwhelming tide of desire that threatened to sweep her along with it. Everything about him, from the feel of his rough hair under her fingers to the crush of his chest against her breasts to the steely strength of his arms as they held her and his legs as they pressed against hers excited her madly. She loved the smell of him, the taste of his mouth, the harsh sound of his breathing. If he didn't take her soon, she was afraid that she would be reduced to begging for his possession. She wanted him more than she had ever wanted anything in her life, more than she had ever thought it possible to want anything. But at all costs, she couldn't reveal to him the depths of what she felt for him. For their child's sake, she had to convince him that it was Donald she loved, Donald she meant to marry. She had to convince Justin that her feelings for him were merely those of the flesh.

Megan arched against him, her head falling back, her body quivering under his hands and mouth. He pressed his lips to the softness of her breasts where they were bared by the decolletage of her chemise, then moved even lower so that he could capture the nipple between his teeth, sucking and biting through the thin lawn until it was rigid in his mouth and Megan was moaning aloud with passion.

"You love me," he murmured, lifting his head and fixing her with eyes that seemed to glow. Megan shook her head helplessly, feeling her treacherous body quivering from head to toe, her nails digging into the nape of his neck as he bent her back over his arm and her eyes hazy with the passion he was forcing her to feel.

"You love me, Megan. Admit it," he whispered insistently, bending so close that she could feel his warm breath on her face.

"No," Megan whimpered, closing her eyes to shut out the sight of that dark, handsome face that blotted out the world. "No."

"You do."

"No. I love Donald."

He snarled as he snatched her up in his arms and carried her over to the bed. Megan clung to him, her breath came in shallow pants; she was afraid to open her eyes because of what she might read in his face. On no account must she weaken—but she wanted to. Oh, she wanted to.

Megan felt the softness of the mattress under her back, and then the hardness of his big body as he followed her down, trapping her with his weight. His hands had burrowed under her hair to rest on either side of her skull, and Megan could feel their strength as he pressed them against her. He was kissing her, his mouth hard and hot and hungry, and she was kissing him back with helpless longing. Her hands caressed his dark head, and her body responded to his stroking hands like a kitten wanting to be rubbed.

"If you don't love me, then why are you shaking? Why does your body arch itself against mine, begging to be loved?" Megan struggled for breath, struggled for some control.

"You—you said yourself that you were a good kisser," she responded bravely, surfacing briefly from the mists she was lost in. "You're—good at other things, too."

Justin leaned back to stare down into her face. His hard mouth twisted bitterly.

"So all you want from me is stud service, is it? Then by God, you little bitch, that's all you'll get."

As he spoke his hands closed on the neck of her chemise and ripped it in two. Megan made no move to

299

stop him as he stripped off the rest of her clothes, and she made no move to cover herself as he stared at her naked body with eyes that seemed to hate her as much as they wanted her. Shivers coursed over her skin as she lay waiting for him, watching as he shed his own clothes with lightning speed. Megan wanted him so much that she could not stop the way her legs immediately opened to receive him, urging him inside her even as he joined her on the bed. He took her with a quick hard thrust, and she cried out. The feel of him inside her was incredible; it was driving her out of her mind. He held himself still, propped on his elbows, watching her as she wriggled and squirmed beneath him. Megan saw the cruelty in that look, and shut her eyes. She couldn't bear to look at him. But her traitorous body wouldn't be still. When he still refused to give her what she craved for, she began to move against him, thrusting her hips up from the bed, twisting and turning in an effort to bring relief to her throbbing body. It wasn't enough. She wanted the strength and power that he knew how to use so well.

"Oh, Justin, please," she moaned at last, unable to hold back the words any longer. "Please love me, Justin."

"You little bitch." He ground out the words in a thick, barely audible voice, and as Megan flickered a dazed look up at him she saw beads of sweat on his brow and his broad, bronzed shoulders heaved with the force of his breathing. Her nails dug into his shoulders, hurting him purposefully as she tried to urge him on. At last, with a vicious movement, he withdrew a little then plunged deep inside her again, then did it again and again and again until Megan thought she would go mad from pure bliss.

"Is this what you wanted?" he whispered tauntingly into her ear as he took her to heaven and back. "Is this what you were begging for, pretty baby?"

Megan heard the bitterness in the words, but she was too caught up in the pleasure he was giving her to more than register it vaguely. His body's effect on her was the most wonderful thing she had ever known; she had never guessed that life even offered pleasure of this depth and intensity.

At the end he was moving like a precision machine, his groans mingling with her cries as she clawed and bit and enveloped him in her body.

"Oh, Justin," she moaned as he thrust into her with all his strength, his arms tight around her, his chest hard and wet with perspiration against her breasts, his mouth swallowing the little sounds she made. Finally she dissolved in a sea of rapture. Feeling the convulsive shudders that racked her, Justin found his own bliss. He cried out her name, thrusting deep inside her one last time. Then he went rigid in her arms, shuddering himself, before he gradually went limp.

After a while he muttered harshly, "Do you still say you love Winspear?" Megan had been on the verge of sleep, but the question dragged her back to consciousness. No! her heart cried, but her mouth stubbornly said, "Yes."

He lifted himself away from her, staring down into her face with hatred in his eyes.

"By God, I'll drive him out of your mind if it's the last thing I ever do!" he muttered thickly. "If it takes me forever, I'll do it."

And he took her again. And again. And again. Until Megan didn't know whether to plead with him to stop or to never stop. Until she ended up doing both, begging him in a voice that shook with the force of the sensations he was making her feel. But never, even at the very height of her passion, did she admit that she loved him, only him, never Donald. The baby inside of her was her talisman, and she clung to that like a drowning man to a raft.

Finally sheer exhaustion made him stop. They both fell asleep almost instantly, and didn't awaken until light was pouring in through curtains which had been only partly drawn the night before.

Justin's eyes were boring down into hers as Megan came slowly awake. She blinked at him, thinking groggily that this was the first time she had ever slept beside him all night to wake up with him in the morning, and thinking too that he looked more like a brigand than ever so early in the morning. His lean jaw was obscured by a thick growth of bristly black beard, and his black hair stood up in little peaks all over his head. He was naked, as she was, and the soft black fur covering the hard muscles of his chest made her want to rub her cheek against it. He was propped up on one elbow, looking at her, and the corded muscles of his upper arm held her eyes for a long moment. Then she looked up into his face, wanting to smile, and saw the golden eyes looking down at her with a queer, half-

302

hurt, half-hungry expression that wrung her heart. Suddenly Megan knew that she had to tell him the truth, whatever the consequences. He had to know why she was so eager to marry Donald, to understand that it was love for their child rather than lack of love for him which was motivating her.

"Justin," she said softly. "You have to take me back to London today. I have to marry Donald tomorrow."

"You can forget that," he said, his eyes hardening and narrowing at the same time.

"Justin, listen to me," she said, shifting so that she was propped up against the pillows in a half-sitting position. Justin sat up beside her, his eyes never leaving her face. "I have something to tell you."

"And that is?" His voice was cold, distant. His eyes were like glaciers as they moved over her face. Megan swallowed, then jumped in with both feet.

"I-I'm with child, Justin."

Chapter 18

He was shocked. Megan watched anxiously as the blood slowly receded from his face, leaving it pasty white under its sun-bronze tan. His eyes flickered as if from a blow, then stared at her as if he was not quite certain who she was.

"Justin?" she ventured timidly as the silence stretched between them. His eyes seemed to focus on her face, then suddenly sharpened.

"Are you sure?" he asked harshly. Megan nodded without speaking. His lips compressed until a thin white line formed at the corners of his mouth.

"Is it mine?"

Megan's eyes flared at the question. Justin saw that angry flash and held up a hand as if to ward off whatever she might be getting ready to say.

"I withdraw the question. Of course it's mine."

Megan glared at him. How dare he question his child's paternity? If he had not immediately taken it back, she would have tried to suffocate him with his own pillow.

The silence between them lengthened. She could feel the tenseness in Justin's big body as he leaned back against the pillows beside her. His lack of response made her feel nervous. What was he thinking? Was he pleased with her news, or was he wishing her and the baby at Jericho? Sneaking a quick look at him, her apprehension increased. He was frowning, his thick black brows were drawn together to form an unbroken line over his eyes. His hands as they rested on the flower-sprigged coverlet were balled into fists.

Finally Megan could bear the silence no longer.

"Justin?" she said again, her voice questioning as she put out a hand to tentatively touch his arm. He pulled it away as if her touch burned him, not looking at her as he swung his legs over the side of the bed and got up. Megan's eyes ran distressfully over his tall muscular form as he walked away, his movements oddly jerky. His wide shoulders were held stiffly, and she could see the corded muscles of his back and buttocks and legs flex as he moved. Naked, he was a magnificent-looking male animal. As she watched him, Megan felt a wave of possessiveness that stunned her with its strength.

306

"Justin!" she called after him urgently as he pulled on his breeches and shirt with a single-minded economy of movement and headed for the door which opened out into the hall. He turned as she called his name, his eyes sweeping over her half-naked shape as she leaned toward him, still ensconced in his bed. His expression was remote, and its very remoteness frightened her.

"I'm going for a walk," he said evenly, his hand on the doorknob. "Get dressed."

And then he left the room, closing the door behind him with a whisper that was louder than a bang.

"Justin!" Megan cried, terror in her voice. She scrambled from the bed and ran to the door, her one thought being that she had to go after him to discover what had brought that terrible bleak look to his face. Her own nakedness stopped her. She could not possibly go running after him like this. Moving with frantic haste, she dressed, but donning the myriad garments that a lady wore before she was considered decent to go out in public, took time. Her chemise was a casualty of the night, but she could not worry about that now. Hurriedly she stepped into her pantalets, and then her petticoat, before at last she pulled her dress over her head. But again the tiny hooks at the back defeated her. She struggled with them, and had just made up her mind that she would have to go downstairs with the back of her gown unfastened when the door opened. She looked up to see Justin slowly enter the room, close the door behind him and lean back against it. His eyes were cold as they looked at her.

Megan abandoned her attempts to deal with the recalcitrant hooks and moved toward him. The coldness of his eyes stopped her while she was still some paces away.

"Justin," she faltered, her eyes searching his in vain for some sign of softening. "Please talk to me."

A tiny muscle twitched at the side of his jaw. It was the only indication he gave that he was feeling any emotion whatsoever.

"I asked you if you were all right some time ago. You said you were. Presumably that was a lie? You already knew that you were pregnant?"

The bold word for her condition made her flush; she nodded using the tiniest affirmative movement of her head.

"When were you planning to tell me?" His voice was almost conversational. Megan's eyes dropped guiltily.

"You weren't, were you? So why did you tell me now?"

Megan's eyes rose swiftly back to his. Here was her chance to explain.

"I wanted you to understand why I have to marry Donald. . . ."

At the sudden terrible flash of rage in his face she broke off, staring at him, her mouth agape. He looked homicidal.

"My God, you don't seriously suppose I'm going to permit you to go through with that, do you?" he rasped.

"Justin, please, can't you see it's the only way? Our

308

baby. . . ." She got no further. Justin came away from the door in a lunge, his hands catching her by the shoulders, his fingers pressing hurtfully into her skin as he let her feel his power. "I could kill you," he said. "I could do it so easily. If you weren't carrying my child, I think I would. My God, were you actually intending to marry another man and pass my baby off as his, with nary a word to me? You vicious, immoral little slut!"

Megan cried out at that, backing away from him as if he'd struck her. He continued to hold her inexorably, his hands tightening until his fingers were digging deep into her flesh beneath the thin silk of her gown. Megan, staring like one mesmerized into gleaming golden eyes that could have belonged to the devil himself, felt a tiny frisson of fear. He looked capable of any violence.

"You're hurting me!" she cried, her hands coming up to close over his wrists. For an instant his hands exerted their cruel pressure, and then he almost flung her away from him, in disgust.

"Get your cloak. We're leaving," he said curtly, moving toward the door.

"Justin, you don't understand!"

The look he gave her was icy with contempt.

"Oh, believe me, I understand very well," he said through his teeth. His free hand came up to close around her wrists, and hold them tightly. Megan whimpered as he deliberately crushed her delicate bones between his fingers.

"Count yourself fortunate that I don't accord the

309

same treatment to your lovely neck," he grated, and then he flung her hands away from him and turned back toward the door. "Get your cloak and come down," he instructed briefly over his shoulder. "And I warn you, if I should have to come back after you, you won't care for the consequences. I give you my word."

And with that, he left the room. Megan stared after him for some time, too stunned even to cry. Then, moving blindly, she gathered up her cloak and followed Justin down the stairs.

This time he put her into the carriage alone, while he rode alongside on a horse procured for him by the innkeeper. At this evidence that he couldn't even bear to be alone with her, Megan felt a dull ache invade her heart. She had made him despise her, and he was making no secret of his distaste. He had not vouchsafed one word to her since he had left her whimpering in his bedchamber at the inn, and to Megan's one last desperate attempt to force him to see the situation from her perspective, he replied with a glance so fierce that she fell instinctively silent. He was not far from violence, she guessed. It would take very little provocation on her part to drive him over the edge. But *I meant it for the best*, she wanted to cry as she watched his dark, brooding figure astride the big bay horse through the dusty window. Why would he not see that?

She was so miserable that she had not even questioned their destination. She did not believe that he still meant to carry her off to his house in Wales, but as it happened, she was wrong. They broke their jour-

310

ney twice; Justin took advantage of the first stop to change into clothes more suitable for riding. Megan was relieved to discover that he had brought luggage for them. Although she was offered no opportunity to change, at least it was good to know that she would not have to wear her evening dress until she could return to London.

As day lengthened, the country through which they rode became increasing hilly. The roads were rough, and she had to endure considerable jolting as the carriage pressed forward with all speed. The occasional roadsigns they passed bore foreign-sounding legends: Thedegar, Tydfil, Aberdare, Neath, and Llanelly. Despite the limited amount of traveling she had done, Megan had no difficulty in recognizing them as the names of Welsh towns. Justin was indeed still taking her to Windsmere.

They kept going until long past midnight. Luckily there was a full moon floating high above the winding dark road, or Megan very much feared that Pryor would not have been able to find the way. As it was, Justin had to ride before them with a lantern strapped to his saddle so that the coachman could see the road.

The last part of the journey was slow, and extremely bumpy. Megan had to press herself back against the seat to keep from being thrown to the floor. At last Megan heard a distant roaring and pounding which after a short while she identified as the sound of the sea.

When the carriage finally rocked to a halt, it was Justin and not Pryor who assisted her to alight. His touch was impersonal as he helped her from the carriage. Megan had at first thought that his assistance was a sign of a lessening in the terrible icy anger he had seemed to feel toward her all day. Now, looking up into his bleak face, as dark and forbidding as the windy night around them, Megan realized that she had been mistaken in thinking that his anger had eased. As Pryor had been fully occupied with preventing the horses from moving too close to the cliff edge, which was perhaps some twenty yards away, Justin had simply done what was necessary. Megan stared up at him helplessly for a moment, then turned her attention to the house.

Her first thought was that Windsmere was huge; her second, that it was dark; and her third, that it looked as much like a haunted house as any place she had ever seen. The stones of which the entire four-storied facade was composed were so deep a gray as to be almost black, and the numerous turrets looked like gnarled fingers grabbing at the moon. There was not a light in any of the windows; the driveway leading up to the ornately carved front door was overgrown with weeds. Megan began to have the awful suspicion that she, Justin and Pryor were the only human beings within miles. Had he actually brought her to a deserted house? Then, remembering his avowed purpose in abducting her, she thought that it was quite likely.

In this, she wronged Justin. He was staring up at the house with a disgusted expression on his face that had nothing to do with her or her condition.

"Go in out of the wind," he said brusquely. "I had no

312

time to inform Mrs. Cork of our coming. Clearly, she is not prepared to receive visitors."

He turned back to Pryor with a brief word advising him of what to do with the carriage and horses, then climbed up on top of the vehicle himself to remove a pair of valises while Pryor continued to stand at the horses' heads. Megan made no move to enter the house without him, and Justin threw her an irritated glance when he rejoined her, a piece of luggage in each hand.

"Come on," he said, leading the way across the last bit of weed-choked driveway to the unswept stone steps which led to the door. Then, as Megan trailed meekly behind, one hand pressed to her skirts to keep them from blowing about indecently and the other holding the hood of her cloak over her hair to shield it from the rain that had just begun to fall, he added, "Be careful where you step. You could fall." It was the first note of concern Megan had heard from him all day.

Justin pounded on the door. Even with the reverberations of his fist on the wooden panel sounding louder than the thunder that was beginning to rumble, it was some appreciable time before the door opened. Justin alternately cursed and pounded, while Megan huddled as best she could under the overhang, which provided little protection from the heavy drops of rain.

When the door opened at last, Justin did no more than glare at the frail little woman who stood clutching her black wrapper at the neck with one hand and hanging onto the barely cracked door with the other before shouldering his way inside. Megan followed him, and stood shivering in the great drafty hall which was lit only by the single candle that the small woman had apparently carried to the door with her before setting it on a nearby table so that she could work the bolt. Justin looked huge and menacing in the nearby dark hall, and Megan was not surprised to see the woman cower from him as if he were some monstrous apparition.

"For God's sake, Mrs. Cork," he snapped. "What ails you? And where are the rest of the servants? This place is as cold and dark as a damned great tomb."

"Is it you indeed, maister?" she quavered in a broad Welsh accent looking only marginally less startled than before.

"Yes, Mrs. Cork, it is," Justin said, making an obvious effort to control his impatience. "Shut the door and rouse the rest of the staff. This lady needs a warm bath, and her supper, and so do I."

"There bain't no other staff, maister," Mrs. Cork said. "They up and went back to Cardiff some three months back. I would've wrote and told you so—if I could write."

Justin cast his eyes at the ceiling. "My God, what next?" he muttered to no one in particular. To Mrs. Cork, he said, "See about heating some water for a bath for the lady, please. And bring up whatever you have in the kitchen to eat—it doesn't matter what it is. And don't bother to carry up the water—I'll come back down for it."

"Aye, maister."

314

Justin plucked an unlit candle from a tarnished candelabra set into the wall, and lit it from the single taper that appeared to be the only light in the entire house. Then, turning to Megan, he said curtly, "Come along, I'll take you upstairs."

Mrs. Cork was already moving slowing toward the back of the house, where Megan assumed the kitchen must be, when she obediently turned to follow Justin as he climbed the wide staircase.

It was impossible to see anything of the house by the light of the single candle, so Megan was left with the impression of vastness and neglect as she followed Justin for what seemed an enormous distance. At last he stopped, opened a door and motioned for her to precede him into a room. Megan did, but stopped short before she had come to the end of the pool of light cast by the candle. She did not much relish the idea of being left on her own in this mausoleum of a place.

But before she could summon the nerve to beg Justin not to leave her, he entered the room behind her, closed the door and dropped the valises he had carried in one hand on the floor. Feeling relieved, she nevertheless trailed nervously in his wake as he moved across the darkened room with a sureness born of familiarity. He seemed to have no trouble locating the huge stone fireplace that took up almost one entire wall. A many branched candelabra sat on the mantle, and Justin lit this, illuminating the room. Then he dropped to his knees before the fireplace and proceeded to lay the fire with wood from a basket on the hearth. Finally he lit the smallest chips of wood in the

315

center of the pile he had made, and blew on them until he had a fire going. Megan moved closer to the growing blaze as he got to his feet, brushing off his hands with a gesture of satisfaction.

Megan looked at him appealingly as his eyes moved over her, raking her mercilessly from her hair, which was curling wildly from the dampness, to the drenched hem of her cloak.

"Get undressed: You're wet," he ordered tersely, as he turned away from her, ignoring the unconscious plea in her eyes. "I'm going downstairs to get the water for your bath. I'll be back in a few minutes."

Megan watched him unhappily as he left the room. Clearly he was not intending to forgive her, or even try to understand why she had planned to marry Donald knowing that she was carrying his, Justin's, child. At least, he wasn't planning to forgive her yet. Maybe, after they had both had a good night's sleep, he might be in a more reasonable frame of mind.

Justin was right. She was wet. Removing her clothes gave her something to do, something to distract her mind from Justin's anger. Luckily, in her haste to go after him that morning, she had left most of the hooks at the back of her dress undone. If she hadn't, she would never have been able to manage alone. And she didn't like the idea of asking Justin to play lady's maid in his present humor.

She had undressed down to her petticoat, which was dry and which, she supposed, would have to serve as a nightgown, when she heard Justin coming back. Her ingrained modesty as much as the chill of the room prompted her to drag a musty-smelling blanket from the bed and wrap it around herself. She had just done so when he walked in without bothering to knock, steaming buckets of water in either hand.

He set the buckets by the door, threw her a cursory glance, and crossed the room to drag a hip-bath from behind a screen in the corner to rest on the rug before the fire. It was dusty with disuse and neglect, and he sloshed a little water into it and wiped it out with a rag before pouring in the rest of the water. Then, without a word, he went out again, to return with two more buckets of water which he proceeded to empty into the tub.

"Get in," he said when this operation was completed.

Megan looked at him uncertainly. "Is this your room?" she asked, not sure exactly how best to phrase the question that was burning a hole in her brain, the question of where he was sleeping that night.

Justin eyed her sardonically. "Does it matter? Get in the bath."

"I just wanted to know," Megan replied defensively, her chin lifting at his manner of addressing her. She made no move to get into the tub.

"If it matters so much to you, yes, it is," he said coolly. "As it was the room most recently in use, I assumed that it would be the most liveable."

"Oh." Megan's voice was small, but her mind was alive with speculation. If he was meaning to sleep with her, then there was the probability that she could persuade him to listen to her in the age-old fashion in

317

which women had always persuaded men.

"Get in the bath," he said again, his voice telling her that he would not brook further delays. Megan stared at him mutely, held back by a ridiculous attack of shyness. After all, the man had seen—and more than seen—every square inch of her body, she told herself, but still she could not quite bring herself to disrobe in front of those cynical eyes. But, on the other hand, she could not quite bring herself to ask him to leave, or turn his back. He would be sarcastic, she knew, and she didn't think she could bear any more nastiness tonight.

With uncanny perception, he seemed to know the cause of her reluctance, because he snorted derisively and left the room. Megan took quick advantage of his absence to shed the blanket and her petticoat and step into the tub. She sank down until the deliciously hot water covered her shoulders, and she rested with her head back against the rolled procelain lip. Her long hair trailed down over the back of the tub to touch the floor. For several blissful moments she remained like that, letting her mind drift while her cold, tired body soaked up the warmth. She was feeling delightfully drowsy when the door opened and Justin came back into the room, a covered tray in his hands.

Instinctively she sat upright, then just as swiftly sank back down again. If Justin noticed the abortive movement, he didn't say anything; he merely crossed the room to set the tray on a table by the bed, then came back to stand towering over her, looking down at her with a brooding expression on his lean face. The firelight was reflected in his eyes, making them seem to glow with a strange golden fire. His black hair fell in a disordered swathe across his forehead, and his broad shoulders and long body cast an awe-inspiring shadow back across the room. Megan looked up at him with a combination of hope and fear, and the gnawing attraction that he always inspired in her.

"Hurry up. The water's bound to be turning cold by now. You don't want to catch a chill." His concern for her well-being should have cheered her, but his words were uttered in such a detached voice that she ached inwardly. Any hope she had nurtured that he might find the sight of her, naked in her bath, softening, died a quick death.

"Did you hear me?" His voice was sharp as she stared at him without moving.

"Yes, Justin," she answered docilely, and as she began to soap her arms and legs with the small, well-worn cake of soap he had unearthed from somewhere, he left the room again. Megan washed her face and body, glad that her pregnancy had not yet brought any outward changes to her firm breasts and flat belly. She meant to make use of her body tonight in a way that would never have occurred to her before Justin had revealed its secrets.

She was scrubbing her face when he came back into the room with his arms full of bedding. As she splashed her face with water, she watched with some amazement as he systematically stripped the Queen Ann style canopied bed in the center of the room and remade it with fresh sheets and blankets. It was such a homely act, and one that she would never have expected from the mighty Earl of Weston. In fact, she would have doubted that he knew how.

He finished the bed and turned back to look at her. She was regarding him wide-eyed, her face pink and shining from the scrubbing she had just given it and the ends of her long hair trailing in the bath. In her bemusement at his adroit handling of the bed, she had completely forgotten her modesty and her lovely breasts were almost totally exposed to his gaze. The sight did not appear to afford him any pleasure. He frowned, picking up a large piece of toweling from where he had dropped it on the hearth earlier, and held it in both hands, spreading it open for her to walk into.

"Out," he ordered briefly. Megan looked at him, felt her cheeks warm, and shook her head. She could not, blatantly, flaunt her nakedness before him. It was one thing to plan, but another to follow through in cold blood.

"Out," he said again, and this time his tone brooked no disobeying. Swallowing, knowing her cheeks must be as red as apples, she stood up and stepped from the tub. Immediately he wrapped the piece of toweling around her, but in the split second before her body was decently covered she had seen his eyes moving over her flesh. But not with desire; Megan thought she read evaluation in that hooded gaze, and her flush deepened as she surmised that he was looking for some outward sign of her expectant state.

As soon as she was wrapped in the toweling, his hands fell away from her. Megan knew a moment's disappointment. She had anticipated that he would dry her. He had turned away from her to stare broodingly into the fire. Megan, watching him, saw tiny droplets of moisture clinging to the rough black waves of his hair, and to the broad shoulders of his claret-colored wool coat. He would be just as wet as she was, and yet he had taken no thought for himself. All his attention had been focused on getting her warm and dry. Despite his anger, he had lavished care on her, as he had always done. Looking at him as he stood staring into the fire, the flames painting his dark face an orangey-bronze and casting his tall, muscular body into sharp relief, she felt a wave of tenderness for him.

"Justin, you're wet," she said softly. Her hands had ceased their drying movements and she stood holding the overlapping part of the toweling together over her breasts. His eyes were hooded as he moved them down her slender body, which the damp toweling did more to emphasize than hide, before turning away again.

"I'll survive," he answered sparely, his attention once again focused on the crackling fire. "Your night gear is in the valise nearest you. Get it on, and get into bed. You can eat your supper there, then go to sleep."

"What about you?"

His eyes flickered in her direction again.

"What about me?"

"Well, aren't you going to undress, and have a bath, and come to bed? I'll let you eat part of my supper." She smiled coaxingly at him, her violet eyes alight with the love she felt for him. He stared back at her, his face stoney.

"Trying to tempt me?" Megan had no trouble detecting the hostility in his tone. She realized that drastic measures were called for if she were to win him from his anger, and pushed all thoughts of modesty aside. She wanted, needed, his love, craved the warm affection he had always shown her. If she had to shed her maidenly scruples to get it back, she would, with scarcely a qualm.

"Yes," she said softly, and moved toward him. Her hands were held out to him as she crossed to stand before him. Without her restraining grip, the toweling slipped to the floor, to be left behind. She was naked and lovely in the firelight, her long black hair rippling over her shoudlers to her hips giving her body an innocent eroticism. Justin's eyes moved over her flesh as if forced to do it; Megan rejoiced as she saw the tell-tale muscle beginning to jump in his cheek. He wanted her, and he wasn't going to be able to deny it or her.

"More punishment, Megan?" His voice was very dry. Megan stood directly before him, her eyes glowing up into his, her flesh glowing too as the firelight played with it. She had expected that he would take her in his arms, but if he would not, then she would make the first move. Without answering, her hands came up to caress his broad shoulders before sliding around his neck. Standing on tiptoe, she pressed herself against him, knowing that her behavior was shameless but wanting him too much to care.

"Hold me, Justin," she whispered. He was rigid beneath her embrace, holding himself stiffly as she

322

rubbed her body against his. Megan felt a flicker of unease as he made no move to do as she bade him. But then, finally, his arms came up, and she let out her breath on a little sigh. It was going to be all right.

But instead of embracing her, his hands were going behind his head to close about her wrists, holding them in a vise as he pulled them down. He held them captive against his chest, his expression bitter as he stared down at her while their locked hands forced a slight space between their bodies.

"Justin," Megan protested piteously. She struggled to free her hands so that she could slide them back around his neck. He refused to release them, holding them with negligent strength against his chest.

"You really hate me, don't you?" he asked almost conversationally. Only the leaping flames in his eyes told her that he was not as cool and in control as he sounded. "Well, my girl, if you think that I'm going to let you put me through a hundred kinds of hell with your little tricks, you can think again."

"Justin, no!" she cried frantically as he released her hands and turned on his heel, striding from the room. He was gone before she could tell him how wrong he was. She didn't hate him, how could he think it? She loved him, and wanted him. Maybe she had been wrong to plan to marry Donald while she was carrying Justin's child, but what other solution was there? Even now, loving Justin as she did, if Donald had appeared before her with a ring and a preacher she would have wed him. For her child. Justin was not thinking clearly, or he would realize that his child deserved better than to go through life bearing the stigma of bastard, just as she deserved better than to spend the rest of her days labeled whore. But if only she herself had been involved, she would have stayed with Justin happily, whether the world called her whore or no. Tomorrow she would have to spell her feelings out in words of one syllable, so that he would understand. Not that she cherished many illusions that he would let her return to Donald. She knew enough about the way his mind worked to realize that he considered her, and the child she carried, as his possessions. He would never willingly let them go. But if she could not persuade him to let her do what was best for their child, at least she could make him understand. She could not bear for him to go on thinking that she was bent on marrying Donald because she hated him, or because she wanted to punish him. She was simply thinking of the welfare of the child. Tomorrow she would tell him all this, she promised herself as she pulled on her nightdress and climbed forlornly into the wide bed. Tomorrow she would make him understand.

But tomorrow he was gone.

Chapter 19

Days turned into weeks, and weeks turned into months, and still Justin did not return to Windsmere. By the end of April, when she was nearly seven months along, Megan's condition had grown very obvious. She bore her embarrassment as well as she could, thankful that Windsmere was so remote that she saw no one save the servants. Justin had left a letter instructing her to consider herself the mistress of Windsmere, and see to the hiring of servants and refurbishment of the household as she thought best. This kept her days occupied, and if at night her thoughts lingered achingly on Justin and an occasional bout of tears soaked her pillow, no one knew it save herself.

Two days after Justin had left, while Megan was still debating the wisdom of attempting to return to London despite his command that she stay at Windsmere for the the duration of her confinement (she might actually have left, except that she had a sneaking suspicion that Justin had commissioned Pryor, who had remained behind, to forcibly restrain her from such an act if necessary.), an enormous war horse of a woman had appeared at the door, announcing that she had come to stay. She introduced herself as Janet Wibberley, said that she had been Justin's old nurse, and said too that he had come himself to find her and dispatch her to look after Megan and the coming child. Megan was slightly comforted by this evidence of Justin's concern for her well-being, but then she reflected that he was probably doing it more to insure his child's safe arrival than for her benefit, so the brief flare of warmth for him faded.

At first she did not know quite what to make of Janet, as the woman insisted on being called. She was nearly as tall and broad as Justin, with iron-gray hair that she wore in a severe bun at her nape, and dressed day in and day out in shapeless black dresses that looked like the very ultimate in mourning. The woman bullied her unmercifully, making her eat when she didn't feel like eating and rest when she didn't feel like resting, but Megan soon discovered that her heart was as kind as her manner was brusque, and she had quite a considerable knowledge of what was best for expectant females. She instituted a program of walks for Megan which she insisted be strictly adhered to regardless of the weather or the girl's inclinations, telling her firmly that she would be glad of her strengthened muscles when it came time for her lying-in. She was also invaluable when it came to managing the household. Newly hired servants who might have been lax in their duties under Megan's inexperienced eye needed only a stern look from Janet to fall to work with a will.

By the time a month had passed, Megan had come to utterly rely on Janet, and had grown very fond of her. The woman gradually came to take the place of the mother she could barely remember. She never said anything to indicate that she was aware of any disgrace connected with the coming child, and indeed behaved as if Megan was Justin's wife and the baby had been conceived in all honor. Megan was grateful for this, and grateful too that Janet made the necessary trips to the nearby town of Tenby. She didn't think she could have borne being seen in public in such a state.

Justin had said in his letter that she was to do what she would with the house, and Megan took him at his word. After the place was thoroughly cleaned, she set about ordering new curtains and carpets, overseeing the re-painting of rooms and the re-arranging of furniture. Windsmere would never be a cozy family home, but at the end of three months time, it had a stately beauty that Megan grew to love. Every room bore a touch of her personality, and Megan considered the house her home. She refused to allow her thoughts to wonder if Justin would permit her to stay there after the birth of the child. It was, after all, one of his family estates and at some point in the future it was bound to prove an embarrassment to him to have his mistress and illegitimate child installed therein. She supposed, when she allowed herself to think about it, that he would in time buy a small house near London for her and the baby. Or he might send her abroad, as she had some hazy idea that this was a common solution among men of Justin's wealth and position for removing girls they had ruined. If only he would permit her to keep Janet, she would fall in with his wishes without demur. And, of course, she must be allowed to keep the baby, but she had no real fear that Justin would try to take it from her. Despite the disgust he had shown toward her, he was not a monster, and only a monster would try to separate mother and child. Besides, what would he do with it? The only thing that worried her was that he might confess the whole to Alicia, and somehow browbeat or persuade her into taking the child and passing it off as their own. Just picturing cold, haughty Alicia mothering her child was enough to make Megan ill with fear, but she told herself that the possibility was so remote as to be unworthy of a second's consideration. Justin would not do such a thing to her, and if her tried, she would flee to the ends of the earth to protect her baby.

She loved this small person inside her more with each day that passed. At night she would wrap herself around her womb, cradling the baby within, drawing comfort from its presence. From a horror and a disgrace, it had become the hub of her life. Justin had left her, but he had given her this child to take his place. She loved it with all the fierce emotion she would have showered on him if he had let her, and with a special sweet caring that was the child's alone. In all her life, she had never had anyone that was utterly hers to love. This baby was flesh of her flesh, bone of her bone, sheltered and nourished by her body. She would protect and cherish it with all her strength, and give her life for it if necessary.

The only communication she had from Justin was at Christmas, which she celebrated quietly with Janet and the servants. She had more than half expected Justin to come down from London, where she understood from Janet he had returned, but he did not. Even to herself she would not admit the depth of her disappointment, or her hurt when she opened the smallish square box he had sent to find that the lovely amethyst and diamond pendant was accompanied only by his engraved card. Not a word, not even a signature personalized the gift. After that one look, Megan had locked the pendant in a drawer, and did her best to never think of the lovely jewel.

By his absence she came to believe that he had finished with her. He had clearly not forgiven her for planning to marry Donald whose face she could barely recall, and pass off their child as the issue of that marriage. At the time Megan had thought that it was the only possible solution, but now she was honestly glad that Justin had prevented it. In fact as long as she remained retired from the world, there was no one to shame her. What would happen after her child was born, after he or she became old enough to ask questions, she did not know. For now, she could only live one day at a time.

The first of May came and went, and Megan was now so big that she had difficulty getting out of over-stuffed chairs. Her slender build and small stature made her bulging belly glaringly obvious even beneath the lightweight smock-like dresses that Janet had made for her. On this particular day, as she took her accustomed walk along the cliffs, she was dressed in one of her favorites: a deep blue dimity with a high, ruffled neck and no waist. The elbow length sleeves and flowing skirt were edged in deep flounces. Her hair was arranged in a cool chignon on the top of her head, but the brisk breeze which blew endlessly from the sea had teased myriad curling tendrils loose to frame her face. Her feet, in accordance with Janet's suggestion, were clad in simple flat-heeled sandals that minimized the swelling that her hands and feet had become prone to as her pregnancy advanced.

Windsmere was situated high above Carmarthen Bay, and Megan never tired of watching the ever-changing moods of the water far below. Today the sea was as blue as her dress, with rolling waves wearing peaked white caps ceaselessly throwing themselves at the rocky shore. Enormous gray rocks edged the tiny beach like giant sharks' teeth, but today their somber warning was softened and beautified by the hundreds of bit of crystal imbedded in their steep slopes that sparkled like dewdrops in the sun. Grass grown soft

330

and green with spring carpeted the ground to the very edge of the cliffs, and it was on this that Megan walked, a faint smile on her face as she watched a fishing boat far out to sea.

The unmistakable sound of approaching carriage wheels made her turn, and shade her eyes with her hand. It was the only house along this road, and there was no where else in the vicinity to which anyone could conceivably travel. Apparently her privacy was at an end, and she put an instinctively protective hand over her rounded stomach as she contemplated facing strangers' hostile or pitying stares.

There were two vehicles, and as they bowled toward the house Megan had no trouble recognizing either of them. The arms depicted on the carriage door told her that she had not made a mistake, but she didn't really need to see the painted shield with its sword and sleeping tiger to identify the vehicles. Justin's tall figure, as he tooled the curricle toward the house, was unmistakable. Her eyes fastened on him with hungry avidity. She could no more have stopped looking at him than she could have vanished on the spot.

He didn't see her, she surmised as he drew his horses to a halt in front of the door and leapt down, throwing the reins carelessly to his small, wiry tiger who had been riding up behind him and had run around to the horses heads as soon as they stopped. As the second vehicle, the traveling carriage lumbered up behind the curricle, it occured to Megan to wonder who he had brought with him. Not, surely not, Alicia?

Her mind was set at rest on this point as two men

climbed out of the carriage. From this distance, Megan couldn't be sure, but she thought one of them might be Charles. She could not hazard a guess as to the identity of the other.

At the thought of what Charles and the other man must think of her condition, Megan nearly groaned aloud. She knew that Justin must have apprised them of the state in which they would find her. He was not so insensitive as to expose her and them to the horrified embarrassment that her pregnancy would invoke, but still she dreaded having to meet them, to talk to them and watch them pretending that everything was as it should be. She was a fallen woman, no longer acceptable in polite company; she knew it, and they knew it.

She could not go back just yet, but continued her walk along the cliffs. Her arms curved in an instinctive, unconscious gesture around her belly.

Justin came after her, as she had half hoped and half dreaded he would. She had turned back toward the house, but was still some distance away, when she saw him walking toward her. His long legs had been eating up the distance between them, but as he saw her eyes on him his stride slowed. His hands were jammed firmly in the pockets of his biscuit-colored pantaloons as he approached with measured steps.

Megan's feet faltered and stopped as he drew near. Blindly she turned to stare out to sea. From the corner of her eye she could see his eyes run swiftly over her burgeoning figure. Some nameless emotion seemed to flicker through him as he took in her swollen belly, but

332

it was gone before she could identify it.

"Megan." His voice sounded oddly husky.

"Hello, Justin." She risked a quick look at him, and as she met his eyes, her cheeks crimsoned. Inwardly, she cursed the betraying color, but there was nothing she could do about it.

"Janet tells me that you've been well."

"Yes."

"You look well."

"Thank you." This stilted conversation, which could have been exchanged between two strangers, made her want to scream. She gritted her teeth, tilted her chin in the old defiant gesture, and turned to face him. Her eyes glinted proudly.

"Why have you come, Justin?" she asked directly. His mouth twisted as he returned her stare steadily.

"Did you think I wouldn't?"

"I hadn't thought about it at all," she replied with less than perfect truth. Not for anything would she grovel at his feet, giving him the satisfaction of knowing how many nights she had been unable to sleep for thinking about him, or how many lonely tears had wet her pillow. His eyes narrowed slightly at her response, and the bitter twist of his mouth deepened.

"I have a message for you. From Donald." His tone bit.

"Yes?"

"He said to tell you that he'll be waiting. Of course, he still imagines that you're a sweet little virgin devotedly nursing your dying aunt. No doubt, if he were to learn the truth, he'd be very quick to change his tune."

Megan refused to let him see that the words which were intended to hurt had been right on target.

"Is that what you came to tell me, Justin?" Her voice was cool. Megan was proud of her unfaltering poise.

Justin hesitated a moment before replying. Megan was too preoccupied with maintaining her facade of calm unconcern to take note of his hands as they balled into fists in his pocket.

"No," he said finally. "I came to marry you."

At this statement Megan felt her breathing stop. She stared at him dumbfounded, afraid to believe her own ears. Justin threw her a quick, hooded look, then turned himself to stare out to sea.

"I was able to get an annulment," he said as though she had asked him a question. "The grounds were lack of progeny and denial of conjugal rights, I believe. My lawyers handled it. Alicia is understandably upset, but the ton has rallied to her side, and she is playing to the hilt the part of the woman wronged. It is my guess that she is having the time of her life painting me as a depraved monster whose vicious assaults left her unable to face the thought of bearing children and all that it necessarily implies. And I made her a handsome financial settlement. She will never want for anything."

Megan felt a pang of pity for Lady Alicia. In her place, Megan knew that her heart would be broken.

"Poor woman," she murmured. Justin threw her another of those hooded looks.

"Don't waste your pity on Alicia," he said shortly.

334

"Believe me, beneath all her posturing she is as glad to be rid of me as I am to be rid of her. She would rather lose my title than be forced to share my bed again."

Megan turned to look at him. "Is that how you got her to agree?" she asked faintly. Justin nodded curtly. "Yes."

Megan said nothing for a long moment, inwardly shuddering at his ruthlessness. She had no doubt that he had terrified Lady Alicia until she was willing to agree to do anything.

"I brought a priest with me, and Charles procured a special license. We can be married this afternoon."

He turned to look at her. Megan stared back at him silently, her eyes enormous in her small face. She had dreamed of marrying Justin for months, and had longed for this fairy-tale ending to their story. But when she had pictured marrying Justin, it was not to this man, a hard, cold stranger, who didn't love her.

"Why are you doing this, Justin?" Her voice was expressionless as she battled with hope. Even now, if he would say just one word of love, she would fall into his arms. His eyes flickered down her body and back to her face.

"I should think that is obvious."

The little flutter of hope died. "Yes," she said, and moved past him, walking steadily in the direction of the house. After a moment Justin fell into step beside her.

"I assume that means you'll marry me?"

Megan flashed him a brittle smile. "Why not? At

335

this point, any husband is better than none, and you do have the added advantage of being my baby's father."

He didn't like that, she could see. As she saw his almost imperceptible flinch, she felt fiercely glad. His cold acceptance of his responsibilities had cut her to the quick. Even if his pride was all she had hurt, she needed to watch him suffer.

Megan prepared for her wedding like a sleepwalker. Janet met them at the door as they returned from their walk, showing as much emotion as Megan had ever seen her reveal. But the pleased excitement died out of her eyes as she observed the strained silence between the two of them. Megan's face was cool and remote, while Justin's was set in harsh lines. This wedding was clearly not the joyous occasion Janet had anticipated, and as she whisked Megan up the stairs to change her dress, she ached for what she knew the girl must be feeling beneath the hard shell of ice that seemed to encase her.

"What will you wear, dear?" Janet asked when they were alone in Megan's room. The girl needed bucking up, not mollycoddling; if this wedding was not what she would have chosen, and Janet puzzled at that, because she would have wagered a month's pay that Megan was in love with the Earl, it was still vitally necessary. Megan should be grateful that the Earl was an honorable man and willing to stand by her at such a time. Many, nay most, in his position, with all he stood to lose, would not.

"You choose, Janet," Megan said with an indifference that was not assumed. In truth, she thought one of Janet's black dresses would have been most symbolic of the way she was feeling.

Janet did not cluck and fuss over her, as many another would have done, and Megan was greatful for the phlegmatic way she went about the business of helping her to dress. The gown she chose had of necessity to be waistless, but it was very pretty, a lavendar organza strewn with posies of pristine white flowers. The neckline was square and just high enough to be demure, while the sleeves were short and puffed. A simple white ribbon was tied beneath her breasts, and its ends fell down over her rounded belly in a charmingly frivolous style. Janet threaded another white ribbon through the tumble of curls on the top of her head, and her toilette was complete.

"The pendant my lord sent you for Christmas would be a nice finishing touch," Janet suggested in a neutral tone as Megan surveyed her reflection in the dressing table mirror.

"No!" Megan said fiercely, her eyes flashing with the first sign of emotion that she had shown since agreeing to marry Justin. Janet's eyes flickered speculatively at her vehemence, but she wisely forebore to push the point. If Megan chose to go to her wedding unadorned by jewels, it was strictly her concern.

As a final touch, before the two women went downstairs to join the gentleman waiting in the parlor, Janet thrust a white prayer book into Megan's hands.

"Instead of flowers," she said stolidly. Megan tried not to wince at the reminder that Justin had not cared

337

enough about this wedding to provide her with the traditional bouquet.

Megan hesitated outside the parlor door, suddenly embarrassed at the thought of facing Charles and a priest with her protruding belly unmistakeable proof of her depravity, but Janet would stand no nonsense. With a brief hummph, she pushed open the door, and Megan was left with no choice but to enter. She was thankful for Janet's stalwart presence behind her as the eyes of all three men turned toward her.

She could not bring herself to look at Justin, and so missed the sudden flare in his eyes as he caught sight of her. She focused on the priest. Her cheeks flushed hotly as he moved forward to greet her, his eyes tactfully fixed on her face instead of her waist. Megan held her head high, although it cost her an effort. But she refused to lower her eyes. Her pride wouldn't let her.

"My dear." He took her hand, which she had automatically extended, and she saw that his eyes were not censorious, but kind. She smiled at him, a small tremulous smile, and he pressed her hand reassuringly before releasing it.

"This is Reverend Peake, Megan." Justin was beside her, although she stubbornly refused to look at him. Charles was on her other side, and she turned to him with a feeling of inevitability. Here was a man who had known her from childhood, who had really been more of a father-figure to her than Justin despite Justin's role as her guardian. He had seen her as a little girl in pigtails and short skirts, as a schoolroom miss with a big bow in her hair and ink-stained fingers, as a budding young lady—and now like this. Her humiliation was complete as she looked into his face. It was only partially eased as she saw that his eyes, like the priest's, were kind.

"You're looking very lovely, Megan," Charles said gently, leaning over to kiss her cheek.

"Thank you." Megan had been afraid that she might not be able to speak around the lump in her throat, but her voice sounded amazingly clear. As Charles straightened away from her, Justin made a sudden impatient movement beside her, and Megan looked at him at last.

He was dressed in the same dark blue superfine coat and biscuit colored pantaloons that he had been wearing earlier, but he was freshly shaved, and he had run a brush through his unruly hair. He was looking so handsome that he stole her breath, and Megan could not suppress the little pang of pure agony that shot through her as she met the familiar tawny gold of his eyes. If only he loved her.

"If you're ready, Reverend, I'd like to get on with it." He broke eye contact first, speaking to Reverend Peake with a respect that did little to camoflage his abruptness.

"Certainly, certainly," the priest said, moving to stand before the window. "If you'll come over here, my children."

The actual ceremony passed in a blur for Megan. All she could remember of it was the coolness of her own voice as she made the traditional promises to Justin, and his own clipped responses. There was a vivid mo-

339

ment of clarity when Justin took her hand and slid an exquisite gold and diamond band on her finger. Megan felt the warmth and strength of his hand holding hers, and the cold slide of the metal on her finger as he staked permanent possession of her, all the way through to her soul. Then Reverend Peake pronounced them man and wife, and it was over. Justin didn't even kiss her.

Megan pleaded a headache and fled upstairs to her room immediately after the ceremony. Justin made no demur at her retreat, and from the bleakness of his face Megan guessed that he, too, would have preferred to be alone. But hospitality dictated that he offer his guests a drink, and he did so with punctilious courtesy.

Janet came upstairs to see if she needed anything, but Megan pretended to be resting, and she went away again. But in truth, Megan was far too keyed up to even sit still. She paced restlessly around her room, turning her thoughts over and over again to the events of the afternoon. She was Justin's wife now, Countess of Weston. Her child would be his legal heir. Had ever anyone's circumstances changed so much in the course of a few hours? This morning she had been a social outcast, virtually certain to be publicly shunned if she were foolish enough to show herself outside the confines of Windsmere. Now, by the simple yet profound act of making her his wife, Justin had restored her respectability. More, he had elevated her to the highest echelon of society by the mere bestowal of his name on her. No one would dare ostracize the

Countess of Weston. Oh, they might talk behind her back, and she might meet with a few cold shoulders from the highest sticklers amongst the ladies, but for the most part people would be prepared to turn a blind eye to what had occurred before the wedding. The golden circlet on her finger had set all to rights, and Megan knew that she should be delirious with joy over this story-book ending. Instead she felt lonelier and more miserable than she ever had before in her life.

Watching the sun as it began its colorful descent behind the western horizon, Megan suddenly knew that she had to get out of the house. She would go for a short walk, and maybe by the time she returned she would have things sorted out in her head. There was no escaping Justin now, however much he might despise her, however much his open contempt might hurt. She and her child belonged to him as surely as if he had purchased them in a slave market.

She walked along the cliffs, instinctively going in the opposite direction to the one she had taken earlier. The sun was going down in a pinwheel of pinks and oranges, and the sea reflected the brilliant colors, throwing them back at the sky. Megan stopped walking and concentrated on watching the ever-changing display, thinking that if she focused all her energy on the sunset she would not have to think or feel.

She was still standing rooted to the top of the cliff, staring out to sea when Justin found her. It had grown quite dark, and the cooling breeze was gradually transformed into a stiff wind. Megan had unconsciously wrapped her arms around herself for warmth; she was so lost in her thoughts that she was not even aware of Justin's presence until he dropped his coat over her shoulders.

"You shouldn't be out here; you'll catch a chill." His voice was rough; his hands returned to his sides almost as soon as the coat's bulk touched her flesh.

Megan said nothing. Her hands reached up to hold his coat closer as she turned back in the direction of the house. She could see it, a dense black shape in the gathering twilight made small by distance She had not realized that she had walked so far. As she moved, Justin fell into step beside her. It was some time before he spoke.

"We have to talk," he said harshly. Megan looked at him.

"Talk," she said. He threw her a glance full of dislike, and jammed his fists into his pantaloon pockets.

"I want you to know that you don't have to worry about taking up your duties as my wife. I'm returning to London tomorrow."

"I see," she said politely. Inwardly she felt relieved. Maybe if he left, this horrible aching pain would go with him.

"You may draw upon my funds through the bank in Tenby. I'll have Charles send them written authorization. And, of course, any bills you may incur should be sent to me in London. Buy whatever you like for yourself and the baby. Money is no object."

"Thank you. You're being very kind."

Her politeness seemed to anger him. She saw his

342

jaw clench as if to bite back whatever he would have said, and his nostrils flared in a way she had learned meant that he was on the verge of losing his temper.

"I suppose next you're going to thank me for marrying you." His tone was bitter. Megan thought that over for a second.

"I should, shouldn't I? You've gone to a great deal of trouble to make me respectable again. But you really needn't have done it, you know. If you hadn't interfered."

"By God, if you mention Winspear's name to me I won't be responsible," he broke in fiercely, his hands shooting out of his pockets to grasp her shoulders through the thickness of his coat. Megan stared up at him, feeling strangely triumphant. Although her words had not been premeditated, she was pleased that they had goaded him into such a response.

"Donald loved me," she said softly, deliberately.

"If I'd had any sense, I would have let the fool have you," he muttered thickly. Then he added, his voice louder, "And if you hadn't been carrying my baby, I would have. After I got tired of you in bed, of course."

Megan's face whitened, and her eyes blazed. She had known that the child was his sole reason for marrying her, but to have him tell her so brutally hurt nevertheless. And she hated him for hurting her.

"You swine," she choked furiously, her eyes shooting venom at him. "At least Donald would have waited until we were decently wed before he took me to bed. You seduced an innocent schoolgirl whom you hadn't the faintest notion in the world of marrying.

343

Donald may be a fool, but believe me when I say that I'd rather be married to a fool than a blackguard like you!"

Before the words were entirely out of her mouth he drew back his hand and slapped her. Megan felt the sting of his palm against her cheek and gasped. Immediately her hand flew to cradle her abused cheek, and tears welled to fill her eyes. She stared at him, barely able to believe that he had struck her. He looked as stunned as she felt.

"I see now why Lady Alicia was so eager to be rid of you," she spat, jerking herself free of his hands. "Did you beat her, too?"

"Megan!" He called after her, sounding anguished, but Megan was already running away from him along the cliffs. She was nearly blinded by tears, and her gait was clumsy, weighted down as she was with the child. She knew he was coming after her, and that he would certainly catch her. Sobbing, she refused to stop, refused to admit the inevitability of defeat.

"Megan!" He was closer, and she redoubled her efforts at escape, running with her head down while her stomach heaved and her breath came in sobbing pants. For the sake of the child, she knew she should stop, but she couldn't seem to do it. She wanted to run and run forever.

She stepped on a rock, invisible in the darkness, and her foot twisted. Megan felt herself falling, braced herself for the jarring encounter with the ground—then panic—it didn't come. She was pitching sideways over the edge of the cliff.

The last things she heard were Justin's frantic shouts, and the sound of her own scream.

Chapter 20

Pain dragged her back from the darkness she was lost in. She screamed as something tore at her belly, then screamed again.

"My God, send for a doctor!" A ragged voice bellowed near her ear, and she recognized Justin's frenzied tones. She wanted to call his name, to beg him to help her, but that clawing agony came again and she could only scream helplessly.

"Megan!" He sounded like he was going out of his mind. Megan could feel the strength of his arms around her, the heat of his chest against her side, and realized that he was carrying her. Her lashes fluttered up for a moment, and she saw that he was bounding up the long flight of stairs that led to Windsmere's second floor. He was taking the steps two at a time, cradling her convulsing body against him. With her head hanging limply over his arm, the world was a bouncing kaleidoscope of shapes and motion. She shut her eyes again, moaning.

"Dear lord, what happened?" The voice was Janet's.

"She fell about six feet over the cliff; thank God there was a ledge to catch her. When I brought her up she was unconscious, then she started screaming. You heard her. I think she's losing the baby, and God knows what else is wrong with her." He was moving as he threw the words at Janet, and Megan heard the sound of doors opening. Then she was being lowered to a bed. Justin's arms slid away from her, and she wanted to catch at him, to beg him not to leave her. But the thing was at her belly again, ripping into it. She screamed, clutching the precious burden that she carried. Something was trying to steal her baby, to wrest it from her body and carry it off where she would never see it, never hold it.

"No!" she screamed, drawing her knees up to her chest and wrapping her arms over her belly as if to hold the child inside her. "No, no, no!"

"Megan!" She had never heard such raw emotion in anyone's voice as she heard now in Justin's. She wanted to respond to it, but she couldn't. The clawing hands were reaching again for her baby.

"Can't you do something for her?" At Megan's

scream Justin rounded on Janet. She was staring with horrified eyes down at the writhing body of the girl on the bed, but at Justin's expression of frantic helplessness she quickly pulled herself together.

"Get out of the way, my lord. The baby's coming," she said authoritatively, and bent over Megan. Her hands were steady as she pressed them against the girl's heaving belly.

"She needs a doctor." Justin had never felt so frightened in his life. Megan and their child might be dying before his eyes, and there was nothing he could do to help them. And he had caused it.

"Mr. Stanton has gone for one. Is she—may I be of help?" Reverend Peake's soft, compassionate voice came from the doorway. Justin turned to stare at him, barely registering the group of servants that stood gaping behind his black-robed form. Slowly he realized that the priest was asking if he should administer the rites for the dying.

"No!" he roared, glaring at the man. His expression was demonic. The gathered servants backed a pace as one. Reverend Peake bowed slightly, and took himself off downstairs.

"I'll need two of you girls to help me. The rest of you get back to your duties. Flora, put some water on to boil and bring it up to me the minute it does so. Ann, bring clean sheets, towels, whatever you can find. Immediately." Janet's brusque orders dispersed the servants at once. She bent again over Megan's body, which had gone ominously limp. Quickly she checked the girl's pulse, and then began to unbutton her dress.

Justin stood watching at her side, his fists clenching impotently, his face pale.

"What can I do?" he asked. Janet looked at him, her eyes level.

"Nothing, my lord," she said, her tone firm despite the sympathy she felt for him. "This is no place for a gentleman. It would be best if you went downstairs. There is nothing you can do but wait."

Justin stared at his old nursemaid. "I'm not leaving her," he said. Janet looked into his eyes for a long moment, then nodded curtly.

"Then stay out of the way," she said. The words had no sooner left her mouth than Megan started to scream again.

All through the night and on into the next day Megan labored to bring her child into the world. The doctor arrived at last, dragged from his bed by Charles, and could only shake his head at the condition of his patient. He, too, tried to banish Justin from the room, but Justin refused to be dislodged. Megan was his wife, and he was staying. No one short of God himself could wrest him from her side.

It was toward morning of the second day. Megan's screams had been growing progressively weaker until they were little more than rasping moans. Her face was ashen, drained of every vestige of blood as it tossed and turned on the pillow. Her nightdress was wringing wet with sweat, and her hair was soaking, too, as it lay in tangled knots against the bed linen. She lay on her back, with her knees drawn up; her body was bare to the waist. Justin sat on one corner of the bed near her head, rhythmically bathing her face with a cool, wet cloth. He had not eaten or slept, or left the room for any except the most urgent of nature's necessities, since he had carried her upstairs. Janet and Dr. Lampeter worked frantically over Megan's exhausted body. Finally the doctor shook his head, and looked up.

"I'm very sorry, my lord," he said heavily. Justin looked up at him in sharp fear; his hand froze in the act of dipping the cloth back into the basin of water. If he had been white before, in that instant he looked like a living corpse.

"It is up to you," the doctor continued in the same tone. "I cannot save them both."

Justin stared at him blankly. Dr. Lampeter's eyes had profound sympathy in their depths.

"Your wife or your child, my lord," the doctor spelled out quietly. "Which is it to be?"

Justin felt as if a large hand was crushing his heart. He shut his eyes briefly, picturing the son he had not known he loved until that moment.

"Save my wife," he said bleakly. Then, his movements jerky, he got up from the bed and crossed to the window, staring blindly out into the night while the doctor did his work.

An hour later it was all over. The child was a boy, the son Justin had wanted for years without knowing that he did so. He was perfectly formed despite the fact that he was but eight months. The umbilical cord was wrapped tightly around his neck, which had suffocated him as he passed down the birth canal. If Justin has chosen to save his son at the expense of Megan's life, the doctor would have had to cut the child from her belly, and Megan, exhausted by the long labor and loss of blood, would almost surely have died.

Megan had not regained consciousness by the time the child was buried early the next morning. Justin, haggard from lack of sleep and sorrow, dressed in sober black, stood with his head bowed as the tiny body of his son was lowered into a small grave dug during the previous afternoon. Charles stood a little to one side and behind him as Reverend Peake conducted the brief service. Except for the servants, who stood at a respectful distance, he was the only other mourner. Janet had elected to remain at Megan's bedside. Megan was still not out of danger, and someone stayed with her constantly.

Megan would have to be told when she awoke, and he would have to be the one to do it. The thought haunted Justin all through that afternoon and into the night. By losing control that evening when he had slapped Megan's face, he had killed his son as surely as if he had shot him. Justin knew it, and the grief and guilt he felt were not helped by the fact that only he and Megan knew precisely what had transpired before she had fallen over the cliff. If she hadn't hated him before, she would hate him as soon as she found out about the child, Justin knew. He dreaded telling her, and yet it was his responsibility. He could not, would not, shirk it.

He sat by her bedside all night, alone, his face bleak and his eyes brooding. Janet had left him only reluctantly, alarmed by his looks after the small funeral. She, who had known him for years, had wiped his infrequent tears in the nursery and done her best to curb his boyish excesses, had never seen him look so sad and defeated. Her heart went out to him, and to the pale, still girl in the bed. Janet alone, of all the household, had known how much Megan's baby had come to mean to her. She knew the girl would be devastated by her loss.

Dawn was painting the sky a pale rosy pink when Megan's eyes opened at last. Justin had not slept, and he was seated in a chair near the bed, staring out past the open draperies at the beautiful promise of the sunrise. He looked exhausted and sick to death. Looking at his dark profile, silhouetted against the growing light outside the window, Megan had a horrible premonition. Only a tragedy would make him look like that.

"Justin," she whispered, barely getting his name out past lips that were dry and cracked. She was half afraid and half hoping that he wouldn't hear her, but he turned to look at her instantly. As he saw her eyes wide upon him he got slowly to his feet, and came to stand beside the bed, his movements those of an old, old man. With the lighted window behind him, he was a tall, dark shape looking down at her. Megan's eyes fastened with painful intensity on the deep shadows which obscured his face.

"My baby. . . ?" The question was a mere breath of sound. If he answered as she somehow knew he was going to, she wasn't going to be able to stand it.

There was a pause that seemed to stretch for years, but could in reality have lasted for only a couple of heartbeats.

"We lost him." Justin knew of no other, more tactful way to say it. In truth, there was no way that would lessen the pain that he knew the loss of their child must inflict upon her. He watched her pale face turn even whiter, watched the beautiful violet eyes widen as if from a blow, and instinctively reached down to cradle her in his arms. To his everlasting agony, she turned her head away. His hands dropped to his sides without touching her.

"Please go away," she said in a voice as cold as stone. Justin had known how she would feel toward him, and yet even that pre-knowledge had not prepared him for the shaft of raw pain that went through him at her words.

He wanted to plead with her, to beg her forgiveness, to cry like a child on her bosom, but he did none of these things. Instead, his heart breaking, he turned silently on his heel and left the room, sending Janet up to take his place.

Megan's grief was like a fog around her, preventing her from seeing beyond its dense boundaries. Nothing and no one had any reality for her over the next few weeks except her loss. She felt as if a part of herself had died, and she mourned for it as she had never dreamed she could mourn for anything. She knew that Justin was suffering, and yet she couldn't reach out to him, comforting him and drawing comfort from him in turn. It took every ounce of her strength to exist from day to day.

It was Janet who got her out of bed at last, and bullied her into resuming her daily walks outside. Instinctively she avoided the cliffs where she had loved to walk before, instead she followed the road that led toward town for some little distance before turning back. Once she went as far as the small graveyard, and stood for a long time looking down at the mound with its tiny stone lamb that marked the resting place of her son. She didn't cry, and she didn't go there again.

Janet accompanied her on all these expeditions, and with the part of her mind that still concerned itself with mundane activities, Megan realized that she was never left alone except at night. And then either Janet or one of the maids would sleep in the adjoining sitting room, with the door ajar in case she should need something.

It was June, and the weather was beautiful. Part of Megan wildly resented the picture-perfect days that dawned with such vitality while her child lay in a cold, dark grave. She could not cry for the loss of her son, but she could rage against the fate that had taken him. And this she did, silently, bitterly, every hour of every day.

Justin remained at Windsmere. This would have surprised Megan if she had been capable of being surprised by anything. As it was, he was nothing more or less to her than a terrible reminder of her grief. She avoided him, and if he looked haggard and ill the few times she chanced to see him, she didn't notice it. There was no room in her heart for anything but pain.

Charles went away briefly, and then returned to Windsmere. Megan noticed neither his coming or going. She never saw him. All her meals were taken on a tray in her room, and except for her daily walk she kept strictly within the confines of her suite.

It was late one night more than five weeks after the loss of the baby that Megan awoke to lie staring up at the canopy above her bed for what seemed like hours. She had not been sleeping well, and she supposed glumly that this was going to be another one of those nights when she would lie awake until it was time to get up. Then, for the first time in a long while, it occurred to her that she didn't have to just passively lie there. She could get up, move about the room, even go outside for a walk if she was careful not to waken Janet in the sitting room. For a while she turned the possibilites over in her mind, marveling at the notion that she actually had an alternative to lying sleepless, and then she made the ultimate effort and got up. Moving stealthily, she retrieved her wrapper from the foot of the bed and pulled it on, tying the sash loosely around her waist which was nearly as slim as it had been before. The very act of belting her waist brought her lost baby poignantly to the forefront of her mind, and for a moment Megan hesitated, on the verge of going back to bed. She did not really feel up to a midnight walk, after all. And then her natural strength asserted itself. She would go for a walk. It was a small thing, but a necessary step in recovering from her grief.

She crept downstairs, not wanting to wake anyone and have to suffer through their inevitable questions, and moved silently toward the front door. To her surprise, a few candles still flickered in their sconces, and as she moved closer to the door she understood why: Everyone was not yet in bed. She heard voices, mascu-

356

line voices, coming from the rose parlor, on her left. As she drew nearer to the door of the room, which had been left slightly ajar, she recognized those deep, harsh tones as belonging to Justin. Automatically she stopped just outside, leaned lightly against the wall and listened.

Justin was talking to Charles, and from the thickness of his speech and slight slurring of his words, she guessed that he had been drinking.

"You think I haven't told myself that?" Justin was saying bitterly.

Charles' voice was quiet as he replied. "It's Megan you should be telling."

"How can I? She despises me and with good reason."

"Justin. . . ." There was a wealth of sympathy in the word.

"God, Charles, I've made such a mess of it." Justin's voice was suddenly muffled, as if he had dropped his head onto his hands. "I wanted her so much, I couldn't keep my hands off her. I knew better, I hated myself for it, and yet I couldn't help it. I swear by all that's holy I never even meant to touch her. I just couldn't help myself. She was so lovely and so sweet. I never wanted anything in my life as much as I wanted her. And she wanted me too—said she loved me. Hero-worship, I suppose, though I wouldn't let myself think that at the time. Whatever it was, I took advantage of it. She was a seventeen-year-old bloody virgin, and my ward, and I took her to bed. Afterwards, when I realized what I'd done, I felt about two inches high. The whole bloody thing was my fault entirely. She didn't even know I was married. Can you believe that?

357

Seems that in all those years we were visiting her, neither of us ever mentioned Alicia. That's when she started to hate me, you know: When she found out about Alicia. I can't say that I blame her. There's no excuse for what I did. I ruined her life and killed my own baby."

"Justin. . . ." Charles tried to break in, but Justin's words tumbled out one over the other, as if now that he had started he couldn't stop.

"Just once, I told myself. Just once, something for me. I wanted her, and I took her. I put her through hell, Charles. I hurt her, and I shamed her. God, do you know how she came to fall over that cliff? She was running from me. I hit her. You're right to look at me like that, it was a dastardly thing to do, but I was so jealous that it was eating me up inside, and before I even knew I was thinking about it, it was done. She was running from me, and she fell over that cliff and she lost our baby. I suppose I'm lucky it didn't kill her, too. God, Charles, take my advice and don't ever fall in love. It hurts like hell."

As Megan listened to this tortured speech, she felt as if a great beam of light had broken through the fog that had surrounded her. She had never thought of Justin's side in all this—never even imagined that he was hurting so badly. From the raw agony in his voice, she realized that he had suffered every bit as much as she. He had loved their baby, too, and he blamed himself for its death. Maybe that made his pain even greater than hers. And from the sound of things, he loved her, too, despite all that had happened.

Suddenly she realized how selfish she had been since the baby's death, shutting herself away with her grief, refusing to realize that Justin needed her. He needed her. That thought brought with it the first glimmer of joy she had known in weeks. She had hurt him, and only she could comfort him in his pain.

At least she could ease his guilt about the baby. Her fall had been as much her fault as his. She had not really been running from him—that single slap had hardly constituted a brutal assault—so much as she had been fleeing her own emotions. And with a child on the way she should have known better. Perhaps their son would have lived if her pregnancy had gone to full term; perhaps not. Janet had told her about the umbilical cord around his neck, and that could have happened at any time. It might possibly have corrected itself in time, but neither she nor Justin nor anyone in the world could be sure of that. The loss of their child had been the will of God. But it did no good to rail against such a blow from fate. It had happened, it was over, and she and Justin still had the rest of their lives together. And Megan realized, with a sudden lifting of the dense gray misery which had enshrouded her, that more than anything in the world she wanted to live the rest of her life with Justin.

A tiny part of her grief had been magnified by fear. She had been desperately afraid, without even knowing that she was afraid, that, now that the baby, the reason for their marriage, was gone, Justin would regret it. He had sacrificed so much to make her his wife—destroyed the whole fabric of his life. It would be years, if ever, before he could resume his seat in the House of Lords, before he could walk into his club without whispers following him, before anyone in society would even mention his name without associating it with scandal. He had done all this because he was an honorable man, and he had gotten her with child. Would he have done it for her alone, if she had not been expecting? Was his love for her strong enough to drive him to such measures for its own sake? Secretly, she had feared not. But now she remembered him asking her to marry him the night Donald had announced their engagement. He had offered then to get a divorce, if she would wait for him. And, because of the baby, she had turned him down. But if there had been no baby, she would have waited forever. But, without knowing about the baby, he had asked her to marry him, fully aware of the consequences to his good name and his future position in society. How then could she doubt his love for her?

But he could, and did, doubt hers for him. Since the baby's death she had been deliberately avoiding him, blind to his pain, too caught up in her own grief to give a thought to his. She winced at the thought of him suffering alone with his grief, believing that she held him responsible for what had happened, mourning their child and her too. It was too late to turn back the clock, as she would have given anything to be able to do. She could not undo what had been done.

But she could go to him now.

Chapter 21

The rose parlor was lit only by a pair of candles that flickered feebly from their brass holders atop the mantle. The hearth below was dark; there was no need for a fire in June. The elegant looped curtains of deep rose brocade with silver fringe framed a settee covered in matching fabric. It was on this that Justin sat, his long legs with their booted feet sprawled out across the patterned oriental carpet. His head rested tiredly back against the ornately carved wooden trim that edged the top of the settee. One arm curved to balance a glass on his thigh; the other dangled out of her sight over the edge of the settee. He was dressed in severe

361

black pantaloons and a plain white shirt that was open at the throat. The shirt was sadly rumpled, as was the rough darkness of his hair. His face was turned slightly away from her, and his eyes were closed, the short thick eyelashes standing out starkly black against skin that had lost much of its healthy sun-bronze over the last few weeks. He did not hear her come in.

Charles did. He was seated opposite Justin in a little silver chair, looking slightly out of place against its daintiness. He, too, was dressed only in a shirt and pantaloons, and he, too, held a glass in his hand. But his eyes were open, focusing on Justin with concern. As Megan pushed open the door and glided quietly into the room, his head swung round and he looked at her. A variety of expressions chased themselves across his face.

He got to his feet immediately, and would have said something except that Megan signaled him to remain silent with her finger against her lips. But her warning was useless. Justin heard Charles stand up, and his eyes opened inquiringly. When he saw the reason for Charles' abrupt rise, saw Megan standing there with her blue-sprigged wrapper held close around her throat, his whole face tightened. Dark spots of color rose to burn tellingly in his cheekbones as he stared at her without speaking. Then his inbred courtesy came to the fore. He set his glass down on the low table in front of him, and rose to his feet.

"What are you doing out of bed at this hour?" Justin's voice was harsh. Megan looked at him for a moment without speaking, her heart contracting as she noted how his clothes hung on his large frame, and how gaunt his face had become. He was still her handsome Justin, but he looked as if he had been ill. And Megan knew that he had been, and still was. He was suffering from the same illness that had held her in its thrall until his tormented words had broken its grip: Heartsickness.

"I couldn't sleep," she answered him quietly, then looked at Charles. "Charles, would you excuse us? I want to talk to Justin."

"Certainly." Charles set his glass down on the table, too, and began to move toward the door. His eyes rested fleetingly on Megan's face as she watched Justin, and he looked satisfied at what he saw there. As he reached the door, he turned back for a moment. "Tell Megan what you've just been telling me," he said to Justin, his voice low, and then he went out, pulling the door closed behind him.

Justin stared at the closed door, then shifted his eyes to Megan. His expression was guarded. He didn't say anything, but stood rocking back and forth on the balls of his feet, his hands jammed deep in his pockets. After a moment it became obvious that he had no intention of saying anything. If the chasm between them was ever to be bridged, Megan saw that she would have to be the one to bridge it. There was no place for pride in love, as she had painfully come to realize. And looking at Justin standing there for all the world like a small boy dreading further punishment, she knew that she loved him so much she ached

363

with it.

"Won't you please sit down? We have to talk." She moved forward as she spoke, and seated herself in the chair Charles had just vacated. Its delicacy exactly suited her small frame.

Justin gave a harsh crack of laughter.

"I seem to remember saying the same thing myself not too long ago," he muttered, making no move to sit down. A momentary shadow crossed Megan's face as she remembered when he had used those words to her: The night she had fallen over the cliff. He winced at the sudden pain in her face, and suddenly sat down again on the settee.

"Say whatever you have to say," he said wearily, his eyes tired as he looked at her. "I deserve it, I know. I caused it all, right from the beginning. Nothing you can possibly say to me can be worse than the things I've been saying to myself."

"Justin." She wanted to fly to him, to put her arms around him and never let him go. He looked so alone. But she sensed that he was not yet ready to accept her love. There were a few points that had to be cleared up between them. "You are no more to blame for anything that happened than I am. Do you really think you seduced me, darling? If you did, let me tell you that there was never anyone more willing to be seduced. I used to lie awake at night, imagining what it would be like between us. And I never even got close: the reality was so much better. The memory of our first night together is something I'll treasure all my life. You made it so wonderful for me, Justin! Do you think I don't know that it wouldn't have been like that with anyone else? When Lord Ivor kissed me—and Donald—" Something flashed warningly for a moment in Justin's eyes at these recollections, but Megan resolutely went on; they had to have complete honesty between them now. "They made my skin crawl, Justin. You were the only one I ever wanted."

"You were going to marry Winspear. You told me you loved him."

Megan leaned forward in her eagerness to convince him.

"I only told you that because I thought it was the only way you'd let me marry him. And I wanted to marry him because of the baby. I loved our baby so much, Justin. I didn't want it to have to be ashamed all its life, to grow up with the stigma of illegitimacy hanging over its head. It never even occurred to me that you might be able to marry me in time; it seemed like Donald was the only alternative I had. But even before you came back, I was glad that you hadn't let me marry Donald. I realized almost as soon as you left me at Windsmere that I would have been miserable with him—without you."

"Do you mean that?" His voice was very low, but his eyes began to gleam with what looked like hope as they met hers steadily.

"I swear it, Justin. I only wanted you. I still want you."

"I never said, I'm sorry I hit you. I could have cut off my hand as soon as I'd done it; I will cut off my hand before I'll ever do it again. I'd rather slit my own

365

throat than hurt so much as a hair on your head." The words were a whisper, and Megan had to strain to hear them. But they were well worth straining for. She smiled at him, her mouth tremulous, her eyes misty with sudden tears.

"Darling. . . ." she began, but he interrupted her, talking fast, his voice husky.

"When—you lost the baby—I wanted to die. I caused it, and I knew you'd hate me for it. And when I thought of you hating me, I wanted to die."

"Darling. . . ." This time she went to him, not caring whether he was ready for her or not. She bent over him, putting her around his broad shoulders, holding him tightly. He stiffened, and then his arms came around her waist, pulling her arms down onto his lap. He burrowed his head into the soft curve between her neck and shoulder. An enormous lump rose in her throat as she stroked his thick hair.

"Please don't hate me for it," he muttered against her skin. "I know I deserve it, but please don't hate me."

"Justin." Megan had difficulty getting the words out past the lump in her throat, but she knew she had to. She had to do what she could to mitigate the awful burden of guilt he carried. "Justin, darling, listen to me. The way the baby died—you musn't blame yourself. You shouldn't have slapped me, and I shouldn't have run from you, but even if neither of us had done those things, we might still have lost him. Janet told me that there was no telling how long the cord had been around his neck. It could have been that way for weeks, and there was no guarantee that it would have been any different whenever I'd given birth. Even if I'd carried the baby the full nine months, Justin, he still could have died the same way. Do you hear what I'm telling you? It wasn't your fault any more than it was mine: We must simply accept it as the will of God, and go on from there."

"I don't deserve you," he said thickly, lifting his head so that he could look into her face. Megan felt tears brim her eyes as she saw the suspicious brightness of his. With an unsteady finger she touched the single moist path that traversed the lean darkness of his cheek.

"Maybe not," she said with a husky little sound that was part sob, part laugh. "But you've got me. Forever, if you want me."

"If I want you. . . ." His voice broke, and he pulled her tightly against him, pillowing her head on his shoulder and holding her as if he would never let her go. "Oh, God, if I want you . . . !"

And as he cradled her on his lap his muttered words gave her to understand that he wanted her very much indeed.

Chapter 22

Sometime during the night Justin picked her up and carried her up to his bed. He undressed, then came to join her in the soft warm darkness, his arms going around her to draw her close against his side.

"Go to sleep," he muttered, pressing his lips against the silky moistness of her forehead. Megan, already drowsy, feeling as if she'd come home at last after a long journey, did.

When she awoke it was broad daylight, and Justin was gone. Megan blinked bewilderedly for a moment, wondering if she had dreamt the events of the night. The very fact that she was in Justin's room, in his bed, convinced her that she had not. They had reconciled during the night, and he had left her in the morning. Staring down at the pillow next to her own, tracing the shape of the indention made in it by his beloved head, she had a sudden inkling of where he might have gone. Justin had been suffering the tortures of the damned for weeks. Intuitively she guessed that he had gone to face a particular demon, and in the process try to come to terms with it.

She got out of bed hastily, grabbed her wrapper from the floor where Justin had dropped it, and hurried along the corridor to her rooms. As she approached she saw that Janet stood in the open doorway, a worried frown creasing her face. When she saw Megan coming toward her, her look of relief was almost comical.

"Did I worry you, Janet?" Megan asked contritely, approaching the door. Janet moved aside to let her enter the room, turning to watch her as she withdrew a dress from the wardrobe and then began to strip off her wrapper and nightdress.

"A little, my lady." The wryness of Janet's voice told Megan how very much of an understatement this was. Megan smiled at her, then registered that, for the first time since Justin had married her, it had not felt strange to hear herself addressed as "my lady." With an inward grimace she guessed it was because she now felt she had earned the title. Last night she had become Justin's wife in truth; oh, not in the legal sense, their marriage had yet to be consummated, as Megan just that moment realized, but in her heart and soul. He was no longer her guardian, the inaccessable Earl, or the experienced and charming man who had taught her the devastating pleasures of the flesh. He was simply Justin, the other half of herself: Her husband, and her love.

"I'm sorry," Megan answered, pulling a single white petticoat over her head and then doing the same to a simple cambric daydress of palest lemon. No longer would she wear the dreary mourning that she had donned each day since the baby died; her life, and Justin's, was starting anew. She meant to leave behind all reminders of the past. Janet came to help her, twitching the dress into place and fastening the hooks at the back while Megan fidgeted impatiently.

"Do you want me to come with you?" Janet asked quietly as she did up the last of the hooks. From her tone Megan knew that Janet somehow had divined a good part of what had taken place while she and most of the rest of the world had been sleeping. Megan turned to smile affectionately at her.

"No, thank you, Janet," she said, and barely paused to splash her face with water and run a brush through the curling tangles of her hair before heading out the door.

Justin would have walked, she guessed, but she was in a hurry. She jogged impatiently from one foot to the other while Walter the stableboy harnessed a horse to the trap. She didn't like to think of him facing his demon alone. Then the trap was ready and Megan was seated inside it, clucking to the bay horse who moved out in a brisk trot.

It was another beautiful summer day. The sky was a bright halcyon blue with fleecy white clouds scudding across its surface. A gentle, salt-tanged breeze blew in from the sea. The grass was green, and the road cut-

371

ting through it was a light, sun-baked brown. Small clouds of dust were churned up by the horse's hooves, and by the wheels of the trap.

The small church with its attendant graveyard stood on the crest of a gentle hill. Megan slowed the horse to a walk as she approached, then stopped it altogether, dismounting and securing the reins to a post provided for that purpose. Her hunch had been correct, she could see. Justin stood, head bowed, over their son's small grave.

Moving quietly, she opened the wrought iron gate and passed through it, crossing the neat paths between the mounds until she stood behind him. Unlike herself, he still wore his mourning. The fine wool of his black coat was smooth across his broad shoulders, and his black pantaloons faithfully delineated every powerful muscle in his legs.

She said nothing, but came to stand beside him, placing a gentle hand on his arm. He opened his eyes then and looked at her steadily for a moment without speaking. Megan felt her love for him glowing like a lamp throughout her body. He must have read it in her eyes, because the tawny-gold depths of his own warmed as he looked down at her. Still wordlessly, his arm slid around her waist, and he pulled her toward him until she stood with her face pressed against his chest and her hands clutching the front of his coat. As he enfolded her in his strong arms next to the tiny mound that was all they had left of their son, for the first time since the child had died Megan was able to cry. Justin bent his head so that his face was pressed against her hair, murmuring soft words of comfort and endearment as he rocked her back and forth as if she were a hurt child.

It was a long time later before Megan's tears subsided, and she lay resting against his chest. She felt oddly healed.

"Justin," she said presently, pulling back a little so that she could look up at him. One arm stayed around her waist, but the other went to the pocket of his coat, from which he extracted a snowy handkerchief. He used it to tenderly wipe the tears from her cheeks. Then he held it to her small nose.

"Blow," he instructed, the beginnings of humor quirking about his mouth. Megan did as he told her; grimacing, he folded the handkerchief, and pocketed it.

"Now," he said. "You were saying?"

Megan smiled at him. Her lips were tremulous, but her eyes were at peace.

"I love you very much," she told him clearly. He looked down at her for a long moment, his mouth straight and firm in his dark face. The look in his eyes made her want to cry again; it also made her want to laugh and sing and shout with joy.

"I love you, too," he said at last, his voice low. Touched to the heart, Megan reached up to lay a gentle hand against his cheek. He turned his head so that his lips burned into her palm.

"Let's go home, darling," she whispered lovingly.

His arm was warm about her waist as she led him from the graveyard.

Epilogue

It was fifteen months later, and a gentle September rain was washing the second floor windows at Brant Hall. Megan was leaving the nursery, where she had just finished feeding her three-month old daughter, Alexandra Justine. At Megan's insistence, the little girl had been named for both Justin and his mother. But if she had known that Justin would persist in calling the child Alex despite her protestations, she would have chosen something less prone to corruption. Megan had a strong suspicion that their daughter would object to being stuck with a boy's nickname when she had grown up sufficiently to recognize the difference, but by then it might well be too late. Even Janet had taken to calling the baby Missy Alex. And nicknames of that sort tended to stick.

Megan walked into the bedroom she shared with Justin, intent on washing her face and brushing her hair before going downstairs again to consult with Cook about dinner. Brant Hall was Justin's ancestral home, a beautiful estate in the middle of Worcestershire where Justin had grown up, and his wife Megan was very much the mistress of it. She had learned to be a capable, assured housekeeper, and her days were taken up with the hundred and one myriad tasks involved in running a house of such size. Deciding on a dinner menu was just another of those daily chores.

She had gotten halfway across the room before she registered the pungent odor of a cheroot drifting lazily through the air. Her hand flew to her throat in an instinctive reaction as she whirled. Justin was sitting in a chair beneath the window, his feet propped lazily on a small table, and smoke from the cheroot that dangled negligently from his fingers, swirled about his head.

"You scared me to death," she gasped. His eyes moved over her with casual possessiveness, taking note of the lovely picture she made. She was a woman now, not a girl, and a dazzlingly beautiful one. The simple chignon into which she had twisted the silken mass of her hair suited her, lending a sweet maturity to the porcelain-perfect features. Her breasts and hips had blossomed to a womanly fullness, while her waist retained its girlish slenderness. He felt a stabbing ache in the region of his groin, and his mouth twisted in a wry smile. The effect she consistently had on him never ceased to amaze him, and it seemed like years since he had been able to make love to her as he was dying to do. During the last two months of her pregnancy, the doctor had advised him to abstain, and since the baby's birth he had been too fearful of hurting her to even suggest it. It was almost funny that he, who had never rated celibacy as worth any more than a passing sneer, should have been celibate for nearly half a year and made no attempt to do anything about it. He could have gone up to London and eased himself with any of the all too willing ladies there, or even tumbled a local maid as many a man in his position would have done. But he wanted no woman but his wife, which was the best justification for marital faithfulness he knew. She had cast a spell over him, his violet-eyed little witch, and she still held him hopelessly in her thrall. He was ruined for all other women, and the knowledge both piqued and amused him. But he knew that he would remain celibate until Megan was able to become un-celibate with him.

"Sorry," he replied to her accusing look with a glinting grin. Megan came to stand beside him, leaning down to press a soft kiss to his mouth. He caught her hand in his, and drew her down to his knees. She allowed him to pull her down willingly, resting comfortably back against his chest.

"What are you doing home at this time of day, anyway?" she asked, smiling up at him as he took a quick puff on his cheroot. He had become vitally interested in agriculture, and spent most of his days supervising the care of various experimental crops that he had planted throughout the estate.

"It's raining, my love, in case it has somehow escaped your attention," Justin pointed out, his hand fondling her waist without his even being conscious that it did so. "Surely you wouldn't want me to get wet?"

"A little rain never brought you home before," Megan pointed out, her finger tracing idle circles up his shirt front. He had removed his coat and neckcloth, and was dressed only in a plain white cambric shirt, buff pantaloons, and boots. Her teasing finger reached the open collar of his shirt, sliding beneath it to twist little curls in the fine mat of hair just below his throat.

Justin grinned a little lopsidedly. "Maybe I just thought I'd check on my two beautiful girls."

Megan made a face at him. "Alexandra's taking a nap, and I'm getting ready to decide what to have for dinner. Do you have any suggestions?"

Justin's eyes met hers, and he laughed. "None that you could serve up in the middle of the dining room table," he answered, leering at her. Megan snuggled against him, feeling the sudden hardness of him beneath her thighs with a quick upsurge of excitement. He had been forbearing and patient for months, and she was more than grateful at the care he had taken of her. But now she was quite recovered from what had, admittedly, been a rather difficult birth and his body was warm and hard against hers.

"Justin," she murmured, her fingers toying with the top button of his shirt.

"Ummm?"

"Aren't you going to kiss me hello?"

He looked down at her curled up on his lap.

"I don't think so," he replied after a moment. But he made no move to stop her as she slowly freed one button from its hole, and then another.

"Why not?" she sounded disappointed, but her eyes were smiling as they met his.

"Because right now I'm not in just the right mood for kisses."

"Oh." Megan had his shirt unbuttoned to the waist, and as she spoke she nuzzled her mouth against his skin. She could feel the tensing of all his muscles at her action.

"Justin."

"Ummm?" His voice was beginning to sound faintly hoarse. Megan smiled to herself, and opened her lips against the salt-tanged skin of his chest, tasting it with her tongue.

"Neither am I."

It took him a minute or so to absorb the meaning of that, and then she could feel the sudden increased tempo of his heartbeat beneath her mouth.

"My darling, it's too soon." The huskiness of his voice told her all she needed to know. She smiled against his skin, saying nothing as she sensuously ran her tongue down his taut abdomen to the waistband of his pantaloons.

"Megan." The word was a half-hearted protest as she slid off his lap to kneel before him on the floor, her hands busy at the fastenings of his pantaloons.

"If you want me to stop. . . ." she murmured innocently, the wicked little glint in her eyes the only hint she gave that she was teasing him.

"God, if you do I think I'll strangle you." This half-humorous, response made Megan chuckle. She eased his pantaloons down just far enough so that she had access to the part of him which interested her most at the moment. As she touched him, her cool little fingers closing around him, he groaned. He had taught her well before her pregnancy had temporarily ruled out further intimacy between them. She knew what gave him pleasure, and as she stroked and caressed him she gloried in his heightened breathing, in the rapid rise and fall of his dark-furred chest. She loved the scent of him and the feel of him beneath her hands. Suddenly she wondered about the taste of him. Many, many times he had given pleasure to her in that way, but he had never suggested that she do the same to him and she had never thought of it. Now she did. She bent over him, and heard him gasp with a fierce little stab of triumph.

"That's a filthy whore's trick," she heard him growl after a moment, and his hands were on her shoulders, pushing her away from him. Megan looked at him, surprised. He had been enjoying it immensely; she knew too much about his physical responses not to realize that. Then, as he slid down beside her on the floor, she caught the teasing glint in his eyes and smiled back at him.

"Who taught you that?" he continued in the same menacing growl, but she wasn't fooled. He was still breathing fast, and his eyes had the hot, excited glimmer that she knew from experience.

"You did," she answered truthfully, reaching out to touch him again. "Don't you like it?"

"No." He was pushing her back down against the floor. Megan went willingly, her hands on his shoulders pulling him down with her. "I love it."

She grinned at him. "I thought so."

"Too much," he added grimly. "I don't think I can wait any longer."

"I don't want you to," she answered, her eyes as soft as her voice. He was leaning over her, his eyes passionate as they met hers.

"My darling, are you sure you're well enough?" The hoarseness of his voice told her of the control he was exerting. She smiled at him, shaking her head at the same time. Her hands crept up over his shoulders to curl around his neck.

"What does it take to seduce you, Justin?" she murmured provocatively. "Do you want me to beg?"

"Yes," he answered promptly. She laughed up at him, moving her body so that it was pressed intimately against his. The bare flesh of his stomach and thighs burned her through the figured silk of her dress.

"Can't you hear me, Justin?" she whispered, pressing herself even closer against him. "I'm begging."

"God, I love you," he muttered, and at last lowered his head to claim her lips with his. His kiss was hard and yet tender, taking and giving at the same time. Megan opened her mouth to him willingly, touching his tongue with hers, exchanging caress for caress. Her arms were locked hard around his neck, and as she felt his hands slide beneath her to work the fastenings of her gown she sighed blissfully. The familiar quickening excitement began to spiral maddeningly inside her, radiating out along her limbs, making her tingle and yearn for him.

"Good Christ, why do you women have so many damned hooks?" he groaned against her mouth, and

Megan giggled helplessly despite her own rising excitement at the frustration in his voice.

"To keep things interesting, of course," she responded pertly, and he bared his teeth at her in a mock snarl.

"I'll make things interesting for you, my saucy wench," he said, and promptly abandoned the hooks to jerk her dress and the chemise beneath it down to her waist. Megan gasped with surprise at his action, then felt color wash into her cheeks as he stared down at her breasts. They were beautiful, full and soft and creamy white, tempting enough to eat.

"These look like strawberries," he muttered hoarsely, bending his head to flick each nipple in turn with his tongue. They instantly quivered erect under the erotic tutelage of his mouth. "But they don't taste like strawberries. They're much, much better."

As his mouth divided its time between her lips and her breasts, his hands were coming up under her skirts to tug at the ribbon fastening of her pantalets. When at last he got them untied, he pulled her pantalets down her legs and tossed them aside. Then he pushed her skirts up around her waist. Megan felt the rough scratchiness of the carpet against her bare bottom, and her eyes flickered open. Justin was looking at her, eating her body with his eyes.

"God, you're beautiful," he whispered, and suddenly all the teasing was gone from his eyes. His mouth came down on hers, and he settled himself over her body. His weight pressed her into the carpet, crushing her against the unyielding floor beneath, and Megan loved it. Boldly, she rubbed her breasts against his hair-roughened chest, exciting herself as well as him. His hand slid between her thighs, fondling her; sensations so intense that they drove her nearly mindless swamped her. She writhed against his hand, wanting him. And then she reached for him, guiding him to her, opening her legs and panting in her eagerness for his possession. He held back for a moment, wanting to prolong the pleasure for both of them, but then with a groan he gave in, plunging deep inside her with no more preliminaries. Megan welcomed his entry with a hoarse cry, her legs locking around his waist, her fingers stroking his hair and shoulders and back and anything else she could reach. His hands were beneath her, cupping her buttocks, lifting her so that he could plunge deeper and deeper inside.

"Justin!" she cried out when she could stand his exquisite torture no longer. "Oh, yes, Justin: Yes!"

With a groan he stifled her cries with his mouth. The violent contractions that racked them both seemed to go on forever.

It was a long time before Megan opened her eyes to find Justin propped up on one elbow beside her, looking tenderly down into her face. She smiled at him.

"That was wonderful," she said huskily. "You're wonderful."

He grinned, his white teeth cutting a bold slash across his dark face.

"Thanks for the recommendation, lady," he murmured teasingly. "Need I add that all the ladies tell me that?"

Megan doubled up her fist and brushed it playfully across his chin.

"Conceited oaf," she muttered lovingly. She knew perfectly well that he had eyes for no one but her, and he knew she knew it. She started to say so, but then a clock chimed from some distant part of the house.

"My goodness, I had no idea that it was so late. Cook must be wondering what on earth has happened to me. Let me up, Justin, or it will be ten o'clock before we get anything to eat tonight."

"I find my appetite's gone in another direction entirely," he grinned, holding her in place by the simple expedient of rolling on top of her again. Megan protested, but she couldn't keep from laughing at him.

"It's just occurred to me that it might be a good idea to give Alex a little competition before too long," he said, with a mock thoughtful air. "What do you think?"

Megan pretended to ponder.

"Well, I always heard that only children get hopelessly spoiled," she answered demurely, her smile belying the seriousness of her tone.

"Oh, do they?" His eyes glinted wickedly down at her. "In that case, it will be my pleasure to provide Alex with half-a-dozen brothers and sisters."

And it was.